GODZILLA AND THE SONG BIRD

ALSO BY MANZU ISLAM

Fiction
The Mapmakers of Spitalfields
Burrow
Song of Our Swampland

Non-fiction
The Ethics of Travel: from Marco Polo to Kafka

In memory of my brother Ashraf,
with whom I grew up in a town like Mominabad.

ACKNOWLEDGEMENTS

Kamala Achu helped me with editing while providing shelter during manuscript drafting. Riaz Hasan Faruk assisted with sensitive reading and alleviating my worries about certain aspects of this book. Mags Chalcraft and Naz Yacoob offered their friendship and encouraged me to pursue my passion for writing. My children, Amalia and Tomal, and their families, Kareem, Charlotte, Kamilo, Ruben, Inara, and Marla, have always been there for me with bonds of love and care. My siblings – Sharif, Lipi, and Rupa – supported me in good and bad times. Jeremy Poynting supported me from the beginning of my writing career; he understood my projects and helped me shape them. I am grateful to him.

MANZU ISLAM

GODZILLA AND THE SONG BIRD

P E E P A L   T R E E

First published in Great Britain in 2024
Peepal Tree Press Ltd
17 King's Avenue
Leeds LS6 1QS
England

ISBN13: 9781845235871

Supported using public funding by
ARTS COUNCIL
ENGLAND

CHAPTER 1

'Little bird, you were born between the gecko and the fly,' his grandmother told him.

'Am I a monster, Dadu?' asked Bulbul.

'Monster? Mind you, half and half is not a bad thing. Especially between a lizard and an insect. Imagine the things you could do. Slither the ground and fly the blue. All at the same time. Oh, what fun you'd have. But I was thinking of your birth-time, my little bird,' said Dadu.

'Oh, was it a monster time, Dadu?'

'Good question. Do you see time? Can you touch it? Can you smell it? Yes, yes, it's a monster, all right. Very shameless, too. You'd be a fool to await its coming. Only when it's already left. Gone forever. You scratch your head: *Oh what was that, what was that?* Very funny. It's already gone and never comes back. Anyway, little bird, let us think of the gecko.'

Yes, the gecko: he was a common sight, our old friend tictiki. At first, time lay still in its eyes, unblinking, and then, as if not to turn into a stone, it came ferociously alive, scuttling up the wall at breakneck speed.

It had been a long birthing moment and the mother was struggling. Dadu had gone out of the birthing room, clip-clopping on her padukas for a breather, to cool her face with a slosh of water, to prepare herself for what was to come. On her way back, she spotted the gecko, its large glassy eyes locked on a tiny fly. Strange, she wasn't into geckos, even felt alarmed by them, and yet she stood transfixed as her grandson came into the world and his mother left it.

'Did I kill Amma?' asked Bulbul.

'Who taught you to talk so silly, little bird? You weren't even there to do anything, let alone doing any killing. It's just a little game that time plays. Mind you, it's a very cruel game. I assure you, you were your mother's singing bird. I knew it the moment

I laid my eyes on you. That's why we called you Bulbul.'

'But I can't sing anything, Dadu. When I open my mouth, my throat hurts. Boys tell me I sound like an ugly frog.'

'Stupid boys, what do they know? Your soul sings sweet. Don't you ever forget that,' said Dadu.

★

On this dark, rainy night, lightning offering sporadic glimpses of the Sundarbans, they put him on a dinghy. Ignoring all protocol, Colonel Alam climbed down from the gunboat to push him away. 'Go with Godzilla, Singing Bird. See you in hell,' he said. Bulbul had to row between the dense labyrinths of mangroves to reach across the border. His chances were slim; only a miracle would see him through. The military gunboat kept its searchlight on him as he drifted downstream in the current. Then it was darkness.

It wasn't thunder or lightning that shook him and made him bolt upright. It was the roar of the tiger. If he'd been alert to the shrieks and howls of the macaques in the canopy, he would have realised a tiger was prowling nearby. Perhaps it was Wrath of God, the terrifying man-eater of the Sundarbans. He lay in the dinghy, wrapping his arms around himself, rain dropping on his closed eyelids, kissing his lips. Perhaps Wrath of God was waiting at the end of this narrow channel. He would be easy prey for the wily old tiger; all that was needed was a gentle leap and its teeth would be right in his throat.

The shrieks and howls of the macaques were getting louder. Perhaps it would be better to be eaten by a tiger than have his throat cut by the mullah. He felt calm, accepting the inevitable, letting the rain caress his face. Caught in the current, the dinghy drifted downstream to the sea.

★

Over the years Bulbul heard Dadu's stories and stories about him from Dadu. Sometimes, he even felt that they were his stories.

Apart from Dadu, the only other relative he knew was his grandfather, whom he remembered as an odd and antic figure wearing a three-piece suit, swanking between the paddy fields, sporting a crimson fez, a bunch of golden tassels dangling at its back like the bushy tail of some fabled cat. Despite his odd ways, Bulbul remembered him fondly, still feeling guilt that he had something

6

to do with his death. Now, perhaps, it was the Sundarbans that made him tell his grandfather's stories.

He sat shaking at the tiger's approach as his grandfather had done many years ago. Nothing else would make the macaques jump so desperately from canopy to canopy, their shrieks strangled, as if they would die of their own dread long before the demonic beast came anywhere near them. Suddenly, he heard a deer break through the mangroves and jump into the river, then silence. He knew the jungle was telling him that the tiger had his prey and that everyone could have their ease for the night. Facing the dark sky, Bulbul reflected that it wasn't him but the jungle and the tiger that killed his grandfather.

His grandfather, Syed Amir Shah, was a staunch Muslim Leaguer. It was Calcutta, 1946. The city was seething with communal hatred as India headed for partition. Six years before, the family had moved to the Bow Bazaar area – a bustling place with trams hurtling past its main avenue, an open-air market teeming with cows and men, baijis and prostitutes trading in its dark, hushed alleyways. Although his grandfather didn't think it the most desirable of locations for a man of his standing, he couldn't pass up a bargain: a large, crumbling mansion belonging to an impoverished zamindar – a hard-drinking, afim-khor, aficionado of nautch girls – for the price of an average bungalow. It would be home for his growing family, all living under one roof.

Of recent generations, Syed Amir Shah was the first to venture beyond their natal territory and reach Calcutta; the rest of his kin remained in the swampy Brahmaputra delta region of East Bengal. Suited and booted on a winter's day in 1910, Syed Amir Shah, aged eighteen, arrived in what was then the second city of the British Empire. Of the family's history nothing was certain, though there was a hush-hush whisper that his grandfather was an untouchable Hindu, a cobbler from Patna in Bihar, who ended up in the waterland of East Bengal. But how? Stories, there had always been stories, and one of them had the cobbler as the protagonist in a long, twisting journey that began with a pair of sandals.

As it happened, most of the land in the cobbler's village belonged to a rather pernickety Muslim nobleman – always fussing about the rules regarding halal and haram. As was the custom, the landowner ordered a new pair of sandals to be made for Eid. The task fell on our cobbler, then a young novice. He wanted to make an impression by crafting the landlord fine-looking and comfortable footwear. He sourced the best pigskin he could and poured in all his know-how and flair in the long hours making them. Who wouldn't be pleased with such workmanship on such delicate material? The landlord was no exception. 'You have talent, boy. I say an artist among cobblers, deserving of handsome tips. I'll give you a piece of land to build your own hut. Happy?'

But then things took an unfortunate turn. Under the impression that he was wearing perfectly halal footwear, the landlord not only went to perform the Eid prayers in them but also trod the inner sanctum of his house. The mullah, who taught the Koran to his children, brought the matter to his attention. 'Sir, I see you have a handsome pair of sandals. I must say, very fetching on your noble feet. But if I may be so impertinent…'

'What's the matter, Mullah? Spit it out,' said the landlord.

'Sir, how should I put it? The skin, Sir. It looks from impure things. I mean, Sir, pigs.'

'Pigs?' screamed the landlord.

He had the sandals burnt immediately, and the rugs, carpets and house floor scrubbed and sprinkled with attar. He promised to go to Mecca to perform Hajj. He also summoned the young cobbler and his entire clan to dispense collective punishment on them; they had to pay double the rent and do all the leather work for free for a year. They would starve to death. They wailed and begged for mercy. It was the mullah who came to their aid. 'Sir,' he addressed the landlord, 'your judgement is most righteously just. Polluting the prayer ground with the hide of an unclean beast, especially in the house of a pious nobleman deserves harsh punishment. But if you'd allow me to intercede on behalf of these unfortunate souls, Sir.'

'What's on your mind, Mullah? Let's hear it.'

'Sir, your kindness is bountiful. Perhaps if the young cobbler were to convert, if he takes up our faith, perhaps, Sir, you might find it in your benevolence to forgive them.'

Once converted, the young cobbler found himself in no-man's land. He couldn't stay in the village's cobbler section and other Hindu areas were out of bounds, and the Muslims wouldn't accept him as one of their own. 'Yes, yes, he's one of us now. But to tell the truth, we're not sure. His soul has been mired in heathenism from Adam's time onwards. It can't be cleaned overnight, can it? Besides, the fellow still reeks of unclean things.'

The ex-cobbler had to squat in the market among the beggars and the lepers, until one day he took to the road, headed southeast and, after wandering nearly five hundred miles, ended up in the swampy region of the Brahmaputra delta in East Bengal. The village was called Dambarpur; its predominantly Muslim inhabitants were peasants and fishermen. The young cobbler-convert declared himself a Muslim of aristocratic lineage, a Syed with elaborate Middle Eastern genealogy. 'We're so blessed to have a Syed among us,' said the poor Muslim farmers in the village, 'Are you related to our Prophet himself?'

'You ignorant fools,' said the young convert, 'don't you know that you can't be a Syed without belonging to the Prophet's household?'

'So true, so true,' said the villagers.

He told how his ancestors came from Baghdad, part of a group of Sufi saints, related to the prophet, to spread Islam among the Indians.

'Are you the only son of your parents?' asked one of the farmers.

'Yes, I am.'

'In that case, the power of sainthood must have found its way to you,' said a farmer. 'Honourable Syed, you're our saint now.'

The news spread of the saint and his power to perform miracles, and villagers flocked to his little hut by the river for blessings and cures. When the Muslim landowner of the neighbouring village heard about the saint, he gave him land, had a house built for him, and offered his daughter in marriage. In due course he became a wealthy man and assumed the effortless superiority of a pukka aristocrat. Following him, his son also became a saint, and the grandson, Syed Amir Shah, was expected to do the same. His father brought in a private tutor, a learned mullah, well versed in Koranic studies as well as Arabic and Persian languages and literature. He was to lead prayers at the family mosque and instruct Syed Amir Shah to become a proper Islamic saint. As far as his father was concerned, the mullah was doing a good job. At the age of thirteen, Syed Amir Shah could recite the Koran by heart, knew the life and sayings of the prophet, and felt at home in the vast corpus of Sharia law. The father had no idea that the mullah was a secret admirer of Sir Syed Ahmed Khan, the Feringhee-loving Muslim aristocrat who advocated, as well as Islamic learning, the rational, scientific education of Western enlightenment and mastery of the English language. Under his influence, Syed Amir Shah pursued a modern education and learned English. On his fourteenth birthday, he approached his father who, after a long day of saintly duties, was on the outer veranda with his hookah, enjoying the evening breeze.

'What's the matter, my boy?' his father asked.

'I want to go to the school in town. I want to learn Maths, Chemistry, History and English,' said Syed Amir Shah.

'You don't need those Feringhee subjects. You will be a saint.'

'I want to be somebody, like a policeman.'

'What? No job is bigger than being a saint. Good money and plenty of prestige. You don't have to work hard, either. You touch some heads, bless some water. That's all. You can be as lazy as you like, live a cushy life. And you want to give this up to become a policeman? A servant of the Feringhees?'

Syed Amir Shah pestered his father until he gave in. The school was about six miles from Dambarpur in the nearby administrative town of Kishorepur, with its red-bricked court, police station and magistrate's office. For the next four years, until he finished his secondary education and entered higher secondary education at a nearby college, he would travel twelve miles a day to Kishorepur. During the flood season, he went most of the way by boat and then cycled. He could cycle all the way during the winter and dry season. With each journey to Kishorepur, each class he took, and each book he read, he drifted further and further away from the religious worldview in which he'd grown up. He demanded proof for everything, and if it was not forthcoming he dismissed it out of hand as mumbo jumbo. He even went to his father asking for proof of his saintly miracles.

'Where have you been, my boy? On my intercession, every day

someone's desire bears fruit. You know Matab Ali's son, don't you? The idiotic one. He was mad to become a peon at the sanitary inspector's office. Matab Ali honoured my craft with two fine chickens and a basketful of mustard. He begged me to do something for the boy. How could I refuse? So I just touched his head and sent him away. Now, the boy wears a sola-hat and drags the inspector's donkey from house to house. He's in seventh heaven. Is that empirical enough for you? And didn't you see Kalu's mother-in-law, yesterday? The woman has been virtually dead for years. If Kalu had his way, he'd have buried the old hag long ago. But his wife donates me her kid-goat and two dozen duck-eggs. Ah, mother love, total craziness, but beautiful. Well, you've seen it with your own eyes, right? She went away skipping like a young filly, even talking about amorous adventures. Are they not proof enough for you?'

Not really. He wanted a different kind of proof and explanation but couldn't find the words to express them. He would drop the subject, but bide his time until he left home. His father wasn't happy.

'It pains my heart with extreme heaviness. Unbearable heaviness. My own son is becoming such a supporter of the Feringhee's ways. Very sad. Let me exorcise you, my boy. What's the point of possessing all that saintly power if I can't do a trifling thing for my own boy?'

Syed Amir Shah didn't want to be exorcised. One of his college teachers, a big fan of the Raj, gave him his old suit and tie. 'I don't want you to arrive in Calcutta looking like a junglee. I want you to look like a tiptop Englishman,' said the teacher. The boy hid the suit and tie in his suitcase, and as the train arrived at the outskirts of Calcutta, he changed his pyjama and punjabi and put on the suit and tie. So as not to indulge his pursuit of ungodly materialism and Feringhee ways, his father had given him only enough money to cover his transport costs and a bit extra to last a few days. 'Let the boy see the Feringhee city. Let him get it out of his system. I hear it's a hellhole of spewing smoke, eardrum-splitting noise, and speed everywhere. A damn monster of a thing. Doesn't he know the Feringhees? The most devilish masters of the universe. They are sure to trample him underfoot like a cockroach. Let's see how long he lasts,' said his father.

Syed Amir Shah was determined to last in the city and make it in his own way.

★

Was it only minutes or hours? He had no idea. The boat had drifted gently downstream and become entangled in the mangroves. It was dark and he had no strength to do anything. Luckily the rain had stopped and he fell asleep in the hum of the forest. But Wrath of God was still prowling with hunger in his eyes.

CHAPTER 2

The following day, a pair of honey-collecting brothers found him.

'What are you doing here, on your own?' asked the elder.

'I'm looking for the border. To get to the other side.'

'If you follow the current, you'll end up in the sea,' said the younger. 'To get to the border is difficult. You have to veer right into the jungle. It's like a maze. Even the best of us get lost. Add to your botheration, there are tigers and bandits.'

Bulbul told them how he'd ended up there, how he would be a dead man if he didn't cross the border.

'On the radio we heard the news,' said the elder brother and he showed Bulbul an old, plastic transistor radio, held together by pieces of string. 'You see my little brother here. He gets lonely and likes to listen to songs. I don't care much for them. I like to listen to the river and the wind and the birds. Even tigers.'

'Anyway, what did you hear?'

'There was a military coup. And they killed the leader. So, we understand your situation. But if we take you to the border, we'll be dead men too,' said the younger brother.

'Don't worry, I understand. Just go. I'll try my luck. If I don't make it, I don't make it.'

'Stop this foolish talk. We'll take you,' said the elder brother.

'You don't have to. I mean it.'

'We have to take you. That's the end of the story.'

'Why? You don't know me. You owe me nothing.'

'Does there have to be a reason? You don't owe us anything. We just found you. We'll take you to the border.'

'You might get killed.'

'So what? We've seen your face. We can't do otherwise.'

Bulbul got into the honey-collectors' dinghy and they steered it right into the jungle.

'Have you been to the Sundarbans before?' asked the younger.

'Yes, when I was a boy. With my grandfather.'

'Your grandfather? Why did he bring you to the Sundarbans?'

'Well, it's a long story.'

'We like stories. The longer the better. If you like, you can begin before your grandfather's birth. You can stretch it out using all kinds of fancy. We don't mind. We like stories – good, bad and ugly. No matter what,' said the younger.

'Well, my grandfather lived in Calcutta before partition. Let's begin there. He was very conservative-minded, but he didn't start like that.'

'I don't understand why some people go sour with age. Like time eats away their souls, chewing their insides and only leaves behind some stinky poo-droppings. Take my elder brother here. I know he doesn't like me saying these things, do you, Bora Bhai? But I say that time has only made his soul bigger. Making him love everything, including tigers, even Wrath of God. Your grandfather, with all those smelly things in his soul, I bet he became a tiger-hunter.'

'Yes, it was on a tiger hunt that my grandfather brought me here. But it's a long and complicated story.'

It was low tide and the shores were muddy slopes with crabs and mudskippers. Leaning on his oar, the younger brother stood up to see if he could spot any tiger's pug marks. Suddenly, he slumped down and started to row at a furious pace and his elder brother, swayed by his urgency and fear, matched his strokes. It must have been Wrath of God's pugmarks, thought Bulbul. He gripped the gunwales tight and the dinghy raced through the channels, turning bends at dangerously acute angles. They only relaxed when they reached a wide inlet with dense mangroves covering the shoreline.

The younger brother steadied the course and the elder lit a chillum. Taking a drag and spewing smoke through his nose, the elder said, 'Your grandfather. He became a communalist then?'

'I suppose so. But the funny thing was – at least according to my grandmother, Dadu – his ancestors were low-caste Hindus.'

'I knew it. Converted ones are always the most zealous types. Hating types,' said the younger.

'But aren't we converted too? From one thing to another. From the days of Adam,' said the elder.

'Yes, Bora Bhai. That's why we don't hate anyone, Hindu or Muslim. Whoever, whoever. All are the same. All the same in a tiger's tummy. Anyway, what became of your grandfather?'

'In Calcutta, he became a trainee bookkeeper at a jute merchant's warehouse. Even on hot summer days, he wore a suit and tie. Very English-sahib like. His co-workers wore dhuties, lungies and pyjamas.'

'No, we don't like those trousers. Imagine when nature calls, with all those buttons and zips. Oh Allah, it doesn't bear thinking. And the tie. Did your grandpa fancy hanging himself on that tongue of a thing? He must have been drunk on some devilish Raj-liquor,' said the younger brother.

'Yes, he was. He wished the Raj would last a thousand years. No, until doomsday. My Dadu said he wasn't put off when the English laughed at him, calling him a mimicking macaque, a slimy Babu. He just thanked the English and laughed.'

'I can't believe it, you the grandson of this shameless man. He must have hated Gandhi real bad,' said the younger.

'Yes, he called Gandhi a primitive-wallah. He identified with Mir Zafar and fancied himself a big-time traitor, prepared to flush Bengal and the whole of India down the sewer.'

'Oh poor you. You've bad blood in you. Never mind. It doesn't change anything between us,' said the elder.

'But the funny thing is that later he became a Gandhi-loving nationalist. Wore only khadi-cotton. Even fasted when Gandhi did a hunger strike. Turned into a veggie-type.'

'Some somersaulting gentleman, your grandfather. I suppose one more somersault and he fell back into the Pakistani path,' said the younger.

It was late afternoon and streaks of sunlight squeezed through the mesh of mangroves and skimmed the water. They moored the dinghy by a muddy slope and invited Bulbul to share their food: water-soaked rice and honey.

'You see, we were once three brothers. The middle one was a forgetful type. Very fond of singing. He used to make us see things with his songs. He made his sister-in-law – my wife I mean – cry. He was eaten by a tiger while collecting honey,' said the elder.

'Sorry to hear about your brother. I hope he made it to heaven. Thank you for sharing this precious honey with me. But I don't understand how you can still love Wrath of God.'

'He was made that way. He was just doing his own thing. You can't hate someone for doing his own thing, can you? Can you blame a creeper for climbing your wall?' said the elder.

'So, you're not scared of Wrath of God?'

'Of course, I'm scared. You're made to be scared of him just as he was made to devour you. It's just like that,' said the elder.

'I still can't get my head around it. How can you love something you're scared of? Something that can eat you up?'

'I can't explain it. Love is like that. Very funny,' said the elder.

'Bora Bhai is like that, aren't you, Bora Bhai? People in our village call him a funny head,' said the younger.

After the meal, the brothers shared a chillum of tobacco then took to their oars.

'We'd like to hear your stories. How about your father and mother? They must have loved you like sweet mangoes. No?' asked the younger.

'I don't know. Dadu tells me that they loved me.'

'Oh, what happened to them?'

'My mother died giving birth to me.'

'Sorry that you never knew mother love. Most sweet thing,' said the elder.

'Our mother, she's ancient now, totally blind. She touches and loves our faces, doesn't she, Bora Bhai?'

'Yes, she does. Anyway, what happened to your father?'

'Well, it's a long story, and I have no memory of him either. What I know of him came from Dadu and others. So, it's mainly hearsay. Surely, you don't want to hear a second-hand story.'

'We don't mind even at a thousand hands. A story is a story. Changes of hands only add more truth to it. Isn't that so, Bora Bhai? So, we can't wait to hear what happened to your father.'

'Dadu was a real storyteller. My version will be a pale imitation

15

of hers. But if you insist. Well, my father was a troubled soul. Before he was married to my mother, my father was in love with a Hindu girl.'

'I see. Your father was a rebellious type then,' said the younger.

'My grandfather – then a Muslim leaguer – was horrified. But Dadu reminded him of his untouchable ancestry.'

'Your Dadu is such a truth-telling lady. A dynamite mouth, too. Anyway, your father. What did he do, then?' asked the younger.

'He was forced to give up the Hindu girl. But it drove him to drink. Often, he'd come home drunk and scream that he would become a Christian and eat pigs.'

'Did he eat pigs?' asked the younger.

'I don't know. But he fell apart completely when my mother died giving birth to me. He took to drinking even more.'

'Oh, no. I hope something bad didn't happen to him,' said the younger.

'Something bad did happen to him, all right.'

'Don't spare us any details. We like it gory, don't we, Bora Bhai?'

'It was during the riots in Calcutta, just before partition. I was a baby without a mother. Fearing the mob, no one dared to go out to get milk for me. That day, I was screaming and screaming. My father, drunk on a bottle of whisky, was sleeping. He woke up, cursing me for being born.'

'Not a very nice father, was he?' said the younger.

'He had his reasons. He was in a bad way.'

'Did he keep sleeping then?'

'Well, no. Suddenly, he just ran out of the front gate to get milk for me.'

'Ah, father love. He was risking his life for you.'

'Yes. I can't be sure what happened next. I heard several versions.'

'Tell us the one you heard most. We don't mind if you add some twists of your own. The truth of the story is the truth of the story.'

'I don't know what you mean. Well, my father, once he got the milk, he ran back towards the front gate. But the mob was chasing him with knives, clubs, and machetes.'

'I hope they missed him. I wouldn't want to be caught by that lot. I'd rather be eaten by a tiger,' said the younger.

'Well, they caught him and lynched him,' said Bulbul, feeling a slight tremor in his lips.

'Poor father. Poor you. You became an orphan boy,' said the younger, and began to sob.

'My little brother is like that. Very soft heart. He even cries when the fox takes one of our chicks, don't you, little brother?'

'So, you two don't kill your chickens? Don't eat any meat? Only dal, rice and vegetables?'

'Oh, no. We love meat, especially chicken. Very delicious, you know,' said the younger.

'I give up. I don't know what to make of you two.'

'We are what we are. So, what happened after?' said the younger, wiping his eyes with his gamcha-towel.

'It wasn't good. The mob started throwing stones and fireballs into the house.'

'It must have been very scary for you,' said the younger.

'Remember, I was just a baby. I've no memory of it.'

'Better that way. Some things are better not remembered,' said the younger.

'I wish. But how could I escape it?'

'Acha, very true. We still remember our grandfather, don't we, Bora Bhai? When he was whipped for refusing to grow indigo. It was way before we were born.'

'Sometimes it's like that. Someone else's experience from another time gets under your skin.'

'We're a funny lot, we humans. Anyway, what happened then?' asked the younger.

'The mob was about to break through the gate. Everyone started to scream.'

'Your grandfather was a hunter, wasn't he? Didn't he do something?' asked the younger.

'He did nothing. He was a frozen rabbit under the bed. It was the gardener. He took shots at the mob and dispersed them.'

'The gardener was some man. I like him, but your grandfather...' said the younger.

'He was what he was. I don't want to judge him too harshly.'

'Yes, he was him. I would have been scared too. So, what happened to your father's body?' asked the elder.

17

'It was torn to pieces.'

'Oh no. Allah have mercy on his soul,' the younger, sobbed again.

'Your poor grandfather. Your poor Dadu. What a terrible way to lose a son. Allah have mercy on their souls,' said the elder.

'Someone must have saved you. Otherwise, you wouldn't be here telling us your stories,' said the younger.

'I'm not sure how it happened. I was told it was the latrine cleaners. Most people shunned them, but Dadu loved them. She always kept a good portion for them when she cooked something nice. To my grandfather's annoyance, she would gossip and laugh with them on the verandah. So, with their help, my father's body parts were brought in and buried under the old neem tree in the inner courtyard, next to my mother's.'

'So, a large part of you is still in India then?' asked the younger.

'Yes.'

'Bloody partition. It's the root of so much of our ills. I suppose your family then came over here.'

'Yes, my grandfather brought his family back to Dambarpur, his ancestral village, now in Pakistan. But Dadu wasn't happy.'

'How could she be happy? Leaving her son behind?'

'It's a sadness she carried all her life. But she didn't talk much about it.'

'We understand, don't we, Bora Bhai? If you don't talk, you feed the monster. He grows fatter and fatter inside you. Until he and you become one. That's why we never stop talking about our middle brother.'

'Dadu never stopped talking about their home in Calcutta.'

'Memory thing is a big botheration. It clings to you like leeches. It is sometimes saddening, sometimes sweet like honey. Anyway, what did she talk about?' asked the younger.

'So many things, like the shaded courtyard, the mango tree in blossom, the shadow passing the length of the veranda, the little *doog-doogi* drums of the hawkers in the afternoons, the locked room at the back with its statue of Mother Kali with her garland of skulls, and always the roof with its cool breeze from the Hooghly.'

'Yes, those are honey-memories,' said the elder.

'I imagined them so many times they became my memories.'

'Now, they have become our memories too. We'll tell them to our children and grandchildren. One day, they will own them, too,' said the elder.

Suddenly, the sun dropped behind the mangroves and the mauve of the river gave way to darkness. Searching for the stars, they remained on the foredeck as silence descended on the forest.

'Wrath of God is dreaming,' said the younger.

'Really? What does he dream?'

'Perhaps he's dreaming of how he ambushed our middle brother. He knew he would be coming for that kewra tree, laden with that enormous hive. Foolish as he was, our middle brother couldn't resist whistling a tune. He was far too easy a catch for Wrath of God. Perhaps that's why he's dreaming about it. Tigers like it easy. He leapt across the channel from the dense green fronds of the nipa palms. Perhaps our middle brother had just climbed a step up the Kewra tree,' said the younger.

'We didn't find his head. Only the spine and the breast bones. It was proof enough that Wrath of God enjoyed feasting on him. That's why he dreams about him,' said the elder.

'Wrath of God's a monster. I hope someone shoots him dead.'

'Why? What did he do to you?' asked the elder.

'Bora Bhai is like this. He's funny about the hate thing. He finds it nasty, don't you, Bora Bhai?'

CHAPTER 3

'Dadu, tell me a story?' Bulbul begged.

'Yes, my little bird. But wait for the stars to appear in the sky.'

Five years had passed since they crossed the border into East Bengal. Now, draped in green/white and a crescent moon, it had become East Pakistan. If he'd thought about it, Syed Amir Shah would have found it incredible that he would fall victim to such a savage irony of things coming back full circle. He was destined for it. Fired by his exuberance for Feringhee ideas, he'd been lured away, all those years ago, from Dambarpur to one of the hubs of the empire and the modern world, only to be returned to the same old swampy backwater of the Brahmaputra delta. He still wore punjabi, askan and karakul hats and harboured the wounds of communal violence, but had lost much of his enthusiasm for Pakistan.

'If you'd listened to me, I could've told you,' said Dadu. 'Nothing doing in this land of pure Islam stuff. It'd be too pure for you to digest. Only a morsel and you'd be running to the latrine.'

He'd lost the grandeur of his Calcutta days when they escaped, abandoning his business, mansion, savings and connections. Luckily, his father had left him property in Dambarpur – several tin-roofed huts and an outer bungalow – all in disrepair. Although it was primitive compared to the Calcutta mansion, it could be made habitable. He'd also inherited some excellent arable land and stretches of swamp; if managed properly, they could earn him a reasonable living. But he wasn't interested.

'How can we live here? No electricity. Damn place is dead. Bloody foxes taking it over, howling the place down. Not to mention the snakes. Damn things slither like they own the place. How can any human live here?'

'Correct me if I'm wrong,' said Dadu. 'Your father, didn't he live here? So, he wasn't a human, then? A Londony Feringhee sahib. No doubt, an evil, pig-eating type. He thinks some of us are blood-kin of monkeys, those pink-bottomed howlers that used to raid my kitchen. Not to mention pooing and pissing everywhere. So, your dad, was he one of them?'

'Shut your foul mouth. How dare you speak of my father like that. Pouring venom on his person. He was a saint. And don't bring the Feringhees into it. Anyway, you're too stupid to understand evolution. I've no time for those God-hating ideas, but it's very proper. Scientific, you know,' said Syed Amir Shah.

He couldn't wait to leave Dambarpur, but Dadu wanted to stay there. She only relented when he argued that Bulbul would soon need schooling. For that they must move to a large town. Besides, he wanted to try his hands at the jute trade again. With both ends in mind, he chose Mominabad, the largest town in the region, about ninety kilometres north of Dambarpur.

It was the beginning of the summer months in Dambarpur. There was no sign of rain – only long days of oppressive heat and dust. Sitting on a recliner under a jackfruit tree, Syed Amir Shah had been watching Bulbul, a feral child covered in dust, running wild under the savage sun. At the approach of midday, on a whim, he decided to take him to the pond for a wash.

'What do you want to become? When you grow up?' he asked.

'I want to be a fish-catcher. Catch the largest catfish in the swamp.'

'Fish-catcher? Can't you think of something else?'

'Maybe I'll look after a big cow. Milk her. Many, many buckets.'

Syed Amir Shah shook his head, thinking he should have taken the boy out of this rural backwater much earlier. Perhaps it was already too late to clean him of his shameful inclinations to lowly bumpkinness. He felt remorse for not instructing him properly. Had he done his duty as a grandfather, he could have fostered some higher ambitions. He had to do something, but what? Perhaps he should teach the boy how to swim – surrounded by so much water, the danger of drowning was all too real.

Reaching the ghat to the pond, Syed Amir Shah told Bulbul, 'Get ready, my boy. It's time that you learnt swimming.' He decided on the method that had worked for him, the method his father had used; it involved throwing the learner into the water and expecting him to scramble back to safety. He held Bulbul by his legs and arms, took a swing and threw him into the water as far as he could. Bulbul sank. Nearly a minute went by and he hadn't surfaced. Syed Amir Shah froze. He stood there, in a daze. Fortunately, a village girl, who'd come to fetch water, dived in, pulled Bulbul up and brought him to the ghat. He looked dead. While Syed Amir Shah stood there, still dazed, the girl pressed his chest and breathed into his mouth. Still, Bulbul lay inert. In desperation, the girl, hitching her sari to her knees, straddled his chest. Head bent, she thumped it and gave him another breath, but this time with the full vigour of her lungs. Terrible seconds passed, but at last Bulbul threw up water.

By now the news had reached Dadu. She'd dropped her padukas and come running. She grabbed Bulbul and took him home. She didn't say anything to Syed Amir Shah, but he knew what her looks said. Through much of that afternoon Bulbul slept; he woke up at dusk, terribly hungry. Dadu fried him a giant swan's egg and made coconut bread. While Syed Amir Shah smoked his hookah on the veranda, that night, Dadu spread a soft rattan-mat in the courtyard. On it, she lay face-up on a long, round pillow, Bulbul next to her, both looking at the stars.

'Do you want to hear Behula's stories?' asked Dadu.

'Who's Behula?'

'She's a girl who lived on the banks of Brahmaputra. Just at the bend, near the lines of kapok trees. Where we grow mustard and lentils. You can still see the ruined house. Have you been there?'

'No, Dadu. I'm scared. Rakshasa-demons, raw-eaters and snakes live there.'

'Well, my little bird, the story I'm about to tell is all about them. If you're too scared, I can tell you another story. Perhaps about a baby deer and her mummy.'

'No, Dadu. I love scary. Please tell it.'

'You're not going to wet your bed? Or wake up screaming?'

'No, I promise, Dadu.'

'Well, here goes. Bless the storytellers, bless the long-memory men, bless the long-memory women. It's not a once-upon-a-time story, full of fancy, and make-believe, but about a girl who lived down our way, who cooked, cleaned, drew water from the river, put kohl on her eyes, and dreamt of a man. She eloped with him to live with him in a house by the river bank.

'On the other side of the river, there lived a fish-merchant. He was bad-tempered, mean, and a big-eater with a huge, hanging tummy. He was a funny sight, but no one was allowed to laugh. He had seven sons. Allah only knows how, but all of them turned out to be hardworking, kindly souls, handsome, fit, and modest. One day, poisonous Manasa, the queen of snakes, who grew powerful tilling all things mean-spirited and vain, was taken by a new fancy.'

'You don't like her, Dadu, do you?'

'Never interrupt the storyteller. It puts holes in the memory-time. It eats into the swing and swallows it up. And never mind what I think. It's the story that doesn't like her. As I was saying, Manasa, not happy to be the queen of snakes, gluttoning on fish, frogs and other snakes, wanted to be worshipped by man. So, she demanded that the fish merchant make a statue of her and worship her with tulsi leaves and milk.'

'How does she talk? Does she have a mouth like us?'

'I told you, don't interrupt the storyteller. Who cares if she has a mouth or not? What matters is the story. Does it have mouths? Yes, the story has a thousand mouths. It can say anything it wants.'

'I see. The story. It's like a rakshasa-demon. Does it have many heads too?'

'If you ask questions all the time, I can't tell you the story.'

'Please, Dadu. Promise, no more questions.'

'Proud that he was, the fish merchant refused to worship Manasa. He sent her packing to her hissing den.'

'You told me, Dadu, didn't you? Queens live in palaces. How come the snake-queen lives in a den?'

'There you go again. Already ruining the storyteller, killing her in her tracks. Didn't I tell you the story has a thousand mouths? If one mouth speaks of a palace, the others can speak of shacks. Or, no house at all. Understand?'

'Promise, promise, Dadu. No more interruptions.'

'Manasa sent one of her poisonous subjects, a long, vicious type, darker than coal-dark and it bit one of the merchant's boys and he died all blue. Oh, the same thing happened five more times. The fish merchant was left with only one of his sons, his youngest. His name was Lakshindar. Stubborn as ever, the fish merchant still refused to worship Manasa, and all was set for the inevitable. The merchant's youngest – ah sadness, ah such a nice boy. Desperate, the merchant hired scholars from here, there, and even from across the seven seas.'

'Sorry, sorry, Dadu. What is a scholar?'

'It's impossible to tell you a story. What botheration. A scholar is a book reader. Stories keep them, all hush hush, you know, to come alive.'

'Is he a magic man, then?'

'Do you want to hear the story or not?'

'I promise, Dadu. Never again. No more interruptions.'

'He hired scholars and set them on books – written, spoken, hidden in Pharaoh's tomb. Some books not yet born and screaming to come out. He wanted the scholars to find a way to save the boy.

'So, the scholars are books' mothers. I want to be like them. Reading books.'

'Book reading is good. But you have to be careful about the kinds you read. Back to the story, then. After searching long and hard the scholars found that if Lakshindar had married a girl – unblemished of misdeeds and pure of heart – Manasa couldn't have him killed. Fortunately, they didn't have to look far to find that girl because Behula only lived on the other side of the river. Everything was set and the fish merchant spared no expense for a lavish wedding. Yet knowing that Manasa – vicious and crafty as she was – would try to find a way of killing his boy on the wedding night, he took meticulous measures. He called in the best builder in the land to build a house without holes, so no snake could enter it on the wedding night. Manasa threatened to unleash her snakes on the builder and his entire family. Frightened, the builder agreed to leave a hole of one hair's breadth in the building.'

'How did the builder build such a tiny hole?'

'If you want me to explain everything in a story... Oh, what botheration. It might take me a whole year to tell just one story. Not to mention boredom. Besides, how do I know how he built it? I'm a storyteller, not a builder. Acha, to the story. After the ceremony and the festivity, the newlywed couple was lodged in the newly-built building. When the couple was deep asleep at midnight, Manasa sent her thinnest, cleverest and most poisonous snake to the building. It entered through the hair-thin hole and was about to bite Lakshindar, but stopped, realising that his bride, Behula hadn't committed any sin. Oh, what to do? That snake had no trouble coming up with a crafty ploy. It dipped its tail in the lamp's oil and smeared it on the parting of Behula's hair, so Behula was no longer pure. Now the snake had it all clear to bite Lakshindar.'

'Dadu. Sorry, sorry. Why is putting oil in your hair is a bad thing? Also, Behula didn't do it. It's not her fault.'

'I don't make the rules. It's the men-folks and the Gods. Besides, the story was there long before me. I'm just a memory woman. Just a teller.'

'What happened then, Dadu?'

'What do you think? The snake bit Lakshindar and he died.'

'Oh, no. I don't like that.'

'Story is a story. You don't have to like it or hate it. Anyway, it's too late now. It's time to sleep,' said Dadu. 'We'll continue with the story tomorrow.'

The following day, Dadu sent for the girl who saved Bulbul from drowning. Her name was Kona Das. She belonged to a low Hindu caste of cobblers. Her father had died the previous year of a snake bite. Her mother worked from dawn to dusk, husking rice, grinding spices, making cow-dung fuel, doing odd jobs for the landowning families, and still couldn't make ends meet. Kona Das, who was fifteen then, came with her mother.

'Thank you for saving my grandson. What can I do for you?' asked Dadu.

Kona Das smiled nervously but didn't say anything. Her mother cleared her throat and said, 'You know, Bibi. Since Kona's father died, I've been struggling. I can hardly feed myself.'

'Yes, I know. We women are doomed. With our menfolk and without them. Such is the unfairness of the Gods. Tell me, what can I do for you?'

'Take the girl. Kona is hardworking and knows many crafts. Keep her at home. She can do chores for you.'

'All right, I'll think about it.'

Dadu raised the issue with Syed Amir Shah.

'Keeping a young Hindu girl at home. I'm not sure. It could be a lot of trouble.'

'What trouble? Because the girl is of the cobbler caste? Does she remind you of your grandfather? Poor grandfather cobbler. It'd pain him to know that you're ashamed of him – now that you're parading your phoney Syed in your name.'

'One day you'll kill me with that tongue of yours,' said Syed Amir Shah, and walked out.

Kona Das came to live with Dadu and the family.

In the waterland, there was no sign of the heat and the humidity dropping. Sometimes clouds would gather high up in the sky, dulling the landscape, but no rain. People were struggling to get through the days. Besides, the village was terrified to hear news of approaching smallpox.

Most of the villages on the other side of the river were already infected. On their side, the disease had spread to some neighbouring villages. The villagers went to the mosque for all-night prayers, fasted, and promised animal sacrifices to keep the demon of smallpox at bay, but they knew that only the goddess

Sheetla Devi had this power. Muslim and Hindu elders visited the temple to see the purohit. He agreed that Sheetla Devi needed to be summoned to protect the village.

Three days later, in the afternoon, Bulbul heard the conch shells blowing and the beating of kettle drums. He ran out and saw a group, led by the purohit, circling the village. He joined the children following the group. Bedecked in a blue sari with beads and shells, Sheetla Devi was seated on a donkey, looking very young and pretty despite her three eyes and four hands. Accompanied by kettle drums and conches, with dust rising to a dense, grey whirlpool from the feet of the group, the purohit intoned some Sanskrit verses, sprinkling water from a brass pitcher as he went. Three times, they circled the village. Solemn, but for a faint smile on his face, the purohit finally declared that the village was fortified; an impenetrable wall had been erected and there was no way the demon of smallpox could pass. Unless, of course, sinners in the village were in cahoots with the demon of smallpox. In that case, it would be necessary to identify them, catch them, shave their heads, and drive them out of the village. A shiver ran through the bodies of all those present, especially those of the poor, physically disabled, and those branded mad. It was from their ranks that the victim was usually chosen.

Bulbul came home and told Dadu what he had seen. Overhearing him, his grandfather ranted, 'It's all primitive mumbo-jumbo. It's compromising the boy's brain. And you, Bibi, you're feeding the boy with your nonsense stories. Rakshasas, demons and whatnot. Very damaging for the boy. It's time we take him out of all this.'

'Are you getting back to your Feringhee ideas? Your reason-prison-lightness business? Now, even though you've got your Pakistan, I bet, next, you'll want to bring back – you know – the queen from London, that munshi-loving empress herself, to rule us again. What tamasha,' said Dadu.

That night, Dadu again lay on the rattan mat in the courtyard, her hand fluttering a palm-leaf fan. Bulbul was next to her. Unlike the previous night when they'd shone brilliantly, the stars remained hidden under dark clouds. Bulbul knew he needn't remind Dadu of the story, but he did.

'Now that Lakshindar is dead. Is the story dead, too?'

'No. Just the beginning. Remember, the story has a thousand mouths. If it dies, we will all be dead too. Acha?'

'Determined to bring him back to life, Behula refused to have Lakshindar cremated. Prompted by the urgency of the task, the villagers worked through the night to cut the plumpest and the tallest of banana trees. By dawn, the raft was ready for the journey to the unknown. When Behula, her hair-parting smeared in blood-red vermilion, sat as a lotus on the raft with dead Lakshindar on her lap, the villagers, in a cacophony of conch-blowing, kettledrums and chanting sacred verses, pushed off the raft. While Lakshindar's body rotted, the raft drifted downstream, facing many fearsome storms. After several days, it reached a deserted village.

'When Behula climbed the riverbank, she spotted two young men under a bakul tree with a caged hunting bird beside them. They must be bird hunters, thought Behula, on their way to the swamp, to hunt for koora-birds. As she approached them, she realised one of them was dead. What happened, she asked. Long, long story, said the living brother. They had been resting under the same bakul tree where they were now. It was hot and humid, and in the shade they fell asleep. Without realising it, one brother had slept on a snake hole. The other brother woke up to find his brother dead. Seeing they were in the same plight, Behula invited the living brother to come on board her raft with his dead brother. When I find a way to bring my husband back to life, said Behula, I will help your brother too. Now the four of them were drifting downstream.

'It was midday and Behula needed a wash. Near a bed of hyacinth, she decided to plunge into the river. After swimming under the water, she surfaced between two clumps of hyacinth, and looked towards the raft. She couldn't believe her eyes. She thought it was a mirage at the bidding of the sun, its rays bouncing off the raft's cabin. She closed and opened her eyes several times. The brothers weren't humans, but evil raw-eaters, rakshasa-demons. Like the living one, the dead one stood towering in its huge, gross frame, its fangs dripping poison, its eyes – enormous in the middle of its head – burning like the sun. Snorting like hungry beasts, they were about to devour the dead, rotting body of Lakshindar. How could she bring him back to life without a body?

'Quick as a darting fish, Behula swam beneath the water and

reached the raft. Sensing her presence, the brothers assumed their previous forms: one a nice young man, the other a dead body. Drawing a veil over her head, Behula went inside the little cabin on the raft to change her clothes. She came out with two cups of drinks. First, she told the living brother that she had been administering this drink to her dead husband to slow the body's decomposition. She would like to try it on his dead brother. The living brother couldn't refuse it. She opened the dead one's mouth and poured down the drink. She gave the other glass to the living brother and said it would fortify him for the long journey ahead. He took a sip. Within minutes, both were dead.

'How come they're so stupid to fall for it? And aren't they rakshasa-demons, Dadu? You can't kill them with poison drinks.'

'A story has a thousand mouths. Didn't I tell you that? It can kill anyone with anything it likes.'

'A story. Stronger than a rakshasa-demon? Why doesn't it look fearsome?'

'A story is a thousand times stronger. If it were to appear, it would fill up the entire universe. So it doesn't appear, only speaks. Now off to bed. We'll continue tomorrow.'

The following day, Kona Das arrived with her things in a bundle.

'What can you cook?' asked Dadu.

'We're low caste, Bibi. Wouldn't I pollute you if I cooked for you?' said Kona Das.

'What do you think I am? A sickly little girl? So easily polluted? Anyway, the whole polluting business. Such tamasha. What colour is your blood?'

'Red, Bibi.'

'Mine too. Now go to the kitchen. See what you can find. Make me a snack. Something savoury.'

From then on, Kona Das became inseparable from Dadu. She did chores for her, washed her clothes, ground her spices, helped her with cooking, arranged her room, and became her confidante and travelling companion. She slept in the same room with Dadu, on a rattan-weaved mattress, and each morning, brought her the mortar and the pestle for cracking betel nuts.

Kona Das had prepared fried puffed rice with mustard oil and green chilli. Seated on a low, cane-made stool on the veranda, Dadu was enjoying them, thinking that the girl had an uncanny insight into her desires, knowing exactly what she wanted to eat and how to prepare it to her liking. Hearing the chatter of an approaching group of men, Dadu went inside. She thought they might have come to talk to her about the cultivation and the management of the land and the swamp. Usually, she conducted these talks from behind the front door with the men seated in the inner courtyard. Today, however, the men came to talk to her husband.

Before arriving, the men had decided that it would be Matab Ali who would speak for the group. He was a frail old man with a thin, long beard and a white skullcap, who laboured his way on a stick. He coughed and spoke in a rasping voice, as if choking.

'Bora Shahib,' he addressed Syed Amir Shah, 'you know the smallpox. And so many other dangers and calamities threatening the village. We had floods, tornados, and drought. Even the bad old jinn are menacing us again.'

'What's your point, Matab Ali?' asked Syed Amir Shah.

'Our purohit, our mullah, our keeper of jinn. And, of course, the hard work of the snake-man and the medicine man. They're all trying to safeguard the village. But, Bora Shahib, sad to say, it's not enough.'

'But what can I do?'

'The power of sainthood. Your father and grandfather protected our village. For two generations we lived free of calamities. We were the envy of the entire swamp country. Bora Shahib, I don't want to be disrespectful. You've your own reason for not following the saintly path. I blame the Feringhees and their funny ideas. I hear they keep little tubes in their latrine rooms. Like magic men, they put concoctions in them and then look into them with their magnifying glasses. Funny ways to get to the truth of things.'

'So, what are you driving at, Matab Ali?'

'We can't do without a saint in the village. Please, Bora Shahib.'

'I can't be a saint, even if I wanted to. I've renounced it. You know, one can never get it back.'

'We're aware of that, Bora Shahib. We're not thinking of you. It's your grandson.'

'You mean you want Bulbul to be your saint.'

'Yes, Bora Shahib. The boy has a look. And the aura. We feel the power of sainthood – how can I put it? – trying to spurt through him. Like a fountain.'

'I don't know. The boy needs to go to school now. If he wants to be a saint when he grows up, it's up to him.'

Despite further pleadings, Syed Amir Shah wouldn't budge; he was determined to take Bulbul to to school in Mominabad. It was only a few months before the beginning of the school term. Syed Amir Shah travelled to Mominabad to rent a house, a godown for his jute trade, and to look for a suitable school for Bulbul.

After the traumatic experience of the swimming lesson, Bulbul was afraid of going to the pond to bathe. But one midday, at Dadu's prompting, he accompanied Kona Das to the pond. At first, he just walked along the water's edge and wet his feet down the gentle slope, but then she persuaded him to climb on her back. She waded up to her waist and dipped in with Bulbul clinging to her. Slowly, over the next few days, Kona Das taught him the basics of swimming. Dadu said, 'At least you won't die drowning.'

It was still hot and humid, but dense, dark clouds were gathering low in the sky. From time to time there was lightning and thunder too. Perhaps the monsoon was almost there. In the afternoon, accompanied by Kona Das, Bulbul went to the swampland, reduced to a murky shallow pool, to see the annual fishing event in which most of the men and boys of the village participated. They came with their bamboo, bell-bottomed polo-traps, and stood along the width of the shallow water of the swamp. Then they advanced slowly and, at each step, sank their polo-traps into the mud, catching any fish in their path. Encouraged by the sight of a woman and two young girls among the fishers, Kona Das waded in with her polo-trap.

'What are you doing here?' asked the man beside her.

'Fishing like you. Like the woman and the girls over there.'

'That woman and the girls don't count. She's a beggar woman. Very loose morals. The girls are her daughters. Mad types. They're outside the law. Things like shame don't apply to them, like they don't apply to a beast,' said the man.

'I'm untouchable. I don't count either,' said Kona Das.

'You've a sharp tongue for an untouchable,' said the man.

She ignored him and kept pace with the others in her line, plunging her polo-trap into the water.

Standing on top of a mound, Bulbul watched. It was getting darker and lightning was coming nearer and becoming frequent. It scared him that he couldn't call Kona Das. She'd moved far from the shore and was invisible in the darkening swampland. He left the mound and took shelter under a giant raintree. At first he didn't catch on, but the roar of the fishing group told him the rain was here, and within seconds, it was sweeping the raintrees. Despite the protection of the dense foliage, the slanting rain was soaking him. Kona Das came running; she had caught two catfish. She, too, was soaked. Monsoon was here and they would have downpours for weeks on end.

That night, Dadu and Kona Das cooked the catfish. Syed Amir Shah was still away in Mominabad. After the meal, while Bulbul snuggled next to Dadu under a khata-quilt in the bed, Kona Das lay on the pati-mattress on the floor.

'Now that rakshasa-demons are dead, was Behula safe, Dadu?' asked Bulbul.

'Not so soon, my little bird. She has more trials ahead of her, for she hasn't yet faced the female ones. Rakshasi-demons. They can be more crafty. More vicious,' said Dadu.

'That's not fair.'

'Fairness doesn't concern the story. It likes to spin more and more trials to test you. Find out what you're made of.'

'How come the story is so nasty? More vicious than a rakshasi-demon?'

'Don't forget it can kill any rakshasa/rakshasi-demon. And save you, as it has saved Behula. She'd have been dead and gone long ago if it weren't for the story. No one would remember her.

'Behula's raft was making a good progress downstream in a fair wind. Suddenly, she saw a huge barrier ahead of her – water touching the sky and frozen into an impenetrable wall. There was no way the raft could pass through it. Lakshindar's body was decomposing fast; without preserving a good portion of it, she could never bring him back to life. So, what to do? She was getting desperate. She moored the raft at the water's edge and climbed up the banks, hoping to find help. All she saw was a little girl, wearing

31

white, and weeping. What's the matter? asked Behula. I was with my Baba and Ma, said the girl, travelling in a boat to see my grandmother on the other side of the swampland. Then, a rakshasi-demon, pretending to be a little girl, gained our trust, and while my Baba and Ma slept, she ate them. Why didn't she eat you? asked Behula. Oh yes, she gobbled me up too, said the little girl, but she had to vomit me out. It was my amulet. See, it's still around my neck.

'Feeling pity for the girl, Behula invited her to the raft, saying she would find a way to cross the barrier and take her to safety. Time passed, the night came, and the barrier was still there. Behula was praying, calling on all the gods and ancestors for help, but to no avail.

'As night fell, the little girl said she needed to go ashore on a call of nature. So, off she went. When she hadn't returned for ages, Behula got worried. She lit the hurricane lamp and went to search for her. She hadn't gone far when she heard a noise coming. She hid behind a mound to see what was happening. It was a dark night, and the little girl in white glowed like a thousand fireflies. She was hunching over something. Suddenly, Behula saw her transformed into a fearsome giant. She was as tall as the sky. Her orb-like eye on her forehead lit up the landscape. Her long, matted snake hair hissed and her giant teeth gnashed. She was dripping buckets of saliva and snorting. Then she got down to her raw eating: devouring buffalos, cows, and goats. Behula couldn't take any more; she rushed to the raft. She knew that the barrier was the rakshasi's doing and that she was biding her time to devour her and her husband's body.'

'Why didn't the rakshasi eat them immediately?' asked Bulbul.

'What can I do if the story wants to take its time? I can't force it, can I? Also, the story wants to give Behula a chance. See, it can be kind too,' said Dadu.

'Behula opened the sacred scroll her mother had tucked into her trunk for her journey into the unknown. She read that a blue glow on the throat was a sure sign that the bearer was the queen among the rakshasi demons. There had been such a blue glow on the little girl's throat. Her type were the most difficult rakshasi demons to kill, though the scroll provided precise instructions.

'When the girl returned, all sweet and demure, Behula pretended she suspected nothing. She was worried that the rakshasi-demon might eat her dead husband's body, but then thought: perhaps after such a large meal of raw eating, she wouldn't be tempted so soon. Behula memorised how to kill the rakshasi demon queen. Still, no time to lose. She left the raft, climbed the river bank, ran along it some distance, then climbed down and dived into the water. She was going down and down to a depth beyond measure, and there in silence, in darkness, cold, strange creatures, their eyes glowing, looked at her. Finally, she saw the palace as described in the scroll. There she would find a bluebird in a golden cage inside it. She knew the only way to kill the queen rakshasi demon was to break the bluebird's neck.'

'How come Behula can hold her breath for such a long time? Isn't she human?' asked Bulbul.

'Yes, she's human. It's the story's gift to her. She deserves it, don't you think?' said Dadu.

'As she entered the palace, she was assailed by the most frightful noise. Everything shook as if caught in an earthquake. From an open door, she entered the palace, down the long corridor and several anterooms, until she reached a vast hall. She hid behind a small wall. Finally, she saw the snake. It was at least a thousand feet tall, its girth the measure of several houses. It was guarding the bird. An army of strange beasts brought in five elephants and a dozen pigs and offered them to the snake. It gobbled them up. Behula knew it would be impossible to sneak up to steal the cage with the bluebird. The snake was vigilant to the slightest vibration, faintest smell and, despite its size, it was lightning quick. It never rested or slept, always guarding the bluebird – the soul of the queen rakshasi-demon. Behula took out her flute and started to play.

'I didn't know she had a flute,' said Bulbul.

'If everything is spelt out, the story would die in its telling. Understand? Besides, the flute is a gift from the story.'

'Can I have some gifts from the story?'

'Don't be greedy. It has already given you a gift. The gift of listening – a very highly esteemed gift. You're enjoying the story, aren't you?'

'Hearing Behula's flute, the snake stood up all its thousand feet, spread its hood and hissed a tempest that blew out all the lamps and scattered the furniture. It was ready to strike Behula. Undaunted, she went forward, playing her flute. Soon the snake began to wobble, falling to the ground as if a mountain had collapsed. It began to snore, deep in sleep. Taking her chance, Behula gathered the cage with the bluebird and returned to the raft. Putting clumps of hyacinth on her head, she peeked into the raft. The queen rakshasi demon was still in the little girl's body, but seemed to be finding it difficult to restrain her urges. She was licking the festering wounds on Lakshindar's body.

'When she saw Behula climbing the raft, she became sweet and innocent again, but seeing the bluebird her mood changed. She assumed the fearsome aspect of a rakshasi demon, advancing to devour Behula. Quick as a storm wind, Behula broke the bluebird's neck before the rakshasi demon could reach her. In a flash, the giantess fell into the water, disintegrating into dust. As soon as she was dead, the water barrier came down. Finally, Behula was on her way again, drifting downstream.'

That night, Bulbul fell asleep hearing the rain. For days and weeks the rain kept falling until the swamp and the village became one giant waterland. It took Syed Amir Shah months to return from Mominabad. The good news was that he'd managed to rent a house for them, a godown for his jute business, and located a possible school for Bulbul.

The night before they were to travel to Mominabad, Bulbul asked Dadu to finish the story.

'Story is endless, but I'll finish it tonight for you, my little bird. Yes, Behula drifted downstream, reaching a shore where a washerwoman was beating clothes. She heard Behula's story and took pity on her. She happened to be the aunt of Manasa, the snake queen herself.

'Is that another of the story's gifts?' asked Bulbul.

'Don't be so cocky. You want to hear the end of the story or not?'

'Well, then. The washerwoman took Behula and her rotting husband to the palace of Manasa beneath the deepest waters. It was a gilded building of a blinding yellow hue, cylindrical towers, some reaching the sky, repeating themselves to infinity, and covered with carvings of snakes inlaid with emeralds, rubies and sapphires. Stationed around the palace were millions of snakes, their fangs twitching to strike, their muscles tensed to coil and squeeze out the life of any living body. At the washerwoman's request, Manasa granted Behula an audience. At midnight, with thousands of oil lamps burning, Manasa sat on her throne with the other gods and goddesses beside her. All waited for the gong to strike, and when it did, Behula started to dance. Throughout the night she danced, blood pouring from her feet. It was a dance the likes of which the gods had never seen; they were in tears. At dawn, Manasa stopped her. I give back your husband's life, she said. Take him home and live happily ever after.'

'What is ever after time, Dadu?' asked Bulbul.

'How do I know?' said Dadu, 'It's a story's secret. It told me nothing. Absolutely nothing about it.'

The following day, a large sampan moored at the ghat. Syed Amir Shah, Dadu, Kona Das, and Bulbul climbed on board. Villagers came to see them off, and the elders waded into the water and pushed the sampan on its way, across the swampland, then taking the Brahmaputra, its tributaries upriver. After four days and nights of punting, rowing, and being propelled by the wind in the sail, they reached Mominabad.

CHAPTER 4

Some ninety kilometres upriver from Dambarpur, along the banks of the Brahmaputra, Mominabad was built by the colonisers as a regional administrative centre and a hub of the jute trade. Many of the red-bricked buildings of the colonial city survived. Syed Amir Shah had rented a small house near the centre and a godown by the river. It was a bustling place with thousands of rickshaws and bicycles but only a few cars. Most belonged to government officials; only two were privately owned. Syed Amir Shah had chosen an English-medium, missionary school for Bulbul – a remnant of the colonial days.

Dadu wasn't happy about it. 'You tried the Feringhee ways. Look what happened to you. Full of loose screws, making a racket in your brain – full of hugger-mugger confusion.'

'I want the best school for our grandson. Everyone knows that's the English school. It will groom the boy for power.'

'What power? Pakistan power? Total tamasha,' she said. 'Already, it's robbing us of our own tongue. You want the boy to be shameless? Lovey-dovey with them. They'll spit on him. Yes, the way the Feringhees spat on you.'

Some students had recently been killed in Dacca for demanding recognition of Bangla, and discontent was brewing in Mominabad, too, with demonstrations and rioting. When these forced the schools to close, Bulbul felt relief. From day one, he had been picked on by other boys, town-grown from well-to-do, aspiring families, an ordeal that lasted until he left that school five years later.

He had been born in the largest and most modern city in the British Indian empire, but six years in Dambarpur had shaped him into a country boy, as if his blood smelt of paddies, cow dung, and the swamp's muddy waters.

'Does your mother cook with cow dung?' the boys teased him.

'I have no mother. She's dead,' said Bulbul.

'Was she a beggar woman? No food to eat. Was that how she died?'

Bulbul couldn't take the taunts anymore; he ran out of school and went home. His grandfather was cross with him, but Dadu told him, 'Next time they pick on you, punch them hard. Make them bleed, those rascal sons of Satan.'

His grandfather took him back to school. For punishment, he was put in an empty classroom and made to write on the blackboard, filling it up, rubbing it clean to begin all over again: *I am as stupid as a little heron.* At first he was upset about doing this mindless task, but with each repetition, he felt cleverer. It was the teacher who was dumb for choosing this punishment. How could he not know that herons were intelligent birds? Hadn't he noticed their infinite patience in ambushing fish, and ways of finding the topmost branch of a tree to sleep at night – where even the most nimble predators couldn't reach? Yes, he would be a little heron any day.

The boys laughed at the way he spoke Bengali. Even the teachers poked fun at him: Our little bird pipes jolly good rustic tunes, very bucolic. What should we call him, boys? teachers would ask the class. Bumpkin, Sir, the boys would chorus. We can't have bumpkinness in this school, can we? Go home and shed your uncouth ways of speaking – otherwise, all our efforts to groom you for power and wealth will fall, dare we say, into a shithole.

He had worse difficulties with English. Whereas most of the boys had private tuition in the language, he had none. Dadu berated her husband. 'You sent our grandson to a Feringhee school. Did you bother to think about it? No. I'm up to my eyes with your bragging that you speak English like a pukka sahib. Bha, bha. Why then, not give the boy a bit of the Feringhee tongue? It's vulgar and sounds like a howler, but the boy is suffering. It's like throwing him into a den of snakes with nothing, not even a stick.'

Estranged from his teachers and fellow students, Bulbul paid little notice to his lessons, made the least possible effort at his homework, and often skived. Some days, he would head for the river. During winter months, he would wander through the dunes, dig himself under the sand as if he were a burrowing animal, perhaps a mole, then look up at the sky and see the vultures catching the thermals and circling higher and higher and disappearing in the blue. How nice it would be to be a vulture and get far, far away. Sometimes, he would wade through the water, looking at tiny fish shoals for hours. If he were a fish swimming with so many friends, there would be no school, taunts and bullying. When afternoon came, he would go home. He would lie about his absence, but the school would demand letters from his grandfather, and he would be punished again when they failed to appear. He had to stand on a high bench for hours, perching over his classmates and pulling his ears. His peers would vie with each other to mock him: Look at the bird; he wants to shit on us from high up. He would laugh inside, thinking that would be a good idea.

In summer, he would wander the lush bushes along the river, looking at plants and trees, their trunks, branches, leaves, barks and flowers, and imagine their roots, their underground lives of mazes and secret connections. If he turned into a tree, he'd relate not only to other trees and their roots, but also to the birds, the insects and the bees that fed and nested in them. After the rain, when the river would be full, he would watch the boats and dolphins. He would wait for the wind to pick up and the waves to form little humps of galloping water and fold into each other. He would keep his eyes fastened on them until they died down into a flat current again.

One spring when the dunes were still above water, playing truant, he hid in one of the sandy caverns, but instead of burying himself in the sand, he went for a swim. He took his half-pants off and ran into a channel, took a dip, then floated on his back. No vultures circled the sky that day, only some scattered clouds. He thought he was alone. He had no idea another classmate was also playing truant and hiding in one of the dunes. He saw Bulbul running into the river without his pants on.

The next day at school, he didn't notice the whispering going on until a boy passed him and said, 'Stark naked, ha, ha shameless bird.' Soon, it became a chorus. That was just the beginning; the story became more colourful. One of the exaggerations had Bulbul not only naked but shamefully touching himself. Soon, boys would be piping as soon as they saw him: 'Touchy-touchy bird, pee-pee, dicky-dicky, ding-dong much.'

He found it impossible to attend school and stayed away on all sorts of pretexts, but his grandfather, still committed to grooming him for power, took him back. He developed a stutter, which his teachers and classmates used to inflict further pain on him. One maths teacher, famed for his cruelty, would call him out to solve a problem on the blackboard. Bulbul would be so tense, his legs shaking, butterflies in his stomach, his head spinning, he wouldn't be able to solve the simplest task. The maths teacher, his shifty little eyes squinting above his fussy little moustache, would hit the cane loudly on the desk and say: 'A dung beetle, no, no, he's got more brain than you, a maggot, yes, yes, you're a maggot, a stinky little maggot.' He would then ask Bulbul to read the math problem on the blackboard out loud. Choked, gasping for breath, he would struggle to say a primary number and fail. 'You're a tongueless thing, not even worthy of being a maggot,' the maths teacher would say. All Bulbul could think of was becoming a maggot and wriggling his way out of the classroom, but he never had such an easy escape. He would be made to kneel and pull his ears.

Among the boys was one who made it his vocation to torment Bulbul in all kinds of ways. He was rather meek-looking with thick glasses and a tick that made him jerk his head every so often. When other boys got bored teasing Bulbul and went out to play, he would stick to him during break times, repeating the well-established insults and invent some of his own. No wonder your mum is dead, he would say; she couldn't take the shame of having you. He would make Bulbul hand over his pocket money and lunch.

One day, Bulbul and the meek boy with thick glasses were taking a mock exam, sitting beside each other. Head down and under his breath, the boy kept taunting him. Suddenly, Bulbul rose to his feet, held his pen up, and stabbed the boy in his shoulder. The boy bled and started to cry. Bulbul wanted to run away, but the school guard, a giant man with a severe moustache, caught him. He was caned and expelled from school.

He was happy to be expelled, but his grandfather lobbied the teachers and the school committee to take him back. Though Dadu did not know the severity of the taunts that Bulbul faced, she thought that he must have had a good reason to lash out. She told her husband, 'Feringhee school doesn't suit the boy. No, it doesn't. I bet it's full of meanness. Admit him somewhere else.'

'You know nothing, Bibi,' said Syed Amir Shah. 'The boy needs to be toughened up. Otherwise, he'll remain a namby-pamby bumpkin.'

It took his grandfather six months to persuade the school to take Bulbul back. During that time, keen to keep an eye on him, he took Bulbul to work at the godown, showed him the bales of jute bought from the growers in villages and loaded off the boats at the river ghat, then reloaded again for buyers in distant parts of the country – some even destined for foreign parts.

'Why jute? Why is it called the golden fibre?' asked Bulbul.

'Profit, my boy. I buy from the peasants and sell it to merchants, to manufacturers. It makes me a handy profit. Those merchants and manufacturers also make profits. In fact, the more hands it passes through, the more profit.'

'But the peasants who grow it get less than anyone else.'

'Yes, my boy. That's the rule.'

'It's not fair.'

'If we don't buy their jute, what'll happen to the peasants? They'll starve to death. We can't have that, can we?'

Despite feeling that his grandfather's trade wasn't fair, he was happy to be with him. In fact, those were his happiest moments with his grandfather. On the way to the godown, Syed Amir Shah would take him for breakfast at a restaurant. He would have ghee-fried parathas with bhuna goat, glasses of sweet milk, and sometimes even laddus and rasgollas. If he was in a good mood, Syed Amir Shah would give the lunch brought from home to his supervisor and his assistant, and take his grandson out to a restaurant. Bulbul would always order chicken biryani.

Above all, his grandfather helped Bulbul with his studies. He showed him the tricks of solving maths problems and taught him English. Unlike his teachers, his grandfather was patient with him and encouraged him. 'I know a genius when I see one. Yes, my boy. A genius is waiting under your skin. You just have to give it a nudge and it will pop out for sure.'

In the afternoon, if trade was going well, Syed Amir Shah would take a break, and they would go on a boat trip. He would tell Bulbul about his hunting adventures with the English sahibs, of his Calcutta days. Sometimes, he would drift into talking about his son and daughter-in-law. Even Dadu said little about his parents. Looking at the flowing water of the river and now and then dipping his hand into it, Syed Amir Shah would tell Bulbul how clever his father was, what a bright future had lain ahead of him, and how beautiful and dutiful his mother was, and how both would have been so proud of him. 'Don't forget. They loved you,' Syed Amir Shah would say. In those moments, avoiding his grandfather's eyes, Bulbul would bite his lips and look at the clumps of hyacinths drifting past the boat, but his grandfather would edge close to him, rub his head and say, 'I love you too. You'll shine in life.'

One Monday morning, as Bulbul and his grandfather were heading for the godown, they saw a crowd milling around, nervous, talking as if they had received some ominous news. Syed Amir Shah went to the crowd to ask what was the matter. The world is to end, said someone, on Friday at four in the afternoon.

It had all happened at early morning prayers at the grand mosque, led as usual by the imam. On weekdays, only his most pious and sincere devotees attended, whilst most, having to go to work, performed prayers at home. Those who attended prayers that day remember that the imam, a man reputed to be of the highest spiritual virtue, looked somewhat other-worldly. In fact, for days leading up to that morning, people said he had been looking distracted, as if summoned from elsewhere. He would sit for hours in a meditative pose, muttering something about which no one had the faintest clue, nor the language used. He was evidently embarking on a rare spiritual journey.

After morning prayers, the imam fell into a deep sleep. At first, his devotees thought he had fainted, but were too scared to try to revive him. Suddenly, he woke up and declared that the world would end this coming Friday, precisely at four in the afternoon.

He said no more. The devotees rushed out to spread the message, urging people to prepare themselves. Syed Amir Shah respected the imam and thought he wouldn't say something like that lightly, but he was sceptical. For a moment, he wished he'd gone along with his father's wishes and become a saint. If he had done so, he would have immediately known the truth. He toyed with the idea that perhaps Bulbul had inherited his father and grandfather's saintly powers. He asked Bulbul, 'What do you think? Is the world going to end on Friday?'

'No,' said Bulbul.

His grandfather didn't ask how he could be so certain but was sure he was right. At lunchtime, he popped into the shrine of Mominabad's saint near his godown by the river, which had a large following. He talked to the shrine's caretaker, a man reputed to be a powerful saint in his own right. He assured Syed Amir Shah that if the world were ending on Friday, he would have had some inkling of it. He had none. So, after several more inquiries, and using the rational habits of his youth, he concluded that the world probably wouldn't end on Friday at four in the afternoon.

Opinion in Mominabad was divided. Some dismissed the idea and got on with their daily lives. Some took it seriously and devoted their time to repenting their sins, praying, fasting, and staying huddled up with their families. Some didn't really believe but lacked the courage to dismiss it; they didn't pray and fast any more than usual but secretly repented their sins and stayed off bad deeds.

The response of the jute merchant, Keramot Ali, who had his godown next to theirs, was unusual. He was neither a devotee of the imam, nor a pious man. No one knew if he had any faith except making money, and he was the most successful jute merchant in Mominabad. Syed Amir Shah didn't like him and thought he lacked education and culture, the refinement of a gentleman. Despite his considerable wealth he spent hardly any on philanthropic activities.

Keramot Ali declared that on Friday he would hold the most opulent party Mominabad had known, to which everyone was invited. He sold his business, house and everything he possessed, and withdrew all his savings from the bank. He erected a giant marquee in the green field at the edge of the town. He printed thousands of leaflets saying: *Come to the end of the world party, have fun and go out in style*. He hired hundreds of youths to go door-to-door in every neighbourhood to distribute the leaflets. He hired the band of the local cinema, its drummers, bagpipers and players of brass instruments, to go around the town with a huge banner advertising the party. From dawn to dusk they marched down every street and alleyway playing loud, happy tunes and displaying the banner as if advertising a cinema premiere. Keramot Ali himself, dressed in his finest silk sherwani with elaborate embroidery and precious jewels and a bright red pagri on his head, walked the streets inviting rich, poor, men, women, Muslims, Hindus, Christians, and even communists. He came especially to Syed Amir Shah's godown to invite him and his family.

'It would be an honour to go to eternity together,' Keramot Ali said, 'and why not have fun and go in style? Allah will be pleased for honouring his judgement.'

Syed Amir Shah accepted the invitation out of politeness, though he didn't want to be associated with such a vulgar affair. On Thursday evening, as he was leaving his godown, Keramot Ali ran in, breathless. He repeated how he would be honoured to spend his last minutes on this earth in his company.

'What if the imam's prophesy doesn't come true?' asked Syed Amir Shah.

Keramot Ali scratched his nose and said, 'It's got to be true. I feel it in my bones.'

On Friday the believers and devotees of the imam packed the mosque; others stayed with their families, fasting and praying and waiting to hear the conch of doomsday. Nonbelievers, sceptics, doubters, and those who almost believed in the imam's prophecy but not quite, and those who, like Keramot Ali, accepted the truth of the prophecy as incontrovertible but wanted to go in style and having fun (almost half the population of Mominabad), gathered at the vast marquee.

Dadu professed not to believe in the prophecy but took to fasting and praying just in case. Syed Amir Shah sat on the veranda and smoked his pipe. Alone in his room, Bulbul thought that perhaps he was foolish to dismiss the idea, and feeling a sudden panic, ran to his grandfather and asked to be taken to the party.

'I thought you didn't believe in the prophecy. What changed your mind?'

'I don't know. But we can't miss the party,' said Bulbul.

The marquee, the size of a town, was decorated with all kinds of flowers, silk draperies, balloons and colourful lights. There were hundreds of long tables with red, hand-crafted nakshikhata cloths and cushioned, high-backed chairs in rows. For those who wanted to sit on the ground, there were thick woollen carpets – also red – and round pillows with velvet covers. Strategically placed bands played kawali and gazal, Bengali folk songs, Bollywood dance music, and much else. There was ample room for those whose spirits took hold of them to whirl, shake, gyrate and jump with all the freedom in the world. All around the marquee, young men were reciting the Koran.

Hundreds of cows, goats and chickens had been roasted and curried. For the fish lovers, many giant catfish and carp had been fried in the finest mustard oil. For the vegetarians, a mountain of aubergine and okras had been bhajied. There were ten different types of dal for everyone and an endless supply of pilau rice and varieties of meesties.

Keramot Ali received Syed Amir Shah with an effusive hug, patted Bulbul's head and said, 'You're a handsome boy, aren't you? I hope you're a big eater. Nothing like an end-of-the-world party, eh? We go merrymaking. Jolly, jolly.'

He took Syed Amir Shah and Bulbul to a table where other dignitaries were seated. The party began with a prayer by a mullah who wished everyone a safe journey and said: 'See you shortly in heaven.' It was already one in the afternoon, with only three hours left for the people to eat as much as they could, sing, dance and make merry. Of course, no alcohol was permitted, though someone had asked for it: 'To take the party to the next level, to make it truly the mother of all parties, you need a bit of sarab.'

'Yes, yes, I understand,' said Keramot Ali, 'but you don't want to spoil your chances of drinking sarab in heaven for eternity. The finest vintage quality. Have patience. Just three more hours.'

The musicians put their hearts and souls into their performance and cranked the volume up, producing a riotous cacophony. This made the young men shake their bodies, though they quickly drifted away when food was announced. From then on the musicians merely provided a background din. Still, another two hours to go before the world ended. Prompted by this cosmic urgency, most guests felt the compulsion to tuck into all this delicious food before it was too late. Though there were thousands of guests, there was still more food than they could consume, and yet they jostled each other, like a pride of lions on a kill, to fill their plates. Some didn't even bother with plates; they lunged for the roasted goats' legs and began eating as if it were the last supper. Few heard Keramot Ali's announcement that only fifteen minutes were left, let alone heeded his suggestion that perhaps it was time for quiet contemplation and prayers. Some guests had eaten so much they couldn't move; they lay there and began snoring.

Bulbul nibbled on a chicken's leg, feeling breathless and slightly sick. He was imagining that when the end-point came, at the sound of trumpets, the sky would break into pieces and fall on them, crushing everyone to death. He had heard Keramot Ali's fifteen-minute call and ran out of the marquee to see if the sky was already cracking. It was unusually blue and clear, not even a sliver of cloud – only the vultures circling high above. That sight should have reassured him; for when the end was near, the animals would know and wouldn't be circling the sky. But then he thought the vultures might be part of the divine endgame. Perhaps they were waiting for the sky to fall on the humans down below and then clean up the bodies.

When he heard the five-minute call, he ran inside the marquee, still thinking the sky would collapse. He hid under the table, grabbing his grandfather's legs. While Keramot Ali counted the final ten seconds to 4 o'clock, Syed Amir Shah stroked Bulbul's hair and intoned a prayer. At the end of the count, there was a stunned silence, then a few more minutes passed, and finally, a loud cry. It was Keramot Ali. He was screaming: 'I'm ruined, I'm ruined.'

When the world didn't end that afternoon, the mob hurried to the grand mosque to lynch the imam, but he had already slipped out wearing a burka. Bulbul returned home holding his grandfather's hand. Dadu said, 'It serves that Keramot Ali right. He's a nasty piece of work. He deserves utter ruin. I'm glad that Allah has obliged him.'

It was two months since the doomsday party, and Bulbul was still off school, as happy as before to accompany his grandfather to the godown. But his grandfather, though his jute business was doing well, wasn't a happy man. Few knew him in Mominabad, and he wasn't regarded as highly as he wished.

When one of the two private car owners, a man who owned grocery shops and markets, was giving a party to celebrate his daughter's wedding, all the notable families except Syed Amir Shah's were invited. Bulbul's grandfather had had enough. He printed out leaflets and distributed them throughout the town. He, a man of an ancient aristocratic lineage, who had hunted with British sahibs, would go to the Sundarbans on a tiger hunt. Dadu started to buy white saris, telling the beggar women, 'I'll be a widow soon. My old fool of a husband, his head has gone all wrong. He is preparing himself to be a tiger feeder. Oh, Allah, have mercy on me.'

Undaunted, Syed Amir Shah had invited all the respected families in Mominabad, except the man with the private car. He spared no expense, erected a tent in the garden and employed the finest cook to prepare goat biryani. Dadu would have nothing to do with the party. 'What to say? I'm afraid the same fate will befall the old fool. The same as Keramot Ali.'

Sitting at a table right in the centre of the tent, as if he were a bridegroom, Syed Amir Shah showed off his double-barrelled shotgun, told stories of his hunting exploits with the British sahibs, and told of his aristocratic lineage, which could be traced back to the Prophet Muhammad himself. One mischievous young man standing among the crowd by the table, cleared his throat: 'I hear British sahibs were fond of hunting wild boars and having them roasted on the spit. I wonder what hog meat tastes like.'

'How would I know? Are you a communist or Hindu-lover or something? I'm a Syed and a proper Muslim League man.'

Bulbul, sitting next to his grandfather, felt anxious for him. His grandfather's lips shook and globules of sweat gathered on his forehead, which he dabbed at frantically with his pristine white handkerchief. Bulbul blurted out: 'My grandfather's father came on a tiger's back from Arabia. He hated pig-eating more than anything else, so does my grandfather. Do you know that he keeps company with the Jinn and killed a king cobra with his bare hands?'

The young man laughed and was about to say something sarcastic, when he saw his father, the owner of the second private car, approaching.

'Forgive the insolence of my son. I blame the ungodly professors at the college. Yours is an esteemed Syed family. Your presence truly blesses our town. I see your grandson takes after you. A handsome fellow. No doubt also very brave.'

Syed Amir Shah sat back with a self-satisfied smile, then he looked at Bulbul and said: 'Yes, my grandson is very brave. I am taking him to the Sundarbans with me on the tiger hunt. He'll be my eyes and ears.'

Bulbul nearly fell off his chair. This was news. Of course, Dadu was against it, but Syed Amir Shah stuck to his decision despite her vehement protestations. 'The boy is too soft. He needs a bit of toughening up. It will be an adventure for him. He needs it, especially after what happened at school,' he said.

'Besides tigers, the jungle's full of evil things. Nothing there for humans. If anything happens to him, I'll divorce you,' said Dadu.

'Bibi, you know nothing. It's one hundred per cent safe. Do you think I would do anything to risk the life of our grandson?'

As preparations for the hunt went on, Bulbul felt fear and excitement in equal measure, as he did on the morning when, accompanied by a cook and a servant, he left with his grandfather for the Sundarbans. There, they met up with the professional hunter who had been paid handsomely to help with the hunt. He had constructed a shelter between high branches of a large sundari tree and tethered a goat down below. If things went to plan, some tiger was bound to be lured by the goat's bleating, and when that happened, it was simply a matter of taking aim and pulling the trigger from the shelter. 'It's a foolproof method,' said the hunter, 'even the most cowardly and incompetent can't fail. You, Sir, are undoubtedly a champion shooter and bravest among men.'

At dusk, the hunter and his men hoisted Bulbul, his grandfather and the servant boy up the tree to the shelter. The hunter offered to stay, but Syed Amir Shah told him, 'Don't worry about us. Go and have pleasant dreams in your bed. Come and witness a great kill in the morning.'

The grandfather put cartridges into his double-barrelled gun, asked the servant boy to serve him tea from the flask, and leaned back on the trunk to see the last rays of orange in the gaps in the canopy. When night fell, in the full moon, the tethered goat was still visible on the ground below. The night wore on in silence, with hardly any wind and birds back in their nests. In between taking sips of tea, the grandfather kept looking down, cocking, un-cocking his gun. Then, the goat began to bleat as if it had sensed danger. The grandfather sat upright, clutching his gun. Bulbul and the servant boy, their teeth chattering and their bodies in spasm, held onto each other. From the canopy of nearby trees, macaques began their shrill cry. On the ground below, chital deer took flight, rustling the bushes. Everything now told of the approach of a tiger.

It was there, enormous, crouching in front of the goat. Syed Amir Shah, his hands shaking, took aim. Suddenly, the tiger growled, leapt on the goat, and disappeared into the forest. Instead of pulling the trigger, his grandfather fainted at the tiger's growl and lay precariously dangling from the branches. Despite still shaking and wetting their pants, Bulbul and the servant boy held onto the grandfather. In the morning the hunter didn't ask any questions; he smiled as if he had figured out what had happened. He gave Syed Amir Shah his salaam and said, 'Not to worry, Sir. Everything is fine. It's part of the service.' He had arranged the necessary proof of a successful tiger hunt to go with him.

Back in Mominabad, people gathered to welcome Syed Amir

Shah, the brave tiger hunter. He showed off the trophy of a tiger's pelt with its massive head and gaping canines but remained rather grim-faced and reticent. No one knew who spilt the beans, but soon the rumours of Syed Amir Shah's fainting at the tiger's roar began to spread, propelled by the laughter of the tea-stall gossipers. They called him the Fainting Sahib. No one questioned Bulbul, but the poor servant boy got the sack. At first, Syed Amir Shah, donning his suit and fez, braved the streets, but soon, the laughing eyes of the people got to him and he stopped going out, then took to his sick bed and died within months. Keeping vigil by the dead body, Dadu wailed, 'I knew that one way or the other the tiger would get him. At least we'd have been spared shame if it were by his teeth. Allah have mercy on my old fool's soul.'

Whenever he thought of his grandfather, Bulbul felt he had killed him because it was he who had spilt the beans.

Following his grandfather's death, Bulbul went back to his old school. Now, the boys had something new to tease him with. They taunted him, 'Bulbul, you poor little bird. You like nothing better than fainting, like your grandpa, don't you?' Sometimes, they would catch a fly or a grasshopper and dangle it up close, almost brushing the tip of his nose. 'Look at the monster. Oh, so scary. Our little bird is fainting.' Mostly, they would shout, 'Look, there's a tiger!' and fall to the ground.

When he left that school at eleven, Bulbul felt liberated.

CHAPTER 5

After spending the summer months in Dambarpur, where he was as happy as he ever was, Bulbul was back in Mominabad. Now, the household consisted of Dadu, Kona Das and himself. Though only eleven, Bulbul had to take on some of the 'manly' tasks: running errands in town, doing daily food shopping from the open market, slaughtering chickens and paying utility bills. Since Syed Amir Shah's death, and the consequent loss of income from the jute trade, Dadu couldn't afford the town centre house. She rented an old two-bed, damp, dilapidated brick-built house in a densely packed poor neighbourhood on the edge of town. Bulbul had one small room to himself; Dadu and Kona Das slept in the other. The veranda at the back served as a cooking and dining area. It had a small courtyard with a tube well and a chicken coop. Next to it, Dadu had planted a tulsi bush for Kona Das to do her morning puja. Dadu also asked the neighbourhood potter to make a statue of goddess Kali for Kona Das; it was placed on a shelf just behind the cooking area. Each morning, while Dadu performed her morning prayer, Kona Das would sprinkle water from a brass pitcher on the tulsi and ask for its blessings, and then she would join palms before the statue of Kali and do her puja.

He hadn't stuttered since he left his old school. With no male guardian, Bulbul went alone to the neighbourhood Bangla-medium school and registered himself. It was a large school with two shifts: the first started at six in the morning and ended at one in the afternoon; the second began at two in the afternoon and ended at nine at night. Students were required to attend half the year on one shift, and the rest on the other. This suited Bulbul well because it gave him time to fit in all his chores.

For the two months of the summer holidays, he travelled back to Dambarpur with Dadu and Kona Das. Sometimes, Dadu would leave Bulbul during the school term in the townhouse alone, especially from his fourteenth year onwards. She would travel to Dambarpur with Kona Das to supervise the land's cultivation and manage the fishing season in the swamp. It was the only way Dadu could pay for the townhouse and keep Bulbul at school. She arranged with a neighbour – a widow with a young daughter – to cook for Bulbul and keep an eye on him. Bulbul, playing the man of the house, felt more than capable of looking after himself.

It hadn't always been easy, especially his first kill. Unexpected guests had arrived, and Dadu asked Bulbul to slaughter the cockerel. He had known it since it was a little chick; he had seen him grow into a top bird with its high, red crest. He would climb to the top of the coop and crow in the morning and from time to time throughout the day. He would protect the hens, call them when he found juicy insects and worms, and cluck around them. Bulbul would laugh when he saw him puffing his chest out, strutting along, doing his limbering steps on the parapet, then jumping

49

down on the ground, where he would drop his wings, going in a semicircle around the tulsi tree, clucking and crowing. He was wary of Bulbul and sometimes downright aggressive, running to peck him, jumping high into a fly-kick to claw him. 'Don't mind him,' Dadu would say, 'he wants to be the only boy in the house.'

Now there was a new young cockerel to look after the hens, Dadu thought the old one would be a good treat for the guests. She would slow cook it with naga chilli and green papaya. She called Bulbul to the courtyard where Kona Das held the cockerel upside down, gripping tight around its wings. Dadu gave him the knife, saying, 'You're the man in the house now. Go and do it.'

Holding the knife in his right hand, he grabbed the cockerel's head, pulling it towards him, and tightening the neck. Then their eyes met – the cockerel staring at him, the way it did whenever it attacked him with its beak and talons. Now it was as if it was daring him to do it. Detached from his body, driven away beyond the moment, Bulbul stood there, holding the cockerel's head.

'Are you going to do it?' asked Dadu, tightening her lips, and shaking her head. First glancing at Dadu, Kona Das looked him straight in the eyes, gave him a little kick on his shin, and nodded her head. Bulbul woke as from a deep sleep. Saying bismillah, he put the knife to the cockerel's throat, pressed downwards, and jerked his hand forwards and backwards. Blood spurted in his face. Kona Das dropped the cockerel on the paved circle around the tube well. Unable to get up, its head almost severed from its neck, the cockerel flapped about, blooding itself and the paved area. Flinging the knife away, Bulbul ran back to his room. He didn't come out when the guests enjoyed the cockerel. After the guests left, Dadu came into his room with a plate of rice, dal and aloo-vorta mixed with fried red chilli and mustard oil. She sat on the bed, rubbed his head, and said, 'My little bird, this is one of those things. Cruel things. Like your circumcision. We do funny things, no? To survive. Like a fox. Or even a hog.'

Bulbul pretended to be asleep. Dadu asked if she should tell him a story, like when he was a little boy. 'I cut the cockerel's throat. No more baby stories,' he said. But he took the plate of rice from Dadu's hand and began eating.

During that night, unable to sleep, he wondered why it had

never bothered him before when he saw others slaughtering a bird, when he sank his teeth into their flesh, savouring Dadu's delicious chicken curry. Perhaps, despite knowing what was involved, he had turned a blind eye to the gory reality, as if he weren't a beast among a community of beasts. Dadu had brought him to face it squarely, his kinship with the foxes and the hogs.

Then he thought he'd had enough of the damn cockerel: from now on he would slaughter them like it was nothing more than brushing his teeth with a neem twig. Still unable to sleep, and remembering Dadu's comment, he drifted into the time of his circumcision. It was in Dambarpur and he was five years old. Until then, his birthdays came and went; no one bothered about them, but that year, his grandfather wanted to mark it with a celebration. Dadu wasn't keen. 'It's a Feringhee custom. I've never known anyone celebrating it. Is not coming to this earth enough? Why make a fanfare of it?'

She relented when he argued that Bulbul was old enough to have his circumcision done and agreed he should have a festive day for the occasion. The monsoon was there, and flood water from the north was coming down and making the rivers and swamps a single waterland, except Dambarpur, which floated like an island in a sea of water.

Syed Amir Shah rented a large boat with a spacious cabin. He announced that his grandson would have his circumcision done and that any five-year-old in the village could join him – he would provide both the procedure's cost and the care for the boy's recovery. Four parents came forward with their five-year-olds. 'Thank you, Syed Shahib, thank you for your generosity,' they told him, 'our boys are blessed. To take their first step to manhood in the company of your grandson – our little saint.'

Syed Amir Shah invited the entire village to a feast; he had a large bull and six goats slaughtered. Since the ground was wet, they cut a forest of bamboo to make a platform in the field, which was on higher ground in front of the outer bungalow. All around that field, water was lapping, as if it was out to devour it.

Villagers squatted on the bamboo platform, ate the bull and the goat curry with a mountain of rice, and prayed for Bulbul's and the other four boys' safe passage to manhood. Villagers remarked how this feast reminded them of the olden days when Syed Amir Shah's father and grandfather practised their saintly vocation, and such gatherings were regular events. With tears in their eyes, some wished for the return of those days. The village would be blessed if someone from the Syed family became a saint again.

The large boat used for the circumcision was attached by an iron hook to an ancient simul tree standing tall over the landscape, some distance from the compound, half of its trunk submerged. Inside the boat, at the far end, screened by a curtain, the guni-man-skin-cutter had set up his surgery: two face-to-face, low wooden stools, and next to them a lamp burning, over which, on an iron rack, lay the tools of his trade.

First on the list was Bulbul. A new lungi was tied to his waist, and a gamsa-towel wrapped around his bare shoulders. It was still raining heavily. Someone held aloft a large umbrella, and his grandfather put Bulbul on his shoulder and carried him to the dinghy. 'It's a passage for all our male members, you know, one we all have to make to take our places in the community of men. I know it's a bit painful. But you're brave and I'm proud of you.'

Bulbul didn't say anything; he clung to his grandfather as tightly as possible. Soon, they arrived at the dinghy and got aboard. Someone gave it a push, and the dinghy floated into the muddy water, then the boatman plunged his oar. Syed Amir Shah sat on the bow with Bulbul on his lap, his body arched over his grandson to protect him from the rain. The wind made the water choppy. Bulbul felt sick.

When they reached the boat, they took off Bulbul's wet lungi and gamsa-towel, dried him, and took him behind the curtain where the guni-man-skin-cutter awaited him. Syed Amir Shah kissed Bulbul on his forehead and left him there. This surprised him because his grandfather rarely showed such physical affection. The kiss eased Bulbul; he was much less afraid of what lay ahead.

As soon as he sat on the low stool, a man put his arms under his thighs from behind and held him tight. Facing him, seated on the stool, the guni-man-skin-cutter held the skin of his penis with the fingers of his left hand and pulled it towards him. He took a thin bamboo strip from the rack over the fire and put it into the flame for a few seconds. Then, with a quick movement, he cut off

Bulbul's foreskin. He felt a sharp pain and gave out a muffled cry.

Now, in his bed in Mominabad, he thought that perhaps the cockerel felt something similar when he cut his throat. No, the cockerel must have felt a thousand times worse because it bled to death and became meat for them to feed on and he had recovered within weeks.

After the procedure, his wound bandaged, he was put on a bed on the other side of the curtain. He heard the cry, the wailing of the four other boys, and then they were placed next to him in the boat's cabin. They stayed there for the next two weeks, mostly lying in bed, the rain lashing the cabin and the boat swaying in the waves. From time to time Syed Amir Shah visited, bringing food and treats. Once, he came with ice cream, and Bulbul and the boys were so excited that they forgot their ordeal for the rest of the day.

In those days, Bulbul and the four other boys had to endure the pain because no one thought of painkillers, but they didn't complain. Though Bulbul didn't know the boys, he felt reassured in their company, as if going through the ordeal together lightened his pain. Syed Amir Shah never came to play games or tell stories, but some other fathers took turns to amuse the boys. One dad would mimic various animals and the boys had to guess them. Despite not being quick enough to name any animals first, Bulbul enjoyed the game. Afterwards, he would spend hours imagining the various animals of the waterland, especially the birds that called from the reeds and rice paddies, which he had never seen. He liked to imagine them with bright yellow feathers, so bright that people would go blind seeing them. Perhaps that was why they didn't show themselves to humans. The other fathers would take turns telling stories at night until the boys fell asleep. Strange, he thought, he had never seen any of them since their time in the boat. Perhaps, while he came to Mominabad to go to school, they went to help their fathers in the fields, ploughing lands, harvesting rice, or laying traps in the swamp to catch fish. They would be farmers like their fathers, but what would become of him?

Bulbul felt more at ease in his new Bangla school. No one picked on his country accent or acted the fainting-sahib routine to shame him, yet he was cautious about making friends. He kept to himself for the first few months, always alert, and observing the other boys. He was well into his second shift at school when he made his first friend.

He was now also well used to open-market shopping. He could look at a fish and tell if formalin was used to preserve it; he knew how to look at the gills to determine their freshness. He still had problems with bargaining: he would become self-conscious and not dare to pitch a low price to begin the game of wit and nerves. He would be unnerved by the make-believe incredulity and baffled looks of the sellers – seasoned practitioners at the game – as if he were an idiot and wasting their time in pitching such a low price, which was already higher than those of other buyers. Instead of joining in the bargaining banter of sarcasm and counter-sarcasm, he would be tongue-tied and lower his head in shame. The sellers would drive home their advantage, and he would pay a higher price just to escape as quickly as possible. Even so, he learned ways of dealing with the situation.

For one thing, the sellers got to know him and his ways. Though they didn't stop taking advantage of him, they became mindful of his vulnerability and let him off relatively lightly. Afterwards, they would sigh, and tell each other, 'What to do? The silly boy. I don't have the heart. Really, I don't want to cheat him more than fifty per cent. I wish I weren't cheating him at all. But business is business. Poor boy.' He got to know the sellers who would cheat him the least, and developed the courage to walk away if he felt the price was too high. All in all, he became a reasonably adept shopper.

He wished, though, he could forget his first day in the market, but how could he? He was lost even before he approached a stall. The sellers could sense his nerves, his naivety, the way he carried his body, and the way he clutched his shopping bag – like an injured prey waiting to be hunted down by a lion pride.

He feared to approach any of the stalls, even the vegetable or salt sellers' stalls, when a fish seller called him, softly. Only later did Bulbul realise why no one was around his stall. At the time, he was happy no one was there to see him make a fool of himself. The seller gave him such a smile that Bulbul felt he was standing before a man of honesty and sincerity. 'Young Sir, are you in the market for a fine fish? Of course, you are. A fine gentleman like you. No doubt most discerning. I bet you're after a reasonable price, too. Why not? A man of good taste loses every time without prudence. You, Sir, seem to have both qualities in abundance.' He showed him a large carp.

'I can't afford such a large fish. I have only five rupees to spend.'

'Normally, I sell a fish of this size and quality for twenty-five rupees, but I'd like to have a discerning gentleman like you as a long-term customer. You get my point, Sir? Yes, take it home for five rupees. Your parents will be proud of you.'

Bulbul couldn't believe his luck; he handed over the five rupee note and almost ran home, imagining that Dadu would be so proud of him. It was Kona Das who first spotted the disaster. 'Oh, ma. Bulbul Da, what've you done? It smells. The fish is rotten.'

'Kona Boo, you know nothing. This is a bargain. Look at it. Such a nice fish. A very kind man sold it to me. He gave it away, practically for free. He likes me, you know.'

'Of course, he likes you. He swindled your five rupees for a rotten fish. Of course, he likes you.'

Dadu didn't say anything; she sent Kona Das to dispose of the fish in the municipal rubbish bin. Locked in his room, Bulbul felt terrible – how could he be so stupid? Dadu knocked on the door with a bowl of savoury rice. She caressed his face and said, 'You, my precious grandson, my little bird. I'm proud of you.'

Towards the end of his first year Bulbul made friends with Alam Mirza, known as White Alam, and with Sanu Mia, known as Sanu the Fat. Alam wasn't white, only slightly fairer than most of the pupils at school; Sanu, though, was fat. White Alam was the son of the town traffic policeman, notorious for his bribe-taking and extreme frugality. People called him Stingy Traffic Policeman. Despite becoming very rich on bribes, with which he bought several large houses and shops in the town, he dressed like a beggar and kept his family half-starved. His frugality prevented him from taking a rickshaw even on the stormiest days. He was also fearful that rickshaw pullers might contrive some devious accident that would leave him maimed for life but themselves unharmed – damn rascals would walk away unscathed, with grins on their faces. He had reason to be suspicious of the rickshaw pullers because they hated him. For them, the sight of a hooded, hissing cobra was less forbidding than his white-gloved dancing hands at the crossroads in the market square. He extracted bribes from them for all kinds of phoney infringements. His usual was stopping rickshaw pullers for carrying three passengers.

'Grave infringement of the law. Very grave,' Stingy Traffic Policeman would say, shaking his head, 'we take a dim view of it. Extreme dim view.' When the accused man would point to passing rickshaws carrying four or more passengers, he would say, 'Law says rickshaws can carry two passengers, but not three. The Law always goes by the letter, you know. It specifies nothing about carrying four or more passengers. So, these cases do not amount to infringements. Are you too idiotic to understand this elementary logic? No wonder you earn your living by pulling rickshaws.'

'I don't know of any letter, Sir. I'm just a poor rickshaw puller. What am I to do?'

'Good question. I don't know what you've heard about me, but Stingy Traffic Policeman is kind. Some donation in his direction makes him soft. He corrects the infringements. You must know that is a serious business. It takes a heavy toll on one's soul, but someone has to look after you wretched lot.'

He would take the bribe, amounting to half the rickshaw puller's earnings for the day, and let him go. Sometimes he would stop a rickshaw at random, fiddle with the brake and say, 'Not up to the standard specified. This is serious infringement, you know. Merits a very dim view. Do you want to lose your license or what?' Poor rickshaw pullers had no option but to pay up.

During evening prayer at the mosque, Stingy Traffic Policeman would cry his heart out and pray loudly for forgiveness for the bribes he had taken that day. 'Allah, forgive my sins. What's a poor man to do? A bit of extra doesn't harm anyone. Allah, I promise I'll go to Mecca to do Hajj. Maybe I'll become a double or triple Hajji, turn pious-looking with a long-hennaed beard, build a mosque with fine domes and minarets.' He would emerge from the mosque smiling and looking relaxed, and people would ask him why he looked so happy?

He would say, 'I am touched by the grace of Allah. My family and I have eaten very well. I bought a little fish, slightly rotten, for one taka. But it smelt so good. Super delicious, I tell you. We took turns to smell it and ate our rice. Oh, I am so happy.'

'You know how to live it up,' people would humour him. 'You're a great connoisseur of fine things.'

White Alam had inherited his father's deviousness but none of his frugality. He was a deft hand at stealing things – including Bulbul's lunch. Still a bit naïve and fearful of making a fuss, Bulbul had no idea how his tiffin had been disappearing. At lunchtime, he would open the boxes and find all the purees, parathas and bhajis gone.

One day, having lost his lunch, he was going to buy dal puris from the hawkers who gathered at the school entrance, when a sudden call of nature made him run for the latrines. Behind them, he spotted a hunched-up figure among a clump of small trees. He was in too much of a hurry to stop, but when he came out of the toilet, the figure was still there. He gathered courage and surprised him: White Alam gorging on his lunch. He didn't say anything; they just looked at each other. He did not report the thief to the teachers, and the next day White Alam offered him two ripe mangoes, which he'd stolen from a tree on his way to school.

'I'm White Alam, the son of Stingy Traffic Policeman,' he said. 'What do they call you?'

'I'm Bulbul.'

'Ah, the singing bird.'

From then on they became friends. It took him several more weeks to befriend Sanu the Fat. He was exceedingly corpulent and wore his curly hair Afro-style. He was supremely adept at telling stories. Bulbul had seen kids surrounding him during break time, listening to his tales, reacting with horror in their eyes or doubling over with laughter. One day, he tiptoed behind the group to see Sanu the Fat sitting on a pile of bricks at its centre. Boys were offering him their lunches: parathas, purees, bhajis, sweets, and mangoes. He sat in deep concentration as if meditating. From time to time he stirred, gobbled up some of the offerings like a snake, and then went back to his meditative pose. Bulbul feared that he would explode like an over-pumped balloon, but he belched, rubbed his nose, and began telling a story.

Well, Sanu said, it wasn't a story at all but something that had happened; he'd seen it with his own eyes, heard it loud and clear, smelt it, and could still taste it in his mouth. Nothing added, nothing embellished. Could anything be truer than that? Everyone nodded. Well, he was visiting his old grandmother who lived in his ancestral village. It took half a day's train journey, then several hours on the boat, across a haor, to get to it. 'It's very remote, you know. *Things* still live there,' said Sanu the Fat.

'What things?' someone asked.

'Things, my friend. Things.'

He'd reached his grandmother's village in the late afternoon. Once he'd crossed the vast haor from the mooring point, he had to walk several miles with his guide to his grandmother's house. They had to go through a bamboo grove; its rustling unnerved him, as if something was watching him. His stomach clenched. He'd clutched his guide's hand tight. 'They are not happy,' the guide said. Who, he'd asked. 'Them,' the guide said.

Rushing to catch the evening market, the guide left him near the bungalow. His grandmother was at prayer, and the servant boy had gone to fetch the cows in from grazing. He was alone and it was getting dark. When no one had appeared after half an hour, he thought he should look for his grandmother. An ancient tamarind tree, huge trunked, gnarled and tall was between the bungalow and the external wattle fence. He had always been scared of this tree, never dared look up it, even when it was laden with ripe tamarinds. Everyone knew it was home to a fearsome old ghost and its impish family, who weren't pleased to see anyone passing. He thought he would run for it, but froze as the impish family, assuming the forms of giant cobras, hung from the branches and hissed. One came down inches away from his face and spat. God only knows what they would have done if his grandmother hadn't appeared right then with the hurricane lamp. That night, he couldn't sleep because of the noises and hissing on the tin roof of his grandmother's hut. Big boy though he was, he clutched onto her. 'They are not happy,' she said, 'they don't like anyone coming to see me. They're waiting for me to die to take over the house.'

The following day, on the way to the pond, he saw them climbing the bamboo, looking like pink-bottomed monkeys with large fangs and howling. He ran back, shivering. When he reached the pond, accompanied by the servant boy, a quick dip was all he could manage. He was lucky to come out alive because the pond was infested with demon cooking pots with hippo-mouths, who pulled down the legs of unsuspecting bathers and held onto them until they were dead. Luckily, the servant boy was alert to the danger and pulled him out before they could lock onto his legs.

His grandmother was worried. They took against you, my little fatty, she said. They want to scare you off. Despite this warning, he went out to the hoar that night. The haor at moon-light always had a special allure for him. Surely they wouldn't come out on such a night.

He set off, accompanied by the servant boy. The bamboo grove was silent except for a slight rustle of leaves. This time, he didn't feel as if anything was watching him. As arranged, the boatman was waiting for them by the fig tree at the edge of the haor. The boat slid into the silvery water with a gentle splash.

They continued between lotuses and hyacinth clumps. He put his hand into the water, picked a lotus fruit, and the boatman began a song. He saw the bats flying overhead on their nocturnal forage. Suddenly, something jumped out of the water, splashing the boat. No-one knew what it was. 'They don't come out on a night like this. Light doesn't agree with them,' said the boatman, 'so it has to be a fish, a really big one.' No sooner had he said this when a shoal of something moved on both sides of the boat, purring like cats. 'Oh, no. It's not fish,' said the boatman, 'it's them.' He began to row faster. The shoal zoomed away from the boat, leaving the night to silence. Then, suddenly, everything changed.

A giant figure, its head touching the sky, its eyes bright and orb-like, was approaching the boat. Before they could think what to do, it was upon them. It lifted the boat and flung it down into the haor. He had gone flying and found himself on a bed of hyacinth. He lay there and saw hundreds of lights fluttering across the hoar. Oh, it was them, dancing. Then darkness fell. It was the servant boy who found him and dragged him ashore. The following day, they found the boatman floating on the hoar, his neck broken. 'You see, it was them, all right,' said Sanu the Fat.

When the school bell rang, signalling the end of lunchtime, and the crowd of listeners dispersed, Bulbul said to Sanu, 'Nice story. Did you make it up by yourself or did you hear it from someone else?'

Sanu the Fat smiled, 'Don't tell anyone. I heard it from my uncle. He heard it from his friend at the tea stall. But the suckers believe any damn story you tell them.'

'My grandmother told me similar stories when we lived in the village.'

'Did she? Anyway, what do they call you?'

'Bulbul'

'Ah, the singing bird.'

He became friends with Sanu the Fat and White Alam, and they became inseparable. On winter's days, they'd go to the cricket field, not to play or even to watch the match, but to listen to the tall-tale gossipers – the legendary adda-men. Always at the same spot, the adda-men sat on the grass in a semicircle, their legs drawn in lotus position. There was Hakim Khan, the lawyer; Banu Gosh, the doctor; Samsuddin Gazi, the sawmill owner; Abid Ali, the journalist; and Fazle Rabbi, the landlord. Although not rich men, they were comfortably off and had time on their hands.

One day when they went, the cricket ground was full of shouting, cheering, drum-beating, bugle-playing, and whistling supporters. The match was between the Fishmongers and the Butchers, a local derby. The adda-men supported a different team, so they were neutral spectators, simply there to enjoy the game's finer points and partake in some good old adda.

The Butchers had won the toss and decided to bat; the Fishmongers were about to take the field.

'Today, I've a case – a solid murderer. Brute-looking, too, but the chap… My God, the funniest I ever met,' said the lawyer, chuckling.

'You're lucky, lawyer. To a physician, he'd be an intriguing case. A funny murderer, a real find,' said the doctor, looking serious.

'He's not a loony type, Doctor. The fellow is outrageously sane. That's what makes him so funny.'

As the openers – one the legendary Basir Sarder, a giant butcher with a handlebar moustache, who always batted after a bottle of whisky – were heading towards the crease, following the umpires, Hakim Khan launched into telling his funny murderer story.

'He wasn't supposed to kill the guy, the murderer told me, just scare him off. He told me the murderee was the meanest bugger alive in the whole universe. He wasn't human. Not even an animal. He'd asked the man to give him one of his goats. Only one goat, for his life, was that too much to ask? He couldn't believe it, but the mean bugger refused. Even a goat has an instinct for self-preservation natural to all organisms, except the murderee and those damn suicide bombers, my murderer said. So, what was he to do? He put the bugger out of his misery. Some would call it philanthropic work. Only Allah knew what he did for those wretched guys, he said. Someone had to relieve them of the hell they lived in. He said the murdered man even looked like a starving goat. Mind you, he told me, he took one of the man's goats and had it roasted on a spit. The finest he'd eaten. He said he could still smell it on his fingers. It made him feel like he'd just done that naughty thing with his wife. Do you get my meaning, Mr Lawyer, Sir? he asked me.'

'That is not funny,' said Samsuddin Gazi, the sawmill owner. 'Your murderer sounds like a brute. The blessings of millions of years of evolution don't seem to have touched him.'

'My friend, that's what makes him so funny,' said the lawyer.

The doctor scratched his head and mumbled: 'I'm still puzzled by your insistence that it's a funny story. I've found nothing in it to tickle me. Not even a slight chink to spill an ironical laugh.'

They watched as Basir Sardar, tottering slightly at the crease, took guard. In came Bala Ram, the quickie for the fishmongers, and let rip a leg-cutter which missed both the bat and the stumps. Leaning on his bat, Basir Sardar burped, steadied himself, and shouted to his partner at the other end: 'That damn Bala Ram, he's a demon in a man's skin; he's sending me three balls, all in one bowl. How can a man bat against such devilish trickery?' His partner shouted back: 'Yes, Sardar, the two outside balls hail from your whisky. Just send the middle one to hell.'

'Ah, Basir Sardar. His batting skills are as refined as his butchery,' said Abid Ali, the journalist; 'his sixes are as explosive and brutal as his cleaver-work on a bull's rump. He achieves a rare affinity between the bat and the cleaver. The man is a true genius.'

Bala Ram ran in for the second ball of the over and slung down the shiny red orb. Basir Sardar saw three little missiles assailing him, but he was ready to send them to hell. He whacked the middle one with a balletic swing of his bat and the ball flew high and across the boundary line. Cries of jubilation and beating of drums erupted from the butchers' quarter.

Fazle Rabbi, the landlord, his mouth open, followed the ball until it landed and said, 'You know I'm a bit partial to exaggeration. It's the vice of my imaginative temperament, but it's no exaggeration to say the Sardar's shot – how can I put it? – was like Indra's thunderbolt.'

'Very true,' said Abid Ali, 'I'm a peddler of facts. If I had an imagination, I would have said the same thing.'

'Don't underestimate yourself, my friend. Your comparison of the bat and the cleaver was almost poetic. Besides, in your journalistic pieces, facts sing with rare melody. You're our bard of the real,' said Fazle Rabbi.

'Thank you, my landlord friend. Unadorned facts is all I aspire to.'

The following two balls were also sent sailing over the boundary line, one to long-on, the other to square-leg.

'I tell you, those are no whisky shots. He must be on the local brew today. The wicked Bangla mot,' said the doctor.

But with the fifth ball of the over, Bala Ram slung the ball down and uprooted the middle stump. On the way back to the pavilion, Basir Sardar said to his partner, 'Damn Bala Ram. He's a master devil. He must have been on ganja the whole night.'

After Basir Sardar's departure, the game returned to a sedate contest between ball and bat. The gossipers looked around and were pleased to see the three boys behind them. They loved an audience, especially of young ones, who would, one day, take over from them and keep the art of adda alive.

Banu Gosh, the doctor, an amateur angler, began a tale of his recent fishing exploits, 'Art of fishing and cricket is the same, really. They both teach you the virtues of patience and timing. You can learn more about human flourishing from them than from reading Aristotle. But this time, I wasn't prepared for the cunning of the fish. If he'd been human he would have been a leg-spinner and adept at the googly.' He paused, and Fazle Rabbi, the landlord, took a closer look at the boys. He recognised Bulbul, which prompted him to tell his own story, interrupting the doctor just as he seemed to have found the thread of his fishy tale. 'Something like this doesn't happen often, but it happened to me. I was going to the village to inspect my land,' he said.

'Sorry, landlord, that I couldn't lend you my car. The damn thing is giving me too much botheration,' the doctor interrupted in turn. He'd recently bought an old banger and become the third private car owner in Mominabad.

'If I'd had your car,' said the landlord, 'I wouldn't have had that experience. And what a remarkable experience it was. One in a million. I may be prone to exaggeration, but what I tell you is absolutely true and needs no adornment. You see, I was on a rickshaw on a deserted country road by the forest's edge. The rickshaw had a puncture, and the damn puller couldn't fix it. As my village wasn't too far, I decided to walk. I had only turned two bends when I sensed the beast. It was a country tiger.'

Bulbul's heart sank. He wanted to run away, but his friends had been caught in the tale and wouldn't budge. He kept his head down and played with blades of grass.

The landlord continued. 'He emerged from a bush and was on my trail. Perhaps it wasn't as large as a Royal Bengal – the kind our fainting sahib encountered in the Sundarbans – but it was large for a country tiger and meant business.'

Bulbul knew what was coming. Why else would the landlord be telling a tiger's tale if not to have fun at his grandfather's expense? Poor grandfather! Sure, he had some funny ideas, but Bulbul loved him. He wished he could become a tiny insect, camouflaged among the grasses, and crawl away.

'Facing a tiger, a man's true mettle is tested,' said the landlord. 'That damn tiger – a real sneaky bugger. He stayed invisible among the bushes but was gaining on me. As he was about to leap, I caught the branch of a bakul tree and swung up. I went to the topmost branch and stayed there. But the damn tiger lay under the tree as if meditating on eternal questions. A philosopher among tigers. But he was after my flesh. Filling his belly first, then contemplating higher thoughts afterwards. Certainly, no Gandhian. He'd have no truck with pacifism and nonviolence. He was all about pure appetite. Anyway, hours went by, then days, and he was still there, waiting.

Sure, I was hungry, but unlike some sahibs, I didn't faint.'

'Which sahib, do you mean?' asked Abid Ali, the journalist.

'I don't want to name names. Especially with the youngsters listening. Who knows, the gentleman's grandson… he could be among them.'

'We mustn't pay any heed to gossip and rumour. Loose mouths might have spilt them out of spite. Facts, my friend, facts. We must stick to facts,' said Abid Ali.

'Yes, that's so. I'm all for verification. Shall we ask the grandson? I hear he was with our sahib when that unfortunate event occurred. So, he would be the best placed to speak the truth.'

It was more than Bulbul could bear. He sprang up and bolted. His friends hesitated, then followed him.

CHAPTER 6

If it weren't for Dadu, Bulbul wouldn't have met Scientist. At least not so soon after arriving in their neighbourhood on the edge of the town. Sooner or later, everyone needed Scientist: he was an all-purpose mechanic, builder, illustrator, painter of signs, and counsellor on most matters – from the delicately private to the abstrusely official. He knew several languages, possessed an encyclopaedic knowledge of most subjects, and was an amateur dramatist and cinema buff. He was the eldest of a family of eight: six brothers and two sisters. The rest were tall and well-built, considered handsome; Scientist was born a dwarf – only two and half feet tall and so thin you could almost see through him. His voice was high, and he spoke slowly and softly. Whereas his brothers were lazy and didn't earn anything, Scientist worked long hours and made enough to support them all. Like him, his sisters were hardworking and versed in many crafts; they were snapped up as wives as soon as they came of age.

Dadu had an old Murphy radio, which she began using after his grandfather died. While he was alive, she didn't listen much because he had the first choice of programmes and chose mainly news and discussion. When the radio became hers, Dadu only listened to music and drama. News was a man's thing with their squabbles and wars. 'Little boys playing with their willies,' she would say to giggles from Kona Das. She kept the radio on most of the day, except when she was praying, and in the evening she would give herself entirely to it, drifting to sleep on a story or a mellow song. When she heard Dadu snoring, Kona Das would get up from her half-slumber and put it off. Sometimes, Dadu would get exasperated with a character in a drama, giving them advice or a piece of her mind. Kona Das would nod to show agreement. She also joined Dadu in humming songs. In his room, Bulbul, annoyed at their duet, would try to block it out with a pillow pressed against his ears.

When the old Murphy, struggling for some time, broke down completely, Dadu became irritable, even picking on Kona Das for no good reason. After a restless night, she asked Bulbul to take it to Scientist to repair it.

Bulbul was waiting in the workshop, cluttered with machines and junk, half-painted signs and paintings. He knew of Scientist's reputation and thought he knew what he looked like, but was taken by surprise when he walked in through the beaded curtain. Without looking at Bulbul, Scientist used a stepladder to climb onto his chair, then looked him straight in the eyes.

'I'm Bulbul. Syed Amir Shah's grandson.'

'I know who you are.'

'How? We never met.'

'Your face has its architecture. Your eyes tell stories. And I've met your grandfather. Does that answer your question?'

'I don't follow. Acha, how did you meet my grandfather?'

'He came to see me after that tiger affair.'

'Why?'

'That's between me and your grandfather. I must say, though, the treatment he received was most unfair. People don't know about tigers and the power they pack into their roars. They emit a lot of energy to vibrate the air around them. A tremendous force. It can easily bring a macaque down from a tree – even a man. Anyway, what can I do for you?'

Bulbul showed him the radio and told him it needed repairing.

Without examining it, Scientist said it would be done and told Bulbul to return in two days.

When he arrived to collect the radio, Bulbul found Scientist working on a billboard. He had already painted figures on a canvas, now he was applying finishing touches to the lettering. It was for a government-sponsored family-planning campaign. In one corner, a large family had been drawn in drab colours – children looking like a swarm of rats, dishevelled and malnourished. The caption read: *a large family is an unhappy family*. In the other corner, a family with two healthy, well-dressed children was depicted in bright colours. Its caption read: *a small family is a happy family*.

'What do you think of these?' asked Scientist.

'The people look like real people. It's amazing how you draw human faces. I like the happy family the best. Nice looking people and nice colours.'

'It's rubbish. Pure propaganda. No artistry there, only imitation. It's selling your soul to the devil. I'm ashamed of it.'

'I don't understand. I wish I could draw human faces like that. So real.'

'When you grow up, read books, then you'll understand. Do you read books?'

'No. I don't like reading. I hate what they give me at school.'

'You have to read school books to pass the exam. Without that you'll be joining the labouring classes. If your grandfather was still here, he wouldn't be very happy. But there are other books, books that feed your mind. If you don't bother with them, you'll stay at the same level as a howler monkey. Do you want that?'

'I don't know. I like monkeys. They get to swing from trees. They groom each other really nicely. In fact, I'd rather be a monkey.'

'You're missing the point, young man. Listen to me. You can be a monkey if you want, but read books.'

'I haven't found a book I like.'

'Keep your eyes open. I promise you, you'll find it. By the way, do you like films?'

'My grandmother took me with her several times. I didn't like those films. People just cry. I've seen some Bengali films with my friends. Guys chasing girls around the trees. Dancing and singing. I don't like them much, either.'

'I, too, don't like those films. I go for the morning shows, on Fridays. Have you been?'

'No. What kinds of films?'

'Oh, foreign films.'

'I don't understand how foreign people speak.'

'You don't have to follow the language. They are full of action and adventure. Just follow the pictures and imagine.'

'I'll go this Friday, then. Oh, no, I can't. I've got to go to the mosque to do my Friday prayer.'

'That's fine. The show is on really early in the morning. It finishes well before prayers. I'm going this Friday. In fact, I've already seen the film. I liked it so much I'm seeing it again.'

'What's it called?'

'*Godzilla*. A Japanese film. Well, a bit tinkered with by the Americans. A fat American is added. A journalist. He translated most of the film into English. I hear it has compromised the film a bit. But thanks to that, I could follow it.'

'Would I be able to follow it?'

'You went to an English medium school before, didn't you?'

'But I didn't learn much in that school. It was horrible.'

'Was it? That's a pity. English would have given you so much more of the world. Culture, knowledge. Anyway, as I said, you can follow most of the film without the language. But if you want, I could explain. You know – a bit about the background.'

'Yes, please.'

'Well. It's about the nuclear bomb. Do you know about it? The Americans dropped two on Japanese cities. Thousands died. Still people are dying today. Radiation poisoning. Very dangerous.'

'I heard something about it. My grandmother was talking about the Devil's bomb. She said that's how Allah's doomsday will come. But I didn't understand much.'

'Your grandmother is right. Things are worse now. The Americans and Russians are developing hydrogen bombs. Many times more destructive than those the Americans dropped on Japan. The way things are going, I'm afraid the world's destruction could come any day. It's the American hydrogen bomb tests in the Pacific Ocean that drove Godzilla to the surface. He's actually a living bomb. His breath is full of nuclear emissions. Very dangerous.'

Before Bulbul left with Dadu's Murphy back in working order, Scientist gave him a magazine in English, which he couldn't read, but it had a lot of photos of nuclear tests and the destruction they caused, and the planes and missiles that delivered them.

By the time he went to see *Godzilla*, his nerves were in tatters. He wasn't sleeping well and had little appetite, even when Dadu cooked his favourite things. He was always looking around as if expecting to see a ghost. Dadu called the doctor. 'He goes around like a scaredy cat, like something is after him. Maybe he's possessed by a demon. What do you think, doctor?'

'Possessed by a demon? That's nonsense, Bibi. There must be a scientific explanation for the boy's condition. I'll examine him with the utmost rigour.'

The doctor found nothing wrong with Bulbul physically, so concluded that it was due to some psychological disturbance.

'So, tell me. What's been happening?' the doctor asked. 'What's scaring you? Is it something to do with your daddy? Or perhaps, your mummy? Or perhaps you are having funny feelings. Down there, in your little man. Nothing wrong at your age to have funny dreams about girls. Do they want to cut it off? Is that it?'

Bulbul hadn't a clue what the doctor was talking about.

'You can talk to me frankly. No one will know. Very confidential. I've been a boy, too. I know how these feelings can be very scary. Oh, yes, it was scary for me.'

'It's the bomb. The nuclear bomb. Hydrogen bomb.'

'What? What about the bomb?'

'There are enough of them to kill us all. Make the whole world full of poison. Burn it up. Break it into pieces. The people who have them are greedy and mad and always quarrelling. We could be under a mushroom cloud any moment. Doomsday any day.'

'Come on, young man, you're running away with your imagination. I bet you dabble a bit in poetry. Hush, hush, secretly, yes? We've all been there. You heard the imam's prophesy? Of course, you did. I saw you with your grandfather at Keramot Ali's Doomsday party. Has the world come to an end? No. So, don't worry. Just concentrate on your studies. As they say, those who study get to ride horses and cars.'

Bulbul thought the doctor was talking rubbish and wondered

how such a stupid clown got to be a doctor.

During the day it was bad enough, but at night the terror doubled in menace, haunting him with a particular deviousness. He would open a tiny chink in the window, expecting to see a mushroom cloud, lifting like a fountain, spewing out radioactive poison to kill everything. What was that light over there? Perhaps it had already started by the river; it was only a matter of seconds before it reached him. Ya Allah, what to do? It must be an awful way to die. Perhaps he should go to Dadu's room; she would know what to do. At least they would be together, Dadu holding him when it burnt, tearing him to pieces, poisoning him. He couldn't breathe. He was feeling sick. Why were those evil people playing with this thing? Perhaps the doctor should go and tell them off, tell them not to play with their little men down there, but who would listen to him, he's such an idiot. Suddenly, a sound. What was that? No doubt it was their planes, like they did in Japan. Ya Allah, they've dropped it, perhaps on the other side of the river. He dived under his bed, shivering.

Dadu was sleeping, but Kona Das was wide awake. She thought she heard something coming from Bulbul's room. She came to investigate. 'Bulbul Da. What are you doing under the bed?'

'It's the bomb. I don't know if it's nuclear or hydrogen. But they've exploded it. We're all going to die like the Japanese.'

Kona Das held him, washed his head with cold water, circled a candle lamp around it, and asked for Kali Mai's protection. He eventually fell asleep. But in the morning, he was edgy again, looking over his shoulder for signs of the bomb. On a clear day, he would go to the riverside, from where he could see far into the distance, as far as the peaks of the Himalayas and would wait to see the poison cloud drifting his way. What was the point of running? Perhaps he should dip under the river's water, but would he be safe there? No, nowhere to hide, only death, horrible death.

But by the next night he wasn't thinking about the bomb. What was the point? What would happen, would happen. Tomorrow was Friday, and he would get to see *Godzilla*. Just a monster film. He would be a little scared – that was the point. You paid to get scared, and afterwards he'd have a good laugh about it.

It happened on that night with a breeze fluttering through the open window, and draped in moonlight, he was drifting gently into sleep. A tiny streak of light was streaming in through the ventilator, coming towards him. How could he have been so stupid not to realise that it was from a nuclear explosion, perhaps from somewhere near. Everyone would be dead by now, the whole world charred and poisoned. How terrible his lungs felt; it was eating away his insides. Perhaps it came to visit like a cat through the ventilator because it wanted him to suffer before killing him. He tried to scream and call for Dadu, but he felt choked. Drops of saliva trickled from the corners of his mouth. At last, it came and rested on his ankles, spreading its weight with a barely audible purr. He knew he wasn't asleep or dreaming. It was searing his skin, melting his flesh and bones and sending radioactive poison through-out his body, burning into his stomach and flooding his intestines. He wanted to retch out his whole insides but could not. Nor could he move. It pawed its way to his chest, clawing to get to his heart. Dadu, the bomb is killing me, he wanted to scream, but couldn't force his breath out. It sat on his chin, ready to finish him off, pumping its noxious poison into his mouth, into his nostrils. Perhaps this was the end of everything: Hiroshima and Nagasaki all over the world. Straining his body to breaking point, he screamed: 'Dadu!'

Both Dadu and Kona Das came running. 'What's the matter, my little bird?' asked Dadu. But Bulbul didn't look like someone who'd just had a nightmare. He was wide awake and calm.

'It's the atomic bomb. No. A hydrogen bomb,' he said.

Dadu was worried because she had no idea what he was talking about. Perhaps the boy had gone mad. In the morning, she called the doctor again, who reassured her: 'Nothing to worry about, Bibi. Adolescent boys, you know. Full of funny, funny new feelings. In the profession we see this all the time. Testosterone rampaging around their organs. Prone to feverish imagination. He'll be fine.'

He felt fine enough to attend the Friday morning show with Sanu the Fat and White Alam. It was the final showing of *Godzilla* after a four-week run. There had been only a handful of viewers, film buffs like Scientist for the first two weeks. In the third week, the house was full. Now, thousands of people were jostling for a ticket in a hall of just three hundred seats. As he had for other popular shows, Sanu the Fat used his bulk to push his way to the ticket counter. He took off his shirt, rolled up his lungi, and pushed his body against the crowd to edge forward. He was making good progress and was within a yard of the box office when the sold-out sign went up. Black market tickets were available but at three times the regular price, which Bulbul and his friends couldn't afford. Dejected, they sat down for tea at the stall in front of the cinema and could hardly bear to look at the happy punters with tickets going inside the hall. They were about to leave when Bulbul spotted Scientist getting off a rickshaw and heading for the back entrance, without even a sideways glance. Without hesitating, Bulbul ran after him.

Scientist didn't look surprised, as if he had been expecting to find Bulbul in just such a predicament. He told him to call his friends and follow him, which they did, up the winding stairs to the projection room. The projectionist didn't seem surprised to see Bulbul and his friends, either; perhaps Scientist had already arranged it with him. While the projectionist threaded the film on the reels, Bulbul and his friends sat beside Scientist.

If Scientist hadn't told him, Bulbul wouldn't have noticed the nuclear connection. He felt sorry for all the destruction and the pain of the people, but, apart from one or two moments, he wasn't scared by Godzilla. He felt sorry for the monster, who as well as being forced out of his underwater home by the nuclear test, was infected by the radioactive poison, which he emitted through his breath. Poor Godzilla – no wonder he was angry.

After the film, Scientist just nodded to Bulbul and hurried away before the rest of the audience could leave the hall. Later, Bulbul learnt that Scientist always came to the cinema at the last moment, would only watch the films from the projectionist's room, and left before the audience emerged. Whilst people who knew him gave him proper respect, there were strangers who couldn't resist picking on him. 'Hey, dwarf. I hear you lot are as randy as goats. Is that true?' His friend would say, 'Don't be stupid. The dwarf is diseased, all shrivelled up inside. With his tiny little fellow down there, he couldn't do anything. His parents must have been into unnatural things to produce him. Allah's curse for sure.' Another would say, 'Dwarves have brains the size of goat shit. No, even smaller. Do you understand, dwarf? Hey, you ugly dwarf, do you understand what we're talking about? No. Obviously not. You're like a vegetable, aren't you? A tiny, rotten one.' Sometimes, they would push him, spit at him, and pull his pyjamas down to poke at his private parts.

From the cinema hall, Bulbul and his friends went to the mosque for Friday prayers, but they couldn't stop talking about the film. White Alam had been scared by the monster. During the show he had looked away several times, hidden his face under his arm, and jumped at the terror's unexpected appearance.

'I don't fall for Sanu the Fat's ghost stories, rakshasa-devil stories. My father calls them village folk things. Superstition. Totally untrue. But Godzilla is real. It scares me.'

'Why don't you suggest to your father he should see the film?' said Sanu the Fat.

'You know my father. He wouldn't spend a rupee on a film. Films are frivolous, the vice of spendthrifts.'

'Ah, your father. One of a kind. The man is a true legend. Never mind. It's good for you. You'll get to inherit the fruits of his frugality, though maybe you won't be able to digest them. You know, swallow the bribes,' said Sanu the Fat.

'Are you serious? They're all legit. Hundred per cent halal. He deserves more. His clients are only poor rickshaw-wallahs. How much do you think they're able to pay him?'

Sanu sucked his teeth, rolled his eyes, but stayed quiet when he saw the imam coming their way.

'It's a place of Allah. Not a place for gossip. If I hear you lot again, I'll throw you out.'

Shaking his head, the imam returned to the minbar from where he would lead the prayer, but he had posted his assistant, a young mullah with a goatee-no-moustache, behind the pillar to keep an eye on the boys.

Unaware of the spy, they began chatting again.

'I didn't like the girl. What's her name? You know, the professor's daughter?' said White Alam.

'You mean Emiko?' said Bulbul.

'Yes, her. She's double-faced. A slut. How could she break off with Serizawa? The poor scientist. He gave his life to save the world. He wasn't good-looking enough for her with his bad-eye and patch, so she ran off with a cinema idol type. Pure slut.'

'Oh, I see. You like Emiko. You'd like to do hanky-panky with her. Is that it? That you're jealous,' said Sanu the Fat.

White Alam wanted to say something but stopped. The imam was stampeding towards them like a bull elephant in musth.

'I've had enough of you nasty boys. Talking about films in the house of Allah. Worse than idol-worshipping-heathens. Get out!'

They were not unhappy about this. They could get on with the main event that followed a visit to the cinema, though, before that, they needed to have lunch. On Fridays, Dadu always cooked something special, and while performing his Friday prayers, Bulbul would think about this and pray for the imam's long sermon to end. He knew it would be goat because he'd bought a kilo of the finest meat from the open market. Yet it would still be a surprise because Dadu could cook it so many different ways.

It was a goat rezala with pilau rice – and bhajis, vortas, achar and dal that day. Bulbul had already asked Dadu if he could invite White Alam and Sanu the Fat, and she said yes. After serving them on a rattan mattress in the inner veranda, Dadu and Kona Das left the boys to enjoy themselves. As usual, Sanu the Fat went into his own zone, as if he had given his body and soul to some fantastic music, perhaps a bhatiyali sung by a boatman on a lonely shore. Ignoring the side dishes, he served himself a mound of pilau rice and goat rezala, fishing out the largest meat pieces and all the lumps of fat. Feeling awkward at the silence at the table, Bulbul tried to start a conversation, but Sanu was so engrossed in his eating that he didn't hear a thing.

White Alam, deprived of good food by his father's extreme frugality, was also gorging on the dishes. His was a more anxious greediness that lacked Sanu's passion. 'If my father saw such a serving of good food, he'd have a fainting fit. He'd consider it extravagant, a waste of money. Don't tell my father that I've eaten goat rezala with you; he'd see it as encouraging bad habits. Eating well is like opium addiction, he says. You get hooked. Indulgence in delicacies and rich flavour is the surest way to destitution.'

'Your father's one of the wealthiest men in Mominabad. What he's going to do with all the money he's saved? asked Bulbul.

'I don't know. No one can raise the subject with him. He talks about security and peace of mind. Uncertain times, he tells my mother.'

After lunch, they went to the field next to the old colonial college and lay on the grass under the giant raintree. In the silence of Friday afternoon, mingling the hot sun and cool breeze, it would have been easy to drift into sleep, but Bulbul was thinking of the next main event of the day, when Sanu the Fat would tell the story of Godzilla.

Since he'd started going out to see films with his friends, it wasn't the film that was the main event but Sanu's retelling of it afterwards. The films were simply the alibi for his performance. Almost always, he made the story more engaging and amusing than what they'd seen on screen.

This, though, was Sanu's first foreign film, and Bulbul wasn't sure if he had followed the storyline or the nuances and complexities of the characters. Up until now, he'd only seen over-the-top melodramas with their cocktail of romance, comedy, song and dance. He was about to ask Sanu what he thought of *Godzilla* when White Alam cut in. He produced a packet of King Stork cigarettes he'd stolen from the tea stall in front of the cinema. It was only recently, on the sly of course, they had been smoking. Both Bulbul and Sanu opened their eyes as if they'd come face-to-face with an object of rare pleasure which, despite being risky, or because of it, offered the promise and the thrill of growing up.

Indeed, even in his early days as a smoker, Bulbul felt a strange erotic sensation every time he lit a cigarette – especially on his own. He would feel aroused, as if his body was being touched by the most alluring of things. He would slink away to the riverside, hide in the dunes and, alone in the world, would light a cigarette. Trembling, he would take off his lungi and whirl around naked until he fell to the ground, rolling in the sand until a tremor coursed through his body, and then, like a crocodile, he would slide into the river. He couldn't help a nervous laugh, imagining his former English-medium classmates' reaction if they saw him. In what obscene performance would they cast him? Sometimes, he would lock himself in the outside latrine and, squatting on the open hole, light a cigarette. Even there, the intense loneliness of the forbidden would flood his veins with erotic sensations. He never felt this way when he smoked with the others.

Now, glancing around nervously, they moved away from under the shade of the raintree and squatted like a gang of criminals in the bush, well hidden from the path that ran along the field. White Alam was first to light up, then Bulbul, and finally Sanu. He said, 'I suppose you want to hear the story of Godzilla,' and he roared like the fearsome monster.

To be fair to Sanu, it wasn't just slapstick and parody at which he excelled. As an actor seasoned in melodrama and weepy-tragedy, he could also evoke unbearable pathos. At first, his retelling of the film doubled Bulbul's terror. It followed him, not just in the play of shadows creeping along the empty streets lined with the ruins of once flourishing businesses, and now given over to Mominabad's rubbish and carrion eaters, but in the dark corners of his mind. At the cinema, Bulbul had kept control of his feelings, even when he watched the scenes in which the woman, with fear and resignation on her face, clutched onto her baby girl and wished herself and her daughter dead; or the terrible scene when poor Serizawa, already spurned by his betrothed, cut the lifeline to the mothership to sacrifice himself to save humankind. These scenes had moved him, but Sanu the Fat's retelling had undone him, bringing tears to his eyes.

But it was the laughter he provoked that proved the most enduring legacy of Sanu the Fat's retelling. Even though the last thing he wanted to do was to provoke laughter, he couldn't avoid it. It was a gradual affair. First, he stood up and tried to add an extra fizz to his fearsome roar, but it came out as a squeaky little grunt, and the more he tried to produce a blood-curdling roar, the squeakier it became. A spasm ran through Bulbul's and White Alam's bodies, but they managed to control it. Then Sanu started to imitate Godzilla's thumping footsteps, trying to simulate not only the sound of the monster's enormous weight creating huge craters on the ground, but also the sound of exploding nuclear bombs. But the ground was muddy after a recent spell of rain, and the harder he thumped, the more squelchy the sound became. Bulbul and White Alam looked at each other but still suppressed their laughter. Then, Sanu imitated Godzilla's rampage through Tokyo. He hunched over and, squeaking and squelching, lumbered like a frog performing a bizarre mating ritual.

'Godzilla!' said White Alam, and he and Bulbul broke into laughter. Soon, the three of them were rolling in the mud, laughing. From then on, one of them had only to say Godzilla, and they would be in stitches. That word would set them off even in the middle of a serious argument. No one else would have a clue what they were laughing about. They used 'Godzilla' to stand for almost anything, as if this word had replaced the entire dictionary. At school, their classmates began to call them Godzillas.

One day, the old boti-cutter, which Dadu and Kona Das used to clean fish and cut meat and vegetables, had gone blunt. The door-to-door sharpening-man had not done a good job the last time he'd called, so Dadu and Kona Das struggled to cut even fish heads on it. Learning that Scientist also did sharpening jobs, Dadu sent Bulbul to him. No problem, said Scientist. Then he asked Bulbul what he thought of *Godzilla*. He was baffled when Bulbul laughed.

'It's not a laughing matter. *Godzilla* is not a comedy. It doesn't even have comic interludes.'

Bulbul said sorry to Scientist for his inappropriate laughter, but did not explain why he'd laughed.

'Don't worry, I understand. Extreme fear often produces nervous laughter.'

Scientist then asked him if he had seen anyone loitering outside his workshop. Yes, Bulbul had seen two men: a junk collector and a door-to-door peanut seller.

'Do they really seem like that to you? Think carefully before you answer.'

'No, not really,' said Bulbul. 'Who are they? What are they doing here?'

'They are spies. They're sent to watch me and notice who comes to my workshop.'

Since the military takeover of 1958, Mominabad, like the rest of the country, felt suffocated. Political activities were banned, and most democratic and progressive politicians had been arrested or driven underground. Martial law courts meted out harsh punishments to people at all levels of society. Some didn't even know for what they were being punished. Most of the newspapers had been banned, and those that remained faced severe censorship. Secret police in plain clothes watched almost everyone and everything that went on.

For Bulbul, it seemed incredible that nine years had passed since he arrived in Mominabad. It was just over a year to go before he left school. Despite neglecting his homework and not showing much interest in learning, he was well-liked by his teachers. 'Such an intelligent boy. A potential A grade. What a waste of talent,' teachers would say. Well, what could be done about it? Honestly, they tried, but you could do only so much; it was all too common with an orphan boy. What could you expect with an uneducated old grandmother at the helm? Yes, he was fated for turbulent waters and hazardous shores; it was a miracle the boy had turned out to be so good-natured and polite.

With the dealing out of summary punishments with batons and rifle-butts on the streets and in the markets, even the tall-tale gossipers, the connoisseurs of adda at the cricket ground were subdued. After the time when one of the gossipers poked fun at his grandfather, Bulbul had avoided them for several cricket-seasons. Mostly, though people hadn't forgotten his grandfather's hunting debacle, no one cared to mention it anymore. Besides, Bulbul was no longer a timid little boy to be cowed by the gossipers. And listening to their adda was a temptation he could not resist.

As always, he was with Sanu the Fat and White Alam. This time it was a mid-table match between the Police and the Municipal Clerks – two notoriously stodgy teams. Despite winning the toss on a good batting wicket, the Police decided to bowl. As usual, they put their two military medium pacers on in tandem. They were bowling steady line and length, over after over, and the clerks were content to block them with their textbook forward-defensive strokes, except for some occasional nudges for singles.

Even the gossipers, who usually went ecstatic over a well-calibrated forward defensive, unpacking the shot with their esoteric cricketing knowledge, were losing interest. However, it was precisely at such dull moments that people expected them to deliver their most memorable adda performances. Today, they were looking at each other sheepishly, looking down at the grass as if counting the blades was a fascinating pastime, taking ages to peel peanuts and undo pan-cones, and sighing. Who could be sure that someone in the crowd wasn't a spy sent to eavesdrop on their conversations and report them to the military authorities? Imagine being arrested and sent to that ancient dungeon of a jail, hemmed in by open sewers and the mountain of a rubbish dump, where, even if you were spared electric shocks to your testes, you would be eaten alive by mosquitoes. Not the most suitable environment for gentlemen of leisure like themselves, people who were used to the cultivation of higher thoughts and subtler feelings, the finer things in life. There was no doubt that military types were utter Philistines; they were bound to mistake their dedication to adda for laziness, not to mention subversion.

It was Abid Ali who broke the silence. 'Anyway, as they already have it in for me, I might as well go down speaking.'

'Journalist, it's your privilege,' said Hakim Khan, the lawyer. 'Exercise your freedom. For a man of adda, his tongue is everything. If it's arrested – it doesn't bear thinking about. Surely, the day of the apocalypse will be at hand. But, my friend, you must consider us, too. If you go down, you'll take us with you.'

'Of course, I'm mindful of that. I promise you, I'll talk with a forked tongue. Satire, parody and allegory will be my way.'

'Suppose there is a spy watching us. And if he reports that you'll speak in that manner, won't that give the game away? Won't everything you say or write be scrutinised for satire, parody, and allegory? And then, the very suspicion of these rhetorical figures in your speech might incriminate you,' said the lawyer.

'Yes, in theory, that might happen,' said Abid Ali. 'But in practice there are grey areas that most regimes tolerate. Even the most insecure and paranoid ones. Unless, of course, you're talking about the likes of Hitler or Stalin.'

'Your strategy might be subtle, but there are limits. Eventually such subtleties will get on the nerves of the man of power. He might, then, come for you with a vengeance – perhaps for your head, as has happened to so many artists and poets down the centuries,' said Fazle Rabbi, the landlord.

'I don't claim to be an artist or a poet. Not by a million miles a Mayakovsky or Lorca, but I'm willing to take that chance.'

'Journalist, tell us one of your forked-tongued stories. Use allegory, satire, and parody as much as you like. We are happy to give you feedback,' said Samsuddin Gazi.

On the field, the cricket continued at the same old boring pace. The spectators, mostly the co-workers of these two services, who had been compelled to attend by their superior officers, were getting restless. At the lunch break, on the excuse of stretching their legs, they wandered off the ground and never came back. The gossipers, though, as a matter of principle, never left a match, however tedious, and since listening to the gossipers was their main reason for being there, Bulbul, Sanu the Fat, and White Alam stayed, too. Seeing only the boys in their vicinity, Abid Ali felt reassured that there wasn't a spy around and he could speak as freely as he wished.

'Since we are among ourselves, I can speak frankly. No need for satire, allegory or parody. Who wants indirection and laughter when plain language and facts will do? However, since my friend, the sawmill owner, has requested it, I'll give it a go. It will give me practice in speaking with a forked tongue. Perhaps it's the only way we can speak and hope to see the next day in desperate times like ours. So, it's a horse story, then.'

'I like horses,' said Bulbul, daring to interrupt. 'Their speed, their strength. Our history teacher tells us it wasn't so much the warriors but the horses that gave the Mongols their vast empires. And in the morning shows on Fridays, we've seen Red Indians become at one with their horses. Becoming a horse – it must be an amazing feeling.'

He surprised himself by intervening in the gossipers' conversation. Where had this sudden boldness come from? It was as if someone else spoke through him. The strangest thing was that he'd never thought about horses before, let alone expressed his feelings about them. Now, he was feeling exposed, shaking inside. He wanted to run away.

'You're a clever fellow, aren't you?' said Banu Gosh, the doctor. 'What's your name? You have a fine facility with the gob. A vivid imagination, too. One day, you'll make a fine adda man.'

'Bulbul, grandson of Syed Amir Shah.'

'Of course you are,' said the doctor. 'What tamasha the idiots got up to. You know, with that fainting-sahib nonsense. Very unfortunate. As far as I'm concerned, your grandfather was a good man. You know, he did a decent thing by not killing the tiger. He should be praised for it. For his moral courage. Tiger numbers are falling. Very worrying news. The world will be so much poorer without the tiger burning bright in the forests of the night.'

Seeing that the conversation was going off on a tangent, Samsuddin Gazi reminded them they were waiting to hear the journalist's horse story.

'Yes. Let us begin, then,' said Abid Ali. 'Perhaps I should begin with the formula *Once upon a time*. I don't like it, but this might suggest that my story is a fairy tale for the entertainment of little children, a work of pure fantasy, and affords me extra protection. If a jealous informer takes my story to the military top brass as evidence of subversion, circulated in the allegorical guise of an equine story, he might be rebuffed. How can a story that begins with *Once upon a time* be serious? They might say to the informer: Who do you think we are? Straw men? To be blown away by a mere children's fantasy? We are as real as they come. Our power has the force to shape things. We're here to bring discipline and order to our unfortunate nation, and be a shining example to all Islamic countries. Perhaps even surpass Turkey.

'Well, back to the horses, then. A herd of wild horses lived in the marshes to the east. Among them was a feeble-looking horse, lacking in stamina for long treks and not very fast either, but he had a keen pair of eyes, a mischievous sense of humour, and he knew how to tell a good story. Wise ones called him Long Tongue.'

'Is that you? I mean, Long Tongue. In disguise. Is it allegorical or something?' asked Sanu the Fat, emboldened by Bulbul's earlier intervention.

'It's not within my remit to answer such questions. Use your judgment, my young friend. I can only say that Long Tongue has nothing to do with me. Anyway, it's good to see young people like you taking an active interest in adda.'

'Godzilla,' said Sanu the Fat, and Bulbul and White Alam laughed.

'What's so funny about that?' asked Samsuddin Gazi, the sawmill owner.

'Nothing. It's private between us,' said Sanu.

'Ah, a boys' in-group thing. Don't you remember when we started out? We used to say "beef" for everything. One of us just had to say "beef" and we'd kill ourselves laughing. We substituted it for any word in the dictionary,' said Banu Gosh, the doctor.

'Yes, yes, those were the days. Our own private language,' said Fazle Rabbi.

'Logically speaking, of course, you can't have a private language, but I know what you mean. Those were happy days,' said Banu Gosh.

The journalist picked up the horse-story again.

'For some time now, the herd had been facing difficulties. There was some rowdiness in the ranks, and the old males, who'd held onto their alpha status for too long, were squabbling for their share of food and mating rights. Perhaps the atmosphere was a bit more chaotic than usual, but the herd had always found a way of resolving its differences. Sitting on the second rung of the ladder, enjoying a fair share of food and females, but not feeling so confident, were the horses in charge of security. Apart from maintaining order among the ranks, they protected their rich pastures from rival herds. They were known as the Enforcers.

'One night, the Enforcers decided to move. First they rounded up the old alpha horses, who offered no resistance and applauded the takeover.

'"Someone had to do it. We can't have disorder, can we?" said one of the old alpha horses, deciding it would be best to offer their best pastures and females to the Enforcers.

'Yet, the Enforcers bit them, kicked them with their hind legs, then drove them into the ancient death hole, where they starved and became bones. Any dissent met summary punishment. Those who were deemed un-correctable were driven into the ancient death hole to add to the piles of bones. The self-appointed chief of the regime was Marshall Big Horse, a paranoid and psychotic horse who gave himself so many medals that he needed an extra-long coat to accommodate them all, which swept the ground as he moved, leaving a trail of dust behind him. He would drive away any herd member who looked at him in the wrong way, ate more food than himself, and looked at his females – even just a sly and cursory glance – into the death hole. He would neigh for hours, extolling his virtues. Any herd member who didn't flap its ears to show approval, even a bit less enthusiastically than deemed necessary, was pushed there, too. Sometimes, he would drive a horse into it for no apparent reason. He would send his hench-horses, the elite members of the Enforcers, to grin at other horses and whisper – DEATH-HOLE – which was enough to keep them in line.

'Terrified of Marshall Big Horse and the death hole, the horses in the marshes kept their mouths shut, pretending not to have seen or heard anything. They were grateful to be alive. Long Tongue, though afraid, was thinking of doing something.

'One day, Long Tongue, beset with so many questions, his nerves on edge, went for a run. He didn't want to do something stupid to add to the mountainous pile of bones, but what could he do? Perhaps he could spin a comic tale about a big billy-goat. Marshall Big Horse, in his vanity, would never see himself as the double of a goat – a pebble-pooing smelly thing, rightly, destined to end up as a heap of red meat on the plates of those upright, two-legged beasts that even monkeys were ashamed to accept into their fold. Marshall Big Horse couldn't imagine that even a deranged horse could liken him to a goat. On the other hand, low-ranking horses in the marshes would know who that goat was and roll on their backs, laughing at him. How was he to present the story of the big billy-goat? How could he make it provoke that laughter?

'While rehearsing various stories, Long Tongue was thinking, well, it's very silly, really, but why not have the big billy-goat sleeping in his pebbly-poo, then send a low-ranking goat to sneak up on him and tie a torch to its tail and set fire to it? That would push the big billy-goat into hopping on his hooves and screaming: *Douse me, douse me, mama goat is burning my tail.* But he couldn't imagine anyone laughing except a few silly little fillies who would giggle at anything. Then Long Tongue thought of going to the mound in the marshes' centre, and summoning all the grazing horses to gather there. He would talk to them, but no more silly slapstick. He would have the big billy-goat wear a long pink coat, with medals weighing him down, his henchmen, tight-lipped under their shades, running either side of him. He would be lumbering and smelling foul despite pouring gallons of perfume on himself. He would have the big goat declare: See, I'm power itself; if I wished, I could puncture your bellies with my ultra-sharp horns, a gift from the god-goat for his chosen one. And don't forget that the god-goat is practically geriatric now, can't get it up anymore, perhaps he'll die soon – long live the god-goat! – so he'll have no option but to hand over his omniscient power to me, though I have that already. Yes, I can see what you desire, what you dream about, the bubbles that go around inside your heads, but I overlook your little pranks. You see, I love you all, my little goat-children. Father is here, yes, yes, I'm here to sacrifice myself to bring joy to you all. At that moment, Long Tongue imagined, his fellow horses would lower their heads to hide their faces and chuckle. It would be the high point of his allegorical number, but he couldn't go through with it. It remained a fantasy. He was too scared of Marshall Big Horse and the Enforcers.

'Long Tongue was heading back to join the herd. As he turned a bend around a forest of tall grass, thinking of nibbling their white flowers, twelve Enforcers jumped on him and goaded him in front of Marshall Big Horse, who, surprisingly, looked rather benign.

'"Long Tongue, long time no see. How have you been?"

'"Very good, Sir. We are flourishing more than ever, thanks to your benevolence."

'"Very good, very good. I'm here to serve all of my children. But what has been on your mind?"

'"Nothing much, Sir. A lowly horse like myself, Sir, what else could I think about except food? I have been thinking of white flowers. They looked delicious."

'"Of course. I myself am partial to white flowers. But before that you were thinking of something else, right? I saw goats. Something about goats. I was distracted by some fillies – I'm sure you agree that multiplying our numbers is an essential duty. Yes, I was distracted, so I lost the thread. Couldn't follow your thoughts properly. You see, even an omniscient mind has its limitations. So, would you like to enlighten us about the goats? Nasty creatures."

"'Yes, Sir. Nasty, smelly creatures. Very cruel, but funny too."

"'I know. But why would you be thinking of goats? Perhaps it amuses you to consider a goat as my double. You chuckle to yourself. Am I right?"

"'How absurd. How can a noble horse such as yourself, Sir, be likened to a goat? Only a mad horse would be tempted by such thoughts."

"'Yes, you spoke my very words. Uncanny. Thank you, Long Tongue. I like you. So, you're a mad horse. It's your judgment, not mine. I always say a bit of confession makes our job so much easier. Call me a humanist of the old school. I wouldn't say I like the use of barbaric methods to get to the truth. I always say truth is truth, even if it dwells in the secret chamber of your mind. Anyway, what are we to do with you, Long Tongue? We like you but we don't want a mad horse among us, do we?"

'All the Enforcers shouted: "No, Sir, we don't."

"'Long Tongue, embrace your destiny. Be noble as a horse should be. I'll think of you as a white flower," said Marshall Big Horse, who went back to his copulating duty.

'The Enforcers resumed where they left off: biting him, kicking him. Long Tongue could hardly see with blood pouring into his eyes. One of his legs was broken. Still biting and kicking, the Enforcers drove him to the death hole. At its rim, they turned their backs on him in a semicircle. Timed to perfection, they lifted their hind legs and kicked him to join the bones.'

Without anyone being aware of it, the match had ended. No one was around except the gossipers and Bulbul and his friends. It was getting dark. Already a swarm of banana bats was flying so low overhead that they could hear their wings swish.

'It's a terrible story, Journalist,' said Samsuddin Gazi, the sawmill owner, 'I thought your allegory business was meant to save his neck. What's happened to your grey areas? Are you saying that all men of power are, deep down, a bit of Hitler or Stalin?'

'Maybe.'

'Journalist, my friend, I might be a bit brutal with my criticism – I hope you don't mind,' said Hakim Khan, the lawyer. 'Frankly, this double allegory of yours doesn't work. First, horses are meant to be the doubles of humans. Then the goats, those of horses. So, the goats serve as twice-removed mirrors. Broken and upside-down mirrors of human follies. No one would laugh at this. Yes, Long Tongue's plight might bring tears to some soft and soapy souls, but it wouldn't jolt anyone to the realisation that something ought to be done, that one should stand up to a psychopathic dictator.'

'Thank you, Lawyer. Thank you for being frank with me. I told you I'm a journalist, not a poet,' said Abid Ali.

'Long Tongue was doomed to the fate of whatever human figure he's supposed to represent. Doomed from the very beginning. I must say some of the details are rather clumsy. It gives too much away of the story's human provenance. It would arouse the suspicion of any dictator who, however dim, would realise that Long Tongue was poking fun at him,' said Fazle Rabbi.

'Thank you, Landlord. You make me think again. Perhaps satires, parodies, and allegories are not the best methods. At least not in my hands.'

'I have this suspicion,' said Banu Gosh, 'that perhaps clever people hide behind such rhetorical figures. Pretending to talk back at power. Patting themselves on their backs as if they've done something ethical and critical, but knowing full well that they can go on with their dandyism, with fine talk, fine music, and fine food. But sometimes, though, they're caught out, especially by the truly paranoid types. We know too well these sad stories of the poets. Poor Long Tongue. With Marshall Big Horse he never stood a chance.'

'Thank you, Doctor. My friends, you've made me realise what I should do. Not go hiding behind fancy rhetoric. I'm a journalist. I should speak plain and simple truth. Name names and take the consequences. Hopefully, you won't suffer on my account. I assure you, I'll take sole and full responsibility,' said Abid Ali.

'So, you're going to speak against General Ayub Khan?' asked Bulbul.

'Yes, my young friend. Can I have a few words with you in private?'

'Certainly,' said Bulbul.

'Do you know Scientist? He lives in your neighbourhood.'

'I know him. He lives only a few minutes from us.'

'Can you give him a message from me? Can you tell him that I want to meet him?'

'Certainly. About anything in particular?'

'I'll tell him myself. Wait. Perhaps you could mention that I want him to do a few posters for me.'

Next day, after school, Bulbul went to see Scientist, but he wasn't in, so he went to White Alam's house where Sanu the Fat would meet them. From there, they would walk to town, along Ganginarpar Road to the railway station, enjoying the sights and sounds. On their way back, they would stop at the town hall, pop into the United States Information Services (USIS) library and stay on for the early evening newsreel.

When White Alam and Sanu the Fat visited Bulbul, Dadu always offered them something: mangoes, jackfruits, samosas, puffed rice, meesty-sweet, palm bread or whatever she happened to have at home at that time. Bulbul knew he would get nothing at White Alam's house, so he popped in a tea stall to buy some dal-puri for the three of them. Inside, the atmosphere was tense; there were hushed conversations with people looking over their shoulders. Bulbul's ears pricked up when he overheard Abid Ali's name. Grave and hesitant, the tea-stall regulars leaned closer over the table to whisper that the journalist must have gone mad to take such a suicidal risk. Perhaps, as regulars, they would be subject to collective punishment, because each morning, on his way to his office, the journalist stopped by for a cup of tea – always no sugar, no milk, but with a piece of ginger.

'He loved his ginger. He really did,' said one of the regulars.

Not daring to ask, Bulbul wondered what Abid Ali had done to incite such a hush-hush and jittery conversation. Perhaps he had followed through on his words in the afternoon edition. He left the tea stall, went to White Alam's, and found him helping his mother in their vegetable patch.

In White Alam's room, Bulbul asked if he'd heard anything about Abid Ali. He hadn't, so they decided to investigate when Sanu the Fat came over. Bulbul was feeling nervous, thinking that something terrible must have happened. Hoping to put him at ease,

White Alam let out their familiar cry of Godzilla, but now all Bulbul managed was a twitch of his lips.

White Alam's father – Stingy-Traffic-Policeman – was back from duty. They heard his agitated voice from the veranda. Soon, he came into the room carrying a newspaper.

'Have you seen this? What tamasha. It'll be the ruin of our town.'

'No, we haven't,' said White Alam.

'I've told you so many times, didn't I? These adda-men are trouble. But who listens to me? No one.'

Bulbul glanced at the headline: 'General Ayub Khan is a tyrant, a devourer of democracy. Down with him and his corrupt cronies.'

'Day after day, you go to the cricket ground,' said White Alam's father. 'You sit behind them. Listen to all kinds of garbage. If the police find out that you fraternise with the adda-men, it'll ruin us. You'll be expelled from school and thrown into jail. The journalist is an idiot. From now on I forbid you to go to the cricket ground.'

With White Alam grounded, Bulbul went out with Sanu. Abid Ali's press office was located on the north side of the town, just after the town hall, at the beginning of Ganginarpar Road. Bulbul and Sanu walked past the press on opposite sides of the road, as if on a casual afternoon stroll. Usually, Bulbul would stop to listen to the press's clickety-clack and smell the ink wafting out of it. The entire operation of *Fresh News* – the town's only newspaper – was located in a tin shed. Besides being its only journalist, Abid Ali was its owner, editor, and printer. Two boys helped him print and distribute copies to various newsagents, grocery shops and tea stalls throughout Mominabad. Some old customers would pop in to collect their copies in person and, if Abid Ali was in, they would discuss the news with him over a cup of tea. Abid Ali never made any money from *Fresh News* – sales just about covered the running costs. His adda friends suggested he should take advertisements – from honourable sources, of course – but Abid Ali refused. It would compromise him as a journalist and an editor. If he weren't a bachelor, and if it weren't for the inheritance that he received from his father, he would struggle to make ends meet.

As they passed the press's tin shed, they saw its front had been flattened, as if a bulldozer had crushed it. Soldiers were loading bits and pieces of printing machinery into military trucks. Bulbul wondered what had happened to Abid Ali; he hoped he'd escaped.

Even though Ganginarpar Road was buzzing, they weren't in the mood to enjoy its sights and sounds. Passing the cinema hall, they checked the billing. On Scientist's recommendation, they had been waiting for the return showing of *20,000 Leagues Under the Sea* and saw it would be on the coming Friday. If they hadn't been feeling anxious about Abid Ali and slightly fearful for themselves and the town, they would have taken a closer look at the poster, showing a sea monster dragging a submarine down to the bottom of the sea with its huge tentacles. The poster alone would have launched Sanu the Fat into an imaginary trailer, which would have been more amusing than the actual one. They merely noted the announcement and moved on.

Before the clampdown, political parties and civic organisations would have been dotted along Ganginarpar Road. Their spokespersons, standing on boxes, would have been giving rousing speeches. Now that politics was banned, advertising campaigns, street stalls, medicine men and freakshows had taken their place. The boys stopped when they saw the return of the Donkey and the Dwarf show, which they'd enjoyed for its mix of slapstick hilarity and biting political satire – ventriloquised by the dwarf as if the donkey were speaking. Now, all trace of political criticism had been excised, and the slapstick wasn't funny without it.

On the way back from the station they popped into the USIS library, not to read books, newspapers or journals but, as usual, to leaf through the glossy magazines for photos of women in bikinis, sunbathing or swimming – a rare chance to satisfy their curiosity about what a woman's body might actually look like.

Bulbul hoped this would take his mind off his forebodings about Abid Ali. Ah, the women were so alluring! He flipped through until he came upon a photo of a young woman with dark hair. Most of the women were blond, with broad smiles, as if they knew how attractive they looked. The dark-haired girl was in profile and she wasn't smiling.

He wasn't sure why he was drawn to her. Perhaps because she didn't seem conscious of being in front of the camera, perhaps she was on a family holiday, and her little brother, without meaning to, had pressed the button on his camera to take this picture. She was wearing a bluish bikini with starry white dots on it. She was looking out to sea, at the blue water, the vanishing horizon, and feeling sad because, despite being surrounded by her family, there was no one to hold her, caress her body and tell her how beautiful she looked. She was just a photograph in a magazine, but Bulbul thought she was letting her body fall like raindrops after a long dry season.

He had no idea that the librarian was standing behind him.

'You dirty boy. Ogling at women in bikinis. Did you come here to touch yourself? If I catch you again, you'll be banned from the library forever. Now get out before I call the security!'

Feeling shamed, he and Sanu hurried out of the library and headed home, but stopped in front of the demolished press building. Abid Ali was standing on a box, denouncing the military dictatorship and prophesying its demise, how it would soon be thrown into the dustbin of history.

'Mark my word, ladies and gentlemen. If you think I'm here to talk about goats and horses, you're mistaken. These creatures are far nobler than our big-man dictator. If we put them in the same bracket as this all-too-human tyrant, we surely demean them. Do you hear me, my brothers and sisters? Even if you're locked inside your houses, inside the dark chambers of your souls, I'm here to name names. Yes, he's called General Ayub Khan – the most diabolical sidekick of the devil himself.'

No one was there to listen to him, and seeing Bulbul, Abid Ali told them it was too dangerous to stay around, because the military must be on their way to arrest him. Bulbul begged him to make a run for it. He should go to Dambarpur. Dadu would happily look after him, hide him. If they came for him, he could disappear into the swamp where, during the dry months, he could lie low in the vast rice and jute fields. After the monsoon, he could melt into the sea of water.

It was too late. Military jeeps were almost upon them. Urged on by Abid Ali, Bulbul and Sanu the Fat ran and hid behind a parapet. From there, they saw the military tying Abid Ali's hands and manhandling him into a jeep and speeding away.

CHAPTER 8

Several weeks had passed since Abid Ali's arrest. Harassed by the goons belonging to the student front of the Pakistan Muslim League, Banu Gosh was under pressure to leave home and emigrate to India. To that end, the goons were trying to whip up communal tension, but Mominabad's inhabitants, their lives so enmeshed for centuries, didn't take the bait.

'We've heard it all before. Hindus tearing the pages of the Koran and wiping their bums with them. Muslims slaughtering cows in the temples and peeing on the goddesses. And always the tales of violation of each other's sisters, mothers, and even grandmothers. Yes, we've heard them all before,' people would say. 'Who do they think we are? Moronic swine to be duped by this same-old, same-old? Oh, no. We know our neighbours. We've been sharing food at each other's Eids and pujas. And tasty treats they are.'

The people knew that all the goons wanted was to get their hands on Banu Gosh's house – a well-preserved colonial bungalow with a garden full of exotic trees from Europe, and a pond teeming with fish, where the doctor practised his angling. For him, an angler's fingers on a line required just as much skill as a sitarist's on his instrument's strings.

'Have you experienced the sublime?' he would ask his adda friends. 'You don't have to go to the Himalayas. Just hook the elusive one. Even if he's tiny, you experience your body deluging with strange sensations.'

Having failed to whip up communal riots, the goons launched a stoning campaign. Throughout the day and night, stones would fly in from all sides of the house, into the courtyard, roofs, veranda, the garden and the pond. One morning as she stepped out of the veranda to offer puja to the tulsi tree, one of the stones landed on the doctor's wife, smashing her shoulder blade. Banu Gosh, though a thoroughly secular man, momentarily became religious and thanked Lord Rama that the stone hadn't hit his wife's head. Of course, he was scared, but he was determined not to be hounded out of his home, from the land of his ancestors.

'Torn from these roots and memories,' he said, 'I would become a hollow man without even a shadow.'

His friends took turns to sleep in his guest room, to reassure him that adda-men, even if death hailed them, would never abandon one of their own. Bulbul wanted to do something but didn't know what. At least he should visit the doctor's home to show his solidarity, tell him, 'We boys want you to stay. Doctor, if you leave what will happen to adda?'

The police, still wanting to avoid any communalist slur, and to prove their impartiality and professionalism, were taking the matter seriously, and had deployed their best officers and latest methods to get to the bottom of the stoning. They got nowhere. How could they? The goons had already cramped all the spaces, from private homes to market squares, with their version of the event, their own brand of truth. Usually not very talkative and certainly not enamoured of complex explanations, the goons suddenly seemed to have hit upon a rare moment of illumination. They aired the view that all you had to do was think through the matter rationally and leave aside volatile feelings and wild hypotheses. Wasn't it obvious that it was the work of evil spirits, demons, rakshasas, and an unruly jinn?

'They don't want them here. Very unfortunate but what can we do?' the goons said. Everyone in Mominabad knew that it was the goons who had been stoning the doctor's house and wouldn't stop until the doctor and his wife crossed the border into India. But as time passed, people in Mominabad were able to stand up to the goons less and less.

Bulbul, accompanied by Sanu the Fat and White Alam, was on his way to the doctor's house. Reaching Ganginarpar Road they stopped by the tailor's shop. Having become fatter recently, Sanu had ordered a new shirt and wanted to pick it up. It wasn't ready, and the tailor shook his head, saying, 'It's a difficult job. So much flesh to cover. The stitching needs to be extra strong to make allowance for the strain of your bulk. Many more hours of labour needed. You need to pay five rupees more.'

'You saw my size. You measured me. Now you want more money. What's the meaning of this?' said Sanu.

'Sorry. I can't always foresee the hours needed. Call it an old tailor's failing. Very bad, very bad, I know, but five more rupees should do it. I've made a special cutting on it. You'll look very thin and handsome in it.'

'I just want a shirt. I don't care about looking thin and handsome. I rather like my bulk. Your demand is an outrage, blackmail!' Sanu stormed out while Bulbul and White Alam stayed on to bargain with the tailor to have the shirt done for two more rupees. 'Come back in an hour and the shirt will be ready,' he said.

Back on the road, Bulbul and White Alam were looking for Sanu, but couldn't see him anywhere. Distracted, they hadn't noticed Keramot Ali, the jute merchant, until it was too late to escape him and his long monologues, which they couldn't make head nor tail of. 'Buy me a cigarette,' he demanded.

Since his doomsday party, Keramot Ali's life had taken a downward turn. His friends had deserted him, and, facing the prospect of being homeless, his wife had moved back to her father's house with his children. Now he lived rough and survived only by begging. He'd grown a long beard and dreadlocks down to his buttocks and taken to speaking in English, of which he'd shown no knowledge in his previous life. Mominabad speculated that he must be possessed by an English ghost, perhaps of a colonial sahib, otherwise, how could you explain his uncanny mastery of their tongue?

Bulbul and White Alam bought him a cigarette. He took a puff, looked at Bulbul and asked, 'Do I know you, boy?'

'No. I don't think so.'

'Right, I don't know you. But you should know me. Do you know who I am?'

'No. I don't know you.'

'You should be ashamed, boy, not knowing the One who came down the mountain to speak the truth. You see, I went to see Him, to play a game of dice with Him and to ask Him some questions. But He was dead before I got there. I feasted on his carcass. He tasted awful – gave me a runny tummy for days. Are you sure you didn't come to my Doomsday party?'

'No.'

'I understand. Well, now that He is dead and gone what are you going to do?'

'Don't know.'

'That's why I came down the mountain. To tell you the truth. Did you know that things go round and round like a bicycle wheel? Each time, the same, the same. So, boys, every time you do something, don't give a fuck about it because that one time is like all the times before and all the times to come. Do you get it?'

'No,' said White Alam.

'You're one of those last-men-idiots? Smelly donkey-bottoms? Licking shit out of money-note and feeling jolly-good-happy? Let me tell you something. Do I care that I blew the lot on the Doomsday party? No. I rejoice in it. What's a man who's the One to do but throw a dice. So, I did. Head or tail, the same, the same. I take my lot like that man-womanish, boozy-man-fakir. Boozy, boozy, modh-khor, I whirl my locks and dance and make merry. Always, oh dear me, Amor fati.'

'What? You want to fart?' asked White Alam.

'Yes, yes, always, yes. Your grandaddy farted. Your daddy-man farted. You look like a farty fellow too. Same stinky fart for eternity.'

Bulbul and White Alam wanted to escape his ravings, but didn't know how without raising his ire; he might get violent and sink his teeth into them. Luckily, Sanu the Fat turned up; he always knew how to handle a difficult character, even a mad one.

'Don't worry, Mr Doomsday Man. We are going to fart like nobody's business, the same, old stinky fart. Like our grandaddies. And we'll love it. Happy? Now leave us to get on with our farting.'

As they walked to a cafe on Ganginarpar Road, Bulbul and White Alam thanked Sanu for rescuing them. Looking around warily, they sat at a table at the back of the stall and ordered three glasses of sweet milk. White Alam offered to pay for them; he'd stolen a few loose coins from his father's latest bribery-earnings. 'My father was very happy today. He came home with his coat pockets bulging. He gathered his earnings into a pile on the dining table and looked at them for hours, like a sadhu meditating, then fell asleep. Truly, the pile was so high and fat that he'd never notice. So, I did a Godzilla on him.'

'You're a true son of your father,' said Sanu the Fat. 'Hopefully this milk is not contaminated by the spirit of thievery and won't poison us. We don't want to die before our time, do we?'

Having had their first sip, they'd eased up a bit when six goons marched in, all sporting dark glasses, with bulging muscles bursting through their identical shirts. They would have looked comical if tales of their menace hadn't preceded them. They sat at a table next to Bulbul and his friends and ordered black tea with lemon and ginger.

'Should I put a bit of sugar, Sir?' said the serving boy.

'No, you idiot. Can't you see we're into healthy bodies, healthy living and, of course, healthy minds,' said one of the goons.

Bulbul and his friends were silent, their hands shaking, not even daring to lift their glasses to take a sip of milk. Sanu the Fat was thinking of saying something funny or flattering to the goons, perhaps praising their muscles, their dark glasses and their sense of style, but he couldn't muster the courage to say anything.

At last, one of the goons spoke. 'We have been watching you. You've been very naughty, haven't you?'

'Sir, we haven't done anything. We are good boys. We esteem you very highly. Hundred per cent respect, Sir,' said Sanu the Fat.

'Yes, yes. We earn our respect. But we have been seeing you a lot. Always behind the adda-men at the cricket ground. No doubt digesting all their rubbish. Now what brings you to this part of town? Nothing to see here, is there?' said another of the goons.

'Nothing, Sir. We just came for a walk to the centre and a glass of milk,' said Sanu the Fat.

'Don't play games with us. That's one thing we don't like. People who tell lies. You came to check on that adda-man, that idiotic doctor, that bloody Hindu, didn't you? The guy is spoiling the decency of our town. He lives like a lord at our expense. Pure wickedness. He ought to be sent back to India. Don't you agree?'

'Sure, Sir. Hundred per cent. Wasn't the doctor born here? His father and grandfather too. Doesn't someone have to come from elsewhere, you know, to be sent back? We agree with you, Sir. Hundred per cent,' said Sanu the Fat.

'Fat pig, don't try to be clever with us. Are you a Hindu lover or something? No matter what anyone thinks, the Hindu has to leave. Go wherever he wants as long as he doesn't hang around here. Anyway, the devils and jinn are making very, very sure that he leaves.'

'We are relieved that the divine has intervened, Sir. Very opportune.'

'Off you go! You don't know how lucky you are. If we catch you hanging around here again, poking your noses into our business, we'll break your legs, then your arms. Very slowly. Don't be fooled by our suave and sophisticated appearance. We're known for extreme violence. Understand? And don't let us see you at the cricket ground again. Behind those damn adda-men.'

'Yes, Sir,' said Sanu the Fat and the three of them rushed out of the stall and almost ran back to their houses where they stayed after school for the next few days.

A lot of things had been playing on Dadu's mind, including that her old Murphy was playing up again. She needed to have it fixed, so she sent Bulbul to Scientist. When he arrived at the workshop, he was surprised to see the spies were inside, helping him. One was sweeping the floor, the other held a bicycle frame for Scientist to work on. Seeing Bulbul's perplexed look, Scientist explained that since these good people had to do a job, they might as well do it in the comfort of the workshop. Why make them suffer the rain or the afternoon heat? Here, they could have teas and snacks and write their reports with everything done tiptop and professionally.

'Yes, yes,' said the spies, 'we do everything tiptop. Our Scientist is a proper gentleman. He even put us to sleep. Sorted our minds. We are very happy.'

Once the bicycle was fixed and the sweeping done, Scientist told the spies, 'Your job is done for the day. Excellent report, some clever turns of phrase. Almost poetic. Your superiors will be very pleased. Now go home. Play with your children. Nothing like father/child bonding. It's very good for their development.'

After the spies had left, Scientist told Bulbul that he felt sorry for them; the poor fellows had to do this shitty job to feed their children, but he had to protect himself too. He had to sweet talk them into believing they could report everything they saw and heard, that nothing untoward was going on, was there? Just a poor mechanic and a painter toiling to make a living. No one came to talk politics or entertain any thought of subversion.

'Well, I had to hypnotise them a bit. Give them the right

suggestions. All very proper. No compromise on the protocol, so that they don't get confused. They are good guys, really.'

'Why send them away then?'

'Can't take chances. Can't trust them completely. Perhaps they think that I am in their power, a fool who fell for it. Sometimes the world is truly crazy.'

Bulbul told him Abid Ali had wanted to see him before his arrest.

'I know. He's already sent me the message. About the posters, wasn't it?'

'Abid Ali had a press. Surely, he could've done the posters there. Why would he ask you?'

'Good question. Perhaps he knew that he would be arrested. Perhaps he thought that mere words were not enough. People see what's happening more clearly in pictures. They're part of my craft.'

'I see. But I don't understand. If he'd already sent you the message about the postering, why would he ask me to bring the same message to you? What was the point?'

'Perhaps it wasn't the message. He didn't want you to be a mere messenger. Perhaps, he wanted you to get involved.'

Bulbul returned home feeling unnerved. Why would Abid Ali want that? Didn't he know the dangers? Perhaps he would end up in jail or be beaten by the goons. Breaking his hands and legs, very slowly. He couldn't talk to Dadu without sending her into a full-blown panic. Perhaps he should talk to Kona Das, but she wasn't in the house. He asked where she was.

'I don't know what's happened to that girl. She's never home. Acting very funny. I fear she might be up to no good. I'm worried sick,' said Dadu. Yes, recently Kona Das had been sneaking out at odd hours, looking distracted, dozing off, singing to herself, and most worryingly, going silent, contrary to her usual talkative self. What was wrong with her? He had to find out what was really going on. If anyone could dig out the goings-on in the neighbour-hood, it would be Sanu the Fat, and he assured Bulbul that he would get to the bottom of it.

'It's a bit delicate. Understand? Keep it to yourself. Even White Alam mustn't know. Godzilla, yes?' said Bulbul.

'Acha, if you want. But I don't understand why I must keep it from White Alam. Aren't we three the Godzilla brothers?'

'Yes, we are. Just make an exception on this for a while.'

That night, after her prayer, Dadu went to bed and the house was silent except for the whining of mosquitoes. When Bulbul heard footsteps, he went to investigate. He surprised Kona Das as she was letting herself out.

'Kona Boo, where are you going?'

'Where do you think? Out. I'm suffocated in this house. No one to talk to. All Bibi does is pick on me.'

'I'm sorry, Kona Boo. What can I do? Perhaps, we can go to see a film. Have you ever been to the cinema?'

'No. What can you do? Nothing. Just leave me alone.'

'If you want. I'll ask Dadu not to pick on you. But where are you going?'

'I'm going to meet up with the cobbler's wife. She and I are of the same caste. We understand each other. We talk together and laugh. Anything wrong with that?'

'No. But be careful. You never know what evil stalks the streets, especially at this hour.'

Over the next few days, as a result of Sanu's efforts, and on the back of his own endeavours, spying, eavesdropping and speculating, Bulbul was building up a picture of what Kona Das was up to, though he knew he had only a fraction of the story and could be way off the mark.

Bulbul recognised that Kona Das had been feeling restless for some time now. But she must know that Dadu cared for her; she had enough to eat and a roof over her head. Her workload wasn't heavy in a household of three grownups – and Dadu put in as much work as she did. He did outside chores, errands, and some of the 'manly' tasks at home. What was making her unhappy then? Perhaps she was lonely. Perhaps she wanted a baby, a husband. Perhaps she needed a community of her own kind, faces to read off her story and even share a common misery with. But the fact was she wasn't heading for the shanty to spend time with the cobbler's wife. She was going to Teeny Mulla's shack, located inside the graveyard.

A madrassa-educated cleric, Teeny Mullah was small, sported

a scraggly beard, and wore a white punjabi and a skullcap, which always looked stained and dirty. He smiled easily, but the more he smiled, the more nervous he looked. He helped wash dead bodies, wrap shrouds, dig graves, conduct the final service before the bodies were buried, and lead the prayers for visiting relatives. His shack, located deep in the vast, sprawling graveyard, was so eerily dark and spooky that even the cutthroats didn't dare venture there after sundown. Apart from providing his lodgings, the graveyard committee didn't pay him anything; his income came from donations from the relatives of the dead. But these weren't enough, even for a single man. He supplemented his income by giving Koranic lessons, evening waz-talks at religious gatherings, and slaughtering cows and goats on Eid-ul-Adha.

It was through an Eid-ul-Adha that Kona Das first met him. Dadu had a goat to be sacrificed, and Teeny Mullah was happy to do the job. It was the custom for a mullah to be fed after he had done the ritual slaughtering. In fact, this was the most challenging part of his job: to eat a full meal at twenty different houses in one afternoon. Committing the entire Koran to memory was hard, but nothing compared to the drills he had to go through to eat twenty large meals in a single afternoon. 'If you can master that,' he would say, 'you can withstand anything Shaitan throws at you.'

Usually, Dadu would ask Bulbul to attend to male visitors, but by the time the mullah arrived, he'd gone out to enjoy the festive day with Sanu the Fat and White Alam. So, Kona Das had to serve the meal to Teeny Mullah. Looking shabby and timid even on an Eid day, the mullah got down to the ten different dishes of the meal; he had to eat a reasonable amount so as not to offend, but he was struggling. That particular Eid fell on a sweltering summer's day, and the call at Dadu's house was the last of his twenty jobs. He had performed nineteen slaughters and eaten equal numbers of large meals. Seeing him gagging and sweating profusely, Kona Das began to fan him.

'Can I have another glass of water?' he asked.

His nerves were on edge in Kona Das's presence. He was manoeuvring his body to ensure his eyes didn't stray into hers. Any meeting of their gaze, even accidental, might push him down a slippery chute to hell.

She returned with the water more quickly than he anticipated and she caught him, red-handed, emptying the dishes into his shoulder bag. Startled, he blurted out, 'Black. For a black woman, you're comely.' He grabbed his bag, gravy leaking into his clothes, and ran out.

The night when Bulbul began to discover for himself the truth about Kona Das's absences, she hadn't headed directly to Teeny Mullah's shanty. From the house, through a gap in the crumbling sidewall, she slid behind a bush, where she transformed herself into a man. She put on a lungi, a long black punjabi, wrapped a pagri around her head and attached a bushy beard. Perhaps this was Teeny Mullah's idea and he had sourced the props for her to become a man. Bulbul was sure the beard was the work of Scientist; no one in Mominabad had the skills to make such a natural-looking piece. Next time he saw Scientist he would ask.

After meandering along several streets, Kona Das entered the graveyard from the opposite side to its public entrance. Since no one dared to enter the graveyard after dark, it was perfectly safe for her secret rendezvous. Still, she hadn't passed unnoticed. People talked about seeing an elegant young mullah in black heading towards the graveyard. Perhaps he was Teeny Mullah's spiritual interlocutor, and they'd be discussing how to uphold the faith, the finer points of Sharia law, and how to move an audience to righteous fervour in their waz-talks.

Bulbul followed Kona Das, fearing for her every time she passed someone in the street, because it would be a terrible scandal if her true identity were discovered – an illicit liaison between a low-caste Hindu and a mullah. Discovery would unleash unsavoury passions: she might be lynched on the spot by a mob, paraded through the town, her head shaven, for corrupting a man of religion, she might even be branded a whore with a red hot iron for corrupting Mominabad's youth. It would play into the hands of the goons who would start a communal riot as cover to send Banu Gosh packing to India and grab his house. Bulbul was relieved to see that no one recognised her.

A bit calmer now, he followed her along the meandering roads to where she entered the graveyard. Because of regular power cuts, Mominabad had been even darker than usual, the graveyard doubly so, except for a flicker of light coming from the mullah's shack. Bulbul felt a growing dread: this would be the place of demons and devils if they lived anywhere on earth. He was trembling, wondering where Kona Das found such courage to venture here. Though Teeny Mullah didn't stand to pay as high a price as Kona Das, it was still risky for him. If people found out, his career as a mullah would be over, and he'd be driven out of Mominabad.

Bulbul ran home and went to bed, but couldn't sleep. It was well past midnight when he heard Kona Das letting herself in. The next day, while Bulbul was having his breakfast on the veranda, Kona Das and Dadu were peeling and cutting vegetables.

'Only a few more months, my little bird. When you finish your time at school, I'm going back to Dambarpur. Never coming back to this cursed town,' said Dadu.

'I want to stay here. I want to do higher secondary education. Where would I stay?' said Bulbul.

'I never see you studying. You're not into book reading, are you? So, why bother with higher secondary?'

'I want to stay here. My friends are here. What would I do in the village?'

'I can't afford to pay the rent anymore, my little bird. Can't keep the house here. You can help me cultivate the lands, manage the fish stock in the swamp.'

'I don't know, Dadu. I don't want to become a peasant.'

'What's wrong with being a peasant? I'm a peasant. Am I shameful to you?'

'There's no point talking to you, Dadu. You twist everything.'

'I also want to live here. I don't want to leave Mominabad,' said Kona Das.

'You too? Have you been conspiring together? Behind my back? Anyway, where would you stay? How are you going to make a living?'

'I can stay in the shanty. The cobbler has a patch. I can build a shack there. There's plenty of work as a domestic. I can clean. I can fetch water. I can cook. I can look after babies,' said Kona Das.

'Yes, yes. You're a queen of everything. Go and be a domestic in other people's houses. See, how they treat you. Anyway, I get it. You two want to abandon me. That's what I get for looking after you. Ya Allah, it's my destiny.'

'Alright, Dadu. Don't be so dramatic. I'll come to Dambarpur and become a peasant. Happy?' said Bulbul.

Kona Das didn't say anything. Perhaps she was thinking of Teeny Mullah, dreaming of making a life with him, having a baby in their own house.

'Ya Allah, it's my destiny,' repeated Dadu and got up to bathe.

When Dadu left, Bulbul looked hard at Kona Das.

'Bulbul Da, why you looking at me like that?'

Bulbul said nothing; he gathered his things and set off for school. In the afternoon, he went to see Scientist. He asked about the spies. Where were they? What had happened to them? After a series of good reports, Scientist explained, the military had been reassured that the workshop was simply a place for mechanical fault-fixing, occasional mind-fixing, painting and advertising campaigns. No subversives came there, only obedient and law-abiding citizens, all very loyal to the General and his governor. The spies had been withdrawn and posted elsewhere.

'I don't get it,' Bulbul said. 'Mind-fixing? I thought the very mention of that would set their alarm bells ringing. Enough to send their superior officers to investigate.'

'You're not as stupid as you look, are you? Yes, it triggered their panic buttons as I knew it would. The chief of their regional military intelligence – some major – came to see me.'

'How come you're not in trouble, then?'

'Well, he was an educated man. Did his training in England and the Soviet Union. I'm sure he knew all about the techniques of brainwashing. Since the coup they have been using them, with some success. Anyway, he was obviously alarmed. He wanted to know all about the mind-fixing. He said he didn't doubt my loyalty, but he was intrigued. I told him that it sounded more alarming than it actually was. Just a few soothing words. Just a way of relaxing people, take their minds off things.'

'What happened then?'

'He wanted to see for himself. Wanted me to do some mind-fixing on him. And, of course, I couldn't pass up that opportunity. I relaxed him a bit and put him to sleep. You know, the usual protocol.'

'What did you tell him? What stories?'

'I took him back to his native Punjab, as a little boy. You know, mummy/daddy stuff. I know it's crap, but it works every time.'

'Now, I get it. You got the spies to put the mind-fixing in their report. Very clever. You knew it would bring the Major in. In the meantime, you researched his background, didn't you?'

'Well, we can't do our job without allaying the major's suspicions.'

'What job are you talking about?'

'I'll come to that in a minute. But what brought you here today?'

Bulbul asked Scientist about the beard: had he made it for Teeny Mullah? Well, he hadn't made it for the mullah; it had simply been gathering dust in his workshop from last year's municipal play for which he designed all the props and costumes. When the mullah asked for one, he retrieved it and gave it to him. He wasn't expecting much, but the mullah gave him a fair price.

'Did he tell you what he meant to do with it?'

'No, he didn't. I suspected that he wanted to play a little fantasy game. We all have secrets and underground lives, haven't we? It's his affair. I didn't want to pry.'

Bulbul stayed silent for a while, biting his lips, still debating whether to tell Scientist or not.

'You've something on your mind. Come on, spit it out.'

'I don't know how to put it. It's rather delicate. Kona Das – she lives with us. Recently, she's been acting very funny. She's sneaking out of home at night. Goes to see Teeny Mullah in the graveyard. I'm really worried for her.'

'I see. So, they're having an erotic liaison. A low-caste Hindu woman and a mullah. You've reason enough to be concerned.'

'I don't understand how it's happened. Kona Das, always so sensible and the mullah, so timid. Why would they take such risks? It beats me.'

'How old are you?'

'Almost sixteen. Why?'

'Well, the passions of the body. You must have experienced their force. You know what I'm talking about, don't you?'

Bulbul wasn't expecting this line of questioning and it triggered an acute unease, as if Scientist was trying to peer into his shameful secrets. He stayed quiet, biting his lips.

'All right, you don't have to say anything. I understand. By the way, have you read any Wordsworth?' asked Scientist.

'No. My English teacher always bleats on about him. I haven't paid any attention. Boring.'

'You should have listened to him. You might have learned something. Perhaps, you would have heard these lines: *Our bodies feel, where're they be, Against, or with our will.* What do those lines tell you?'

'I don't know. Is it something like our bodies can run ahead of our minds?'

'You have a good brain on you. Don't waste it. Take your studies seriously. Read books. Anyway, does it answer your question?'

'Are you saying that Kona Das and Teeny Mullah, despite themselves, are being driven by their bodies?'

'Exactly. My lips are sealed. Hopefully, no one else will find out. If anyone does, all hell will break loose. We'll have a serious situation on our hands.'

'You wanted to tell me about a job. What is it?'

'Well, it's not a job. It's our moral duty. If we don't do it, we'll dishonour Abid Ali.'

'You mean the postering campaign? Even though you got rid of the major and the spies, it's still risky. We might be thrown in jail.'

'Yes, we might be. But what do we do? Doing nothing is not an option. If I could do it alone, I wouldn't ask anyone. Even if my physical limitations weren't a factor, a job like this requires at least two people.'

'I don't know. I'll have to think about it.'

'Alright. I won't do the posters here. A friend of mine offered his shed behind his grocery shop. It's in an alley off Ganginarpar Road, just after the water tank. It's called Anything From Anywhere. I'll begin in three days' time. At midnight.'

'You mean Goni Mia's shop?'

'Yes. In three days' time. Precisely at midnight.'

On the way home, Bulbul felt guilty about not giving a clear answer. Scientist needed his help, otherwise, he wouldn't have given him all the details: the place, the day, and the time. It was too scary. Perhaps Scientist could find someone else to help him. He didn't want to be bitten to death by the mosquitoes in jail or beaten up by the police, by the goons, or both.

Back home, Dadu was waiting for him with the evening meal. She asked where he'd been. He lied that he'd visited the USIS library to see a newsreel about American rockets entering space.

'America, you wouldn't believe it, Dadu, such a nice country. Everyone has a car, flowers everywhere, beautiful mountains. People are very white and beautiful too. Very clever to send rockets into space – you know, where you see the stars and the moon.' But Dadu wasn't impressed.

'It's all lies. No one can go near the moon or stars. It's all vanity talk. A bunch of Nimrods. And don't take me for a fool. I've seen plenty of white sahibs and memsahibs in Calcutta. What made you think they're beautiful? Yes, I've seen them. Pale as anything. You can see through their skins. Like them female petny-devils. Very ugly. Anyway, you shouldn't be wasting your time watching those things. You should be studying, my little bird. Read school books. Your exam is not too far.'

'What's the point of studying if I'm to become a peasant in Dambarpur.'

'Excuses, excuses. If you're not careful, you'll end up badly, my little bird. A landless peasant. Starving belly and all. And don't forget your grandfather and all he did to send you to school. You have to pass your exam for him. His soul will be very unhappy if you don't.'

In his room, after dinner, Bulbul was thinking about Kona Das. He knew Scientist wouldn't open his mouth; he trusted Sanu the Fat, completely, but if he carelessly let it slip to White Alam… He shouldn't worry about it even if that were the case. White Alam would keep his mouth shut. Reassured by this thought, he was preparing for sleep when Kona Das knocked on his door.

'Bulbul Da, can I come in? I want to talk to you about something.'

'What is it, Kona Boo?'

'You know what's going on, don't you?'

'Yes. What you're doing is crazy. It might get you killed.'

'Maybe. It's better than growing old and dying serving Bibi and you.'

'I don't need anyone. You or Dadu. I can look after myself. And what do you see in that Teeny Mullah? The man is an idiot and ugly. Besides, as a man of religion, he's a total hypocrite. You know, before marriage and all that.'

'Bulbul Da, you don't know him. He has no one in the world. Lonely like me. We have done nothing sinful. He recites Koranic verses to me. I don't understand them, but he has a beautiful voice. He tells me I remind him of his mother. She was black like me.'

'Yes, yes, that's all very well. But what's going to happen? You can't keep it a secret. All hell will break loose if people find out.'

'I don't care. They might set fire to me. Kill me. So, what? Anyway, he's going to marry me.'

'So, you're going to convert? Become a Muslim?'

'No. Can't I get married and stay who I am?'

'I don't know the law. But he's an Islamic mullah. Have you considered that?'

'I know he's a mullah. But he cares for me. He'll do anything for me.'

'Let's see about that.'

It had been a long day and he felt exhausted, but how could he sleep with all this going on? What should he do about Scientist's poster campaign? Could he be so foolhardy, not to say suicidal, like Kona Das, to look for some empty walls for posters in the dead of night and risk everything?

CHAPTER 9

Despite not sleeping well, he woke up early, before the confluence of the crows, the dawn chorus from hell.

'Why so early, my little bird?' asked Dadu.

'I'm meeting someone. I don't want to be late.'

'Do I know that someone?'

'Him? I don't think so.'

'What business has he with you?'

'He's giving me a book.'

'I hope it's not a funny book with dirty pictures.'

'You have a funny head, Dadu. Only words. Happy?'

'The only books you should be reading are 'in-books', school textbooks. Especially now the exam is so near. No 'out-books' like frivolous novels and poems. They are a waste of time.'

'It's an in-book. It might help me with my exam.'

'I hope it won't teach you any trickery. How to cheat at exam. Ya Allah, these days... you lot, my little bird. No studying. No reading books. Only trickery and cheating. Anyway, who's this stranger? He could be a dangerous type.'

'I'm off. It's getting late.'

'Be careful, my little bird.'

Long before the military coup, Mohan Ganguly, a legendary communist since colonial times, had gone underground. General Ayub Khan, who'd come to power with the backing of the number one superpower, had shown his gratitude as a zealous commie-hunter. As well as party members and sympathisers among the intellectuals and in artistic circles, even fellow-travellers among ordinary people were hunted down and locked up in prison. The secret services, the police and the military all vied for the trophy of the prized head of Mohan Ganguly. No one, though, had come close to catching him; he'd had a long apprenticeship in the art of disguise and dodging his pursuers.

He hadn't come from the downtrodden; his was a privileged upbringing. Not hardship, exploitation, hunger or resentment against the higher-ups drove his politics. He was the son of a zamindar; his father was known for his opulence, gained from his cruelty in collecting taxes from the poor peasants who lived in the countryside surrounding Mominabad. Like Buddha, as a young boy, Mohan was a sensitive prince and much taken by the allure of a spiritual life; he had wanted to become a fakir. His father, thinking that the materialism of a big city would kick the spiritual fantasies out of the boy, sent him to Calcutta. It didn't take Mohan long to become a materialist, but of the wrong kind. At Calcutta University, he became part of a Marxist reading group. Inspired by the idea that betraying his own privileged class would be a supremely ethical gesture, and seduced by the logic of historical materialism, which he nurtured as if it were lyric poetry, he'd come to an almost religious conviction that revolution was necessary and inevitable. He'd fought against British imperialism and was imprisoned in the penal colony on Andaman Island.

Realising that the arena for his activism should be his birthplace, he'd returned to Mominabad, mobilised the peasants in the countryside, led a rebellion against his father's estate and seized his land. The colonial police and the army had crushed the revolt and Mohan had gone underground, surfacing only during periods of tolerance, which were rare and brief. When partition came in 1947, his family moved to India, but he stayed on, to continue with the struggle.

Disguised, he would roam the town and the surrounding villages, mobilising the peasants and workers, and joining various campaigns for civic and political rights. He would be a beggar, a mullah, a snake charmer, a peanut seller, or a boatman ferrying passengers across the river. People would have no idea who he was unless he revealed himself, telling them I'm Comrade Mohan Ganguly, I am here in these grave times to tell you the truth, and add my voice, my body to your struggle. He lived like a fakir who had taken a vow of chastity and poverty, but he couldn't conquer his weakness for cricket. It was at the cricket ground he'd spotted Bulbul, listening to the adda-men. He, too, enjoyed the adda-men as much as the cricket. If his disguise was that of a peanut seller, he would pitch his stall near them. They had no clue who he was, selling peanuts, watching cricket and listening to their talk.

Mohan Ganguly thought that Bulbul had the potential to be a revolutionary. He had no real basis for this judgement; it was intuition. He sent a young comrade with a pockmarked face to make contact with Bulbul, who was sworn to secrecy; no one must know of their meeting, not even his best friends. The pockmarked youth told Bulbul that Comrade Mohan Ganguly wanted to give him a book.

'I don't know Comrade Mohan Ganguly, and I'm not into book-reading,' said Bulbul.

'He knows you. He also knows that you're not into reading books.'

'So what am I to do with the book, then?'

'It's up to you. But the book has a path.'

'What kind of path?'

'That's for you to discover.'

Bulbul was intrigued; he was also excited that he might get to meet this enigma and legend.

'If you are interested, come to the teeth-man's show in the afternoon. At the station compound. A comrade will meet you there.'

Bulbul felt overwhelmed. Too many things were pulling at him, claiming his entanglement. True, he didn't care much for his exams and he wasn't happy about the prospect of leaving Mominabad for Dambarpur, but he could take it. If he needed to be a peasant, then he would be one. He didn't know what he wanted to become; he couldn't identify any passion or vocation. One of his teachers had said to him, 'Even an idiot, a dimwit wants to become somebody, has some outlandish fantasy like becoming a film star or a circus clown. You, our singing bird, you want to become nothing.'

What was really playing on his mind was Kona Das's affair and the terrible mess she was in. It would end badly, but what could he do about it? Then, there was Scientist's postering campaign. If he decided to go on it, he faced arrest and a beating. He hated to admit it, but he was scared. Then his conscience screamed at him: You selfish boy, you don't give a damn about Abid Ali, or Scientist, who is so nice to you. Yes, but if he could understand why he should get involved and what he felt, everything would make more sense. Then he would be prepared for whatever price he had to pay. Now, on top of it all, he had to deal with the matter of Comrade Mohan Ganguly's book. He was flattered that such a legend would bother with someone like him. If it were just a book… but it was meant to take him down a path. Yes, it promised adventure, but beyond that, would it be the right one for him? Meeting Mohan Ganguly was as dangerous as going out with Scientist on the postering campaign. Besides, Scientist could be in league with Mohan Ganguly. Perhaps, they were working together to get him into their fold. Why would the authorities spy on a mere mechanic and painter? Perhaps, Scientist had told Mohan Ganguly about him. Otherwise, why would Scientist go on about reading books? It was too much to make sense of. If only he could talk things over with Sanu the Fat and White Alam, it would ease his burden somewhat, but he had been sworn to secrecy about both the postering campaign and the book. He felt he was being transported to a different world without any say in the matter.

Despite his doubts, he went to the station compound in the afternoon to see the teeth-man's show. Surrounded by a large crowd, the teeth-man stood behind two sacks full of teeth. Some were so large they could only have come from the mouths of giants or dinosaurs. Shaking the sacks, the teeth-man launched into his spiel. His thin, sticklike frame was bouncing, as was his matted crop of hair, and his voice hissed from his toothless mouth: 'Honourable gentlemen, the teeth-man is here to service your needs, serving you from way before partition time. Perhaps your grandfathers' ancient molars are among the specimens you see before you. I safeguard them like a Raja's rubies or a memory-keepers' long stories – stories that your grandfathers knew and to which they paid heed most piously. Yes, teeth, like storm-hit trees, wobbling at their roots, are givers of the most terrible pain that Allah so assiduously manufactured for damned visitors to hell. Am I lying, honourable gentlemen? Speak up! If I lie, I'll pack my bags and become a naked fakir in the forest. Someone has to speak the truth, yes? The pain of rotten teeth is only the surface, a symptom of deep, festering badness which is devouring you from the insides out, making your stomach go bad, running down to your nether end, down that unspeakable channel, forming stagnant sewers of unutterable smelliness. That's because your liver, kidneys and heart are getting poisoned, and you fear visita-tions from the master of badness himself, the grim reaper. And then there's your manhood, gentlemen – a delicate subject for sure, deserving of the most hush-hush consideration – but truth is truth and it must be spoken. Yes, your manhood, once so robust and so full of uppity motion, and now, oh dear me, going somewhat dormant, becoming a limping master that nothing can arouse, not even the seventy-two houris of heaven awaiting the righteous. If you fail to have your bad tooth extracted immedi-ately, all these misfortunes, gentlemen, will be your lot, one hundred per cent guaranteed.

The teeth-man picked up an ancient-looking, heavy-duty pair of pliers and stood by a tall, rickety stool. His assistant, a man of enormous height and girth, as toothless as his boss, came forward to stand beside him. Already, people were jostling for position. Even Bulbul, though in tiptop shape, having a complete set of sturdy teeth, and as yet untouched by sexual anxiety, began to feel the need to be treated by the teeth-man.

Suddenly, the giant assistant pulled a man with a white beard from the front of the queue, sat him down on the stool, grabbed him tight from behind, and asked him to tilt his head back and open his mouth wide. The teeth-man set to work. Bending slightly, he grabbed a tooth and pulled with all his strength, as if trying to uproot a banyan. Blood spilt on the patient's white beard, turning it red.

Just as the teeth-man was about to display the result of his work, Bulbul felt someone tugging on his shirt. He followed a man away from the crowd into an alleyway. The man whispered that Comrade Mohan Ganguly had a book for him.

'What kind of book?'

'A good book. A pathway to enlightenment.'

'How would I recognise Mohan Ganguly? I don't know what he looks like.'

'Don't worry, he'll have his eyes out for you.'

'Where should I meet him?'

'At dawn tomorrow, on the other side of the river.'

'That's a vast area. Can you be more specific? I might not find him?'

'You will find him. If you don't, you're not ready to take the path.'

Bulbul wasn't ready but felt he couldn't turn back. He gathered a handful of cereal rice and hard date-palm sweets and wrapped them in plastic bags. It was still dark in the early morning when he left the house. As he reached the alley that would take him to the riverside, he bumped into Sanu the Fat and White Alam, who both shouted 'Godzilla!'

Bulbul managed to laugh.

'What are you up to? Where are you going? Are we going to the morning show?' asked Sanu the Fat.

'I don't know. I might skip the film. What is it?' asked Bulbul.

'It's *Ben-Hur*. Mega epic. Full of funny Romans. We're going to have a Godzilla time. You can't miss it.'

'Sorry. Dadu is sending me on an errand. Kind of urgent. Have a Godzilla time.'

Feeling guilty for the lie, he ran to the riverbank, eased himself in and swam across. On the other bank, though he couldn't see it, he knew a vast plain lay before him. He sat down to eat his rice cereal and the date-palm sweets and waited for the morning sun to burn the mist. While munching, he remembered the story he had told himself the night before when he was tossing and turning in his bed. It was well past midnight, and the neighbourhood drunk, Mr Henna-beard was shouting in his Feringhee-style Bengali, singing in his high-pitched female voice about the exploits of Clive and the East India Company. As usual, the dogs barked and chased him until they, too, fell silent. He wasn't sure if he had fallen asleep in that silence, but he was out on an adventure with his catapult.

It was about midday on a deserted country road. Seeing a yellow bird hidden among the broad green leaves of a jackfruit tree, he followed it. Silent as a jaguar he tiptoed under the tree with his catapult, his eyes focused on the yellow. As if its bright yellow plumage wasn't enough to draw attention to itself, the bird began to sing a sweet melody, perhaps to summon a mate. From then on its fate was sealed.

He was firmly locked onto the bird, when suddenly a gust of wind shook the tree and the yellow bird flew away. A leaf from the tree was blown along the ground and he felt compelled to follow it down a narrow mudbank to a huge simul tree. How careless of him not to bring any water in this heat and humidity. He would have ended the story right there if it hadn't been for the goats. There they were, the billies, the nannies and the kids, up in the simul tree as if waiting for him.

The top billy, with a fetching goatee, killer smell and a pair of lethal horns, was guarding all from a high branch. The kids were hustling their mother nannies for milk and grabbing at their udders. He had to look twice to spot a solitary nanny, her udder full of milk, perching among the middle branches. Who knows what had happened to her kids; perhaps they'd been taken by foxes or curried by humans. She was his chance to quench his thirst, but the top billy wasn't in the mood to let him have his way. Strength for strength, he was no match, but the brain under his skull was cunning and devious. He spotted a ditch. He catapulted the top billy with a marble. Not bothering even to bleat, the billy brushed it aside and jumped down to lock horns. He hid behind the tree trunk, threw another slingshot at the billy and ran to stand behind the ditch. Enraged at his insolence and thinking that this puny creature was no match for him, the billy gave chase. He pulled faces at the billy and taunted him: 'Come and get me, you low-ranking weakling.' Head down, his horns pointed, the billy gave chase. Seeing the mighty billy fall into the ditch, bleating like a scared little kid wasn't a pretty sight. He said, 'Sorry, sorry, brother billy, sorry to have thrashed you with such unscrupulous methods, but what could I do? Being born a human, with my puny arms and legs, small teeth, soft head with no horns, I could only win against you by playing dirty. I hope you will understand.'

He climbed the simul tree and sat near the nanny with the udder full of milk. The nanny sniffed at him and stood still as if he were her lost kid. He crouched under the udder and grabbed a teat between his lips, and suckling and suckling, he fell asleep. Now, he wondered why he had told himself such a strange story.

He took a narrow mudpath between jute fields, his footsteps just a faint tremor on the ground, as if in harmony with the burrowing earthworms beneath his feet and the paddy fields of ripening rice whose yellowing leaves were feeding on the orange sun. Then he emerged onto a dry riverbed. Was this the right path to the communist? He entered a dark mango grove, his legs trembling, salt sweating down from his forehead to his lips. Was he ready to meet the communist and read his book? What if the book told him to turn his back on the ways of his grandparents, his parents and the familiar landscapes where he knew the paths, where he could be blindfolded and yet reach the end of time? He ran and ran, dodging between the trunks. He felt that his legs were about to give up on him when he saw another vast plain before him, planted with mustard, yellow stretching as far as he could see. He squatted among it, closed his eyes, and smelt the sweet aroma with its faint tang of tobacco. Opening his eyes, he saw a tiny, torn fragment of paper, then another some distance away. So many of them. He realised that the pieces traced the path. He followed them all the way back to the beginning, to the entrance to the jute fields, and began again, along their loops and circles, round and round. He felt dizzy, but he didn't give up because he now realised that at the end of this labyrinth, he might not meet the communist but he would have his book, and that it would open another path, another journey for him. He gathered the torn pieces of paper into the plastic bags he'd brought his food in and returned home. He went straight to his room. He heard Dadu clip-clopping her way on her padukas. He had just enough time to hide the bags under his bed before she walked in.

CHAPTER 10

He was tense and nervous, slunk around the house and bolted himself in his room. Dadu knew he was up to something. She used all her tricks to draw him out. She called him, 'My little bird, shall I make you some date-palm bread? Extra sweet, the way you like it.'

'I don't feel like sweet things now. Maybe tomorrow.'

'How about catfish curry? Fenugreek and double chilli.'

He was hungry and his mouth was watering but he was determined not to fall into Dadu's trap. She stayed silent, and he thought she'd given up. Then she used her master stroke: 'My little bird, I'm not feeling well. My heart is doing funny things. Won't you come and sit by your Dadu?' He had to do her bidding. He sat by her while she breathed heavily, feigning illness. He asked if he should fetch the doctor, but she dismissed the idea, as if it was an excuse to escape her. He massaged her feet – which never failed to perk her up. She seemed to be drifting into sleep when she suddenly asked, 'You went to meet someone, didn't you?'

'I knew what you were up to,' he said, storming off.

He waited for that eerie time of night when everyone was asleep to retrieve the plastic bags from under the bed. He was about to spill the contents on the floor when he heard Mr Hennabeard singing his boozy number. He waited for him to pass and the dogs to quieten down. He knew Dadu would have left him food under the terra cotta dome on the veranda, perhaps a catfish curry and palm bread for pudding. He should have felt hungry; apart from chewing some rice cereal, he hadn't eaten anything the whole day but didn't feel like eating. He emptied the bags on the floor: a heap of torn pieces of paper. They weren't from a book of printed pages, but ruled sheets of paper with fragments of beautiful calligraphy. What was he meant to do with them? Surely the communist didn't expect him to read these? Even words were broken up, let alone sentences and paragraphs. Was the communist playing silly games with him, taking him for an imbecile? He kicked the heap and the pieces scattered across the room. He should burn the lot and be done with this nonsense. He paused, remained immobile like the gecko on his wall, then he went on all fours collecting the pieces. At last, it dawned on him that they weren't torn but carefully cut pages from a notebook, forming at least a hundred jigsaws – one each for a page. He laughed. Was the communist testing him to see if he was up to the task? He set about finding the matching grooves for each page; it wasn't easy without a picture and colour to match. He went on and on through the night, defying hunger, exhaustion, desire for sleep and pushing his reasoning and intuitive powers to the limit. He was so absorbed in his task that he didn't hear Dadu's padukas clipping down the veranda. He froze at the knock on the door.

'Are you still up, my little bird? What are you doing?'

'Nothing, Dadu. You go to sleep.'

'I hear rustling. Like a giant rat going around your room.'

'I couldn't sleep, so I was exercising to tire me. Happy now?'

'I see you didn't touch your food either. Has someone put a spell on you? I'm calling the exorcist in the morning.'

'You just overreact, Dadu. Big drama-walli you are. I'm fine, just let me be.'

Reluctantly, Dadu went away. He knew she wouldn't sleep the rest of the night, imagining all kinds of catastrophes. He wanted to go to her and massage her feet until she fell asleep, but he had to get on with his task. Why not be like his friend the gecko up on the wall, as if born to leave no trace of sound upon the earth? Yes, why not? He went around the room, again on all fours, matching the grooves of each page. Page after page. Once they were done, he stuck them into his unused exercise books. He heard the

114

morning azan, the racket of the crows, and worked on it until he finished in the late morning.

He slept until the afternoon and only woke when Dadu kept banging on his door. He thought of hiding the exercise books under his bed but decided against it. It would be the first place she'd look when he went out. He took a plank from the bottom of the old almari, put the exercise books inside, and nailed the plank back. He spent the rest of the afternoon with Dadu and Kona Das. Dadu did not bring up what he had been up to; he massaged her feet and told her about Godzilla.

'I get it. It's an old demon and rakshasa story. Once upon a time type, yes? You didn't have to go to the cinema for that. I could've told you one. Remember how I used to.'

'No, Dadu. Godzilla is real. It came with the bomb.'

'We better hurry up, then. Go to Dambarpur. I know this type of town monster. Lives off garbage and electricity. It wouldn't come looking for us in Dambarpur.'

Not getting anywhere in his efforts to explain Godzilla, he returned to his room to get some rest before going postering with Scientist. He woke at about ten and was tempted to take a peek at the communist's notebook, but felt that he wasn't ready for it yet. Perhaps he should leave it until after he left school.

He would go out at half-past eleven, enough time to meet up with Scientist at Anything from Anywhere by midnight. He had an hour or so to kill; he might as well dip into his textbooks, look through some notes and tackle a maths problem. He still told himself he couldn't care less if he passed or failed his exam but felt he ought to make some effort for his grandfather's sake. He opened his history book but soon got bored with the dates, wars, kings and queens in the rise and fall of dynasties. He began studying the walls and ceiling, tracking between damp patches, between shadow and light, until his eyes settled on the gecko, its eyes locked, perhaps on a tiny insect. He might never see what the gecko saw, but how could he not feel at one with its silence, its immobility? It was then that he heard Kona Das letting herself out of the door, on her way to see Teeny Mullah in the graveyard.

He reached Anything From Anywhere before Scientist. Goni Mia, the owner, let him in and led him to a shed. They sat on either side of a hurricane lamp, the shadows patterned by the lamp's metallic frame still and silent.

'Can you whistle?' Goni Mia asked.

'No,' said Bulbul.

'We can't do without a security protocol. Can you do a goat?'

'Yes. I can do a goat.'

'Give me three short, sharp bleats.'

Bulbul obliged.

'You are natural, boy. Pure goatiness, if ever I heard one. Next time you come, give me three bleats. Only then will I open the door. Anyway, do you know what you're letting yourself in for?'

'What do you mean? Just helping Scientist. You know, putting up a few posters.'

'You haven't a clue, have you? How well do you know Scientist?'

'He's an amazing artist. He knows so much, and can do so many things. He can even fix minds.'

'Yes, yes, he's all that. But he's human too. Just like anyone else. Anyway, you might wonder how we became friends. Scientist, a man of learning and culture, me a simple shopkeeper. I've no learning. I'm not even into cinema. We've been friends since we were children. I was Scientist's only friend. Who else would make friends with a dwarf, except me?'

It was already well past midnight and Scientist hadn't shown up. Outside, the wind picked up and hissed through the shed, slightly rippling the shadows.

Telling him to take it easy, Goni Mia offered Bulbul cookies and bananas. Where to begin on Scientist? Goni Mia scratched his face and shook his head. There were so many stories that even the *Mahabharata*, with over two hundred thousand verses, wouldn't be enough to contain them, but how about Scientist in love? Most people saw only a dwarf, Allah's curse, an abomination, and even a mentally-handicapped one, stupid for sure if not a raving mad, someone who ought to be shackled for their safety. Even those who knew him saw only a freak-genius who could fix and sort almost anything, but never a human like themselves. His interests in cinema, theatre and painting were private passions he shared with very few.

'How about politics? Does he know Mohan Ganguly?' asked Bulbul.

'I'm sworn to secrecy. But I suppose Scientist doesn't want to keep you in the dark. Otherwise, he wouldn't involve you in the poster campaign. You've his full trust. I also suppose that Mohan Ganguly thinks likewise. Otherwise, he wouldn't have chosen you, given you the book.'

'How do you know about that? I haven't told anyone about it, not even Scientist.'

'Well, Scientist, Mohan Ganguly and I go back a long way.'

'I knew it. It was Scientist who told the communist about me. Asked him to give me the book. What do they want of me? To get me killed or thrown into jail?'

'I must admit there are dangers. You're implicated in all this. But they trust you. They love you.'

'Why? I haven't done anything to earn this. I have no political views.'

'Scientist is a good judge of character. He saw something in you. Anyway, he has no political views, either. I mean affiliations. He has a lot of passion and a strong sense of right and wrong. If he'd lived in earlier times, he could have been a prophet like Nabi Isa.'

'I've no passion. I don't care about justice. I wish they hadn't dragged me into it.'

'Are you sure it wasn't you who dragged yourself into it?'

Bulbul stayed silent, thinking that perhaps Goni Mia was right.

'You're already involved. No point in beating yourself about it, is there? Just focus on how to get along with it. That's what Scientist had to do. He was full of love for others, and wanted to be loved too.'

As the wick in the lamp burnt down, enveloping the shed in darkness, Bulbul waited to hear if Scientist found love, and wondering who would love him?

'If not love,' Goni Mia continued, 'he had chances of companionship. Over the years, he had no shortage of marriage proposals but from families with dwarfed and mad daughters. They saw him only as someone to offload their burdens onto. He'd say,

117

"Where have all the women with normal minds and bodies gone? I didn't know they'd become extinct." Hearing this, these families couldn't contain their outrage. "Damn uppity dwarf, who does he think he is?" they'd say. "He'll need a ladder to see her face if he marries a normal-bodied wife. Bloody dwarf needs to be taught a lesson. If he's got anything down there, cut it off, make that motherfucker a hijira." There were marriage proposals from families with daughters with normal bodies and minds, but they were poor and greedy. They wanted radios, bicycles, pieces of land, and lots of cash for their daughters. Our friend Scientist would say, "I hope she finds a worthy husband. She deserves to live like a queen."

'So, giving up on the idea of companionship and love, he poured his passion into his work, learning, arts and cinema. But there was a girl, a cousin of mine. She was normal-bodied but headstrong and volatile, given to daydreaming. She even dabbled in poetry. Her family was worried. Who would marry such a dreamy girl with no practical sense? Yet, many families wanted her for their sons. You see, she was known for her beauty. When prospective bridegrooms and their families came to see her, and some relative would ask, "What dishes would you cook for your husband?" she'd say, "I don't like cooking. The kitchen is not a place for a modern woman." She'd tell them she had no skills like knitting and sewing. She'd even ask if the boy knew any poems. The visiting families couldn't get away quickly enough.

'Her parents, shamed and angry, would lock her up and wouldn't give her any food. But they couldn't break her. I had to sneak food into her room so she wouldn't starve. Eventually, her parents gave up the idea of marriage and told her she had to pay her way. So she went from house to house looking for cleaning and washing jobs, and offered to teach children how to read and write. But no one would employ her. "We don't want a mad one like you in our house," they would say. It was I who persuaded our mutual friend that he should take her on.

'She cleaned his workshop, mixed his paints, and generally helped him. Soon, she could do some repair jobs on her own and fill in the background colours of his paintings. But it was her poetry that made the biggest impression on him. He asked her if

118

she went to the cinema. She told him that her father wouldn't let her because he considered films the devil's trickery, leading to shameless behaviour.

'Once they were at ease with each other, he'd ask her to recite a poem. He said they were a bit sentimental, lacking poetic grace, but suddenly, when he was least expecting it, there would be a line that would intrigue him. I still remember one he told me:

Look, a black rain sliding

Down a green mango

Under it hangs a tongue

Quivering, it waits to lap me up.

He said he spent the whole night thinking about it. Why was it a black rain? Was it to signal her invisibility, an insignificant female who had to stay hidden from the world? Was it an image of a rebellious female spirit bent on undoing the habitual order of things? Or was it sexual energy looking for a body to consummate her destiny? He wasn't sure, but it incited his passion, his need to touch her. Perhaps, he thought, it was the whole point of the poem, to speak to him, of their desire for each other.

'The day after reading that poem, she didn't show up for work. There had already been whispers about something immoral, disgustingly perverse, going on in Scientist's workshop. "Ya Allah, what's the world coming to?" the neighbours said. Her family felt ashamed and locked her up. That made our friend more sure than ever that he loved her. He lost interest in his work, paced his workshop, and spent sleepless nights thinking of her. He told me he never thought love would touch him, but there it was. A strange feeling, but he felt blessed.

'I told him to drop it. Even tried to take him on a boat trip and show him the kingfishers along the banks to distract him. Told him how beautiful they were. "Kingfishers," he said, "they don't need my eyes. They are beautiful all by themselves."

'How about a film then, I suggested. Another time, perhaps, he told me. I didn't know what to do. He asked me to take a note to her. Reluctantly I agreed. He wrote: I think of black rain all the time; it falls on me when I'm awake and asleep.

'When he hadn't heard back from her, I had to tell him she was in a terrible state. They were refusing to let her out and she was refusing food. She smuggled a note to me. It said: "Black rain has found a tiny clay bowl, crafted with love. She's happy to fall into it and stay there. For spring, summer, autumn and winter."

'I had to tell him she was getting very frail. She wouldn't touch any food, wouldn't open her mouth. Only Allah knew how long she would last. Our friend wanted to go to her house and propose marriage. I tried to talk him out of it and told him it would end badly. He took no notice and went there.

'The father threatened to call his neighbours, who would lynch him. I'd followed him and dragged Scientist back to his house. He told me the last thing he wanted was for her to suffer and asked me to take another note begging her to start eating. She told her parents she'd only eat if they let her go back to work for Scientist.

'For days, it continued. Her family wouldn't let her out or agree to her marriage to the Scientist. She continued to refuse food. Each day she was becoming weaker. Our friend, in sympathy with her, took to fasting. Soon, her father stopped taking her food, smoked his hookah on the veranda, and counted his beads. I sneaked food to her, but she refused. "If I eat, it'll be on my own terms. Only when I'm out of this prison or marry Scientist."

'I talked to the father on his behalf. I said, "The Scientist earns good money. It's true Allah hasn't given him height but he compensated him very generously, showered him with so many gifts and talents. You must know that he is the most learned, capable and wise man in Mominabad. Your daughter, she's a special one, too. Artistic temper and all that. Only a man like Scientist would understand her. She would be very happy with him."

'Her father would close his eyes, smoke his hookah, and say, "Go home, my nephew. Take a good rest. You've a lot of work to do. Inshallah, we'll see each other soon."

'I went to see her in the small, dark shed where she lay alone, hardly breathing. I thought she looked strangely relaxed. "Cousin, I'm happy," she said, "lucky too. How many girls have known love in their life? Thank Allah that he brought Scientist to my life." I knew it wouldn't be long. And when it happened, our friend, already weak from fasting, lost his mind. I had to take him to the hospital. He left everything behind when he recovered a bit. He crossed the river, and wandered in the jungles. It was there that Mohan Ganguly found him, hardly alive. He nursed him back to health and brought him back home. That's how Scientist got to know the communist and found his mission in life.'

Even after this long tale, Scientist still hadn't turned up. Goni Mia fumbled to find a box of matches and a candle; he put a new wick in the hurricane lamp and lit it. He lifted a plank on the floor, and showed Bulbul a poster. It was really a painting; it had a black background, plain and uniform like a desert on a dark night. On it was drawn barbed wire in silver. Splashes of bright red paint dripped from it. Underneath was written: *How Long?*

Goni Mia gave the poster to Bulbul. 'Scientist wants you to put it up on the water tank.'

'Are you going to help me?'

'Sorry. I don't do politics. If you've any personal problem, yes, of course, I'd be there for you one hundred per cent.'

'I haven't done any politics either. I'm scared.'

'Aren't we all? But you have to grow up sometime. Do what you got to do, acha?'

Goni Mia helped him with the preparation: he put a harness around Bulbul's waist so that the poster, the bucket of glue and the brush could be hung from it, freeing his hands. He gave Bulbul a hard lump of palm sugar and said, 'Off you go. Don't let your mind play games with you. Just do what you have to do. And good luck.'

Bulbul felt a shiver in the wind as he walked the alleyway that led onto Ganginarpar Road; turning left, he would find the water tank. His heart was pounding; he had never ventured into the town centre on his own this late. Police, military, and the goons – all would be looking for someone foolish enough to be out with seditious materials. No one, except insomniacs, would be up this late. The alleyway was empty. After a few tentative steps, he walked briskly and was soon at the end of the alley. He hadn't counted on meeting dogs. They were right in the middle of the path.

Sensing his approach, they lifted their heads and began to growl. He stopped, his legs trembling, waiting for the dogs to make the first move, but they were content to stay where they were. Holding his breath, he edged past them, then hurried on to reach Ganginarpar Road. One or two rickshaws were swishing past, perhaps picking up passengers from the night mail. A few drunks stumbled about, slurring their words. One of the drunks asked if he sold opium; he was desperate for a hit and was prepared to pay a high price for it. The other, thinking that Bulbul was a policeman in plain clothes, saluted him, 'Salaam, Sir. We are good citizens, Sir. Very loyal to the General and his governor. Very loyal, Sir.'

Leaving them behind, still maintaining a brisk pace, Bulbul walked past the water tank along the opposite side of the road. It was too risky to pause as two men were talking in front of it. He continued, stopping just before the street of brothels. Even in the daytime, he would zoom past it, holding his breath until he was on the other side. Apart from the body-business, the street also housed illegal liquor stores selling deadly local brew. Naturally, it was a favourite haunt of the town's goons and ruffians. He was about to turn back when he saw the fearsome bunch of goons belonging to the student front of the Pakistan Muslim League emerging from the brothel street, all wearing dark glasses even at night. If they caught him with the poster, they would slit his throat and dump him in the open sewer that ran along the street. He ran into the alley to his right and was about to crouch at the side of a meesty-shop when someone spoke in a rasping voice: 'Can't you see the place is taken. Find somewhere else.' It was Keramot Ali, who rubbed his eyes and looked at Bulbul. 'Do I know you, boy?'

'No,' said Bulbul.

Keramot Ali stared at Bulbul's face. He shook his dreadlocks. 'You're a liar, a damn liar. You're Fainting Shahib's grandson, aren't you? You came to my Doomsday party and ate my food. Now you deny it all. You're the worst of the last men. Like your granddaddy. You never learnt to play the dice game, did you? Wretched boy. Never learnt the ways of times past and times to come, and amor fati. No, farty-warty thing but the most righteous.'

Bulbul was scared, thinking Keramot Ali would jump on him and tear him to pieces. He made a run for it and, rounding several alleyways, arrived back at the intersection of Ganginarpar Road. He looked around. No one was there; the goons must have gone. Still shaking, he approached the water tank. The two men talking in front of it earlier were no longer there.

He approached the water tank from behind. It was an old

colonial structure, painted red, like everything the British built, though right now, in this light, it was a greyish giant disappearing into the sky. He found the ladder, a series of thin, metallic steps that rose vertically to the top of the water tank. He would surely fall if he attempted to climb it, especially now the wind was gathering speed. In the morning he would be found spattered underneath for onlookers to say: Yes, a definite case of suicide. Who in his right mind would attempt to climb it at night? Another would say, pointing to the poster, a suicide note if ever there was one, dripping blood and saying *How Long?* Poor chap, he couldn't take it anymore.

But how could he let Scientist down? He climbed the ladder, his legs shaking, the harness, the hanging bucket, and the wind making it more difficult. In a trance, as if his body had left him and he was hardly aware of what he was doing, he reached the top and climbed onto the platform with a wooden safety barrier around it. He was about to paste the poster at the front, facing Ganginarpar Road, when he heard a car coming nearer. He lay flat on the platform floor. It was a military or police car. Some uniformed men got out, looked around, and aimed torches at the water tank. His heart was pounding so much he thought he would faint. They were bound to spot him, shoot him down, or drag him to the jail to feed the mosquitoes. Why had he been so stupid to agree to do this damn postering? How could Scientist be so heartless to push him into this? Why was everyone treating him like an imbecile, and that Goni Mia pretending to be a simple shop-keeper without political views? He wouldn't be surprised if he was one of the high-ups in the communist movement.

Luckily the safety barrier hid him, and after looking around for a few more minutes the uniformed men left. Bulbul lay face-up on the platform, looking at the stars, thinking nothing.

With the wind threatening to take him to the sky, he stumbled to his feet, and twisted his body to smear glue on the face of the water tank, then put the poster on it. He climbed down, left the bucket and the brush hidden under a broken rickshaw, and headed home. On the way he bumped into the drunks he'd met earlier. One of them said: 'Look, who's here. I told you, didn't I? You wouldn't believe me. Now have a good look.'

'Yes, yes. Now I see him. You're right. A shooting star. Right from the sky,' said the other drunk. Squinting to look at Bulbul's face, the first drunk asked: 'Are you here to show us the way? Or are you here to blind us with your light?'

Bulbul ignored them and set off briskly, but from nowhere the goons in dark glasses surrounded him.

'What are you doing here, boy? This time of the night?'

Bulbul looked down, his teeth chattering. He mumbled something that the goons couldn't catch. One of the goons laughed and said, 'You naughty boy. You've been to the brothel, haven't you? The first time, eh?'

Bulbul stayed quiet, biting his nails.

'Don't worry. We're not going to tell anyone. We like a boy who has balls. Why don't you come and see us? We're looking for boys like you to join us. The general and the governor can be very generous. Next time you visit the brothel, it'll be on us. Right?'

'Yes, Sir. Thank you, Sir,' said Bulbul and began walking. Once he left Ganginarpar Road, he began to run, and arrived home breathless and feeling sick. He went to the inner courtyard and retched so loudly and violently that he woke Dadu and Kona Das up.

'What's happened to you, my little bird?' asked Dadu.

'Nothing. I had a bad dream. Scary. But I'm fine now.'

Dadu washed his face and rubbed his head until he fell asleep.

CHAPTER 11

Following his postering adventure, Bulbul fell ill, delirious with a high fever for days. Dadu and Kona Das nursed him. When he got better, Sanu the Fat and White Alam came to visit him. 'Godzilla', they said, and the three of them laughed. They told him that several nights ago, a suicidal idiot, no doubt one of Mohan Ganguly's disciples, had put up a poster on the water tank. It wasn't until midday that the municipal authorities got their act together to take it down. 'Sometimes, blundering-bungling-incompetence can be a damn-good blessing, no?' said Sanu the Fat. Early morning walkers were the first to spot it, and many people passed it by. No one stopped, pretending not to look at it, but though only spoken of in whispers, by late morning all Mominabad knew about the poster. Sanu the Fat and White Alam had arrived just in time to see it before it was peeled off. White Alam said to Sanu: 'Tell it for our singing bird here. Tell the story of the poster.'

'It's not a film. I can only tell stories that have already been told.'

'The drawing and the writing, don't they tell stories?' said White Alam, and Bulbul nodded in agreement.

'I suppose it has a story. Let me think. Yes, the guy who put it up must be real crazy. Risking his life for something like that. He's very upset – that's why he took such risks,' said Sanu.

'I see that. But can't you make it a bit funny?' said White Alam.

'You're such a dung-head. Not all stories can be funny. Do you want to hear more or what?'

'Go on. Make me cry then,' said White Alam.

'So, it's a girl in black, wearing a silver necklace. Her brother is away across the desert to sell his camel. She must walk a long way into the desert every evening to collect water. If she doesn't collect water, she and her old mother will die of thirst. It's really desperate. She has no other option but to go into the desert. Each time, though, a bloodsucker who rules the desert waits for her and demands a few drops of her blood. Well, how could she refuse him? Day after day, he is taking her blood and making her weaker and weaker. Now she's so weak she has to crawl to collect water. Still, the bloodsucker demands blood from her. When the brother comes back, he finds both the sister and the mother dead. It's happening all over the desert. Desperate, the brother writes in the sand: *How Long?*'

'If only it were unreal, a make-believe thing like a weepy-film,' sighed White Alam.

'Yes, but we can imagine a happy side to the story. Seeing the brother's writing on the sand, the desert wakes up in rebellion and drives out the bloodsuckers. Here, if you like, we can laugh too,' said Sanu, who got up, put on a funny walk, and made the bloodsucker bleat like a goat as he was dragged to be dumped in the rubbish heap. No one laughed.

'I told you, didn't I? There's no scope for laughter in this poster. Thanks for making a fool of me.'

'Sorry, Sanu,' said White Alam.

Despite the ferocity of the stoning campaign, they told Bulbul that Banu Gosh was staying put and the adda-men were sticking with him. Now, the goons had changed their tactics; they were circulating the story that Banu Gosh was actually a communist, in league with Mohan Ganguly, and was the man behind the poster on the water tank. People in the market were whispering that the doctor would be arrested for being a communist agitator.

Taking the risk of getting beaten up by the goons, Sanu had gone to Banu Gosh's house. Although he looked very tired, the doctor was defiant: 'They can put me in prison, kill me if they want, I'll die on my own land, I'll never leave it.'

The final school exam was imminent, and Bulbul had finally decided to revise. He stayed at home. Dadu fussed over him and cooked all his favourite foods. One afternoon, after lunch, Bulbul lay in bed, hoping to have a siesta before continuing his revision. Dadu came into his room, asking if he had seen Kona Das. He hadn't. She was sneaking out at every opportunity Instead of cursing Kona Das and rushing out to look for her, Dadu stayed by his bed and said, 'How you've grown up, my little bird. I miss the time we had, telling stories. Now, I don't know what to tell you.'

Late that night, Kona Das still wasn't back. She was really getting reckless, as if she wanted to get caught. Unable to focus on his revision, Bulbul went out. Wandering at random, he ended up near Scientist's workshop. Scientist would surely be asleep, but as he turned the corner, he heard three short, sharp bleats from behind a pile of rubble. Strange, he thought, a goat out so late at night. When he heard the bleats a second time, it dawned on him that it was the security protocol Goni Mia had asked him to use. Scientist and a young man emerged from behind the rubble and Bulbul recognised the young comrade who had made contact with him on behalf of Mohan Ganguly. They had been setting off to put up a new poster and, hearing his approach, taken cover.

'Sorry to hear you've been unwell. I should have come to see you, but people get funny seeing a dwarf in their house,' said Scientist.

'My grandmother is not like them. She'd treat you right.'

'Good to know that. Next time.'

Then Scientist asked him if he wanted to come along with them: just one poster on the cinema billboard in front of the railway station. Without giving it a second thought, he said yes, and they set off together, but at the next turn, the young comrade took his leave. Now, Scientist and Bulbul walked side by side with the poster and the glue bucket.

'I know it was tough. Putting that poster up on the water tank. But you did it. I'm proud of you.'

Bulbul hadn't forgotten how angry he'd been with Scientist for getting him to do this, but now, hearing his words, he felt happy. Yet he still wanted to know why Scientist had put him up to it.

'I didn't make you do it. You wanted to do it. Maybe not consciously. I just helped. Anyway, one day, you'll work it out.'

'Is it like how boys in Africa are sent to kill lions with spears? Is it something like that?'

'You mean a rite of passage? I don't know. You'll work it out.'

'What's the poster we're putting up today?'

'You'll see when it goes up.'

'I want to see it now. I want to know what I'm getting into.'

Scientist took Bulbul behind a derelict shed, and crouching on the ground, he unrolled the poster and beamed his torchlight on it. The background was blue, either sky or ocean, but Bulbul's eyes were immediately drawn to the mouth, a gaunt, long mouth without a face in bright yellow. It was stitched shut with coarse white thread. Underneath was written: *Scream*.

'It doesn't make sense. If the mouth is shut, how can it scream?'

'Well, read into it what you will. I hope those who see it will ask similar questions.'

Reaching Ganginarpar Road, they looked around. There were no street lights, and with a dense cloud covering, the only light sources were the flickering torches of late-night stragglers and the dim glow of one or two rushing rickshaws. They only had to dodge these weak, sporadic light beams to stay virtually invisible.

'I wanted to ask you something,' said Bulbul.

'I guessed as much. Otherwise, you wouldn't have come by my workshop this late.'

'I suppose so.'

'So, what's on your mind?'

'I told you about Kona Das, didn't I? She's getting reckless. She's staying out longer and getting careless about her disguise.'

'Perhaps she wants to get caught, to force the issue.'

'What do you suggest?'

'Have a word with Teeny Mullah. See what his thoughts are on the matter. But be prepared that things might get difficult. The goons are getting desperate. They underestimated Banu Gosh. He's a tough nut. They might use the Kona Das/Teeny Mullah affair to whip up communal tension, or take it out on Kona Das.'

They couldn't see the goons, but could hear them from some distance away, bantering loudly near the brothel. They took a detour and turned into an alleyway where it was much darker than on Ganginarpar Road.

'Why are you taking such risks? Putting up posters. Are you a communist?' asked Bulbul.

'Does it matter?'

'I don't get it.'

'If you asked yourself why you went up the water tower, you might get the answer.'

'I did it for Abid Ali, the journalist. I did it for you. I thought that's what you wanted.'

'Can you imagine other Abid Alis, who are suffering his plight? You might not know them at all. Would you put a poster for them?'

'I don't know,' Bulbul said. 'It's too much to ask. Would you act for them, risk your life?'

'I ought to, but I don't know if I can.'

'If you can't. I am sure no one else can.'

They paused before entering Ganginarpar Road again, and in looking out for the goons, they hadn't noticed Keramot Ali standing right behind them.

'Scientist, my main man, my yeah-saying man, fancy seeing you here. How have you been?'

'You know me; the same, the same. Glad that you came down

to us. Was the mountain too lonely for you?' asked Scientist.

'Mountain? Where would I find a mountain in this damn country? Only plains and swamps. Yeah, I have been to haors and swamps. Too many dervishes and fakirs looking for Him and shitting mountains in them places. Too stinky, so I ran away. Glad to know that you are the same, the same. All those self-haters, ass-lickers of Him, don't listen to me. Only you, my main man, the tallest of the tall, rejoice at my words. You and I, do we give a fuck? No, the same, the same, always the same, fucking same. Oh, I'm happy that I blew the lot on the Doomsday party. Yes, yes, I'd do it again and again, fart the fart, amor fati. Yeah?'

He took a close look at Bulbul and shook his dreadlocks.

'Scientist, what are you doing with this wretched boy? He's a self-hater, self-touching, poison-mixer of a last-boy. And a damn liar. He ate at my Doomsday party with his grandpa, that despicable fainting-shahib. Now, he denies even knowing me. Good that I ate Him. Otherwise, Him would've put a red iron bar up his ass.'

'He is a good boy. He's learning the ways of weighty things. Go lightly, lightly, on him. One day, he will be the same, the same. Already, he's getting good at the dice game. Stay well; we must push on,' said Scientist.

'Are you sure the boy is into the dice game? He seems like a nasty, scheming type. Can't believe he takes chances on chance. Well, we'll see. Now, my main man, my yeah-saying man. I'm hungry. Can you buy me some rice?'

'The restaurants are closed. Come to my workshop tomorrow. I'll give you fish curry. Fine catfish with fenugreek. Alright?'

'Don't compromise on the chilli. Plenty hot. Yes?'

Scientist gave him all the loose change he had in his pockets and he and Bulbul took to Ganginarpar Road again.

'Don't mind him. He's mad. Talks gibberish.'

'Why do you humour him, then?'

'Because he's mad, you don't have to shut his mouth, do you? And you never know what truth he speaks in between his pagla-talk.'

Bulbul felt grumpy. Side by side but silent, they headed towards the station. Suddenly, they paused, a chill down their spines. Something or someone was on their trail. Perhaps the goons, the police, or something more sinister. They ran and crouched behind the traffic stand, which, during the day, served as Stingy-Traffic-Policeman's centre of operation, where he directed the traffic and schemed for his bribery earnings. They looked both ways; Ganginarpar Road was empty. Even the late-hour rickshaw pullers had gone. Seconds went by, their breaths stuttering and stopping. A slight wind ruffled the dust as if by the wings of a demon, but they saw nothing. They left Ganginarpar Road, still feeling that something was keeping them in its sight. Face to face with the growling dogs, they ran for it. Finally, they lost them, but looking around they realised they had ended up by Banu Gosh's house. Seeing that the lights were on, and sensing people moving within, they hid the poster and the bucket in a dense tangle of shrubs and knocked on the door. Someone from inside said, 'You got your man. Leave us alone.' When Scientist announced himself, Samsuddin Gazi, the sawmill owner, opened the door.

'How did you get the news so quickly?'

'What news?' asked Scientist.

'The police have taken Banu Gosh on the phoney charge of being a communist. For Him's sake, the fellow is a mega fan of Adam Smith. Boring us to death with *Wealth of Nations* and the invisible hand. Would you believe that they also accused him of the postering campaign? Can you imagine a more absurd sight than the doctor going up the water tower? We love our doctor. Very meritorious physician and a topnotch adda-man, but courage is not his strong point.'

'But he stood up to the goons, refused to desert his homeland and flee to India. I call that courage.'

'Of course, he has plenty of moral courage, but he has a very delicate constitution, you know. Height was a big issue with him.'

Samsuddin Gazi invited Scientist and Bulbul into the sitting room, where the remaining adda-men, Hakim Khan, the lawyer and Fazle Rabbi, the landlord, were reclining on round pillows.

'Totally unjust. The doctor will be sorely missed by his patients. And by us, his adda friends. In his honour and on Mrs Gosh's insistence, we decided to hold an all-night adda. Scientist, join us. You're a true Renaissance man. Your contribution will enrich our adda, make it truly memorable, a fitting tribute to our friend,' said Fazle Rabbi.

'Your young friend is also most welcome. I sense he has the makings of a top class adda-man,' said Hakim Khan, the lawyer.

Scientist and Bulbul sat down on the rug. From inside, Mrs Gosh sent them cups of teas and cookies.

'Much as we'd like, I'm afraid, we can't stay long. We have urgent business to attend to,' said Scientist.

He and Bulbul waited for someone to begin an anecdote, a comment, an observation, a philosophical musing, or self-talk, but the legendary loquaciousness and wit was missing. Glum-faced, as if giant boulders were clogging up their insides, they didn't even twitch their mouths or cough to clear their throats. Silence bound them as if they were drowning together at the bottom of the ocean. Minutes went by, and still no one spoke. Finally, Scientist cleared his throat. 'Friends, no need for words. Your silence speaks amply of the plight that has befallen us. In it, I can hear a sad raga, the rage of a tempest and the tenderness of lovers.'

None of the adda-men stirred when he got up and Bulbul followed him out, picking up the bucket and the poster and heading once more towards the station.

Still they sensed that something or someone was on their trail. They began to run, but after several hundred metres whatever was hunting them was still there and seemed to be gaining on them. They hid in a derelict giant cylinder whose origin and purpose no one knew. 'Whatever happens, we must put up the poster. It might help the doctor. It will prove that it wasn't him who did the postering on the water tower,' said Scientist.

'But they could just peddle the story that the doctor walked out of the prison, did the postering, and went back to his cell. You know, like *The Invisible Man*, the film you told me about. Who's going to stop them? They don't want reality. Only fancy news.'

'You have a point. You have a good brain on you; don't waste it. Read books and cultivate your mind. Yes?' said Scientist.

'If they catch us, what's going to happen?' asked Bulbul.

'Whatever, we have to stick up the poster. We do it for the doctor. Understand?'

Now, the footsteps were very close; they could hear sandals

grating on the sand. Surely, it was the end. Bulbul was shivering and Scientist touched his face to reassure him.

'It's only me. Him-baba,' said Keramot Ali.

They came out from the cylinder. He told them that the goons were prowling the streets and that he followed them in case they caught up with them.

'Do the goons know that it's us?' asked Scientist.

'No. I told them some donkey men, most wretched of the last-types, came to shit in the town.'

'You did well,' said Scientist.

'Don't worry. I'm going to protect you, my main man, the same man. Him-baba would eat up anything that comes to harm you.'

It was too dark to see them, but they heard a group rushing towards them. Keramot Ali told them to run; he would detain them. Realising they couldn't go far before the pursuers had them in sight, they hid behind a rubbish tip. It was the goons.

'Where are the donkey-men? If you play games with us, we'll beat the madness out of you. Understand, you motherfucking shit-head?' said one of the goons.

'Gentlemen, you're stinkier than donkey's shit. Him-baba tells you nothing. Ever and ever, eternally nothing.'

The goons pounced on Keramot Ali, punching him, kicking him and screaming at him: 'You motherfucking loony-brain. You wanted to go through Doomsday in style, didn't you? This is your Doomsday, and we'll give you style.'

'Jolly good. The same the same. Him-baba loves your hands and feet. Oh, how sweet. Give me more until Doomsday.'

Scientist told Bulbul that he couldn't take it anymore; he needed to do something to draw their attention, but Bulbul should run along to put up the poster.

'I can't leave you. They'll beat you up,' said Bulbul.

'I'll be fine. What can happen to a dwarf that hasn't already happened? Go and do the poster for Banu Ghosh.'

'Give them anything they want, but don't let them hurt you. Promise?' said Bulbul.

'Promise,' said Scientist, ruffling Bulbul's hair.

While Scientist began to sing at the top of his voice, *Oh my golden bird, where have you gone, leaving me all alone*, Bulbul, with the bucket and the poster, ran towards the station.

He located the cinema billboard on the roundabout. With the torch he could just about make out the publicity for the current show, a romantic film. The actress was looking at something from the corner of her eyes, her mouth open as if singing, the hero was looking at her with intensity. Using the scaffolding at the back, Bulbul climbed up and pasted the poster, covering the faces of both the actor and the actress.

He threw down the bucket, jumped off the scaffolding, and ran home. Breathless, he was opening the front door as Kona Das arrived.

'Where have you been?' he asked.

'I don't need to tell you. You know already. But where have you been?'

'I couldn't sleep. I went for a walk.'

Through the rest of the night, he tossed and turned, thinking of Scientist. In the morning, he knocked on his workshop door. When he didn't get a response, he walked to his house. One of the brothers told him that he hadn't come home. He went to see Goni Mia; he had no news of Scientist either. Desperate, he visited White Alam, hoping to persuade him to ask his father. Surely, Stingy Traffic Policeman would know his whereabouts, especially if he had been taken to jail. When White Alam cried out 'Godzilla', Bulbul could only give a feeble smile.

'What's the matter with you? You look right godzillered.'

Bulbul told him only that he was worried about Scientist, who seemed to have disappeared. White Alam couldn't promise any-thing: 'You know I don't have that kind of communication with my father, but I will try to find out.'

This time, the authorities got their act together much more quickly; they pulled the poster down within hours of it being first seen. Even so, railway workers on the early morning shift, some passengers for the dawn mail, and the rickshaw pullers who brought them to the station had seen it.

Bulbul slept until lunch, when Dadu woke him. He learnt that news of the poster had spread across Mominabad. The further it travelled, the stranger the story became. By the time Sanu came to see him in the afternoon, it wasn't even a poster.

'Have you heard what happened in the station compound?' asked Sanu. 'Something really bad. Badder than Godzilla badness.'

'Were you there? Did you see it?' asked Bulbul.

'No, but I got it from a reliable source. Extremely reliable.'

'Oh, I see,' said Bulbul.

'You don't believe me, do you? Let me tell you about my source's reliability. The man is fanatical about keeping records. Nothing but written evidence will do for him. Such a meticulous type that five minutes in his company would kill you with boredom. If there were an Olympic event for boringness, he would win gold, hands down. He keeps records of how many times he belches, scratches his bum, poops, has funny thoughts about girls, his member goes stiff, farts etc. The man is an evidence maniac. Nothing but empirical data-mata will do for him. At first I thought he was a pervy type, having about a hundred funny thoughts about girls a day. He said he hardly had any thoughts about girls. He was very worried about that. Apparently, men have eight thousand such thoughts a day. It makes you wonder how we ever get to think about anything else. Anyway, you can see how reliable the man is.'

'Alright. Get on with it. What did he see at the station?'

'With so many rumours, exaggerations, and spicings-up, you need a reliable witness. Some idiots, utterly gullible, believe it was a poster of a mouth stitched up. My witness called them delusional.'

'Come on, Sanu, get on with it.' Bulbul was tempted to say that those delusionals were right, but he restrained himself because it was something between himself and Scientist.

'Yes, yes, but don't ask me to be funny. It wasn't a laughing matter. When my witness read it to me from his notebook, he had tears in his eyes. He saw a severed head – not sure if it was a man or a woman – dangling from a giant fish-hook two feet in front of the cinema billboard at the height of about eight feet. It obscured the face of the hero, but the heroine's mouth was open as if singing. Being a man of facts, he wouldn't say more. But it's not hard to imagine the story. Perhaps the head belongs to a clown, dressed as the General, with medals and all, and he did funny walks in front of a cheering audience…'

'Sorry, Sanu. I don't want to hear anymore.'

'I wasn't trying to be funny. I don't know what's got into you these days. You're so touchy. You know White Alam is in trouble again. His father was cross with him asking about Scientist. What's going on between you and him?'

'What do you mean? Dadu sends me to Scientist to get repairs done. That's all.'

For the rest of the day, apart from having his dinner with Dadu on the veranda, Bulbul stayed in his room. The following morning he went to the graveyard to see Teeny Mullah.

'I'm much honoured that you visit my humble abode.'

'What are your intentions with Kona Das?' asked Bulbul.

'Very good-natured girl. Full of virtues. She'll make an excellent wife to some lucky man.'

'I know. But what are your intentions with her?'

'Absolutely honourable. I've never tainted her sacred temple. She's as pure as she was born. We discourse on spiritual matters.'

'I understand. But what do you want to do with her?'

'I'm a poor mullah. Sometimes I get lonely all alone in the graveyard. I am in need of a wife. If I've your grandmother's blessing, I like to take her as my wife.'

'Do you know that she's a Hindu and untouchable?'

'Yes, I do. I see it as my calling from Allah to save her soul.'

'If she refuses to convert, what would you do?'

'What kind of husband would an untouchable Hindu girl get? I'm poor and humble but a learned mullah. Bragging is not my nature, but connecting with me would elevate her social status. I'm sure she'd be more than happy to convert. She could be a very pious wife. I've already thought of a name. Doesn't Aabida sound beautiful? It means worshipper of Allah. Aabida Begum.'

'Have you talked to her about these things?'

'These are delicate matters. How can a prospective husband raise such questions? If you don't mind, I would be eternally grateful if you'd have a word with your grandmother.'

'You should be talking to Dadu, not me.'

Bulbul came home and leafed through his books and notes for the exam. After lunch, when Dadu went for her siesta, he asked Kona Das to come to his room.

'What's the matter, Bulbul Da?' she asked.

'Teeny Mullah is serious. He wants to marry you. What do you think?'

'Did he say that? I've been waiting for this moment. Yes, I'd like to be wedded to him.'

'Good. He can now ask for Dadu's blessings. Have you realised that you have to convert?'

'What? No one mentioned that. Why should I convert?'

'Kona Boo, sometimes you can be so silly. Do you think a mullah would marry you without having you converted?'

'I'm not marrying his religion, but him,' she said.

'Well, think about it,' said Bulbul.

In the evening he went to see Goni Mia. Finally, he got some news of Scientist. He'd been arrested and was now in jail.

'How is he? Have they beaten him up?' asked Bulbul.

'You know he's gone through the goons, and then the police. It was tough, but he's doing well,' said Goni Mia.

'Can I go and see him?' asked Bulbul.

'I don't know. You're not a relative. They might not let you, but let me see what I can do.'

Two days later, Goni Mia came to see him. It would be possible for Bulbul to see Scientist by pretending to be his brother. It would cost him some money – a prison guard had to be bribed. Bulbul told Goni Mia he would get the money and asked him to arrange to see the guard. He withdrew all he'd saved through the school's banking scheme – designed to instil monetary good sense in the pupils – but it wasn't enough. He went to Dadu.

'Dadu, you know the exam is coming soon. I want to pass it for grandfather, I really do, but I need to buy some books.'

Dadu gave him the money, and together with his savings, it was enough to bribe a prison guard.

On the morning of his appointment, Bulbul sneaked out, dodging Dadu, because he didn't want her to see him with the tiffin carrier. He wanted to buy a takeaway lunch for Scientist. He wasn't sure what Scientist liked but felt that his taste wouldn't be very different from his own, so he bought bhuna goat, dal puri, aubergine bhaji, and meesty-sweet. He arrived at the prison long before his appointment at midday.

At the prison gate, he told the guard on duty that he'd come to see his brother, Scientist, for whom he was bringing a home-cooked meal. 'Do you have a permit?' asked the guard.

'No. But I've got a special arrangement.'

'Have you? Are you a fool? Aren't you aware that the military is in charge now? Very stickler for rules they are. Understand? You look like a nice boy. So, if you want, I can do something about the tiffin carrier. It's very risky; I might lose my job, but I'm a big softy for brother-love. Leave the tiffin carrier with me, I'll get it to your brother.' Bulbul handed the tiffin carrier to the guard, who called a colleague to take his place, and disappeared inside the prison. Seeing the new guard's kind face, Bulbul told him he'd come to see his brother.

'Do you have a permit?' asked the new guard.

'No,' said Bulbul.

'You look like a nice boy. Love your brother very much – yes? I'll do you a favour. Make me an offer, and we'll come to a special arrangement. You'll get to see your brother right away. He'll be so happy.'

'I've already made a special arrangement, Sir.'

'What? You bribed a member of the prison guard. It's a criminal offence. Get lost. If I see your face a moment longer, I'll throw you in prison.'

Bulbul moved away from the prison gate and sat under a tree. About midday, thinking that a change of guard might have brought his man to the gate, Bulbul approached the stern-looking guard standing at ease with a rifle and told him that he was there to see his brother, and that he had a special arrangement.

'Yes, yes, come with me,' said the guard. He led Bulbul into the small sentry room. Inside, he put the gun's muzzle against Bulbul's chest and pushed him against the wall. 'You came to make fun of us, didn't you? Now make me laugh,' and he pushed the muzzle harder. The sharp pain made Bulbul almost double up. He then ordered Bulbul to pull his ears and do sit-ups.

'You don't stop until you make me laugh,' said the guard. After about thirty sit-ups, his stomach aching, Bulbul still didn't know what to say. Fire in his eyes, the guard raised his rifle butt as if to hit his head.

Bulbul cried out, 'Godzilla!'

'What's that, boy?'

'He's the bomb, Sir. Nuclear bomb. He walks funny, Sir,' and he tried to imitate Sanu the Fat's funny walk. The guard slapped his face and said, 'It's not funny, boy. It's the most tedious thing I've heard and seen. Extreme boringness.'

He told Bulbul that if he didn't want his eyes gouged out, he should give him everything he had on him. Bulbul handed him his pen knife, a present from his grandfather on his circumcision, and a few rupees.

'Are you sure you have nothing more?' said the guard, pulling out a lolly from Bulbul's shirt pocket, 'What's this? You playing cheeky with me, boy?' He gave Bulbul another slap, unwrapped the lolly, and started to suck it.

'Keep on doing sit-ups. Faster, boy. You can't escape me until you make me laugh.'

His teeth chattering and his lips shaking, his mind gone blank, Bulbul was like a cornered animal waiting for the final blow. The guard poked his belly with the gun. 'My mother, Sir. She died giving birth to me,' he blurted out. There were a few seconds of silence, then the guard burst out laughing. 'That's funny, boy. Real funny. In fact, the funniest I heard in ages. Off you go.'

Not willing to give up on seeing Scientist, Bulbul waited under the tree. After an hour, he saw a guard approaching with a baton. He lowered his eyes, waiting for the blows.

'Are you the Scientist's phantom brother? The one who made a special arrangement?'

'Yes, Sir,' said Bulbul.

'You need some magic, boy.'

'I don't understand, Sir.'

'You're a dim one, aren't you? How do you propose to turn yourself from a phantom brother into a real one?'

'Special arrangement. I made a special arrangement, Sir.'

'Look, idiot boy, what do you expect me to be, a bloody magician? Do abracadabra, jadu-madu tricks? Such nonsense. Anyway, I now declare you Scientist's blood brother. Happy?' The guard told Bulbul to follow him, and though nervous that the guard might turn on him, he followed.

'Relax boy. I've given you my word. In our line of work, trust and honour are everything. Understand?'

In the interview room, Bulbul was shocked to see Scientist hobbling in on a crutch, his left hand bandaged, his face bruised.

'They beat you up bad. Was it the goons or the police?'

'It doesn't matter. How are things? Seen any morning shows lately?'

'I'm fine, but I'm worried for you,' said Bulbul.

'I'm wonderful. I'm enjoying myself here. Having Abid Ali and Banu Gosh for company, you can't get bored. We are having stimulating conversations. Pity that they haven't seen *Godzilla* and don't go to the morning shows. Mosquitoes are a bit annoying, though, but the poor creatures must survive. Donation of a few drops of my blood towards them is the least I can do.'

'That's a funny way of seeing things. Anyway, how come you ended up with the doctor and the journalist?'

'Well, we don't belong to a political party. So, they put us together with the common criminals in a large dorm. It's enjoyable with the criminals, too. Oh, the stories you hear from them. Almost as good as the films on morning shows.'

'I'm not sure. Did you like the lunch I brought?'

'What lunch?'

'I sent a tiffin carrier with one of the guards.'

Scientist laughed. 'Well, I haven't seen it. But it doesn't matter. Poor guards, as long as they enjoyed it. They deserve to eat well, too.'

'I don't know. When are you coming home?'

'I don't know. But don't you worry about it. And don't waste your time coming to see me. From now on, I want you to study hard to pass your exam. Once it's over, read many books and watch many films on the morning shows. Yes?'

'Officially, you're my elder brother now, so I've got to come and see you.'

'So, don't argue with your elder brother. Just do what I tell you. Until your exam, just study. Nothing else. Then read books and watch films. It's an order.'

On the way home, Bulbul walked briskly, almost running, his eyes blurry with tears. He must do what Scientist told him. With only three weeks to go before the exam, he would not be distracted by anything, but then, at the end of the second week, when he was studying late at night, he heard loud knocking. He ignored it, but it was getting louder and more insistent. Dadu was already up, clip-clopping in her padukas towards the front door. Bulbul jumped up and opened it before she got there. It was Sanu the Fat, who seemed agitated.

'A lot of people are surrounding them,' he said.

'I don't understand. Who, where?'

'In the graveyard. They caught Kona Das and Teeny Mullah.'

'How did it happen?'

'It was Stingy Traffic Policeman. He followed Kona Das from your house to the graveyard.'

'How did he know? Did you say something to White Alam?'

'I don't know. He's our friend. We spend so much time together. Something might have slipped my mind.'

'I trusted you, Sanu. You're so unreliable.'

'Don't just stand there arguing. Go and see what's happened. And bring Kona home,' said Dadu.

A crowd had gathered in the graveyard around Teeny Mullah's shed. He was inside, sitting, head down, on his bed; Kona Das, her sari drawn over her face, was crouching on the floor. A dozen men were inside the shed as well as Stingy Traffic Policeman.

'You've no grownup in your household to represent this Hindu girl?' asked a man with a skull cap and goatee.

'No. I am the man in the house,' said Bulbul.

'Never have I seen such tamasha. We don't tolerate such hanky-panky in our neighbourhood. A mullah and an untouchable Hindu, oh Allah, what's the world coming to? There will be serious consequences,' said a toothless, pockmarked man.

'Very shaming, very unfortunate. But let us not get carried away. Let us find a solution to the problem. We're very reasonable people, aren't we?' said Stingy Traffic Policeman.

'Well, there is only one solution. The mullah has to marry the Hindu girl. Make an honest woman of her,' said the man with a skull cap and goatee. Everyone nodded. It was the only way.

'What's your intention, Mullah?'

'Of course, I want to marry her. Convert her to our faith.'

'Conversion, very righteous. Right solution. Allah's blessings will be on you,' said Stingy Traffic Policeman.

'Hey, girl, what's your intention?' asked the man with a skull cap and goatee.

'It's my wish, too. To be wedded to the mullah.'

'That's settled then. Mullah, arrange her conversion. We'll be witness to the wedding,' said Stingy Traffic Policeman.

Kona Das coughed.

'What is it?' asked Stingy Traffic Policeman.

'I want to marry the mullah. Why do I have to marry his religion, too?'

'What? What do you mean? Mullah is very generous. Some other men would have taken your honour and run. You don't know how lucky you are,' said the man with a skull cap and goatee.

'Yes, I'm very lucky. But I only want to marry Mullah.'

'But conversion is the only way. Otherwise, we are doomed,' said Teeny Mullah.

'Let me be clear. You don't want to be converted to Islam. Am I right?' asked Stingy Traffic Policeman.

'Yes, you're right,' said Kona Das.

'What? I knew it as soon as I saw her. Bloody Hindu whore,' said the toothless, pockmarked man.

From outside the shed a roar went up: Hindu whore, shave her head, beat her up. Sensing the danger, Bulbul stood beside Kona Das and sent Sanu the Fat to fetch Dadu. Teeny Mullah remained seated, head down, on the bed. Stingy Traffic Policeman stood at the door to stop the mob from coming in, but some of the men inside were turning nasty. 'Even a highborn Hindu shits on you, bloody whore,' screamed the toothless, pockmarked man.

'We offered you heaven, and you choose to burn in hell with your untouchable lot,' said the man with a skull cap and goatee, poking Kona Das with his stick.

Suddenly, two men, who looked very gentlemanly and soft, who had remained silent throughout the proceedings, got up and violently brushed Bulbul aside. He fell, hit his nose and it began to bleed. The men grabbed Kona Das by the hair and dragged her along the floor. His head still spinning, Bulbul managed to crawl and bite the men's legs. One of the men screamed: 'Bloody Hindu whore and her damn nasty dog!'

Some of the mob outside now pushed past Stingy Traffic Policeman to enter the shed and kick Kona Das. Teeny Mullah, still seated, began to swing his head back and forth and recite a sura in Arabic. One of the men said: 'Let's take her outside.' Just then, Dadu walked in. Seeing her, everyone froze. She helped Kona Das to her feet and glared at the crowd. 'If any of you dare to touch her, I'll cut your balls off.' No one said a word. Dadu walked out with Kona Das, Bulbul and Sanu the Fat beside her.

Soon graffiti started to appear on the front wall: *Hindu Whore Out! Hang the Whore! You Whore Lovers, Hindu Lovers, Go to Hell* etc.

With so many things going around in his head, Bulbul didn't fall asleep until the early morning, and only for an hour. At first, he thought he was dreaming of Godzilla trampling houses, offices and people underfoot, creating craters in the streets and the fields at the fall of his feet, but Dadu's voice was unmistakably real. 'Get up, my little bird. They're stoning us.'

It must be the goons, thought Bulbul. Stones on the roof were disturbing enough, but the passage through the open courtyard, leading to the latrine, the shower and the tube-well became dangerous. With their umbrellas unfurled, they had to run between the yard and the house. The veranda became unusable and Dadu and Kona Das cooked in the rooms where they slept, and Kona Das had to stop going to the tulsi bush in the courtyard for her morning puja.

Dadu decided they would leave this godforsaken town for Dambarpur as soon as Bulbul finished his exam, which was in a week. They just had to get through the days until then. Remembering his promise to Scientist, Bulbul tried to pick up his revision, but it wasn't easy to concentrate with the stoning continuing around the clock. He was still cross with White Alam and Sanu the Fat for leaking Kona Das's affair to Stingy Traffic Policeman, but when they came to see him and shouted 'Godzilla', he laughed with them. They volunteered to do the shopping and run errands for Dadu because it wasn't safe for Bulbul to go out now. Stoked by the goons, the hysteria over the Kona Das affair hadn't yet died down in the neighbourhood. Sanu told him that Teeny Mullah had done a runner, leaving most of his things behind.

'Sanu, tell Bulbul how Teeny Mullah ran.'

'I don't want to hear it. He can go to hell, as far as I'm concerned.'

Dadu was determined not to be cowed. 'I've seen riots in Calcutta. Those goons don't scare me,' she said. She played her old Murphy at its highest volume and sang along loudly to songs, encouraging Kona Das to join in. She would stand in the open courtyard, stones landing all around her, and scream: 'If you've balls, come and get me. You sons of maggots and cockroaches.' Kona Das and Bulbul had to drag her in.

One afternoon, in a lull between stone showers and the radio not blaring, Bulbul went to sit on the inner veranda. He wanted to savour a moment of silence but couldn't help overhearing Dadu and Kona Das talking. Perhaps they were peeling and cutting vegetables for the evening meal, or, maybe Kona Das was rubbing coconut oil in Dadu's hair.

'Thanks to Allah that you didn't get married to that mullah. He's ugly. You would've had ugly children,' said Dadu.

'I'll die unmarried. Who will marry me now? Even an untouchable wouldn't touch me. Ma Durga, why so cruel to me.'

'Men are total botheration. We're better off without them. I wish we could procreate without them. Total botheration.'

'Bhagwan has given me this womanly body. What am I to do with it? I can't die without knowing its passion.'

'Hasn't the mullah? You know... anything?'

'No. He's too greedy to go to heaven. He didn't want to do anything to spoil his chances.'

'I hope someone castrates him like a bullock. Ugly mullah.'

Bulbul felt guilty about listening to this intimate conversation. He got up carefully, turned to go back to his room, but ended up letting out a loud cry. Though not very large, a stone came flying in and hit his forehead. Blood poured down to his eyes, to his lips, and his shirt. Hearing his cry, Dadu and Kona Das ran to him. Dadu pressed his wound with the corner of her sari, but someone needed to fetch the doctor. Dadu had never been in the town alone, and it would be too dangerous for Kona Das to go out. What to do? She sent Kona Das to knock on their neighbour's back door, but no one answered. Kona Das said she would go and fetch Sanu the Fat, who lived only a few minutes away, but Dadu thought that was still too risky. 'I've seen it all before, in Calcutta during the riots. My son… When communal, religious and shameful things are going on, the beast in man comes out. Reason things, compassionate things get thrown down the shit hole. He becomes more savage than a… snake? No, a snake is much better,' said Dadu.

Desperate and still pressing his wound with the edge of her sari, Dadu led Bulbul to the front gate and hailed a rickshaw to take him to the hospital. He needed several stitches.

When his exam came, Stingy Traffic Policeman offered to accompany Bulbul to and from school. It was a risky undertaking for a man who was pathologically averse to taking risks. The goons, using their connections with the military high-ups, the police chief and the district magistrate, could have had him sacked on charges of bribe-taking, but Dadu was very grateful for his kind gesture. She cooked a duck and pilau-rice and sent it over to his house. Used to extreme frugality, he sat before Dadu's dishes with his family and instructed them to look and smell it while they ate their usual cheap, unappetising meals. 'Oh, such expensive and flavoursome dishes. Mouthwatering, sense-elevating to heaven's level for sure. We have to make them last. By looking and smelling them we are adding delicious value to our meagre dishes. The more time we take, the more value we add. Simple maths, really,' he said.

The food had gone off by the time he allowed them to eat Dadu's dishes. White Alam and his mother were cross: 'We could have enjoyed those dishes. Your dogmatic frugality has denied us.'

'On the contrary, my policy has enhanced our enjoyment of them. We would have finished them in one lunch or dinner. Haven't we enjoyed them over two days?'

'No,' said the mother and the son, 'we haven't enjoyed them. For your information, we suffered them.'

On the first day of Bulbul's exam, Stingy Traffic Policeman arrived on time and hailed a rickshaw. Feeling awkward, Bulbul kept his head down and pressed his body against the outer edges of the rickshaw's sliding, slippery seat. 'Are you upset with me for catching Kona Das?' asked Stingy Traffic Policeman. Bulbul shrugged his shoulders.

'I don't like immoral practices. Morality is a big thing for me, yes it is. Besides, I wanted to force the issue, so that Kona Das could make an honest woman of herself. Call me what you will, I'm an honest and upright citizen.'

The rickshaw puller asked for his fare when they reached the school gate.

'You know who you are talking to?'

'Of course, I know you, Sir. You're the traffic policeman. But if you ride my rickshaw, you're a passenger. If you don't pay, how am I to survive? I've a wife and five children to feed.'

'That's not my problem. With so many infringements of basic laws, you should be paying me to overlook them. I don't know if you've given the matter any thought. Undoing the facts of violation requires a lot of moral courage.'

'I don't know what you are talking about, Sir. You've ridden my rickshaw. You have to pay the fare.'

'You want me to be right and proper now. Well, it's your choice. I forthwith revoke your license for ten basic infringements. I don't have time to list them, but I tell you I didn't get to be Stingy Traffic Policeman without knowing infringements. They crowd my dreams. I thought I would do you a favour and overlook them, but your attitude disappoints me.'

In the end, the rickshaw puller didn't get his fare, and ended up paying Stingy Traffic Policeman for overlooking his unspecifiable infringements.

Bulbul's exams didn't go well, but at least the goons didn't get to beat him up. Dadu wanted to return to Dambarpur as soon as his exams finished, but Bulbul persuaded her to stay one more day. Stoning continued on the house, but by now they'd got as used to it as the leaking roof, power cuts, or the mosquitoes that sneaked in through the net and buzzed in their ears. Then, perhaps knowing they were leaving the next day, the goons gave them a day's grace and the house was quiet.

Before leaving Mominabad, Dadu wanted to cook a special lunch. She invited Sanu the Fat and White Alam. After lunch, they decided to risk going to the college field to smoke cigarettes. When they reached their particular spot, they lit up. Lying on their backs, they blew coils of smoke in harmony, as if to match their moods one last time. Dark clouds were gathering in the sky.

'What do you want to be when you grow up?' asked White Alam.

'I don't think I'll pass the exam. Maybe I'll get a job at the cinema. Usher, perhaps. I'll get to see all the films,' said Sanu.

'And you, Bulbul?' asked White Alam.

'Me. I don't think I'll pass the exam either. Dadu wants me to help her with the farming. I suppose I will become a farmer.'

'How about you, Alam?' asked Sanu the Fat.

'I want to make a lot of money and spend it all. Buy nice things, eat well. Every day, fish, aubergine, meat, meesty-sweet.'

'But the adda-men will be disappointed. They wanted us to carry on with the tradition,' said Sanu.

'Maybe. When we are old, wherever we are, we can come back to Mominabad and become adda-men. Anyway, tell us a story, Sanu. About us,' said White Alam.

'I don't know what will happen to us. I can't tell stories about memories of the future. Perhaps we can go to see a film. I can tell a funny story about that.'

'I'm going back to Dambarpur tomorrow. No time for a film,' said Bulbul.

'We have been Godzilla brothers, haven't we? I'll never forget that,' said White Alam.

Thunder and lightning suddenly broke. They ran through the downpour, stopped by the front gate of Bulbul's house, and together screamed, 'Godzilla!'

That night Bulbul couldn't sleep. He looked at the gecko on his wall, immobile, not even flicking out its tongue, let alone darting at prey. Like the gecko, he felt time had stopped for him. Nothing to remember, nothing to anticipate. He didn't sleep until the early morning and then was woken by the crows. He jumped up, feeling that he must see Scientist before leaving. If only he had something precious to bribe the guards with, but he had nothing. Then he remembered his grandfather's pocket watch, always tick-tocking loud and insistent, as if it wanted you to hear its message that time was passing. He tiptoed to Dadu's room; it was easy to find the watch. He picked it up and ran out. It was still dark. Near the prison gate, he lay behind a tree and waited for the morning light. He hoped that the guard he'd bribed before would come to the entrance, but by late morning there was no sign of that guard. The

146

train to Dambarpur left at midday. When he saw the guard who stole the tiffin carrier with lunch for Scientist, he approached him.

'What do you want, boy? Civilians are not allowed around the prison gate. Get lost.'

'I need to see my brother, Scientist.'

'The dwarf is a serious criminal. No one is allowed to see him.'

'You remember me, don't you? I gave you the tiffin carrier with lunch for my brother.'

'Am I your servant or the dwarf's servant? Why should I take lunch to him?'

'I know you ate that lunch. It's alright. I'm not complaining. I'll give you better things if you let me see my brother.'

'How dare you accuse a member of the police force of stealing your lunch. It's a slander. A serious offence. If you don't bugger off immediately, I'll arrest you. Understand?'

Bulbul waited under the tree, but the guard found him there.

'If you loiter around, I'll have to shoot you. We have firm instructions to shoot any miscreants in the vicinity.'

On his way home, Bulbul didn't care who saw him; if the goons wanted to beat him up, so be it. But the goons were night prowlers, they wouldn't be around until later. When he reached home, he found Dadu and Kona Das waiting for him on the front veranda.

'Where have you been? I've been worried sick. And we have to leave soon for the train,' said Dadu.

Bulbul didn't say anything and walked to his room. Dadu followed him. 'Have you done all of your packing,' she asked.

'Nearly,' he said, and handed over the watch to her.

'It's yours. You keep it. But why did you take it like a thief?'

'I don't know. Maybe I am just a thief.'

Goni Mia offered to take them to the station; he had already called two rickshaws. It was only when they were loading them that Bulbul remembered the notebooks. He rushed back with his bag to his room, opened the plank under the almari and retrieved them.

On the way to the station, he asked Goni Mia, 'Do you have any news of Scientist?'

'Not very good news, I'm afraid. The authorities won't let anyone see him. He's on hunger strike.'

'Why?'

'He wants to be recognised as a political prisoner, rather than a common criminal.'

'I see. How is he doing?'

'He's getting very weak. You know Scientist. He may be tiny in size, but he's very strong inside. If the authorities don't meet his demand, I'm scared he might take it to the end.'

Bulbul stayed quiet; he couldn't bear thinking that Scientist could do this. On the train, he looked out of the window and only when the hawkers and beggars boarded at the next station, did he turn his face to the inside of the compartment.

'What's the matter with you, my little bird,' said Dadu. 'Why do you have tears in your eyes?'

'They're not tears. You know these engines. Vapours getting into my eyes. Maybe some tiny splinters from the charcoal.'

CHAPTER 12

It had been raining since they arrived in Dambarpur. Lodged in the outer bungalow, Bulbul sat on the recliner by the window. He watched the rain making the rice fields in front barely visible and the bamboo groves fringing their perimeters a swinging forest of shadows. He couldn't help remembering the village elders beseeching his grandfather to let him become a saint. If he had followed their wishes, he could have been somebody. It was just as well that he hadn't mentioned it to Scientist, who would have laughed and said: Can't believe it, Bulbul, were you really serious about that nonsense? Did you really mean to be a charlatan, trading in fakery, taking advantage of the weak and the vulnerable?

Scientist would have been right to condemn him, but the tremor of that temptation still rippled through him, hailing him: why not give it a try, see for yourself. Perhaps he should check Mohan Ganguly's notebook, still locked in his suitcase under his bed; it might make everything clear. He brought out the suitcase but decided against opening it. He wasn't ready to face any promise of adventure into the unknown. Some monster might be lurking there to swallow him up. He closed the suitcase and walked out.

Within seconds he was wet. He walked between the paddies, crossed the bamboo groves and began to run. Already patches of haor were underwater. He zigzagged between them, unable to see what lay beyond a few strides. Why should he care what Scientist thought? Did he want to end up a hand on Dadu's farm and her fisheries? As a saint, he could use the power it gave him to rouse the people and lead them to Mominabad to storm the jail and rescue Scientist, Abid Ali and Banu Gosh. He must hurry because he knew that Scientist would take his fast to the end. Ya Allah, don't let it happen. He ran on and on, the rain pelting him until he felt its motion surging within him and he became the wind, gliding over the mud bed at a breakneck speed. He couldn't have avoided sliding down into the deep hole even if he'd seen it. He lay there dreaming of a girl who also slid down a hole, and together they played the dice game that Keramot Ali had been babbling about. He didn't count time, didn't panic, didn't even think about rescue, but he was rescued. After several hours, by chance, a runaway kid goat skipped and sprinted in roughly the same direction as he had done, and fell into the same hole. The owner, hearing it, getting down to retrieve his kid-goat, found Bulbul and brought him back home. He wasn't injured, but the prolonged exposure to cold and wet had given him a delirious fever.

Dadu and Kona Das nursed him, but flustered by his strange behaviour and ravings, his grandmother called the imam, who also dabbled in jinn-craft. Lighting incense, sprinkling rose water and intoning prayers, he sat by Bulbul who, between loud gurglings, began bleating like a goat. The imam blessed a glass of water and tried to make him drink, but Bulbul flung it away and headbutted the imam, who fell to the floor. When the imam rose to his feet, he saw that Bulbul looked as if he was in a deep sleep. He bent down to touch Bulbul's forehead, who opened his eyes wide, his unflinching stare boring into the imam's eyes – almost blinding him. Shaking, the imam stuttered, 'Young master, are you the one? We're so blessed.' Again Bulbul bleated, closed his eyes, and started to snore.

A crowd had gathered outside the outer bungalow. When the imam opened the door, they looked up at him for news, but he remained silent.

'Is he dead?' asked an old man.

'He came back from the dead. Died to be born again, as is the way,' said the imam.

'So, we have a new saint?'

'Yes. Happy news. Yes.'

The crowd rejoiced but Dadu wasn't pleased: 'I thought this family madness had ended. Now it's coming back to haunt us.'

'You should stop it,' said Kona Das.

'If I try, it won't work. He has to do it himself,' said Dadu.

That night, without consulting Dadu, the imam moved Bulbul into an anteroom at the mosque. When Dadu summoned the imam, asking why he had moved Bulbul there, he said, 'We don't want to disturb you, Bibi. With the news of the new saint spreading, people will flock from far and wide. Besides, he needs a team of people to manage the whole thing. I will dedicate myself completely to the saint's service. Two mosque assistants will help me.'

'How do you know the boy is a saint?' asked Dadu.

'I witnessed the birthing moment. Yes, I did. What else can you trust if you can't trust your own eyes? First, he died, yes, yes, he died. Then, he went through several transformations. At one point, he became a goat. Bleatings were unmistakable. They conveyed great meanings, but unfortunately I can't fathom them. Only a saint knows his own meaning. I'm just a humble acolyte.'

'I'll give you a few days. If everything is not proper, or my grandson suffers in any way, I'll very angry,' said Dadu.

After the imam left, Kona Das asked Dadu why she was letting the imam make a fool of Bulbul.

'You've no brains, have you? The boy's not into book-reading, so what will he do? At best, he'll be a poor farmer. Hand to mouth. Always at the mercy of the weather's moods. Struggle, struggle. With that saint thing he can have a good living.'

'Oh, I see. But isn't the whole thing a fake? I know Bulbul Da. He's not into that kind of thing.'

'What do you take me for, a fool? Of course, the whole thing is fake. And that imam – I know a greedy type when I see one. But if the boy makes a good living out of it, who am I to stand in his way?'

Soon, the mosque compound became thronged with seekers of blessings. People came to see the saint from all over the haor country: some seeking miracle cures, others fortunes. No one came empty-handed; besides cash, they offered rice, goats, ducks, chickens, sweet breads, thick milk etc.

Wearing all white, a pagri wrapped around his head, counting beads in his hand, the saint sat on a rug in the anteroom. Escorted by the imam, the seekers would come and touch the saint's feet, who would put his hand on their heads. Within a week, the imam had gathered a long list of testimonies of miracle cures and changes of fortune. A gambler, a habitual loser, won a fortune; an old man, bedridden for years, got back the virility of an eighteen-year-old – he was looking for a young wife.

Before the week was over, the imam came to see Dadu with a bag of cash and a cartload of rice, chicken, fish, and many sweet and savoury foods; and he dragged along three goats.

'What is this?' asked Dadu.

'These are Allah's blessings. For your grandson's work.'

'I don't want these dirty things in my house. If we eat any of this, it's sure to give us diarrhoea. Very bad. But put the cash in that box over there. My grandson can use it in whatever way he sees fit. And sell the goats and put the money there, too.'

'As you wish, Bibi. He's doing fine work, a natural at the job. Helping so many.'

'No doubt he's helping you too,' said Dadu.

'We just take the running costs. A saintly enterprise involves serious logistical operations. Plenty of expenses.'

After a week of saintly duties, Bulbul had a day off; no seekers came and he was happy to be alone. He sat by the window in the anteroom looking out. It was still raining. Water surrounded the mosque, which lay on a higher ground. He went out and stood in the rain as if waiting for something to happen. Out of the mist came a man and a boy. Seeing them, Bulbul ran into the ante-room, but the pair followed him.

'Venerable saint, have mercy on us. We are poor, we don't have much to give you. I've trapped this heron for you,' said the man.

Bulbul looked at the heron, stooping in a cage; it turned its head and fixed him in its gaze. Bulbul felt unnerved.

'You can keep him as a pet. Or, you can eat him. With a gourd, he'd make a fine curry.'

Bulbul said nothing but looked at the man as if asking what he wanted.

'My son. He's blind. But he wants to read books. It's a silly fancy, I know, but what's a father to do? So, I brought him to you. Venerable saint, have mercy on him.'

Bulbul desperately wished he could lay his hand on the boy's head and restore his sight so he could realise his fantasy of reading books. Suddenly, he stood up, grabbed the heron's cage and ran out, wading into the haor, then swimming, keeping the cage above the water with one hand. He was heading towards the outer bungalow which he reached after twenty minutes. He looked at the heron, 'Brother heron, don't look at me like that. I know I've been stupid. Now get on with your fishing.' He released the heron which flapped its wings and flew over the water.

He changed his wet clothes, took out Mohan Ganguly's book and fell asleep holding it tight.

When the imam came to look for him the next day, Dadu was ready for him. 'If you come near my grandson again, I'll pull out the hairs of your beard. One by one. I'm really angry. Understand?'

She brought Bulbul to her hut, where he slept for days. When he awoke, he asked, 'Where's my book?'

'You mean, your exercise books? They're under your pillow. What are they?' asked Dadu.

'They are the bits and pieces of stories that I've collected. Now that I don't have school, I'll read them. Something to amuse me.'

'I thought you didn't like reading,' said Dadu.

He moved back to the outer bungalow, tucked himself in bed and began browsing through Mohan Ganguly's notebook. It was a mixed bag: passages copied from books in diverse genres, often without mentioning the authors' names or the book's title, sometimes, though, accompanied by his own exposition and commentary on them. Even with Mohan Ganguly's expositions, much of the writing was beyond him. He needed to study and learn a lot before he could grasp the meaning of those passages. He was about to close the notebook when he came across a passage that said: *These pages are the distillation of years of study, reflection, meditation, struggles, experiences – both happy and bitter – yet I am still a student, still learning.* It was hard to imagine Mohan Ganguly as a student, but this made him realise he couldn't just read random passages and grasp their meaning immediately. Everything needed preparation, an apprenticeship in learning, practice, perseverance and dedication. To follow the twists and turns of Mohan Ganguly's notebook he needed to follow his path: both in reading – which seemed endless – and in life. This disheartened Bulbul. It was too arduous. Perhaps, book reading and learning wasn't, after all, to be his thing. Besides, he didn't want to live on the run like Mohan Ganguly. He wanted to enjoy life. He closed the notebook and prepared to fall asleep but ended up browsing it again. He read: *Religion is the sigh of the oppressed creature, the heart of a heartless world, and the soul of soulless conditions. It is the opium of the people. Religion is only the illusory Sun which revolves around man as long as he does not revolve around himself.*

He could just about make sense of the 'sigh'. He had seen plenty of people, really down and desperate, praying for deliverance; he had called on Allah at difficult times. Hadn't he recently sought the grace of the almighty to help Scientist? What could possibly be wrong with that? He knew about opium and had seen the wretched condition of opium-eaters in Mominabad, but he couldn't quite work out in what ways religion was an addiction. Hadn't many opium addicts cured themselves by going to the mosque, praying five times a day, and counting the names of Allah on their beads? He was even more puzzled by the rest of the passage. What makes a world heartless? What are soulless conditions? How can man revolve around himself? Thinking that Mohan Ganguly's comments might help, he dipped into them. He seemed to have lost his cool and just ranted: *Bloody mullahs, priests and purohits, and saints and sadhus – worst of the lot – scoundrels conning people, sucking their blood in the name of a big man, who – surprise, surprise – doesn't exist. If I had my way I'd castrate the lot and feed their privates to the dogs.* The violence of these thoughts shook Bulbul; he'd never considered that a man like Mohan Ganguly, who'd given up everything to help people, could think this way. Besides, these comments seemed directly aimed at him: cut his thing off and feed it to the dogs. Yes, yes, he would be right to do so. How could he have been so stupid, so morally depraved to play the saint, and con poor people of their meagre resources? How had it all happened? It was as if he'd walked into a dream despite himself. He could almost hear Mohan Ganguly's voice: but you can't escape your responsibility by blaming it on a dream – that's a cheap old trick. Just be honest, you wanted it – yes? He felt like running out again and disappearing in the haor.

He stayed indoors for the next few days, mostly sleeping or looking out of the window at the rain, when White Alam came to visit him with the exam results. As expected, Sanu the Fat hadn't passed the exam, but he wasn't upset because his mother, by selling the front yard of her house, had given him the money to set up a tea stall by the cinema, where he would entertain his clients by retelling film-stories. White Alam had done well: he would go to the government college in Mominabad for his higher secondary education, then perhaps go on to the university. Bulbul had passed the exam, but his grades weren't good enough to get him into any of the colleges in Mominabad.

White Alam said 'Godzilla' to cheer him up. Bulbul didn't laugh but he was happy to see White Alam – someone to talk to. Apart from going to Dadu's hut to eat, they stayed in the outer bungalow talking. White Alam didn't know what had happened to Scientist, but Banu Gosh had come out of prison. He still had his house and the remaining adda-men met there for all-nighters.

'How about Abid Ali? What has happened to him?'

'He's been moved to another jail. Somewhere in the south.'

After a silence, Bulbul said, 'I got involved in something silly. I don't know how it happened, but I ended up playing a saint.'

'Godzilla! You don't say. I always thought there was something special about you. But I never saw you as a saint. Anyway, what was it like?'

'I don't remember much. It was like I was on drugs. Afterwards, it was horrible.'

'Was the money good?'

'Yes, but it was dirty money.'

'You know the problem with you? Too much thinking. Too much guilt. You should've kept at it. If they make you a saint, it's their problem. They deserve to be milked.'

'I suppose I was tempted but couldn't do it.'

'What are you going to do, then? You can't just stay in this backwater and be a farm hand. You're too good for that.'

'I don't know what I'm going to do.'

As he left, White Alam said they would always be bound by Godzilla times.

Bulbul knew he needed to educate himself before he tackled Mohan Ganguly's notebook. But how? With such poor grades, no college would take him on their higher secondary programme. Over dinner, he told Dadu he wanted to be a book-reader, and attend college.

'If you're serious about it, I'll sell some land to support you. Ah, your grandfather. He always wanted you to become a scholar.'

He explained to Dadu that he might not get into a college with his poor grades, but she insisted he approach his grandfather's old college in Kishorepur.

'If they hear whose grandson you are, they'll take you without looking at your grades. Your grandfather was a famous scholar.'

Now that the land was flooded, he couldn't bike to Kishorepur, about six miles away. He took the bike on the boat for about two miles, then cycled the main road, raised high above the flood water, to reach the town. When he reached the college, he knocked on the admission tutor's door to present himself as Syed Amir Shah's grandson.

'Who have we here?' asked the admission tutor.

'I'm from Dambarpur, Sir. I want to enrol at your college.'

'You have come to the right place. From the village, from the town doesn't make any difference to us. Nor does who your father or grandfather is. We don't give a hoot about such matters. This is an institution for serious scholarship. No place for name-dropping and nepotism. All that matters to us is your potential for serious learning, which we judge by your grades.'

How could he mention his grandfather's name now? He bit his lip and handed over the paper with his results. The admission tutor glanced over it, then said, 'I'm afraid you haven't come to the right place. Judging by your results, you've very little aptitude for learning. Very bad results. Perhaps, agriculture work would be better for you.'

'I want to learn, Sir. Really, I do.'

'Good. May I suggest the New College. I hear they take anyone.'

Bulbul had already heard about New College; it was housed in a dilapidated building, owned by a crooked politician, who, rumour had it, had to bribe the officials to be recognised as a legitimate institution of learning. It was renowned for its shoddy teaching and hooliganism, and no one ever made it to university. Bulbul had no other option, so he went to New College where they didn't look at his grades and offered him immediate admission. The principal himself welcomed him.

'I see a fine scholar. We value and esteem all of our students. We maximise everyone's potential. Whatever you want to be, you can be here.'

'Thank you, Sir,' said Bulbul.

'It's a delicate matter, but I must raise it. Your finances are tiptop, yes? We need a lot of money to run a first-class institution like this. We require advance payment of fees.'

Bulbul, like his grandfather, made the twelve-mile return journey to Kishorepur five days a week. There wasn't much learning and the classrooms were chaotic: students loafed about, gossiped, smoked cigarettes, and fought. The teachers, poorly educated, didn't know how to teach, often slept in the classrooms, and tried to recruit the students into various illegal activities. There were hardly any books in the library, which had been taken over by a gang of skinny dogs who chased away anyone foolish enough to go near it.

The only teacher who made any effort was Basitul Hasan. He was a young man, recently graduated, from a poor family from a distant part of the big haor. He was a serious scholar, but his lack of funds had cut short further studies and his lack of connections closed doors to jobs at a better college. The New College was the only institution that would employ him. He wrote Bengali poetry and was considered very promising in poetry circles.

He was employed to teach English. He, in turn, wanted to shape the students' young minds and inculcate a passion for learning, but his classes were disasters. He was small, shy and spoke softly. In the uproar of the classroom, he was hardly heard. When he turned his back to write something on the blackboard, students would throw paper planes at him. They would loosen the legs of his chair and laugh when he fell. When he tried to extol the virtue of learning English, his students, if they heard him, turned up their noses.

'We don't want to sound funny, Sir. Deshi-people speaking English. Always funny, Sir,' said one student.

'You can discuss many serious and elevated subjects in English,' said Basitul Hasan.

'Deshi-people sound very funny, Sir, when they talk serious in English. It's like a pig, Sir, speaking Einstein. Total bombastic.' The rest of the class, except Bulbul, burst into laughter.

'Can't you find a single reason for learning English?' asked Basitul Hasan.

'No, Sir. It's a Feringhee tongue. They – pardon my language,' said a one-eyed boy, giggling, 'buggered us with their English. Now the Americans are buggering us with it, too. Coca cola, jolly-good, tasty. Only deshi-ass-lickers speak it. They smell bad, Sir.'

'We don't want to smell bad,' roared the class.

'I want to learn English,' said Bulbul quietly.

A student asked, 'What did you say?'

'I want to learn English.'

'Bloody poofter. The British buggered his granddaddy. Now he wants to be buggered by the Americans,' said the one-eyed boy, and the rest of the class guffawed.

After this, it became impossible for Bulbul to go anywhere near the college compound, let alone attend a class. He still made the journey to Kishorepur, but instead of going to New College, he headed for the *Knowledge for Everyone* library. It was well stocked with books on many subjects, though only up to 1947. An old zamindar had set it up. When he left for India after partition, *Knowledge for Everyone* stopped buying books. A few passionate readers, all elderly, managed the library; Basitul Hasan was the only young volunteer. It was there that Bulbul got to know him. Each day after college, at about three in the afternoon, Basitul Hasan would cycle to *Knowledge for Everyone*, and in between his volunteering as a librarian and writing poetry, he would help Bulbul with his studies. He also lent Bulbul post-1947 books from his own private collection. Since Bulbul didn't have any strong inclination for any of the subjects on the curriculum, he went along with his mentor's areas of interest and expertise: English, Bengali, History and Politics.

'Why are you interested in learning and studying?' asked Basitul Hasan.

'It's a long story, Sir. If we are to begin at the tail end, let us say that once a man gave me a book. I tried to read it but couldn't make much sense of it. It made me realise that I need to learn and study a lot before opening the book again.'

'A curious story. Not to say, rather whimsical. Anyway, do you feel this book is meant to show you a path?'

'I don't know, Sir. Perhaps. Something woke me from a long sleep, and that book had something to do with it. All I want to do now is read and learn. Acquire knowledge.'

'You mean rational, secular, and humanistic knowledge?'

'Is that what you call it?'

One Friday, after several months of meeting at *Knowledge for Everyone*, Bulbul invited Basitul Hasan to Dambarpur. Dadu and Kona Das cooked a nice meal with several varieties of fish, lentils and vegetables – all home-grown. Dadu had thought that Basitul Hasan would be an elderly man, so she was surprised to see a small, thin, timid young man. Over the meal, Dadu asked him where he was from, and learning that his village lay in a remote part of the low country, on the other side of the great haor, she thought that the poor boy must be missing mother-love and home cooking. She invited him to come to Dambarpur every weekend so she could look after him a bit.

After lunch, Bulbul and Basitul Hasan went out on a small dinghy, punting and paddling over the watery expanse surrounding the house.

'Your grandmother is nice. If you don't mind me asking, where are your parents? Do they work in Mominabad?'

Bulbul continued punting, saying nothing.

'Sorry. You don't have to say anything. This place is really beautiful. Look at the ducks over there, almost touching the clouds.'

'Don't be sorry, Sir. I wish I knew more. I have no memory of them. Dadu rarely talks about them. All I know is that they died in Calcutta just before the partition. My grandparents crossed the border with me.'

'I don't like you always calling me Sir,' said Basitul Hasan.

'What should I call you then? You are my teacher.'

'If you like, you can call me Bhai.'

'Basitul Bhai. I don't know. It'll take time to get used to it.'

It was getting dark. Birds were looking for a roosting place for the night among the tall trees that towered over the flood water. Basitul Hasan wanted to return to Kishorepur, but both Dadu and Bulbul insisted he stay the night.

'Tomorrow is Saturday. Holiday time. You go after lunch. I'll make bhuna khichuri. Yes?' said Dadu.

'Thank you, Dadu. If I may call you Dadu. I write during weekends.'

'Of course, you can call me Dadu. I'm so grateful that you're teaching my grandson. His grandfather always wanted him to be a scholar. When we lived in Mominabad, he never wanted to read a book. I don't know what has happened to him. Now, he even eats with a book in front of him. Acha, what do you write? Is it bookkeeping or something for the college?'

'He's a poet, Dadu. He writes poems.'

'Poems? I heard poets are a funny lot. Very prone to going mad or something.'

'I don't know where you get these ideas, Dadu. Look at him. Does he look funny to you? Or mad?'

Basitul Hasan agreed to stay, and after dinner he and Bulbul returned to the outer bungalow.

'If you want to write your poems, go ahead. I won't disturb you,' said Bulbul.

Basitul Hasan wasn't in the mood to write so they sat by the window and looked out at half-submerged trees swaying like silhouetted sanyasis under a half-moon.

'Why do you write poems, Sir?'

'No more Sir. Acha? Why do I write poems? I don't know. I just feel like writing them. Perhaps I write poems so as not to cry. Not to die of laughter. Not to get so angry that I might go out and kill someone. Sometimes I want to make people so angry they will tear down a wall with their nails. Perhaps, to reveal that things have other stranger faces, or find a word that sings the melodies of my pulses. Often, I let a rhythm spin in my head, then it catches a word, and together they speak the secrets of things.'

'I don't follow you. It sounds weird. Sometimes, though, funny things happen to me. I don't dare to tell anyone because they might think I've gone crazy. Sometimes when I see a thing – say a gecko, its rest so immobile like a dead stone on the wall as it awaits its prey – I feel so affected by it that my body, without my knowing it, feels that it has turned into a gecko.'

'Now, you've lost me. Anyway, if you could find a word that fits that moment, even if you don't understand it, it could be poetry.'

'I don't know. I can't get my head around it. Let's go to sleep.'

At Bulbul's insistence Basitul Hasan was forced to take the bed while Bulbul took the makeshift one on the floor.

Sensing that Basitul Hasan wasn't sleeping, Bulbul asked, 'You studied English. You teach English. Yet you write poetry in Bengali. I don't understand.'

'Simple, really. I understand the words in English, but their rhythm doesn't sing to me. Not in the way Bengali words do.'

'What's the point of learning English then?'

'It's always good to learn other languages. Another way of seeing things, another set of sounds to impress your senses. In the case of English, what the boys said at college is not untrue. They have a point. Colonial shaping took place through English. Those natives who learned it managed the Empire for their masters. Then, when the Empire was imploding, wearing homespun cotton and singing the praises of home rule, they ensured that they still ran the show afterwards. Now, all over the subcontinent, elite-breeding English schools are flourishing as never before. Business as usual.'

'So, why do you want to learn it? Especially now that the Americans are using it to make us Coca-Cola zombies.'

'Good question. I can only answer it for myself. No one can deny the seduction of what is glamorous and prestigious – which English has in abundance. Your soul burns and you get all worked up to be consumed by the aura of elitedom. You feel your life will be a success, even if you're a wretched sahib in a shit-hole.'

'That sounds nasty. Terrible reason to learn English.'

'I agree. Yet, many people make this Faustian contract.'

'What is that? This Faustian thing?'

'I'll teach it another day. Do you still want me to go on about English and myself?'

'Yes,' said Bulbul.

'It's like taking drugs. You can have a good trip or a bad trip. Or both. In my case, it has been both. I started with the bad trip. Then, when I realised what it was doing to me, it opened the world for me, it became a good trip.'

'I don't understand,' said Bulbul.

'English is the language of two consecutive global empires – unprecedented in human history. As such, there are no bounds to English's voraciousness. It wants to have everything. A true monster. As a result, you can swim along different currents in the monster's belly. My current has been that of writing from other places, in other tongues. If it weren't for English, I wouldn't have access to them. Thanks to English, if I want to, I can read ancient Chinese erotica, Hitler's *Mein Kampf*, or learn about the Kalahari bushmen. But my real interest lies in literature, particularly poetry.'

'If you write Bengali poetry, why should you read those others translated into English?'

'Of course, I read Bengali poetry and learn from it. But the others replenish me, too. For instance, I only recently read Aimé Césaire's *Notebook of a Return to the Native Land*. He is from Martinique and it's written in French. Thanks to English translation it's available to me. So are Garcia Lorca, Maria Rilke, Mayakovsky and Khlebnikov.'

'I don't know much about poetry. Are they good poets?'

'Yes, they are. They have their unique vision and rhythm. I've learnt a lot from them. I like to think of them as my rhythm-mates.'

'I thought it was only in Bengali words that you can feel the rhythm.'

'True. When these poets come to me in translation, I find the English rhythm is strained. I'm affected by them differently. Afterwards, when I bite on Bengali words, their rhythmic flow sends a different tremor through my body, and I end up expressing something slightly different than I originally intended.'

'Sorry, I don't follow. Maybe one day, when I know more about poetry. Do you read any English-English poems?'

'Of course, I do. A lot of amazing poets are coming out, especially in the Caribbean. They put their bodies into English,

161

straining its rhythm to their different melodies and meaning. Obviously, I love Shakespeare – who doesn't? But it was Keats who inspired me the most.'

'I heard of Shakespeare, but not Keats.'

'Earlier you said something that I couldn't quite follow. Facing a gecko, you felt you became one with it, didn't you? Well, now I've some inkling of it. You see, Keats had similar feelings when he wrote 'Ode to a Nightingale'. Listening to the nightingale's enchanting song it would have been tempting for Keats to envy it. Instead, he allows himself, even if briefly, a joyful, musical-becoming of the nightingale. A small window to liberation.'

'I don't follow. The way you put it is beyond me. I don't even understand many of the words you use.'

'Sorry, I'm a terrible teacher. I get carried away with my own train of thought. A bit solipsistic. Sorry.'

'Solipsistic? What's that?'

Before falling asleep, Bulbul resolved never to talk poetry with Basitul Hasan again. It made him feel stupider than he was and it transformed Basitul Hasan into someone other than the modest, timid teacher he knew and loved.

Bulbul planned to accompany Kona Das to her village to see her mother the following day. Dadu was sending a sari as a present and Kona Das had made rice bread with palm sugar. Bulbul persuaded Basitul Hasan to come along with them. On foot, Kona Das's village wasn't more than an hour's journey, but it would take at least twice as long by boat. While Bulbul stood with a pole at the stern, Basitul Hasan sat at the bow, and Kona Das hunched in the middle, facing Bulbul. He was surprised to see her pulling the edge of her sari to veil her face; she looked shy. For most of the journey they maintained an awkward silence. When Basitul Hasan commented that it might rain later on, Kona Das didn't respond, and Bulbul merely looked at the sky.

Near the shore, Basitul Hasan asked if Kona Das's mother had a dog. Kona Das remained tight-lipped, but Bulbul said, 'Why? You don't like dogs?'

'I don't know why, but they always go for me.'

162

'Don't worry. I'll make sure that they don't bother you,' said Bulbul.

They climbed to a compound where several cobbler families lived together. Sensing their approach, some loudly barking skinny dogs came charging at them. Punt-pole in his hand, Bulbul stood in front of Basitul Hasan, shouting at the dogs to back off, but they still circled and barked. When Kona Das shushed them, the dogs stopped and sat some distance away. Several members of the cobbler community came to see what was happening and despite the gap of many years, they recognised Kona Das.

'Oh, how you have grown up. Have you come to see your old house?' asked an old lady.

'It's you, aunty. I thought you were dead,' said Kona Das.

'So many have gone. I don't know why Bhagwan still keeps me here. I am fed up with being left behind,' said the old lady.

'I came to see my mother. Where is she?'

There was a long silence, and then the old lady sighed, and touched Kona Das on the head.

'Come to my house. I'll give you paan and a cool glass of water.'

'First, I must see my mother. Where is she?'

'She's not here. She's gone.'

'Where?'

'One morning, we get up. She was gone. Some say to India.'

'India? We don't know anyone in India.'

Kona Das fell to the ground, pressing the sari that Dadu had sent for her mother against her mouth, and sobbed. Everyone stood in silence. Bulbul didn't know what to do but Basitul Hasan moved forward, almost touching her head.

When Kona Das looked up she sobbed louder.

The return leg of the journey was silent. Basitul Hasan picked a lotus fruit from the water and offered it to Kona Das, who shook her head to refuse it.

Bulbul was glad that Basitul Hasan visited Dambarpur every weekend to stay with him. Otherwise, apart from Dadu and Kona Das, he had no one to talk to. After he'd rejected the saintly role, the villagers avoided him; even at the pond no other bathers would talk to him. If the imam happened to be there, he would speak loudly as if he were talking to himself, but Bulbul knew that it was aimed at him: 'Allah's wrath falls on those who neglect their chosen paths – especially the saintly path. No one escapes judgment, and eternal damnation will be their lot: red-hot rods through their nether ends, rats burrowing into their stomachs, snakes slithering through their noses. Ya Allah, have mercy on them.'

When Basitul Hasan was in Dambarpur, in between composing poems, he would help Bulbul with his studies, over which he was now so obsessed that Basitul Hasan had to drag him off his books for a boat trip. Yet it didn't escape Bulbul's notice that the poet was falling for Kona Das.

For months, careful not to be noticed, Basitul Hasan watched Kona Das serve food, chop vegetables, grind spices, carry water from the pond, dry her hair or just amble in the courtyard. He found a rhythm that matched his poetic pulses in her movement, but he didn't dare speak to her. If only she could read, he would have composed little poems for her, and then, trembling, he would have waited to see her subdued joy as she lipped the lines. Frustrated, he drew a little house surrounded by tall, leafy trees. He left it under her kolshi-pitcher. It wasn't clear whether Kona Das hadn't noticed it or she'd ignored it. Dadu found it. When they came to Dadu's hut for dinner that night, she asked Bulbul if he'd drawn the house. He said no.

'I'm glad. Such a bad drawing. Only a fool could've drawn something like this,' and she handed it over to Kona Das to throw it away with other household rubbish.

For the three weeks before the exam, New College closed and Basitul Hasan moved into the outer bungalow to help with Bulbul's preparation. One day, Bulbul took out the dinghy on his own to clear his head and Basitul Hasan stayed behind. Kona Das came in with his drawing of the house.

'What's the meaning of this?' she asked.

Basitul Hasan was so startled he couldn't speak; he lowered his eyes and bit his pen.

'What's this you've drawn?'

'A house.'

'I know, it's a house. But why?'

He stayed silent, then stuttered, 'It's for you.'

'I don't want any house. And if you think we can have a house together, you are more foolish than I thought.'

'Why not?'

'I'm of the untouchable, hide-cleaner, cobbler caste. I can't read anything. You're a Muslim and a book-reading gentleman.'

'We are just humans,' he said.

'What? Are you mad?'

'We can be what we want to be. Build our little house. Why not?' Kona Das laughed.

'I've heard it all before. When the time came, he wanted me to convert. I'm not falling for that again.'

'I'm not like that. You can stay as you are.'

'It's foolish talk. Where are you going to live? No one would let us live among their communities.'

'We can go to the end of the big hoar. No one would find us there.'

'You want to build a house on water? If only we were fish or waterfowl, but we're not. What are you going to eat there? Air?' Kona Das turned and left.

Following this conversation, Basitul Hasan didn't return to Dambarpur again, but when the day for the exam came, Bulbul was well-prepared for it and passed with top grades. The principal of New College called a special assembly to which he had invited all the who's who of Kishorepur.

'We're very proud of our brilliant scholar, whom we celebrate today. Syed Islam Shah, known as Bulbul. His modesty prevents him from saying who his grandfather was. Everyone knows Syed Amir Shah, a celebrated scholar who made our Kishorepur proud during the British time. Now, we have his worthy grandson making us proud again. Genius runs in the blood, as they say. Yet, a genius needs fertile ground to flourish. I am very pleased that New College was able to offer him such a ground. Modest man that I am, bragging doesn't come easily. Still, the truth needs telling: we furnished him with the rich soil for cultivating his mind, as any serious educational institution with integrity and scholarly ambition should. Only two years ago Bulbul came to us with an abysmal record. Other colleges shut their doors on him, seeing only base metal. But we recognised the gold within. So,

165

kindly spread the word about the achievement of New College. With your help, we can transform many young, base lives into gold, diamond, and whatnot. Please come on board this great alchemical train. And don't forget its name: New College.'

Bulbul felt like vomiting. He ran out at the first opportunity, Basitul Hasan following. They walked randomly for a while, then finally ended up in a meesty-sweet shop.

'It's my treat. What do you want?' asked Basitul Hasan.

'I should be treating you. You've done so much for me. I owe you everything,' said Bulbul.

'Nonsense. It's your hard work and dedication. Not to say your intelligence. It was my privilege to be able to assist.'

'I know how much I owe you. You gave me so much more than helping me get good grades. True, I haven't always understood everything you told me – for instance, about poetry, but you taught me so many things. Thank you, Sir.'

'I thought we'd done with that Sir business. How about some chamcham, jalebis, sweet yoghurt, and a cup of chai to go with them?'

'Thank you. What are you going to do? Are you staying on at New College?'

'No. If I stay I'll either die or sell my soul. I'll go back to my village. Perhaps get a school job there. Anything would be better than New College. Besides, I want to look after my parents. They're old. My father worked in the fields all of his life. Apart from household chores, my mother husked rice, made cow-dung fuel, gathered lotus fruits from the haor. No one in my family ever went to school. I've been lucky to have won competitive scholarships. When I got my degree, my father thought I'd get a good job to help them. But without connections, you can only end up in places like New College. I mustn't complain. There are many people much worse off than me.'

'It's not fair. You're the best teacher I know. Will you still write poetry?'

'I don't want fame, but I'll write, to keep my sanity. Besides, once you get the bug, you can't leave it. How about you?'

'I don't know. I suppose I'll go to the university. Then let's see what happens.'

'Give my respect to Dadu,' said Basitul Hasan.

'She wants you to come to Dambarpur. She wants to cook you a special meal. And Kona Das.'

'Very kind of Dadu. Maybe I'll come when you graduate from the university. If you still remember me then. How is Kona Das, by the way?'

'How can I forget you? Kona Das is fine, but she looks a bit sad. Doesn't talk much. One evening she came and sat by me. She told me that you were the kindest man she'd ever met. She never fails to remember you when she offers her morning prayers.'

That night, back in the outer bungalow, Bulbul opened Mohan Ganguly's notebook and read: *The way to see by faith is to shut the eye of reason.* Under that Mohan Ganguly had written: *Bhagwan died the day I opened my eyes to reason: it woke me up to the most obvious truth that we are things among things: no one else but we make ourselves as we work with our hands, use the brains in our heads, but always in the struggle between have-gots and have-nots. It was let there be light all over again. Strange how I don't remember that day. Was it raining on the day I opened my eyes to reason?*

Dimming the hurricane lamp and turning sideways to sleep, Bulbul laughed, thinking he was finally on the same page as Mohan Ganguly, the communist.

CHAPTER 13

Compared to Calcutta, where he'd been born at the tail end of the British empire, Dacca was a provincial backwater. Still, it loomed on Bulbul as a metropolis of bewildering proportions, spawning fear and excitement in equal measure.

On his way to Dacca from Dambarpur he stopped at Mominabad for a few days, his first visit in about three years. He was staying with Sanu the Fat, who waited for him at the station. 'Singing Bird, welcome home.'

'Home? I don't know where that is, but Mominabad will always be special.'

Outside the station, getting on the rickshaw, Bulbul glanced up at the billboard where, on a terrible night with the goons on his trail, he'd put up the poster of a stitched mouth on the faces of a romantic cinema pair. It was the night he'd lost Scientist.

'What's the matter? It's not a bad town. We had some Godzilla times here, didn't we?' said Sanu the Fat.

'Yes, we had, but I was thinking of Scientist.'

'Didn't you hear? He's released. So is Abid Ali.'

'When did that happen?' asked Bulbul.

'A few weeks ago. Part of the military's clean image campaign. They want to give General Ayub Khan a new face. A good-natured granddaddy-face before the election.'

'For whatever reason they're doing it, it's a good sign.'

'Not quite. I've some more news for you. Finally, they nabbed Mohan Ganguly.'

'Mohan Ganguly? I thought he was uncatchable.'

'Everyone has a chinky-minky in their armour – no? It's the man's weakness for cricket and his addiction to commie-lingo that finally buggered him. Mind you, he was a bit unlucky. They sent a college-educated spy to that match. A new boy of military intelligence and a cricket fan. In the guise of a peanut seller, Mohan Ganguly was doing a good trade and enjoying the cricket. No one suspected a thing. But just as the new boy bought peanuts from him, the batsman played a brilliant on-drive. The ball hugged the grass to the boundary. Unable to resist, Mohan Ganguly cried out: *Ah, this bat and ball contact – the eternal clash and harmony – the supreme dalak!* That made the new boy suspicious.'

'You mean dialectic,' said Bulbul.

'Maybe. Have you been learning commie-lingo? When White Alam told me you'd become a deep book reader, I didn't believe it. Now I see.'

'Talking of White Alam. Where is he?'

'Didn't you know? Somewhere in West Pakistan. He joined the army. Training to be an officer. I wonder what bribing enterprise he'll set up there. He's out to make a killing.'

On the way to the house, they stopped by Sanu the Fat's tea stall by the cinema hall. Bulbul's heart sank when he spotted the goons, four of them, at a side table. Sensing his alarm, Sanu told

Bulbul not to worry; they were on their best behaviour, keeping a lid on their violent urges, eager to present their amiable faces to Mominabad as part of Ayub Khan's charm offensive. Seeing that they were without their dark glasses, Bulbul was a little reassured.

When the goons saw him, they greeted him, 'Young friend, long time no see. How've you been?'

'I'm fine, thank you,' said Bulbul.

'Ah freedom. Aren't we lucky to live in a free state? No need for violent behaviour here. Our president, General Ayub Khan is as peace-loving as a cat,' said one of the goons.

'True, a hundred per cent true,' said Sanu, 'but I wonder if there are mice in the room.'

'Surely, there are no mice here. So, the pussy cat has no business but to purr,' said the same goon.

'Yes, Sir. Hundred per cent pussy cat. General pussy cat. Doing nothing but purring the whole day,' said Sanu.

He took Bulbul to a table some distance from the goons, and served him tea, samosa, and jalebi, which was his stall's speciality. Bulbul could see the jostling crowd and the cinema queue that tailed into the street, and he cocked his head to spot the billboard for the morning show: *Fall of the Roman Empire*.

'Have you seen it?' asked Bulbul.

'Yes, a Roman number. Couldn't follow the lingo, but you don't need that to understand it. You know, to kill yourself laughing. Grown men prancing about with funny haircuts and wearing saris. Hundred per cent nancy boys. And the king guy – he's a real weirdo. I bet he has a thing about his willy. Always anxious to prove his bigness. Every time he looks at you, his smile spits poison.' Sanu leaned over the table to whisper, 'I tell you a secret. The king guy could have been the twin brother of our general.'

Sanu got up to do a round among his customers, sharing banter. One of the customers asked him to tell the film's story. 'You know, the Feringhee film showing now. Give us the rundown. Real funny like.' Other customers echoed his request. Looking unusually hesitant, Sanu glanced at the goons, as if he needed their consent.

'Go on. Make it real funny,' said one of the goons.

'Well, the film has a king-guy for the lead,' said Sanu, 'a real psychopath if I've ever seen one. He's always edgy, poor chap, not a chip but an entire forest on his shoulder. He's seriously lacking down there, and his daddy-man, the old king, wants to chop it off completely. No wonder the guy has issues. Who wouldn't in his place? As it happens in his totally weird family, his sister is the brainy one, but he, the stupid brother, gets to play the king. Do you see the problem, my friends? What do you do if you're seriously lacking both in upstairs and downstairs? You go crazy, wear women's clothes, and walk funny.'

Sanu got coy, moving his backside with exaggerated undulation, and in a harsh, high-pitched voice said: 'I want it big, being the king is not enough for me, I want to be a god, I deserve to be a god.'

'You mean a goddess', said one of the listeners. This prompted Sanu to perform his entire repertoire of funny walks; the punters, including the goons, were doubled over with laughter. 'I want it big,' Sanu the Fat kept whining in his put-on voice, which came out like the hiss of a snake, 'yes bigger than the god's, but the thing is this: does that king-guy remind us of someone?' The hilarity and laughter stopped; only the clicks of the cups on the plates and the breathing of the men could be heard. Undaunted, Sanu went on: 'If the like of that king guy comes and plays god over you, and – pardon my language – wants to bugger you, would you let him?'

One of the goons said, 'We don't know where you're going with this, but we don't find it funny.' Another put on his dark glasses and said: 'Hey, fatty, don't take us for stupid; we know your game. If we weren't feeling benevolent, we would break your bones real slow. Now stop this tamasha and serve us another round.

Sanu the Fat served tea in silence, then came and sat by Bulbul.

'That was a bit risky. I didn't know you'd become so political.'

'I'm not. But you can't play a domestic dog all the time.'

Suddenly, there was the sound of an approaching commotion and some of the customers headed out to have a look. A large crowd was heading towards the cinema hall. Supporters of the opposition candidate, Fatima Jinnah, were on their way to the only public meeting sanctioned by the President-general. Two goons put on their dark glasses and breathed heavily. The other two tried to contain them: 'Orders are clear, so calm down.'

But the two frustrated goons started to break glasses and plates and shout at Sanu: 'You motherfucking fatty, how dare you take advantage of our good nature and poke fun at our President-general? We've long memory you know, so listen up, fatty, after the election we're going to lynch you.'

'Sorry, Sir. Sorry for the misunderstanding. Fatty is a bit foolish. I love the President-general. Hundred per cent. He's like a god to me. Sure, I'm voting for him.' He served the goons a large plate of jilabis, 'on the house, Sir.' That calmed them down. They gobbled up the jilabis and went out.

Sanu's mother was away, so they had the house to themselves. Sanu cooked a huge pot of khichuri and four different types of bhuna meat – beef, goat, chicken, and duck. 'Special treat for us. We eat until we drop.'

A plate of khichuri and a few pieces of meat was enough for Bulbul, but Sanu polished off the rest. 'I tell you something, Singing Bird. There are two types of people in the world. The higher type and the lower type. The higher type live to eat. Best philosophy, no?'

'I don't know. It's more a philosophy for an early grave.'

'You're not becoming a convert to the frugal-living-higher-thinking of Mohan Ganguly? Total loser's philosophy.'

They talked late into the night. While Sanu went to work at his tea stall in the morning, Bulbul popped in to see Scientist. He had to knock on the workshop's door for a while before he responded. He looked much worse than Bulbul feared; he seemed to have shrunk and become much thinner.

'Oh, it's you,' said Scientist in a barely audible voice. His lips and hands trembled, and he braced himself as if not to fall apart.

'Good to see you,' said Bulbul.

'Yes. How are you?' asked Scientist.

'I'm fine. I'm off to Dacca. To study history. And you?'

'Great news. I'm so happy for you. Mind you, I never had any doubt. Me? I'm fine.'

He sent someone to buy meesty-sweet to celebrate Bulbul's university place.

'History, eh? Good subject. Ah, the osprey of time, his wings outstretched, diving down to the past to awaken the dead, soaring up to the living to bloom the future. He's carrying the tempest of our hopes, and who better to ride it than you.'

'I don't know. Anyway, thank you, Scientist. But I'm really worried for you. Come with me to Dambarpur. The country air would do you good.'

'I'm fine. I'm a town-man; the country would kill me. Besides, you should only be thinking of Dacca and your studies. Promise?'

'How can I leave you? I'm really scared. You could come back to Mominabad as soon as you feel a bit better.'

'Trust me. I'm fine. I don't want you to be thinking of anything else. Only your studies. Promise?'

'How can I leave you like this? How can I promise that?'

'You're not listening to me, are you? How many times do I have to tell you that I'm fine? Just promise me you'll go to Dacca and concentrate on your studies. Acha?'

'I don't know. If you insist. Promise.'

'Good. Now, let's cheer up.'

'Alright, but how are you managing? I mean financially?'

'Don't you worry about that. Once I get my hands steady again, jobs will flood in. I won't know what to do with so much money. I'm also thinking of doing some paintings for myself. Full of colours, just colours. So, good times are ahead. Cheer up, yes?'

Scientist looked depleted. When the meesty-sweet came Bulbul wasn't in the mood to savour them, but he nibbled at them because he didn't want to upset his friend.

'If you don't mind,' said Scientist so faintly that Bulbul had to lean closer to hear it, 'I've something urgent to attend to. Perhaps I'll come to Dacca. We can go to a picture gallery together. I always wanted to do that.'

Bulbul headed for Sanu's tea stall. He couldn't shake off how frail his friend looked – at the tick-tock to the end of his time, but what could he do? It wasn't like Scientist to lie to him, string him along as if he were a silly little boy. He had always treated him with far more respect than he deserved. And how not to remember Modu Mia, the woodcutter from Dambarpur? For years, with his sunken eyes and cheeks and his terrible coughs and laboured breathing, he looked as if he would drop dead at any minute, and yet he kept adding years to his life, outliving most of his healthy-looking friends and relatives. Perhaps Scientist would do the same. He had no idea how he had walked so far without realising it, but the clickety-clack and the wafting smell of ink made him aware that he was near Abid Ali's press.

He found Abid Ali at his desk, fine-tuning the editorial for the next edition of *Fresh News*.

'My young friend. What a surprise. Come, come. Sorry, your name has slipped my mind.'

'Bulbul.'

'Of course you are. The singing bird. How are you?'

'I'm fine. On my way to Dacca to study history.'

'Excellent. What would you say a historian's first duty is?'

'I'm not sure yet.'

'Sacrilege and mocking false gods. They are his indispensable instruments for establishing the truth. The same as journalists. But unfortunately my hands are tied now. I'm forced to peddle banalities and platitudes. They watch me like a hawk, and they'll close me down after this charade of an election. Even though ninety per cent of the people are against him, General Ayub will wield his magic wand and win a landslide. Who's the historian who said that the temper of soldiers, habituated to violence and slavery, renders them very unfit guardians of a legal or even a civil constitution.'

'I don't know. Perhaps, I'll be able to tell you in three years. After I finish my studies, I'm considering going into journalism.'

'Good. If you want experience, I can write to a friend in Dacca. He runs a small newspaper. If he takes you on, he'll pay you something.'

'Thank you. I need a job. My grandmother sold some of her land to support my education, but it won't be enough.'

'Remind me to write a letter for you. But it won't be easy to be a journalist with the military running the country.'

'I know. Despite everything, you are doing a good job. And the people in Mominabad read you.'

'What else can I do? I can't just do gossip and banalities. So, I have to resort to indirection and writing about foreign monsters. I've been writing about Papa Doc and his Tonton Macoutes for the last few weeks. Absolute brutes. Hopefully, people are seeing the parallel.'

'Yes, I'm sure they are. Now, to change the subject. I've just seen Scientist. I'm really worried.'

'We're worried too. He's a stubborn man. He won't let anyone look after him. But we adda-men will find a way of helping him. First, we're sending a doctor to him. He'll go there as a potential customer, to offer him a commission – to do a signboard for his surgery. Obviously, they'll get talking. And if that works, medicine and treatment will follow. Since he won't take any gifts from us, we've also lined up a few more people to go as customers and offer to pay him in advance. He might get suspicious, so we've carefully selected people clever with words and play-acting. If this works, it will keep him going until he's well enough to resume his normal trade. His brothers, unfortunately, are idiots. But his sisters love him and will do anything for him. So, don't worry. When are you leaving for Dacca?'

'Tomorrow morning.'

'I'll have the letter ready. Pick it up on your way. It's a good newspaper and my friend is a committed journalist. But like everyone else who wants to tell the truth, he's a bit frustrated.'

Feeling better about Scientist, Bulbul walked to Sanu's tea stall. Luckily, the goons hadn't turned up, and Sanu was busy serving, laughing, telling anecdotes, and bantering with his customers. They went to the restaurant next door for lunch and talked over chicken biryani.

'From now on we're on different paths. I'll always stay in Mominabad and become a mofussil man. And you, who knows where you will end up. I feel your path will take you far.'

'I don't know. Dacca scares me. I don't know anyone there.'

'Just go with the flow. Perhaps travelling is your destiny. But if you ever feel the pull for the old place, I'm always here in this Godzilla town.'

Next morning Sanu took Bulbul to the train station. On the way he picked up the letter from Abid Ali. He asked Sanu to look out for Scientist.

'I never understood the thing between you and him. We never really talked about it, did we? Yes, I'll keep an eye,' said Sanu.

As he approached Dacca, as the brown earth gave way to red, as the paddy fields were replaced by a smattering of concrete, the promise of a modern metropolis, he thought about his grandfather: he must have been scared, too, all those years ago, when he reached Calcutta for the first time.

He went to his hall of residence and was sent to a room he was to share with two other boys, who – like him – were from the provinces. On the afternoon of his seventh day, as he was sorting his books and papers – the day before his first class – he heard a knock on the door. 'Is Syed Islam Shah here?' asked the hall attendant. 'Yes, that's me,' said Bulbul. The attendant handed over a telegram; it was from Sanu the Fat. It read: *Scientist died last night. Allah bless his soul.*

CHAPTER 14

It was a long time since Bulbul had dipped into Mohan Ganguly's notebook. He had almost forgotten about it; for three years it lay wrapped in a cotton gamcha-towel in an ochre clay bowl under his bed, and although he stayed in the same dormitory, he'd changed rooms twice. Each time, he'd placed it, still wrapped, under the bed of his new room and hadn't cared to open it. Now he had finished his course and was moving out of the dormitory, he had to decide what to discard and what to keep of his belongings. He felt anxiety, if not dread, when he picked up the notebook. If a swarm of ants hadn't eaten it away, the humidity would have taken its toll. His hands trembled as he unwrapped it. His fears proved right. Humidity and insects had wreaked their havoc. Many of its pages were dry, brittle leaves, but a few from the middle remained legible.

He read a quote from the notebook: *Everyone thinks of changing the world, but no one thinks of changing himself.* Like many of Mohan Ganguly's citations, the name of its author was missing. No doubt, the author of these lines was a man with a long, unruly beard, who had meditated for many years with exasperation on the ways of young idealists. Mohan Ganguly evidently took these lines very seriously and inserted a long commentary on them.

'Strange that I should find the wisdom of a Christian aristocrat with an anarchist temper, so compelling. This is because understanding historical necessity, the truth disclosed in the impeccable logic of the dialectic, doesn't make you a worthy carrier. You need to cultivate yourself for that – a path no less arduous than a sadhu's long lotus days in a dark, damp and solitary cave up in the Himalayas. It is sad to see so many comrades who are able to make perceptive analyses of history, its social, economic and political processes, and have dedicated their lives to militant struggle, and yet, given the slightest opportunity, are capable of unsavoury passions and action. They let their egos get the better of them, get drunk on the merest whiff of power – even as a local committee secretary. They eye female comrades with lust, and feel no compassion for the destitute, the lumpen ones, just despise them for their lack of consciousness in not rising up against their oppressors. Convinced by the cold logic of historical necessity, they are willing to sacrifice so many lives, as if individual suffering does not matter on the march to reach the goal of history. Draped in the aura of science, this most savage utilitarian thinking can only lead us to hell. Their arrogance and self-righteousness are the most damaging of all. Because they have mastered dialectical thinking and can subject the ruling classes to minute scrutiny and criticism, they feel they have, by this very fact, turned themselves into good men. So, they feel free to commit self-serving acts that benefit themselves and their families, license themselves to be greedy and corrupt, and yet feel holier than thou. So, changing oneself through arduous and daily practice, and keeping oneself under constant vigilance is necessary to keep the impulses of ego and arrogance at bay, and instil the virtue of humility deep in one's guts. If you don't feel compassion for others, as if their hunger is your own, and are not prepared to die their death, you are not a revolutionary. I felt the calling of a revolutionary life in my teens, and along with a scientific understanding of the world, and acting to change it, I have been trying to change myself to be worthy of it. It's a constant battle. I'm afraid I fail often, and my ego takes the reins of my life, giving vent to all kinds of monstrous passions. Sometimes, I get carried away with the feeling that I am the esteemed leader of the dispossessed who ought to listen to me for their own good, that, somehow, I am superior to them because they live oblivious to the real conditions of their existence, while I not only discovered the hidden truth of our lives but live by it. Oh, the delicious arrogance of living in truth.

If ever your eyes fall on these pages, my young comrade, and if you want to embrace revolutionary ideals, begin by cultivating a self worthy of it, otherwise you will only be breeding a monster.'

After reading these lines, Bulbul felt that if Mohan Ganguly had known the course of his life since he started at university, he would have been very disappointed with him. His commitment to revolutionary ideals was perfunctory; he had never joined the Party, only orbited its periphery as a casual fellow-traveller. And he had hardly cultivated the self that Mohan Ganguly had in mind as a proper bearer of revolutionary values. His was a dilettante affiliation, a casual, aesthetic attachment to an offbeat existence, a free-floating bohemian life. Recently, he had become disenchanted with the Party and thought of severing all connection with it. When he raised the issue of the recent Prague Spring, the labour camps in Siberia, his friends in the Party dismissed his concerns as Western claptrap. 'You're nothing but an ass-licker of the imperialists, a bourgeois liberal,' said one young man, 'a hedonist individualist. Come the revolution, you'll be heading for the Gulag.'

'The gulag is in Russia, Comrade,' said Bulbul.

'Don't be a smart alec. Wherever, it will be the place of your worst nightmares.'

'Thank you, Comrade. For not sending me to be shot.'

By the time his friend Noor Azad turned up to help him, Bulbul had packed his bags and was ready for the move. They had rented a small flat in old Dacca; Noor Azad had already moved in. They had met about three years ago, in his first week at the university, when Noor Azad was a promising new voice on the poetry scene. While Bulbul continued his studies, Noor Azad dropped out to pursue his poetic ambitions. He opened a small tea stall in the old town to earn a living and this soon became a meeting place for poets, novelists, painters, student activists, cultural liberals, leftists and journalists. It was one of the few places in Dacca where women felt welcome, and several had walked in. It had no name, but the clientele started to call it Sweet Canteen, and the name stuck. On Thursday evenings, it held poetry/novel/short story readings, discussion of art-house films, new books, paintings, and ideas – which, despite the military regime's professed liberalisation, still needed to be managed with extreme caution.

When Noor Azad agreed to hold a discussion on Marx's *Capital*, the event was advertised as 'Musings of an old Jew on the mysteries of money'. This was a talk to be given by Professor Abul Kalam Gyani – a renowned but abstruse scholar. Dula Raihan, the young undercover agent who attended Sweet Canteen in the guise of a film buff and a painter, was intrigued and terrified.

Dula Raihan was scarcely undercover. Soon after he started to frequent Sweet Canteen his cover was blown. He claimed to know the art-house films of Satyajit Ray and Ritwik Ghatak but fell far short of the knowledge expected of a cineaste. When asked about Satyajit Ray's relationship with Jean Renoir and the influence of Italian neo-realism on *Pather Panchali*, he looked wide-eyed, as if he hadn't the faintest clue. When asked by a woman habitué about the role of Durga in *Pather Panchali*, all he could say was, 'Ray had an eye for girls. Durga is so pretty, oh her large dark eyes, I feel sad for her. Couldn't stop crying.' The woman said, 'Yes, yes, it's a weepy. But comrade, what about Durga's social position? What does it tell us about the role of girls and women in our society?' He could only scratch his chin and say, 'She's a good girl, Durga.' The woman rolled her eyes.

Months had gone by and no one had seen any paintings by Dula Raihan. He would say he was working on 'something very serious. Experimental too.' Soon the regulars would ask him how his serious work was progressing. 'Yes, yes. Very serious. You can't rush it,' he would say. When he felt he had to give some clues about the nature of his very serious piece of work, he said, 'Let's say it's about women from the disreputable parts of town. It's not that I frequent these places of infamy, but someone has to tell their stories. After all, an artist has a social responsibility, hasn't he? I take it very seriously. Yes, I do. You must be very experimental on a subject like this and look for new ways of depicting figures. Pretty faces won't do anymore. So, my figures will have harsh, fierce faces – everything angular, broken up, and made to float on a flat surface.'

One of the regulars gave a chuckle, lit his cigarette, and said, 'Oh the repetition of the same – the mark of a true genius. I bet yours will surpass *Les Demoiselles d'Avignon*.'

Dula Raihan lowered his eyes, then stuttered: 'What's that?'

Even before this incident, convinced he was a spy, the regulars implored Noor Azad to kick the dirty rat out; they didn't feel safe with him around. Noor Azad told Dula Raihan that he had to follow his clientele's wishes. 'Sorry. I have to ask you not to come back again.'

'I admit I'm no film buff or a painter. But I want to better myself. Educate my mind in your company,' he said.

'If this were your sole motivation, everyone would welcome you, but we have reliable evidence that your intentions are far from honourable.'

'I might not be as highly educated as your friends, but I'm honourable. I've never ogled your women clients, let alone solicited their attention. I've always lowered my eyes when addressing them.'

'Of course, you're a gentleman in this regard. But let's not beat about the bush. You are a spy. Listening in on our conversations on behalf of the government.'

Feeling that it would be useless to deny the charges, Dula Raihan begged Noor Azad to be allowed to stay because he needed this job to support his disabled sister and elderly parents. They were just about clinging to life in their ancestral village. He promised to report back to his superiors in ways that suited the canteen's clientele. After a long discussion with the regulars, it was decided that Dula Raihan could stay, but someone would brief him and review his reports. Noor Azad asked Bulbul to take on that task.

A few days before Professor Gyani's talk on *Capital*, Dula Raihan bought Bulbul a cup of tea and said, 'Last time I heard Professor Gyani, he was so bombastic I didn't understand a single word. All I could write was that his thoughts are high, so high one needs a jinn's assistance to understand him.'

'You're not alone. We all have difficulties understanding him. For the professor, the ivory tower is not high enough. He needs a garret above it. Anyway, what can I do for you?' asked Bulbul.

'This talk by the professor on the old Jew and money. I fear I won't understand a word to make a readable report. This time my superiors might not give me another chance. Would you help me write a summary of his speech? You know, in simple language.'

'Alright. Let's begin with the title. What does it tell you?'

'Yes, there was an old Jew in our neighbourhood's annual play. I think he was called Shylock. He's a shifty-looking fellow and laughs funny. At night, he goes out, dining on human flesh – pounds and pounds of it. Then he empties his bowels, shitting money. Piles of it. You burn it, but it doesn't perish. Instead, like a monster, more of it appears. A mountain of money. Then, the money copulates with itself and begets more money. The old Jew laughs funny and dances around his mountain of money. He calls money his father, then his god. He sings: *God begets god, money begets money; how I love money, you're more beauteous than the seventy-two houris in heaven*. He then sits down to shit money, so much of it that he's suffocated under it. He dies singing *Money-god is taking me home, thank you god*.'

'That's the weirdest production of *Merchant of Venice*. I haven't heard anything more bizarre. It's anti-Semitic shit too, but it gets the money just about right,' said Bulbul.

'Now help me please. Tell me what to write about the professor's talk.'

'As you said, the professor is bombastic. He'll ramble on how the old Jew, a master-blaster in the art of Kabbalah, has a rare insight into the secret of things. He will recite mantras like abstract value, commodity fetishism and sublime object of desire as an open sesame to the old Jew's portal of knowledge, which is supposed to reflect the hidden structure of the world. About the money, I've no more to add. Your description of your neighbourhood play sums up the professor's view. Only that the professor will use bombastic language and jargon, which very few will be able to follow.'

When he read Dula Raihan's report, his superior said, 'We don't pay you to write utter gibberish and nonsense. We know that Professor Gyani is an ungodly type and a pukka subversive. Hundred per cent commie-wallah. The man even smells of vodka. But your report is useless in establishing the man's guilt.'

Soon afterwards he lost his job.

Noor Azad took pity on him and appointed him as Sweet Canteen's caretaker and manager. When Bulbul, accompanied by Noor Azad, arrived at their new flat, Dula Raihan opened the door and helped bring his things in.

'Bulbul Bhai, welcome to your new home and new life.'

During his university studies, on Abid Ali's recommendation, Bulbul had worked part-time for *The News*. He started as a general hand around the office, making tea, running errands, then copy-editing, and finally working as a reporter who wrote occasional feature articles. *The News* was connected with the Communist Party, and because Bulbul had become increasingly at odds with the party line, his position became untenable. However, with his first-class honours degree in History, his three years of work experience at *The News*, and the network of connections he had established, he found a new job as a staff journalist at *The People's Voice*, a left/liberal newspaper not connected to any political party. It had the largest circulation among the English-language newspapers in the country.

His and Noor Azad's working days were very different. Bulbul would get up early while Noor Azad was still deep in sleep. On his way to work, he would stop by Sweet Canteen, just a block away, for breakfast. Dula Raihan would bring him tea and they would chat. Dula Raihan would often ask him to recommend a book or a film. He had studied sciences up to higher secondary, then joined the police force, from where he was recruited to the snooping job. 'Bulbul Bhai, I don't want to be an intellectual,' he would say, 'I want to know enough. To get the drift of what you lot talk about.'

'Can you read English?' asked Bulbul.

'Not well enough to read a serious book. I can just about manage a newspaper.'

'Unfortunately, many of the books you should read are not translated. Especially books on ideas. Even in the autumn of 1968, we don't have a translation of *Das Kapital*. Or Darwin's *On the Origin of Species*. Anyway, there are enough books in Bengali to get you going.'

Bulbul's editor at *The People's Voice* was Munir Mahmud. He was tall and fat but had a small head and face, with no discernible neck. He never laughed but squinted when he spoke. He came from a landowning family; his father had been a civil servant for the British, then for Pakistan after partition; when he retired founded *The People's Voice* to represent the values of the liberal, westernised elite. When Munir Mahmud, educated at LSE in

England, took over after his father, he wanted to give the paper an investigative edge, so he recruited journalists whom he judged up to this task – many of whom happened to be on the left.

'I want you to track the student movement,' he told Bulbul. 'It'll be of great interest to our readers. You can do daily updates, then perhaps a weekly column. How does that sound to you?'

'Sounds good to me. Students are at the forefront. Things are building up for an eruption.'

'Yes. I want you to keep abreast of what's happening elsewhere, too, especially in France and the USA. We keep foreign newspapers and journals in our library, as well as the latest books on many subjects. You know, book collecting is one of my passions. Anyway, have a look. They might help you.'

'I'll do my best, Boss,' said Bulbul.

'I don't like this boss business. I'm a man of enlightenment and democratic values. I prefer to be called Munir. But if you feel uncomfortable with that, call me editor.'

'I'll start off with editor.'

'Right, that's settled then. Before you get out in the field, take a few days to get to know the office and your colleagues. Exciting times ahead. The world is in flux, and we'll record its twists and turns. In the future, people will consult our back-copies for a veritable map of the world. Good to have you on board.'

On the way back from the office, Bulbul stopped at Sweet Canteen. He would spend most evenings there and go to the flat only to sleep. He and Noor Azad had decided not to bother with cooking and have their meals at Sweet Canteen. Apart from tea and sweet milk, Sweet Canteen served only snacks like samosas, lentil pakoras, shingaras, puchkas and dal puri but no meals for their customers. The cook, though, cooked for himself, Dula Raihan, and the two young boys who helped him in the kitchen and at the front. All four lived in the shed attached to Sweet Canteen. Noor Azad asked the cook if he and Bulbul could join them.

'For ourselves, we cook poor people's food. Mostly dry fish and coarse rice – with a lot of hot chillies. That might not suit intellectual gentlemen like yourselves,' said the cook.

'We like hot and simple food. Apart from the cost of the food, I'll pay you a bit extra,' said Noor Azad.

When Bulbul arrived, Dula Raihan was at the cashier's desk.

'Bulbul Bhai, how is your new office?'

'Good. It's much busier than my last. The editor – you'd think him a funny guy by looking at him, but he's very serious. He wants to make a new map of the world.'

'A newspaper making maps. I don't get it. Anyway, if he's fair, straight-talking, and not two-faced, that's all you need in a boss.'

'It's too early to say. But he doesn't want me to call him boss.'

'He's a modern type then.'

Bulbul found Noor Azad in a corner at the back of the canteen, where he usually sat to write poems, though on busy evenings he would be at the front, helping the staff.

Bulbul told him about his new boss and the assignment. Noor Azad spoke of his current poetic project. What fascinated him was speed, noisy machines and their ferocious sculpting of a new city. At the heart of this dreadful place, he would locate the poet, a lost, solitary soul on its crowded streets, among its oozing detritus and stench, cut-throats and whores, all manner of low-lives and down-and-outs loitering in the dark. His poet would be a shipwrecked sailor given to games of chance. He might stumble on a raindrop in the course of his aimless wanderings, perhaps caught between slabs on the pavement. He would look at it as if it was a strange, pulsating thing. He would let himself be dragged down by the monster that lurked deep inside it, then surface with an image that would disclose, layer by layer, its elusive essence. He would sing the nameless world into being as the first ancestor poets had done.

'I know, I know. You'll tell me it's all crap. Pseudo-modernism in a sleeping village,' said Noor Azad.

'You said it. You're too good a poet to waste your talent on a Parisian fantasy, and the symbolist aristocracy will always see you as a poor mimic,' said Bulbul.

'Perhaps they will. But it's not a fantasy. I feel I ought to be lost and alienated in a modern metropolis. Wander to map its underbelly. Find new symbols, rhythms and musicality for it.'

'Look around. You're in bloody Dacca. It's still a sleepy village.'

'Perhaps. But shouldn't I stay true to my feelings?'

'You've lost me there. I thought you were a modernist and not a romantic.'

'Maybe I should go to Paris and be doubly alienated – by that machine-age metropolis and by being a migrant outsider. Like Fanon's Negro in Marseille. To be shitted upon and lynched. My objective condition would match my poetic urges. What do you say to that?'

'The pleasures of exile. It's another aesthetic fantasy. You should open your eyes to your living conditions and write about that – as you did when you started. Your poetry was so vital then. It inspired a generation. You can't wilfully alienate yourself when you are not. We're in the midst of an explosion. Students are on the streets. The masses are slowly joining them. Big changes are coming.'

'You're still a communist at heart. I'm not writing some Stalinist social realist shit. No way.'

'I'm not asking you to. I admit you can learn from your Parisian guys, as we've learnt from Brecht. New ways of looking at things. New forms, new techniques. You could be like a Pablo Neruda or Aimé Césaire.'

'I don't know,' said Noor Azad, and he got up to help in the canteen where the regulars had already settled down to their adda session. Resisting the temptation to join them, Bulbul stayed where he was. He wanted to get on with reading about the student movements raging across the globe.

When the customers left at about ten, the cook called everyone to a supper of dry fish shutki and watery dal, the same meal he had been making for two weeks.

'Cook, your shutki is topnotch. Super hot and fiercely stinky. Amrita for the poets. And the dal is runny enough to be the sister of Ma Ganga. Together? What can I say? Even a poet is lost for words. But, as they say, even the most delicious things must be consumed in moderation. After a two-week run, perhaps you should give it a break. Let's eat something else for a change. That way, we can return to your excellent shutki and runny dal and appreciate them even more. What do you say to that?' said Noor Azad.

'I cooked them because I thought you liked them,' said the cook.

'I like them very much. All I'm saying is that after a break I will like them even more.'

'If you like, I'll cook aloo-vorta and thick bhuna dal tomorrow.'

'I'm enjoying shutki and runny dal even though atomic-chilli-bombs are exploding in my guts,' said Bulbul.

'Because it's your first time. Let's see how you feel after a two-week run,' said Dula Raihan.

'I don't cook the same thing for two weeks, do I?'

'Yes, cook, you do,' said Dula Raihan.

'It might look and taste the same to you. But each time I cook something different; the runny dal of yesterday is not the same as today's. I was missing my children yesterday. Today, I'm happy.'

'Oh, dear me, even you're turning into a high-thinking type. Well, I suppose it's the philosophical air of the Canteen. Anyway, your subtleties are lost on me. If you'd kindly cook something that looks different and tastes different – say, the difference between a hot goat curry and a spinach bhaji – we would appreciate that very much,' said Dula Raihan.

'No problem.'

'Thank you, cook. You're the best. A poet among cooks,' said Noor Azad.

After the meal, Bulbul and Noor Azad returned to their flat. Noor Azad opened a bottle of whisky.

'To us,' he said. 'We'll storm the city with our words.'

CHAPTER 15

The flooding had been severe and Dambarpur was barely afloat above the water. Dadu was poorly and in bed, and Kona Das came to receive Bulbul by the hijal tree at the edge of the raised compound, where the boat dropped him.

'Bulbul Da, how are you?'

'I'm fine. You?'

'Time passing. We're getting old.'

Bulbul looked at her and saw that it was true, despite her being only about thirty.

'Yes, time's passing. Sorry, I couldn't come before. After my final exam, I had to get a new job, and a place to live. Nothing is easy in Dacca.'

'Dadu is so proud that you're a B.A. and a big officer.'

'I've got a B.A. degree, but I'm not an officer. Do I look like someone who works for the government?'

'No. With your beard, you look more like a fakir. Bibi won't like it.'

'Do you like it?'

'No. People will think you smoke ganja and wander about. You're a B.A. You should look like a proper gentleman.'

'I don't like gentlemen from the city or the country. We're better off without them.'

'So, it's true. You have turned a communist.'

'No. But I like some of the ideas they believe in. Like everyone should be equal.'

'Equal? I'm not equal to you, and never can be. It's just a fancy idea.'

'That's true. But it can be a reality if we all fight for it.'

'I don't know. Anyway, I hope you're not into ungodly ways. If you are, you could do all kinds of bad things and not feel anything. You wouldn't know right from wrong.'

'You got it wrong, Kona Boo. You can be a good man without god.'

'Can you? I'm not sure.'

After dropping his bag in the outer bungalow, Bulbul went to Dadu. She sat on the bed, waiting for him with palm bread and thick, sugary milk.

'Why are you keeping a beard like a fakir? You'll never get a proper job,' she said.

'I don't need a proper job. I'm a journalist.'

'Journalist? Does it pay well?'

'Enough to get by.'

'With your B.A., you shouldn't just be getting by. You should be aiming to ride a car.'

'I don't need a car. Anyway, how are you, Dadu?'

'My body is quarrelling with me all the time. Very nasty. I wish I could get rid of it soon.'

'You should come to Dacca with me to see a doctor. He'll fix you in no time.'

'I'm not going anywhere. And I don't need a doctor. My body

is very stubborn, but it's beginning to listen to me. It'll leave me alone soon and be gone. Enough of this talk. Have some palm bread and sweet milk.'

Bulbul went back to the outer bungalow; if anywhere felt like a room of his own, it was here. He sat on the recliner and looked out of the window. Just a few yards from the bungalow, from the edge of the compound mound, there was water as far as the eye could see. Scattered trees, their trunks half submerged, were giving their shapes to the water. Suddenly, a slight wind rippled the surface, breaking the shadows, but it passed as quickly as it came, and stillness returned. He was finding it difficult to keep his eyes open and if it hadn't been for Kona Das, who came in with a glass of papaya sorbet, he would have drifted into sleep. While he drank, she stood behind him and gave a little cough.

'Bulbul Da,' she said.

'What is it, Kona Boo?'

'Do you remember Teeny Mullah?'

'That idiot. I'll kill him if I see him again.'

'Bulbul Da, don't be too harsh on him. He's not a bad man.'

'Why are you sticking up for him? He nearly got you killed. Damn, no-good mullah.'

'It was my fault, too. My head wasn't working. I had the funny idea that the two of us could get together. Just he and me as Bhagwan had made us.'

'You're better off without that idiot.'

She told him that after escaping that terrible night, Teeny Mullah had gone back to his home village by the coast in the south. There he made a living by giving private Koranic lessons and was made the assistant to the imam; he was doing well, and there was even a talk among the village elders that one day he, so meek and obliging, would take over as the imam.

'Bulbul Da, I know he's spineless and cowardly, but he's true to his faith and vocation. Being a mullah was all he ever wanted. How could he risk it all by marrying someone like me?'

But he wasn't happy there. He needed a wife, the elders said, and his sister found the right girl for him, not pretty but pious and dutiful, and everything was arranged, but he was getting more and more miserable.

'He said he was foolish to have lost me. But what could we have done? Everything was against us.'

'He wanted to marry you, didn't he?'

'Yes, but I had to convert.'

'Why didn't you then?'

'I can't explain it. I just couldn't do it. I know that being an untouchable, I had nothing to lose. Maybe in my foolishness I wanted him to come to me just as I am. Maybe happiness is not for me, Bulbul Da.'

'What's the point of opening old wounds again? Forget him.'

'I wish I could. Have you heard anything about us?'

'No.'

'He was here. He came to see me.'

'What?'

'He said he would die if he didn't see me.'

'I see. How did he know where to find you?'

'It was easy. He went to Mominabad. Your friend – what's his name, the fat one? He told him to look for me in Dambarpur.'

'Sanu the Fat. Big mouth. He can't keep anything quiet.'

'I'm glad he told him where I am. He left his village in the south, got on his bike and rode and rode. He collapsed in a market, more than a hundred miles away. A travelling tailor found him and offered to be his master, and together they travelled from market to market sewing lungies, making skull caps and mending punjabis and shirts. Eventually, he learned enough of the craft to set off on his own. He put his sewing machine behind his bike, and went from market to market, sewing his way to Mominabad, then to here. At first, he didn't dare approach the house; he sat under the kapok tree. Bibi sent Matab Ali to chase him away, but he wouldn't go. So then she fed the village boys with rice bread and coconut cream and asked them to taunt him and harry him a bit. That cursed mullah is a devil-sent botheration, she said, send him packing to his god-forsaken-nether-land. The boys used vicious words on him, but failing to make him go, they took all his clothes off. He sat under the kapok tree naked. Then the boys put leeches on his privy parts, but he didn't make any sound, just sat there in the rain, under the sun, through the nights among the jackals. All he wanted was to see me. He was hardly breathing.

The vultures were gathering in the kapok trees, biding their time for his dead flesh. It was then that Bibi said she didn't want him to die here. She sent me to him with a glass of water and a lump of hard sugar.'

'What an idiot. What did he want?'

'As I said, he wanted to see me.'

'Did he leave after seeing you?'

'He didn't go too far. He lives in a village market shed and does tailoring there.'

'Do you see each other then?'

'Yes. You know Bibi has her funny ways, but she let us.'

'I know her ways,' said Bulbul.

'She was worried that we'd end up in hell. As an untouchable, hell has always been my destination, so it didn't bother me much. But poor Teeny – he worries about it all the time. He prays and prays to make up for his sins. But what are we to do with our bodies? Why has Bhagwan made us like this?'

'Kona Boo, I'm happy you've found each other. And don't let heaven and hell nonsense spoil it for you. They're just shackles to keep us in line.'

'Bulbul Da, you're a scholar and a B.A. It's all very well for you to say these things. But us poor people, our mouths will rot if we say half the things you say.'

When Kona Das left, Bulbul, still on the recliner, looked out as the shadows of the trees lengthened on the water. He thought about Kona Das and Teeny Mullah, about the strange feeling between them that some call love, which made them risk the passage to hell. At twenty-two, he had yet to experience any of it. All he had were bodily sensations, urges, and sometimes vivid dreams that left him wet and exhausted, but other bodies and other minds were still foreign to him.

He wasn't sure what it was, a moving blob in the distance, beyond the half-submerged trees. As it came closer, Bulbul realised it was a small dinghy. It broke through the shadows and reached the raised compound. A small figure got off, tied the dinghy to the hijal tree, and headed towards the outer bungalow. He was carrying two ducks in one hand, and a bundle in the other. When the man came within a yard of the bungalow, Bulbul realised it was Teeny

Mullah. He looked very different without his beard, skullcap, and long, flowing punjabi. He seemed to have shed the flesh that gave him a certain volume and substance. He knocked on the door and came in. He tried to smile but conveyed only fear and sadness.

'I heard you were at home. I'm here to pay my respects.' He offered Bulbul the two ducks and a newly sewn lungi. 'I trapped these ducks in the haor. I'm a tailor now. The lungi is my work.'

'You shouldn't have brought them,' said Bulbul.

'You're a B.A and a scholar now. I haven't much with which to pay my respects to you.'

While Bulbul stayed on the recliner, looking at the darkening water, Teeny Mullah squatted on the floor. Minutes ticked by in awkward silence. At last, Bulbul asked, 'Can you still eat twenty full meals in one afternoon?'

'I haven't been a mullah for some time. Such things require a lot of practice.'

'Of course. Now that you're no longer a mullah, you should open your eyes to new ways of seeing things.'

'What do you mean?'

'For instance, some people believe, based on scientific enquiry and reason…'

'Scientists are too proud. Mischief makers and sowers of confusion,' Teeny Mullah interrupted.

'First, hear what they have to say.'

'Please don't let me hear anything bad. I'm already drowning in sin.'

'You must hear many sides of an argument, then judge it yourself. Use the reasoning power that Allah gave you.'

'Yes, Allah. He made us from clay and gave us the wisdom to do the right thing.'

'What would you say if I told you that there is very solid and reliable evidence that we evolved slowly and that at some stage our ancestors were monkeys?'

'Tawba, tawba. Ya Allah, forgive me for listening to such sin-talk.' Teeny Mullah ran out, pressing his ears. After a while, he returned and asked Bulbul if he could pray in the bungalow. Bulbul said yes. Teeny Mullah sobbed like a baby as he prayed but seemed calm when he had finished.

'Let us go inside and see Dadu,' said Bulbul.

Dadu was pleased. 'Nice ducks. Go and slaughter them. My grandson hasn't eaten anything decent since he came.'

Teeny Mullah ran out with the ducks. When he came back with their throats cut, Dadu said, 'Don't just stand like an idiot. Be useful. Go and help Kona pluck them.'

Bulbul sat by Dadu on the bed and began massaging her feet.

'My little bird, no-one looks after me. Kona and Teeny,' she beckoned Bulbul to lower his ear to her mouth, 'they're in league with the devil. Busy accumulating bags full of sin. Sure candidates for hell.'

After cleaning and cutting the ducks, Kona Das came to see Dadu for instruction about what spices to use and how she should cook them.

'Don't use any ghee. Ducks are already fat. Just use mustard oil. And bring us some fried puffed rice before you begin. Don't forget to put plenty of green chilli. My little bird likes it that way.'

After he'd served the puffed rice, Teeny Mullah stood leaning against the door.

'Don't just stand around. Go and check on the chickens in the coop. Nasty jackals have been prowling around,' said Dadu. When he left, Dadu sighed and said in a low voice, 'The things I do for those two. They will drag me to hell with them.'

'What have you done, Dadu?'

'Don't be nosy. Tell me stories.'

Teeny Mullah returned and took over from Bulbul, massaging Dadu's feet.

'You're the storyteller. I came all the way from Dacca to listen to your stories.'

'I've no more stories left in me. Besides, now that you're a B.A. and a journalist, you don't want to listen to my silly stories. What do you write in the newspaper?'

'So far nothing significant. Just small reports around the city. Human interest stories. Now I've got a job as a proper journalist, things are heating up in Dacca. The students want democracy and a fair deal for East Pakistan. I'll be writing their stories.'

'General Ayub Khan and his governor won't like it. They are very nasty. Very vengeful. So, be careful.'

'Yes, Dadu. I'm always careful.'

'I hear you turned communist. You even look communist.'

'Do I, Dadu? I don't care for any labels. I believe in democracy and equality, and that we mustn't judge things by supernatural mumbo-jumbo but in the clear light of reason.'

'This clear-light-of-reason thing is pure botheration. It only breeds confusion. So, drop these ideas. I think it's about time you started a family.'

'Family? What do you mean?'

'I'm thinking of looking for a wife for you. And don't you think me a backward type. I'll look for the kind of girl you might want. If you want a clear-light-of-reasoning modern type, I'll find her.'

'I'm not ready for it yet, Dadu. Let me establish myself as a journalist.'

'I hope that's not just an excuse. And don't you dare go for love marriage. It's top-class botheration. You get a little spell of madness and you walk to hell like a zombie.' Dadu looked at Teeny Mullah, who lowered his eyes.

'You can fix me with an ugly old hag in a few years' time. She will be a perfect match for me,' said Bulbul, laughing.

'Not very funny. Love things are like getting carried away like a dog in heat and sniffing flesh. Very uncouth. Then you sing funny little songs to make it all smell sweet. In an arranged marriage, you go about like a bookkeeper. That was your grandfather's job before he went into the jute trade. Perfect system of reason, he used to say. You match everything: family, earnings, education, character, looks. Then happy ever after.'

Remembering the years of bitter rows between them, Bulbul wanted to say *happily ever after like you and grandfather*, but thinking that would be too cruel, he said instead, 'I thought you considered the reason thing pure botheration. Now you're using it to sell me the idea of arranged marriage. You're funny, Dadu.'

'Don't use your book learning against me. Your grandfather used it all the time. You're lucky I've retired my tongue since he died.'

'All right, Dadu. When I'm settled in my new job, you can do your bookkeeping and get me a perfectly balanced wife. Happy?'

When the ducks were cooked, Teeny Mullah helped Kona Das

set out the meal on a rattan rug on the floor. Seeing only two plates, Dadu said, 'Bring two more. We'll all be eating together today.'

Dadu was in high spirits, serving everyone. The duck curry was delicious and the thin red rice from Dadu's own land was a perfect accompaniment. Bulbul ate through several plates, but Teeny Mullah only nibbled a few grains.

'Mullah, you're getting too small and thin. Eat well. I want to see you growing a tummy paunch. Without a gut, a man is not a man,' said Dadu.

'Bibi, I'm not very hungry.'

'Nonsense. You're just having a shy attack. You're among family. Don't forget that,' and Dadu served him more rice and duck, which the mullah gobbled through as if he had been starving. After the duck and rice pudding meal, Dadu climbed onto her bed. Bulbul followed her. Kona Das, who had always slept with Dadu, now slept in the small hut beside the cowshed. 'The girl snores too much. I can't get any sleep. It's better she sleeps in the outer hut.'

'Dadu, your snoring is legendary. I can hear it from the outer bungalow. And now you blame Kona Boo. She never snores.'

'I tell you she does. And why are you becoming like your grandfather? Picking on me?'

Kona Das took her leave; Teeny Mullah stayed behind, sweeping the floor.

'It's getting late, you better get going. How long does it take to row to the village market?' asked Dadu.

'About an hour, Bibi. I'll see you tomorrow. Do you need anything from the market?'

'Bring some sugar. I want to make some sweets for Bulbul. And if you find a large rohu or catfish.'

'It's late and dark. Why don't you stay with me in the outer bungalow?' Bulbul said.

'No. It's better for the mullah to go back to his place,' said Dadu.

Bulbul went with Teeny Mullah as far as the hijal tree where the dinghy was tied. He waited until Teeny Mullah rowed into the darkness before returning to the outer bungalow to go to bed with a book. After an hour, he thought he heard a boat coming in. He saw someone get off a small dinghy and tie it to the hijal tree.

It was Teeny Mullah, and he was heading towards the small hut next to the cowshed.

The following morning, Kona Das brought him breakfast in the outer bungalow. Dadu was lying in because she wasn't feeling well. After breakfast, Bulbul was resting on the recliner, smoking a cigarette. When he heard a knock on the door, he stubbed out the cigarette. It was the imam. He hadn't talked to him since that shameful episode when he played the saint and the imam his acolyte. The imam looked around warily as he entered the bungalow.

'Congratulations on your B.A.. I wanted to come and welcome you yesterday, but I'm afraid of your grandmother. She can't stand the sight of me. As if I'm Shaitan himself. Tell me, was it my fault? You wanted to be a saint, didn't you?'

'Yes, imam. Don't worry. I'll have a word with Dadu. Anyway, how have you been?'

'Very bad. We can't manage the mosque without your grand-mother's support. My children are practically starving. My wife – an imam's wife – has to husk rice for peasant families to support us. We could've made a good living if only you'd stayed a saint. Business was good, wasn't it?'

'As I said, I'll have a word with Dadu.'

'Please do. I hear you're a journalist. Does it pay well?'

'Not very much. But I like it.'

'Perhaps you can reconsider, become a saint again. Both of us would make a good living.'

'Please stop it. I don't want to hear this nonsense again.'

'Sorry. If you don't mind, I would like to raise another issue. Village people are talking, but no one dares to raise it with your grandmother. You see, she owns most of the land in the village, and the farmers rent land from her. You see their position?'

'Yes, I see it. But what is the issue you wanted to raise?'

'It's a bit delicate. Your grandmother is allowing – how can I put it? – a very immoral thing under her roof. That untouchable woman, Kona Das, and Teeny Mullah – total hell-going sinners they are. We are simple, but honest folks. Very upright morals.'

'I've seen no immoral thing going on here. For your informa-tion, both Kona Das and Teeny Mullah are a thousand times more moral than you. If I were you, I'd touch their feet for blessings. Now, if you don't mind, I've something to do.'

About midday, Teeny Mullah came back with sugar and a big rohu fish. Bulbul thought Teeny looked exhausted, probably from all the rowing he did last night – quite a feat. Despite not feeling well, Dadu was shouting out instructions to Kona Das: 'Not too much sugar in the coconut. Don't boil the syrup, just simmer it. Begin by frying the rohu fish lightly with turmeric, then make the sauce. Fenugreek to start with and coriander leaves at the end.' There was dry fish with mooli and fried bitter gourd as well. Dadu wanted Bulbul to have a memorable lunch before he left in the late afternoon.

After lunch, Dadu had the leftovers wrapped in banana leaves, enough to last Bulbul for a few days, to give him a respite from, as she put it, 'god-awful mechanical comestibles'. Before leaving, Bulbul again insisted that Dadu should come to Dacca for treatment, and she again dismissed the idea but made him promise that he would see her soon.

Teeny Mullah took Bulbul in his dinghy to the market, from where he would hitch a boat ride to the southern junction and then catch the night train to Dacca. After punting away from the shore, Teeny Mullah took to the oars and propelled the dinghy into the big haor. He cleared his throat.

'You're a B.A. and a scholar. Could you help me, please?'

'I'm not a scholar. Of course, I'll help you if I can. But what's the matter?'

'I don't see a way out.'

'Of what?'

'You see, I'm still a believer. I pray five times a day and ask for forgiveness from Allah. He's merciful, he might still forgive me. Besides, I can still go to Mecca to perform Hajj. It will cleanse me of my sins. But Kona is still untouchable, an unbeliever. She has no chance of receiving forgiveness. Her sins will always burden her boat, whatever journey she cares to make.'

'I take a different view of these things. Anyway, you're saying that, after all, you might end up in heaven and Kona Boo in hell?'

'Yes. But I don't like it. On this earth we can't be together, except in darkness. Wrapped in sinning and shaming shawls. But in eternity I want to be with her. Now you see the problem?'

'Well, the way I see things, this problem doesn't arise, but I can see that it's a tricky situation from your point of view. You two are destined for two different realms of eternity, whereas you want to be in one. You're in a pickle, aren't you? Any thoughts about how you might get out of it?'

'It hasn't been easy to talk to you about this. Much too shaming. But I put myself through it because I wanted your counsel on it. You're a B.A. and read many books. I believe you can suggest a prudent solution. I can't imagine any other way but only this.'

'Thanks for your confidence. I've some knowledge, but I can't say I'm wise. They are two entirely different things. Anyway, let's hear your way.'

'I want to kill myself.'

'What? Are you serious?'

'Yes, I am. It's the only way. You see, if I kill myself, I'm bound to end up in hell. And Kona is destined to be there. We'll burn in hellfire for eternity, but together.'

Bulbul shook his head but didn't say anything; he dipped his hand in the water and looked up to watch a line of wild ducks flapping their way through the mingling of orange and purple.

'That's just daft. If you want to go to hell, there are better ways.'

'How?'

'Just stop thinking about heaven and hell. Send the damn lot to hell.'

'What do you mean?'

'You know what I mean. Stop praying, stop asking for forgiveness. Stop thinking of going to Mecca. Multiply your sins. Rejoice in them. That way you can have a sure passage to hell, and in the bargain, you'll get to enjoy life here on earth.'

'But I'm still a believer. Allah, in his boundless mercy, might still send me to heaven.'

'Well, he might. But you know what to do, don't you?'

'No.'

'Just kill him.'

'Tawba, tawba. How can you even say that? It's the sin of sin. Boundless sin. Even Shaitan doesn't dare that.'

'It's your choice. Reading books led me on a journey to the end

196

of things or, rather, to the beginning. It's like rowing a dinghy like this one, on a haor like this, then on the rivers, across the seas and the oceans, on and on until you come back here, on this hoar, only to begin all over again, yet you are not riding the same water twice. So much to be done and explored, yet there is nothing to find, nothing to discover, no one to create you, no one to command you, forgive you. There's nothing but this endless journey and the hymns to fire. That's all there is,' said Bulbul.

'You're a B.A. and that's all you can say. Nothing? May Allah have mercy on your soul.'

CHAPTER 16

Spearheaded by the students, the popular discontent reached a boiling point by the beginning of 1969. If he hadn't been a journalist, reduced to being a pair of watching eyes, Bulbul would have plunged into the fray. He had been tracking the mood among the students, their restlessness, their gatherings under the banyan. Under its circular canopy, throwing caution to the wind, they were venting their passion for the coming insurrection. If freedom demanded blood, they were willing to give it in bucket-loads.

Back from Dambarpur, Bulbul was into the swing of his job. Munir Mahmud was pleased with his work, 'Very thorough. Inspires confidence. It seems your sources are solid and reliable too,' he said, squinting.

'Thank you, Editor. I appreciate your confidence.'

'I hear something big is on the offing. When it happens, I want you to be there. An eyewitness report. Nothing added, nothing subtracted. Yes?'

'Yes, Editor. I'll do my best.'

'I don't know whether you've followed the events in the West. I'm intrigued by the students' demands to liberate desire.'

'I've heard of that, but I'm not sure what it means.'

'Anyway, have you heard our students talking in those terms?'

'No. Here, of course, they are preoccupied with universal

suffrage and democracy. Release of political prisoners. A fair deal for East Pakistan and regional autonomy.'

'Ah, we're still in thrall to the Enlightenment. Well, I suppose we must climb the tree before picking the fruits.'

After work, Bulbul popped into Sweet Canteen. Dula Raihan greeted him, 'What's the news from the world? Are we embarking on a revolution?'

'Maybe. Is the talk tonight cancelled?'

'Yes, but Noor Azad Sir said he has a last-minute replacement.'

'Who's that? And what topic?'

'I think it's a journalist.'

'Journalist? I wonder who that might be. Strange, Noor Azad didn't mention anything.'

'I think Noor Azad Sir wants to keep it a surprise.'

Asking for some dal puri and tea to be sent over, Bulbul went to his usual spot to look through notes he was making for writing his column. When Noor Azad came, Bulbul barely looked up to greet him.

'What's the matter? Are you grumpy or something?'

'Nothing. Just doing some work. By the way, who's the speaker?'

'A friend. A journalist.'

'Which newspaper? And does he have a name?'

'Don't be impatient. You'll soon see.'

Already the regulars were milling in the Canteen, ordering teas and snacks but barely hiding their disappointment over the cancelled talk, because the billed speaker – a well-known literati with a wicked sense of humour – was their favourite. Some planned to slip out before the talk began, Bulbul included. Indeed, just before the talk started, audience numbers were so depleted that Noor Azad was in a panic. Seeing Bulbul about to leave he ran after him.

'Where are you going?'

'I thought I'd go to the flat for couple of hours. Then come back for supper.'

'You're not staying for the talk then?'

'I'll give it a miss. Who is he? The speaker?'

'I told you. A journalist. A friend. Please stay. I promise you won't be disappointed.'

Reluctantly, Bulbul took his seat with five others – all men, diehard, lonely regulars who had nothing better to do. To add to Noor Azad's discomfort, the speaker was ten minutes late. He kept running to and fro between the audience and the front of the canteen, sweating profusely. There was a hushed silence when he finally walked in with the speaker. The regulars looked at each other and sat up straight and stiff, drawing their chins in.

'I'm happy to present Dipa Kaiser. You may not yet know her, but she's a radio journalist. Joined the broadcasting corporation about a year ago. She grew up just around the corner and then spent six years in France. She has a degree in anthropology. As you're well aware, it's a last-minute thing. So we're not getting a prepared lecture. It will be more of a conversation on the woman question,' said Noor Azad.

She stood up, a dark, small and thin figure, wearing a plain cotton sari, which was neither starched nor ironed. She had bob-cut hair, not styled or neatly set but loose and tousled. She gave Bulbul the impression of someone soft and vulnerable yet possessing a fierce and steely edge.

'I wish some of my sisters were here. I don't know what you make of me as I stand before you. We women feel that we have had enough of being your shadows, consigned to remain at the bottom rung of the ladder, and subjected to your condescension, not to mention the violence and the discrimination that we suffer daily. Yet, you expect us to stay calm and measure our words with decorum. Unfortunately, no, fortunately, those days of niceties, playing dutiful daughters, have gone. So, what do we do?' Dipa Kaiser paused. Seconds ticked by in awkward silence, and there was nervous shuffling in the seats. Then one of the diehards spoke.

'Miss, I don't understand what you are saying. All I can say is that you look like a fine young woman. Thanks to your parents, you were born with all the blessings of nature. I'm sure you will get a worthy husband from a reputable family with a big-earning career.'

'I don't need a husband. I don't know how to put this across to you. It seems we can't communicate in a meaningful way. I can only say that we don't want to be secondary to you. I want the eye of the law to see me and you on the same rung of the ladder.'

'We've heard of women libbers from the imperialist countries. Funny stuff like bra burning and all manners of unwomanly activities. What are your views? Do they accord with theirs?' asked another.

'When we open our mouths, you want to close them with misinformation and slander. It's your power and privilege. We're always the other, hidden in the bog-land. But many of my kind are emerging from there with our fangs ready.'

'Oh, my God, no. You don't have to be a snake. They're evil creatures. You deserve better. Let's be civilised about it. You seem like a nice and educated girl. I know some of my kind behave badly towards you, but rest assured that all here are against molesting women. It's not a gentleman's way. I know we should be more benevolent towards you. That's the gentlemanly thing to do.'

'We don't want your benevolence. Where did you get the power to dispense benevolence? Have you ever asked that question?'

'You misunderstand. I'm just trying to be nice to you. We're all progressives here. Some of us even know a thing or two about Marx and Lenin. We're very sympathetic to the causes of the oppressed. But it seems you are bent on quarrelling with us. Very unfortunate.'

'As I said, we don't yet have a common language for dialogue. If you, the esteemed audience here, are examples of progressive and enlightened views, then God help us.' Dipa Kaiser stormed out.

Hesitating a moment, Noor Azad ran after her.

The cook served fried bitter gourds and small fish chorchori and mung dal with fish head for supper that night.

'What did we do to deserve such a top-class meal?' asked Dula Raihan.

'Three cheers for the cook. I don't remember when we last tasted these dishes,' said Noor Azad.

'I fear the coming times will be tough, so, I thought we'd treat ourselves a bit.'

'Cook, I don't mind if you cook these items for the next few weeks. You can go super bombastic with your repetition,' said Dula Raihan.

Only halfway through the meal was the matter of the talk brought up. Dula Raihan said, 'I'm sorry the talk didn't go well. The journalist madam didn't look very happy.'

'Yes, it was a disaster. Our speaker was a bit cross, then she found the whole thing rather sad and amusing,' said Noor Azad.

'I hear the journalist madam spent six years in Europe. I don't understand it. Why does she still look so black?' asked the cook.

'Cook, I'm disappointed. I thought you were cleverer than that. Did you really expect her to turn white in six years?' said Noor Azad.

'Well, not completely. But I thought one's complexion softens a bit in a cold climate and looks prettier.'

'Cook, how do you do it? Even Mr Darwin would be gobsmacked. How do you accelerate time to such a mind-boggling speed? At your rate, the snorting pigs that roam the railway yard will evolve to a different level by the time you return from a visit to the latrine. Perhaps they'll engage us in philosophical conversations about the meaning of life. Anyway, despite being black. I think the journalist madam is a fine gentlewoman,' said Dula Raihan.

'Of course, she's a fine gentlewoman. Looks are not everything,' said the cook.

Back in their flat after the meal, Noor Azad said, 'I fancy a drink. Would you join me?'

'Why not', said Bulbul.

Changed into their lungies, they sat on the floor, leaning on pillows. Bulbul lit up, then Noor Azad, with his cigarette dangling between his lips, served glasses of whisky on ice.

'I wish you'd said something at the meeting,' said Noor Azad.

'Yes, I should have. It wasn't that I didn't know where she was coming from. I've been going through my editor's library. He can be annoying, but he has a fine collection, including Simone De Beauvoir. I suppose they were just ideas for me, rather abstract, but when Dipa Kaiser spoke, things came alive. Her words came to me as if from her flesh. I was too startled to open my mouth.'

'Yes, you're spot on, my friend. I felt the same. But it would've been nice for her to know someone was on her side. Against that bunch of dinosaurs.'

'You're right. We let her down. She must have felt so alone.'

Leaning back on their pillows, smoke climbing in a thin, pale dust devil, there was a tremulous silence, each alone in their thoughts. Then along came the insects, whirring their wings, and hanging in clusters in the shaft of light.

'Where I grew up in Mominabad, my room was full of geckos. They would dart their tongues and gobble up insects like these.'

Noor Azad said, 'In my village we used to catch insects like these to trap birds. Tiny little birds with blue and yellow feathers.'

'Memories make us so different. Did you eat those birds?'

'What do you mean? Of course, we ate those birds.'

Silent, drinking topped-up glasses, they drifted into their separate journeys. Now the insects circled their heads as if they wanted to slip up their noses to ride their thoughts. Nosy little devils they were.

'Dipa Kaiser. What did you think of her?' asked Noor Azad.

'She seems very spirited and intelligent. A bit intimidating.'

'You find her scary? If you knew her a bit more, you'd think differently.'

'I suppose. Anyway, how did you meet her?'

Noor Azad tried to raise himself but slipped back on the pillow. Barely able to keep his eyes open and slurring, he said, 'Damn. You do us the honour, my friend.'

His hands were unsteady, but Bulbul filled the glasses without spilling a drop.

'Dipa Kaiser. How did you meet her?'

'Oh, yes. She grew up just around the corner, the old house next to the snake temple. You know, the one with hundreds of betel-nut trees.'

'I didn't know that, but I know the house. Isn't it Ratan Kaiser's house? The sculptor? Ah, I see. She must be his daughter.'

'I'm impressed by your powers of deduction, Sherlock. He's a widower. Dipa is his only child. When they sent him to Paris for three years to serve with UNESCO, he took Dipa with him. She stayed behind to finish her studies. Now you know who she is.'

'So, are mere titbits enough to know another person? Aren't we dark continents to ourselves, let alone to others?'

'Keep it that way. Keep her darker than a dark continent.'

'Why? Why don't you want me to know her?'

'I'm in love, my friend. Dipa Kaiser stole my heart.'

Bulbul lit another cigarette. 'I see. How long has this been going on? What do you see in her?'

'Nothing is going on. I've told her nothing yet. And I've been careful around her. So, she suspects nothing. But if she could peer into my head, well, that would be another story.'

Bulbul poured what was left of the whisky. Reclining back on his pillow, he looked up at the insects. Now only a few were circling the light; most had fallen around him, dead.

'Oh, yes. What did I see in her? Let me start at the beginning. I think it was about two months ago when I saw her for the first time at the Alliance Française. You know, I go there to learn French. We didn't talk, and I didn't think much of her. I noticed only how dishevelled she looked and how briskly she moved. A week or so later, I saw her again. Still, I didn't think much of her except that she looked odd. Most of the women who come to Alliance Française are from posh and well-to-do families, super made-up and in expensive clothes. Not to mention their terrible perfumes that sear your nose and make you want to throw up. Dipa looked her usual dishevelled and brisk self. I noticed that she wasn't wearing any makeup, not even kohl on her eyes.'

'So, it wasn't a love at first sight. And you didn't find her very attractive. Maybe she just wasn't your type.'

'Don't jump to conclusions. Love's paths are mysterious. Anyway, I haven't finished answering your earlier question. Acha?'

'Go ahead. I can see that it will be a story about looking beyond appearances. Digging deep and getting to grips with her inner substance, which, no doubt, will be revealed as composed of unique and enthralling life-forces.'

'Cut your damn pseudo-philosophising. Sometimes you talk crap,' said Noor Azad.

'Sorry. Now, what were you saying?'

'Ah, the third time. It was about two weeks ago. There was a talk on Baudelaire. You know, he and T.S. Eliot are my two main men. Terrible duo, but they are the Virgil/Beatrice who can lead you to the netherland of modernism and glory in man's undoing. Anyway, the talk was given by an old professor of comparative literature at Dacca University. He knew his stuff alright, but his spoken French sounded like a frog's mating calls. Ugly and incomprehensible. To be fair to him, he did confess his shortcomings and asked Dipa to do the reading.'

'So, it's her French that revealed her secret self to you?'

'Well, it was strange. When she opened her mouth – lipstick-less – it had a certain enigma. Couldn't tell whether it was strength or vulnerability. Irony or innocent simplicity. When that mouth spat out those cursed words like *le péché*, *mendicants*, *l'Enfer*, *fleurs maladives*, *femme lubrique*, *spleen* and *ennui*, I felt I was being dragged along to the festering underbelly of a modernist metropolis. I didn't need to go to Paris or London to be undone. Here in Dacca, she bloomed a sick flower before me. And I became sufficiently alienated to be its dirt-digging modernist poet.'

'That's perverse. You wanted a modern city to glory in its misery and forced that image on her. Really sick. Anyway, what's love got to do with it?'

'Calm down. You know nothing about love. When she read those lines, I can't tell you how they hit me. You'll only get an inkling from this poor translation. *Black sorceress, the child of dark nights. My boredom came guzzling in the cavern of your eyes.* That's it, my friend. You can't say fairer than that of a love of a poet in our time. And it was Dipa. My black sorceress. How could I not be madly in love?'

'I don't get it. You're in love with the idea of a wretched city and its decadence. She's just an empty symbol. I doubt if any of it has anything to do with her. Anyway, did you tell her any of this?'

'Are you mad? I asked her what she thought of Baudelaire and she said he was a misogynist shitbag. A pure *merde*.'

'That's it? Nothing else?'

'Well, I've seen her a few more times. Said hello. Once, I think, she almost smiled. Then when our last speaker couldn't make it, I asked her if she would step in. And you know the rest.'

'So, you've never expressed your feelings to her. And she's never given you any sign either. It's like medieval courtly love. You want to be a troubadour of modern times. And she's your Dacca – the unreal city,' said Bulbul.

'Honestly, I never felt anything like this before. I never felt so strongly for anyone. My whole mind aches for her.'

'I see. You can't be in love if your body doesn't ache for her.'

'That's just Cartesian nonsense. I don't believe in that dualistic shit. Why couldn't the mind be the passion of the body?'

Drunk, they dragged themselves to bed. In the early morning hours, while Noor Azad was snoring the house down, Bulbul, feeling thirsty, got up and couldn't go back to sleep. Dipa Kaiser intrigued him, not as some abstract sign of an unreal city, but as a tremulous body that, despite its fragility, was roaring in his thoughts.

CHAPTER 17

It was still misty on his way to Sweet Canteen the following day. Instead of his usual route, he detoured by the alleyway in front of Ratan Kaiser's house and its bordering betel-nut trees. He paused, quickened his pace, and then looked back, hoping Dipa would emerge, looking for a rickshaw. He would only be too happy to help her – run to the other side of the rail tracks to fetch one. But would she think of him as some low-life creep and tell him to get lost? He was relieved to reach Sweet Canteen in double quick time.

'Was a mad dog chasing you? What's the matter?' asked Dula Raihan.

'What? Ah, just thinking that something terrible is about to happen.'

'Yes, I hear. The students are not backing down. They're ready to defy 144.'

Bulbul asked for some dal puri and tea to be sent over. Strange that he should be thinking of Dipa Kaiser when he was about to embark on this most important assignment. He'd have to put himself in the thick of the action to deliver the kind of first-hand report the editor demanded. It might get him killed, if the dice throws went against him. He was scared. Perhaps this, the fear of death, was what made him think of love. It would be terrible if he died without knowing anything of love, but why on earth had Dipa Kaiser got tangled in his thoughts? He hadn't even looked at her properly or met her gaze. If his attraction to her was triggered by something specific, like her scent, the sound of her voice, or the texture of her hair, then it would have made some sense. But none of these factors were in play. Come to think of it, his attraction to Dipa Kaiser was even more ridiculous and abstract than Noor Azad's. Was it jealousy that made him feel this way? Noor Azad was such a poser and pseudo; Dipa Kaiser would surely have nothing to do with him. No, he was the pathetic one, a mean-spirited idiot. Wanting Dipa Kaiser simply because Noor Azad wanted her? Wasn't envy the most uncouth of human passions?

Using the canteen's phone, Bulbul called Munir Mahmud for instructions. He was told not to bother coming to the office but to head straight to the university campus, especially the banyan.

'I'm counting on you,' Munir Mahmud said, 'but I fear things could turn ugly. So, take care. The story won't just be a flash in the pan, it'll run for a while. I want you to stay in one piece to take us through it. Good luck.'

Bulbul ordered another cup of tea to gather his thoughts, before setting off for the banyan. Halfway through the cup, he saw Noor Azad heading towards him.

'What made you get up so early?'

A persistent phone call had woken him; a friend in the know had advised him to stay indoors. 'He fears a bloodbath.'

'My editor fears the same. But he wants me to go out there.'

'Your editor's a fat-ass sadist. He's throwing you into the cobras' pit.'

'I want to be there. I've been preparing for this all my life.'

'You're crazy. Do you have a death wish or something?'

'Maybe. But I know I have to be there.'

'So, you want to kill yourself for your bloody boss. For duty?'

'It's not a duty. It's my calling. Like poetry is your calling. You can't just turn your face from it.'

'Ok. But promise to take care of yourself. Yes?'

'Of course, I want to stay around to see man land on the moon.'

'Oh, no. Why didn't I think of it before? Dipa, she'll be there. She has a crazy streak. She won't hesitate to jump into danger.'

'Don't worry, I'll be there. I'll make sure that she doesn't do anything crazy.'

'But she doesn't know you. I'll have to go. I see no other way.'

'So, now you want to put yourself in harm's way. For what?'

'Dipa Kaiser. She's my calling now.'

On the way to the banyan on the campus, Bulbul asked Noor

Azad if he remembered what they'd talked about last night.

'No. Nothing. We were drunk. I must have talked a lot of rubbish. If you remember any of it, forget it. I hope I didn't say anything to offend you.'

'No. You said nothing to offend me. You only talked about Dipa Kaiser.'

'Oh, how I love her. I can't stop thinking about her. She's the most amazing, most beautiful woman. She takes my breath away.'

Bulbul wanted to remind him of things he'd said about sick flowers and a black sorceress, but he only said, 'Does she?'

On the campus, they headed straight for the banyan. Many students were gathered under its large, circular canopy. More rushed towards it, displaying red and green banners and shouting slogans through homemade paper loudspeakers. Spotting Dipa Kaiser among a group of female students, Noor Azad headed towards her, and Bulbul followed. She wasn't with her soundman but talking and scribbling on a notepad. Seeing Noor Azad, she nodded her head, telling him to wait. After five minutes, she came over and asked, 'What brought you here?'

'Things might get ugly. I'm worried for you.'

'We are on the verge of an uprising. Of course, things will get ugly. I'm a journalist, I'm here to do my job. Don't forget that I was in Paris, May '68. I can take care of myself.'

'You don't know what the police are like here. They've already deployed the paramilitaries. Things will get savage. In the imperialist centres like Paris, it's spoiled students whining about free love and things like that. The police there exercise some restraint. You know, liberal democratic *tamasha*. Here, they'll shoot you.'

'You don't have to teach me about liberal democratic shit. The gendarmes there were real savages. Called me nègre, pulled my hair, beat me up. Do you want to see the marks?'

Noor Azad seemed silenced by the idea of marks on her naked skin. Rubbing his nose he said, 'You're not a negro. Why would they call you negro?'

Dipa Kaiser looked at him with an ironical twitch of her lips.

'I want you to be safe. Acha? Please, don't take any chances.'

'Yes, mama. Now go home,' said Dipa Kaiser.

'Seriously, stay safe. By the way, let me introduce my friend

Bulbul. He's a newspaperman. Staff journalist at *The People's Voice*.'

'The *People's Voice*. Your editor's a creep. Wanted to recruit me. Chauvinist pig, but it's a good liberal paper. See you around,' said Dipa Kaiser, disappearing into the crowd.

Now, dust from the feet of the students under the banyan was creating a screen as dense as the mist earlier in the day. Leaders from different factions went up to the makeshift podium to deliver rousing speeches, and the audience added their musical but apocalyptic slogans. Leaving Noor Azad, Bulbul went among the students, asking them about their demands. They spoke of their determination to break 144 and their willingness to sacrifice, if need be, their lives in a showdown with the authorities. He spotted a particularly militant faction carrying Molotov cocktails and wet cloths and buckets of water in anticipation of tear gas.

Suddenly, without anyone seeming to prompt it, a march set off and snaked onto the roads outside the campus. No policemen were in sight, and the narrow avenue, dusty and lined with leafless trees, offered an uninterrupted passage. The students, tense at first, began relaxing, their voices less strained. Moving among them, Bulbul was gathering comments when he spotted Dipa Kaiser marching among a group of female students. She looked less like a journalist than a militant in her simple, unpressed sari, worn hitched-up like a workwoman in the fields. She was not only adding her voice to the slogans but orchestrating them. He edged closer and seeing him she eased her pace to fall in with him.

'Sorry, your name slipped my mind. With all these things going on. Sorry.'

'Bulbul.'

'Ah, the singing bird. Very nice. Do you think the police will let us pass?'

It had been a while since anyone had called him that. It sounded nice, as if it came out of her mouth laced in sweet breath.

'I don't know. I doubt it. Perhaps they are waiting at the crossroads. By the way, where's your soundman?'

'Oh, I left the radio. Bloody fascists. They wanted me to portray the students as hooligans and miscreants bent on violence and destruction. So, I'm a free agent now.'

'I see. So, you are here as a demonstrator?'

'Not quite. My father has an old printing machine. Really antique. In the shed, back of our house. With some friends, we're reviving it. You know, an underground press. In a time like this, we need the full truth.'

'Sounds good. Please let me know if I can do anything.'

'I might,' Dipa said, and quickened her pace to rejoin the women students. The march turned a bend and entered a long avenue leading to the crossroads. Those at the front of the march could see the police barrier, the paramilitary trucks, and the dreaded red water-thrower. The students, their voices rising in a crescendo, locked arms and moved forwards. Then tear gas canisters came raining down. Within seconds, their eyes and faces stinging, they scattered, gasping as if drowning in a murky pond. Yet, after swilling their faces with the water they carried, and covering them with wet cloths, they regrouped and surged forward. Almost blinded, Bulbul ran to an adjacent field and slumped under a raintree. A student washed his face and gave him a wet handkerchief. He looked for Dipa Kaiser but couldn't see her. Spotting a small group on the ground, he feared the worst, and it was nearly so, for Dipa Kaiser lay there, with Noor Azad nestling her head on his lap and wiping her face with a wet cloth. She had received a direct hit from a canister. Luckily, it had only thumped her shoulder. Noor Azad, who must have been watching her from behind her group, had seen her fall.

When she opened her eyes, she wanted to get up and rejoin the surging group of students but fell back on Noor Azad's lap. Her shoulder was seriously bruised, perhaps broken.

'I'm taking you home,' said Noor Azad, his voice full of concern and care, and Dipa Kaiser didn't protest but looked at him as if she was seeing him for the first time. Bulbul wondered what she saw in him, then scolded himself that this wasn't the moment to feel like this. With the help of student volunteer medics, Noor Azad carried Dipa Kaiser to the nearby hostel. When Bulbul offered to help, Noor Azad told him to go back to the march. 'You're needed there. Go and do your duty.'

After the rain of tear gas, the police baton-charged the students, who responded by throwing stones and Molotov cocktails. Zigzagging through the mass of students, groups surging forward and others retreating, and through the pockets of fire, Bulbul reached the front. Despite the tension, his sense of duty as a journalist and his instinct for self-preservation, he couldn't help but feel upset with Noor Azad. His friend wanted him to return to the march because he didn't want him anywhere near Dipa Kaiser. Suddenly, he saw an armed policeman kneeling on the ground and taking aim. The bullet almost brushed past his shirt sleeve and hit the student next to him, blood spurting all over him. For a moment he thought he'd been shot and by the time he regained his bearings, he saw a group of students picking up the injured man and running away from the front with him. Shaking, Bulbul escaped into the nearby park and from there to the flat.

He wasn't surprised to find that Noor Azad wasn't there; he must be taking care of Dipa Kaiser and, in her vulnerability, making inroads into her soul.

It was afternoon, and he hadn't eaten anything since breakfast, but he wasn't hungry. He changed his bloodstained clothes and soaked them in a bucket, then phoned the office, and the copy editor took the report. A few minutes later Munir Mahmud phoned back. 'Was the shot deliberate? Was it point blank?'

'I can't be sure. I saw the policeman kneel and take aim. The next thing I noticed was blood spurting all over me.'

'That's good enough for me. We'll go for point blank. Sure, they wanted to kill him. A fiery leader and a lefty.'

'It's your call, Editor.'

'It must have shaken you. To see a man killed next to you. Take the afternoon off. Now things are just beginning, you'll be our man at the heart of the story.'

Feeling weary, Bulbul went to his room and locked the door. He wanted to sleep, but how could he when a man had just been killed next to him? He remembered hearing the student leader, a charismatic orator with a poetic way with words, weaving rivers and red petals into a long narrative that evoked the bittersweet romance of rebellion to incite his listeners to martyrdom. Now, he was a martyr. And he should have been there for Dipa Kaiser, but that idiot Noor Azad had wanted him out of the way. He wondered how she was feeling now – hopefully, it wasn't serious, but Noor Azad would use any excuse to impose himself as her nurse and fuss over her. Perhaps even recite some of his bloody poems to her. Bulbul tossed and turned and closed his eyes, but there was still no sleep. How not to think of Dipa Kaiser, those bloody gendarmes beating her, and the marks on her skin. If only he could trace his fingers over them, making new lines and memories. Surely then she would be inseparable from him.

In the evening, he went to Sweet Canteen. It was closed for the general customers, but regulars could knock to be let in. When Dula Raihan saw him, he said he'd been worried for him with all the shootings and tear gas. He was even more worried for Noor Azad as he couldn't find him anywhere.

'Don't you worry. He'll be fine. I'm sure he's having the time of his life somewhere.'

It wasn't until supper time that Noor Azad arrived. He looked fresh, his face flushed, with a self-satisfied grin on his lips. 'Dipa wouldn't let me go. I had to stay until her father came home. Poor thing. She's really shaken.'

'Journalist madam is an England-returned lady. She's not used to our rough ways,' said the cook.

'You mean France-returned? Anyway, journalist madam is not scared. I bet she's tougher than any of us,' said Dula Raihan.

They ate in silence until the cook said, 'What do you think? You two are learned gentlemen. Are we in a revolution now?'

'Yes,' both said together.

CHAPTER 18

The morning was cold and dull, and Bulbul, wrapped under the quilt, wanted to lie in a bit longer, but Noor Azad, at the full tilt of his lungs, summoned him out of bed.

'What's the matter? Why are you huffing and puffing and bringing the house down?'

'The big bad wolf is happy,' said Noor Azad.

'I can see that. Shall we go to the Canteen for breakfast?'

'What? No time for that. I want to be by Dipa's bedside.'

'I see, but she has her father.'

'Father is one thing. A lover is another.'

'Yesterday she was vulnerable. You took her home, and already you're claiming her heart.'

'You don't want me to be happy, do you? When something like this happens, time accelerates. Years can be condensed in the bat of an eyelid. That's the physics of love.'

'I just don't want you to make a fool of yourself. Have you talked to her?'

'I don't have to talk to her. I know it. You know what's so funny?'

'The whole thing is funny. An absolute howler.'

'You know I can't stand romantic poetry. All that lovey-dovey rhyming shit. Sickening couplets about flowers and stuff. The funny thing is I feel like writing one now.'

'So, you plan on trading your sick flower and black sorceress for a perfumed and comely maiden? You are priming yourself for a big fall.'

'Sick flower, black sorceress? Where on earth did you get these ideas? I'd have said you had a sick mind if I didn't know you. Ah, Dipa. If I fall into hell with her, we'll be together in flames of love.'

'That's a sickening metaphor.'

'I don't care. I'd rather be an idiot and an atrociously bad poet than not be in love.'

While Noor Azad headed for Dipa Kaiser's, Bulbul went to Sweet Canteen. He had to knock a while before Dula Raihan, still drowsy, opened the door for him. Since the cook was still asleep, Bulbul made tea for them.

'Bulbul Bhai, if you don't mind me asking, is Noor Azad Sir in love with the journalist madam?'

'I don't know. Perhaps he's a bit infatuated. He's such a fool. They're not compatible at all. It'll be a disaster.'

'Do you think so? I think they could be a good match. Both of them are very modern types. I don't see Noor Azad Sir settling for an arranged marriage. You can tell he's a love-marriage type.'

'Maybe. If you don't mind, I need to finish some work.'

Bulbul finished his tea, scribbled some paragraphs on his notepad, and went to the campus. Now, workers added their numbers to the student demonstrations. He saw very few police in the street. There was even talk of General Ayub Khan and his governor resigning, paving the way for elections and a return to democracy. While following the new, much bigger march of workers and students, talking to the participants and soliciting their views, Bulbul was looking for Dipa Kaiser. He knew it would take her a while to recover, but he wished she was already on her feet and among this crowd. How wonderful it would be to bump into her, walk along with her, shield her from the jostling bodies of surging protesters. Perhaps then their eyes would finally meet.

A commotion from the front of the march rippled to the middle where Bulbul was, and the scattering of the crowd confirmed that the riot police were there. Soon, he received his first water spray from the dreaded red van. It felt like a swarm of tiny little ants crawling all over his skin, stinging as they went. While he took shelter in a dry, open sewer, the crowd regrouped and ran forward, throwing stones and Molotov cocktails. The battle raged for several hours with many injured on both sides, but that day the police didn't fire live shots.

In the evening, Bulbul didn't see Noor Azad at Sweet Canteen, and he only turned up when Bulbul was already in bed in the flat. He hummed around, signalling his joyful self, then knocked on Bulbul's door, who was pretending to be asleep.

'Are you sleeping? Dipa and I, oh what can I say. Pure bliss. If I become an idiotic rhyming poet, who cares. I'm in love, my friend.'

The next day, the crowds on the streets were even bigger, and they came from all walks of life, including a sizable number of school kids who behaved as if they were on an adventure with their friends. The mood among the grownups was sombre; no one spoke about it, but the anticipation of something ominous ahead was visible in their faces. While Bulbul wove between the marchers, gathering their hopes, fears and determination, he kept an eye out for Dipa Kaiser – though if she was there, chances were that Noor Azad would be, too, sticking to her like a leech, ingratiating himself with his saccharine talk, her bloody knight in shining armour.

Long before the crossroads, the marchers met the first of the

213

police barriers. There was no announcement to disperse, but as they neared the barrier, water from the red van came showering down, but did little to deter them. Gritting their teeth, they moved forward, stoning and throwing firebombs at the police, who retreated. Then came the salvos of tear gas, but the marchers were well used to this by now and they continued forward. Bulbul spotted Noor Azad among the dodging legs of the marchers, slumped to his knees, breathing laboriously and vomiting. Bulbul hauled him up and pulled him to the back of the crowd, then to the garden of a nearby house. When his breathing became more regular, Noor Azad asked, 'Have you seen Dipa?'

'No. I thought with her injury she'd be staying home.'

'I tried, but she's stubborn. I must look for her. She'll need help.' He tried to get up, but if Bulbul hadn't caught him, he would have fallen to the ground. Leaving him to the care of the lady of the house, Bulbul returned to the march, looking for Dipa Kaiser.

It was a battle zone. Hundreds of police and paramilitary forces were baton-charging the demonstrators, who stood their ground, resisting with bricks, petrol and fire. It didn't take him long to find Dipa Kaiser; she was crouched in the dry ditch by the road. Her left hand supported by a sling, she gave succour to the fallen with her right. Seeing him, she didn't say anything but gestured with her eyes for him to get down to help a boy whose head was bleeding from a baton blow. While Bulbul held the boy's head in his hands, Dipa Kaiser pressed her handkerchief against the wound. The boy seemed about twelve, skinny, with dark smooth skin. He looked impassively at Bulbul, then closed his eyes.

'Have you seen Noor? We got separated in the chaos. I told him to stay home and write poetry, but he insisted on coming. He has the strange notion of protecting me. Sweet, but very annoying.'

'Yes, I've seen him. A bit affected by the gas, but fine.'

'Good. By the way, you're doing a good job. I'm surprised that your editor – he's such a lecher – is allowing you to tell the truth. You write with such passion. And beautifully too. I love reading your reports.'

Her comments took him aback. He was even more bewildered by how she looked at him. Then they heard gunfire. At first, they weren't sure what it was, but the running and falling bodies left them in no doubt that the police and the paramilitaries were firing live rounds. Panicked, the boy sprang up and took to his heels. He hadn't gone far when he was shot in the back and fell to the ground. Dipa Kaiser threw her sling away and ran to pick him up, Bulbul following. She lifted him by his shoulders, and Bulbul took his legs; the boy already felt limp as dead bodies do. They thought they must carry him to a hospital and began to run. Blood was all over their clothes, their hands and their faces. Suddenly, three baton-wielding policemen were upon them. While two policemen were beating Bulbul, the third tried to snatch the body, but Dipa Kaiser was still clutching on to the boy. She screamed as she received kicks and baton-lashings but wouldn't let go of the body. As if from nowhere, a group of young men raced up to them, and Dipa Kaiser passed them the body and they disappeared as quickly as they'd come. She still lay on the ground, not screaming but looking at the policemen with fire in her eyes, as though she would burn them alive. They left her, a blood-soaked wild woman, where she was. They dragged Bulbul to the police van and drove away.

He was thrown into a tiny cell with a common criminal at the prison. It was a dark, damp and windowless colony for marauding bedbugs and a howling harmony of mosquitoes that never stopped, even when they couldn't suck any more blood. The criminal, a thin figure with a balding head and a goatee, looked like a genial schoolteacher. He greeted Bulbul with a gentle smile; his bright eyes shone even in the gloom. 'I wish I could say welcome, but this is not a welcoming place.'

Bulbul nodded at him, sat on the corner of his bed and looked around. He was pleased to see a gecko, immobile as ever, on the wall.

'Are you a student? I'm surprised they put you with the likes of me. Political prisoners are normally housed in a separate wing. I suppose that's full with so many of you coming in now.'

'I'm not a student. I'm a journalist.'

'I see. But they don't know that. Or choose not to know.'

'They just laughed when I told them I'm a journalist.'

'All that matters is that you know who you are. Anyway, I won't bother you. You won't even know that I'm here. I sleep like a little hedgehog.'

'Thank you,' said Bulbul. 'How can you sleep with so many bedbugs and mosquitoes?'

'Easy. You have to make friends with them. Very approachable creatures they are.'

Bulbul couldn't sleep. Bedbugs and mosquitoes kept a vigil over his body like friends from hell. The criminal, true to his word, was so soundless that he didn't seem to be breathing. Thinking that perhaps he'd died, Bulbul got up to check on him. Before he could place his hand on his forehead, the criminal stirred a little and said, 'Journalist, Sir, are you fine?'

'Yes. I was worried for you.'

'Thank you, Journalist, Sir. It's very nice to be fussed over. I'm so lucky. Don't worry about me. I have this habit. From time to time, I die for a while. Then I always come back.'

'Die? Is this forked-tongue talk?'

'No, Sir. Just straight talk.'

Not sure how to take this answer, Bulbul sat down on his bed, and the criminal assumed his silence as before. A few minutes later, the criminal approached Bulbul with a mosquito net.

'You need this. Until you make friends with them. Shall I put it up for you, Sir?'

'Thank you. I'm Bulbul. What's your name?'

'Nice name, Sir. The bird still sings to me. Especially, when I die. My name? I'm Criminal, Sir.'

'We're all branded as criminals here, but what's your name?'

'I'm Criminal, Sir. That's what I am. Criminal.'

Criminal put up the mosquito net for Bulbul and returned to his bed. With the netting he was at least free of mosquitoes, and being winter it was bearable inside, almost pleasant. He felt he could sleep now but as he rolled on his side, Dipa Kaiser roared into his thoughts. What was he to do with that? He didn't need a wise councillor to tell him the best thing would be to forget her. His feelings for her had no tangible basis, except perhaps his jealousy of Noor Azad. But how could he? Despite the chaos and the horror at the demo, hadn't she, her voice calm and collected yet slightly trembling, said how much she loved to read his pieces? True, he was naïve in the language of love, but even he couldn't be mistaken about how she, with the boy's blood between them, looked at him and wanted to commune with him. Everything would have been more real if he had known the boy's name.

Over the next few days, the news from outside was that more and more people were defying the authorities and that General Ayub and his governor were tottering on their thrones. Such was the passion for vengeance, it wouldn't be enough if they just fell, people said; they should dangle from a rope tied around their necks. Oblivious to the happenings outside, the criminal, quietly as ever, was trying to make Bulbul's life as tolerable as possible. One afternoon, he brought him a papaya from the prison yard, where he had worked as a gardener.

'If you don't mind me asking. How long have you been here?'

'I don't know. Summer comes. Winter comes. Rain comes. They come and go.'

'Seriously, you don't know how long you have been here?'

'What's the point? It's just time. You can't eat time, can you? But that papaya is delicious, isn't it?'

'What are you in for? What crimes?'

'I don't know. I must have done something bad.'

'What kind of bad?' asked Bulbul.

'I don't remember. You see, bad things are not easy to remember. Maybe before I was born.'

'I'm sorry, but that's just nonsense. Anyway, have they taken you to court yet?'

'Court? I don't remember. But they're nice people. Really kind to me. They said they were looking for my papers. If they find them, they will hang me. You see, I'm a criminal.'

'Well, there's a revolution happening. We'll get you out soon.'

'I'm a criminal, I can't go out. Besides, it wouldn't be nice for the guards. They'll get in trouble.'

After a week, Noor Azad and Dipa Kaiser came to visit him. They brought parathas, aubergine bhaji, and meesty-sweet. From the moment they arrived, Bulbul could see that something was different between them – the way they looked at each other, echoed each other's words, and almost compulsively reached for each other's hands. It left him in no doubt that they were a couple in love. It was Dipa Kaiser who brought the subject up.

'It has been so intense. So many things have happened since you've been here. Noor has been by my side all along. We found each other.'

Bulbul stayed quiet for a while, looking at his nails, then he slid his index finger lengthwise along the rough, grainy surface of the table in front.

'We are so happy that we found each other. Dipa and I have so many plans,' said Noor Azad.

'Congratulations. You make a nice couple,' said Bulbul.

Seeing him lying curled up in the dark, the criminal asked him what the matter was, whether he was ill or something.

'I'm fine. We'll be out soon. General Ayub is resigning in the next few days. The prison gates will be open,' said Bulbul.

'But I'm a criminal. This is my home.'

CHAPTER 19

He was only in jail for two weeks. He came out to a different world. What seemed impossible had happened: General Ayub Khan and his governor had gone. He remembered Professor Giyani, in one of his lectures at Sweet Canteen, saying that it was easier to imagine the end of time than a time without the general.

Noor Azad and Dipa Kaiser waited for him at the prison's gate with a garland of sweet morning flowers. Dipa Kaiser lifted herself on her toes to slide it over his head. 'You're our hero. Welcome to the new time,' she said. From the prison, they went straight to Sweet Canteen, teeming with breakfasters and evening regulars who had made an appearance to welcome him. The cook laid out samosas, boras, jilabis and cups of sweet, creamy teas, free for all. People milled around, looking for an opportunity to make a beeline to Bulbul to say a few words. Professor Giyani, carrying the profundity of his thoughts in his enigmatic smile, said, 'We're at the dusk of an inglorious era. It's time, Mr Bulbul, for the owl of Minerva to spread its wings. Such are the workings of dialectics.'

'Thank you, Professor Sir. Sorry, I don't quite get it.'

'Yes, yes, what was I saying? Forget it. Anyway, young men like you are the precursors of new times,' said Professor Giyani, who then hurried out. Dula Raihan moved closer, 'Is the professor bursting your ears with his highfalutin jargon?'

'He's ok. He can't help being the language of his books.'

'Yes, the professor has gone into his books, all right. And got stuck in there. I've heard of words becoming flesh, but not flesh becoming words. Such tamasha. Bulbul Bhai, welcome back. Now that Big Brother has gone, what will we do with so much freedom?'

'I see you've been reading books. In no time you'll be speaking like Professor Giyani. Well, we must use this spell of freedom to ensure that we're free for a bit longer. Yes, freedom for begetting more freedom. Besides, a lot depends on the coming elections.'

'Now that our Leader is free, we'll surely have our autonomy and dignity back,' said Dula Raihan.

'I hope so. But the generals might have other ideas.'

He was tired, so Noor Azad and Dipa Kaiser accompanied him back to the flat. Before going for a nap, Bulbul sat in the sitting room, facing Noor Azad and Dipa Kaiser, side by side on the sofa.

'So good to have you back,' said Noor Azad, 'I've missed you.'

'My cellmate in the prison was a criminal called Criminal. He said it was good to be fussed over. Thank you for fussing over me.'

'Criminal? I hope he wasn't in for murder,' said Dipa Kaiser.

'The funny thing is, rather, the tragic thing is, he doesn't know his crime. Poor fellow, such a nice man.'

'Are you sure he wasn't pretending?' asked Noor Azad.

'I know a poser when I see one. I can name a few in my time. But he wasn't one of them.' There was an awkward silence following this exchange.

'I believe he's genuine. I've heard similar cases. People stay in jail for ages, even dying without ever being charged. Even Kafka would've found these stories hard to believe. My God, the shithole we live in,' said Dipa Kaiser.

'I don't know what it was like for you, but I would've relished being there. Untrammelled by the burdens of the world, I could've focused on my poetry. On just words that would've sung their own songs. You can't say fairer than that for a poet.'

'You turn everything into an aesthetic experience. Nothing matters to you but bloody words. And their hollowed-out shells.'

'Sorry, my friend. I didn't want to belittle your experience. I know it's not fun being in jail, especially our hell-houses.'

'Well, I was only in for two weeks. Not much suffering. Anyway, I admit prison can be a great place for writing.'

'Maybe, but very tough. I don't know how Genet managed to write *Notre-Dame-des-Fleurs* in prison. And, of course, Gramsci,' said Dipa Kaiser.

'There, you see, it's not just pure aestheticism,' said Noor Azad. 'It could be your way out, your path of escape and liberation. If you are shackled in a dungeon, how do you achieve freedom? Imagination and words, my friend.'

'Ok, got the point. But our present situation is all too real. There's no room for fantasy. The boy who was killed at the demonstration just in front of us – I don't even know his name. I don't want to make him a fantasy figure – a myth or a symbol. He was just a little boy. Perhaps his mother is dying of grief as we speak. But how do I remember him for real?'

'I remember him, Bulbul. We had his blood on us. No matter what the world makes of him, he's a real memory for us. Always.'

Noor Azad looked up with surprise, then put his head down. Time ticked by with no one daring to look up to meet the others' eyes, but Bulbul was thinking that if this memory bound Dipa Kaiser and him, and always would, what did that mean?

Dipa Kaiser broke the awkward silence. 'We have some news.'

'I hope good news,' said Bulbul.

'Excellent news. Noor and I are getting married.'

Bulbul was so stunned he couldn't make himself congratulate them.

'Dipa and I want to see each other. Be together. Our society, stuck as it is in the Middle Ages – damn customs and religious hudood – marriage is the only way.'

'Maybe, but you've known each other for such a short time.'

'As I've said before, time moves differently in the physics of love. In an arranged marriage, people don't even know each other until the night of consummation. Can you imagine the horror of that? But sometimes they work, don't they?' said Noor Azad.

'Sorry to be a spoilsport. Congratulations to both of you.'

'I want you to be my main man. Actually, we're only inviting you and a few friends. My family thinks love-marriage is a sin, so they won't have anything to do with it,' said Noor Azad.

'It would mean a lot to us, Bulbul, if you are with us on that occasion. You and my father,' said Dipa Kaiser.

'I'll be happy to be with you two. Congratulations again.'

When he returned to work, Munir Mahmud called him to his office and welcomed him with tea and meesty-sweet.

'A journalist's job at the front is a challenging one. You've served time for all of us. We're very proud of you.'

'Thank you, Editor. I was only in prison for two weeks. My cellmate didn't know how long he's been there or the crime he was accused of. Never been taken to court. Compared to him, my stay seems like a holiday.'

'Maybe. But take it as a badge of honour. It proves your mettle as a journalist. If you want, you can write a piece on your cellmate. It'll help his case. What was his name?'

'That's the thing. I don't know his name. He just called himself Criminal.'

'Maybe you can do some digging and find out. You've done a fine job. I'm thinking of putting you on the investigation team. It'll be a promotion.'

'Thank you, Editor. Investigative journalism. Challenging, but I've always wanted to do that.'

'Well, start with your criminal. I also want you to cover events leading up to the election.'

Back at Sweet Canteen, Sanu the Fat was waiting for him.

'I heard you were out of prison, so I came to see you. It's been a Godzilla time, na?'

'So good to see you, Sanu. I missed you, real Godzilla like.'

Bulbul introduced Sanu the Fat to everyone at Sweet Canteen, and he made them laugh with his stories. Sanu didn't like Noor Azad but loved Dipa Kaiser.

'He's bloody poser, a no-good peacock man, but she's pure homegrown mustard oil. Such a nice woman. She deserves better.' Bulbul bit his lips, but his look made Sanu shake his head.

'I see. You've a soft spot for that woman. You should have fought for her. Like a wild buffalo.'

'We're not rutting animals. She chose him. They are in love. I'm happy for them.'

'Singing bird, I know you. Don't give me that intellectual bullshit. Not becoming of a Godzilla. If you'd said you wanted to gore him to death, I would've believed you more.'

'Let's not talk about this anymore. Let's hear about you and Mominabad.'

'I'm fine. Finally, we are free of the goons. Everyone is out of jail. Even Mohan Ganguly. With Banu Gosh free, the adda men are back to full strength. Sometimes they meet at my tea stall. You should've been there to listen to them. They're taking the art of adda to new heights. And I've some news of my own. Real Godzilla news.'

'Oh, what's that? You're not getting married, are you?'

'Yes. Her father you know – Mizan Ali, the ticket collector at the cinema hall.'

'You don't say – Mizan Ali with the broken cheeks, who we used to bribe to get in.'

'Don't talk about bribes. Stay hush-hush, for Godzilla's sake. The man will be my father-in-law. His daughter is such a nice woman. She can sing many filmy songs. Thanks to Allah she has inherited none of her father's ugliness. In fact, she's very comely. People say she has film heroine looks.'

'Bah, bah. Congratulations, Sanu. I'm really happy for you.'

'Thanks. You have to come. You will be my main man, right?'

'I wouldn't miss it for anything. Have you invited White Alam?'

'Didn't you know? He's in Dacca now. He's just moved in to take up a new post. A captain in the infantry regiment. A big shot army officer in full gear and medals and all.'

'Oh, I didn't know. So, he must be at the cantonment.'

'Yes. I'll be going there soon to meet up with him and invite him. Do you want to come along? We're going to have a good old Godzilla time.'

At the cantonment they had to wait a long time at the security gate for White Alam to fetch them. It was a smart flat on the third floor. White Alam hadn't yet unpacked his things.

'For Him's sake what's the matter with you? You came to Dacca and didn't get in touch,' said Bulbul.

'I tried but couldn't trace you. I phoned your office; they weren't much help. Ask Sanu. Sanu, didn't I ask you to contact Bulbul?'

'Sorry, it's my fault. With the wedding and all, too much on my mind.'

'You're not getting married, are you?' asked White Alam.

'Yes, that's why I'm here. To invite you.'

'Godzilla, I'm so happy for you. I bet it'll be a fat wedding.'

White Alam unpacked a large bottle of whisky and Sanu told him about his bride.

'Sanu, now you two will make a perfect cinema. While your wife sings filmy songs and you act funny, it will be a real Godzilla show,' said Bulbul.

There was no rush because the next day was Friday. So White Alam phoned for a takeaway: parathas and goat kebab. Mindful of Sanu's enormous appetite, he ordered two extra portions. They drank whisky and ate, filling each other with their life stories and anecdotes, and laughed at White Alam's broken Urdu, which he'd learnt while being posted in West Pakistan. At the mention of the posting, Bulbul asked, 'Your generals aren't planning anything fishy, are they?'

'I wouldn't know. I'm only a junior officer. Let's drop that subject,' said White Alam.

To cover the silence, White Alam pressed Sanu to tell a film story, but he hadn't seen anything interesting lately, and besides, they didn't make funny films anymore, not like *Godzilla*. So, no film story then, but he agreed to tell a funny story. After stuffing himself with a few pieces of kebab and emptying his glass of whisky, which White Alam immediately refilled, he stood up. First, he blew wind, as if throwing a long, fierce flame worthy of the monster, but it came out like a little shame from his nether-end, squeaky and stuttering. Undaunted, he turned to his funny walks – at last, the proper Godzilla styling, yes, worth the wait, hundred per cent. Before they knew it, Bulbul and White Alam had belly aches laughing, and Sanu hadn't even started his story.

'Not many people know that Godzilla has so many talents,' said Sanu and he began to speak in a nasal, rasping tone.

'So, he's a snake then. Proper Lord Hiss, but that won't do,' said White Alam, doubled up, laughing.

'Here we go then. Way back in time, there happened to be two brothers living in the same town as our Godzilla-san. Let us call them Habil and Kabil.

'Come on Sanu, with Godzilla, there wouldn't be any town to speak of. He's a town hater. A civilization hater,' said White Alam.

'Do you want to hear the story or not?'

'Sorry. Being in the military, I'm drilled to concreteness and brute facts. But I know a story is a story. Please go on.'

'Yes, yes, brute facts are never brutal enough for you military types. Dashing lot that you are, wearing well-pressed khaki and bayonetting a few women and children here and there, then getting drunk on the fancy of being Papa Napoleon. Perhaps even jingling a few medals on the goose-stepping show. Bah, bah, but why are you lot always looking in the mirror and seeing a handsome saviour of the people? Three cheers for the military. Is that concrete enough for you? Our brothers, Habil and Kabil, were concrete too. How couldn't they have been with their very own concrete problem? Guess who, guess who? Who else but our Godzilla-san who has a head for such concrete issues? Pushing aside all thoughts of violence and raw-eating tendencies, he sat on his giant tail and put on the benign face of a good head-doctor. But even for our Dr Godzilla, this was a hard case to crack. The brothers Habil and Kabil were total degenerate types, hundred per cent loose morals. I wish I had a milder way of putting it, but they were bent on fornicating with their own sisters. Well, we mustn't be too harsh on them. During their time, as you know, there were no other females in the whole world except their two sisters. So, what were they to do with the heavy duty of multiplying our species?

'As it happened, one of the sisters was pretty-pretty and the other downright ugly. No point guessing whom they both wanted to fornicate with. You see the problem? So, they sought the council of Godzilla-san. No problem was problem enough for

224

him. Habil, the younger one, was the first to call. To please the wise doctor, he took two of his finest goats as gifts, which Godzilla gobbled up as soon as Habil went for a bathroom break. Excellent, pleasing gifts, said Godzilla, and belched out a foul breath of rotting carcasses. Habil took it for a breeze from the nearby rose garden. Naughty boy, eh? said Godzilla. You want to fornicate with your pretty sister, and why not? I don't see any rule against it, though that Feringhee Jew had a few things to say about it, utter rubbish, mummy-daddy stuff. Never mind that. You can have that pretty sister of yours, but first you have to tell me something. Yes, of course, said Habil, and he waited, biting his nails for the question. Godzilla, looking even more benign than a head-doctor, asked: What do you see when you look at me? Am I real?

'Don't play with me, O Great One. Of course, you're not real, said Habil. Mere black-and-white trickery of light does not fool me. If you think my head has gone all fuzzy, Habil rambled on, then you're gravely mistaken, Sir. I know what is real and what is not, and you, honourable doc, you are as unreal as they come.

'You're smarter than I thought, said Godzilla. You could make a fortune as a philosopher. Well then, my clever philosopher, since I'm not real, you have nothing to fear and to prove my unrealness – as the Feringhees have it – the proof is in the pudding because it's time to get real and do something about it. Would you please climb into my mouth? Habil looked baffled. I know it's an unreal mouth, said Godzilla, but you can imagine it. Go ahead, give in to your poetic instincts and climb into my unreal mouth. Habil, puffed up with his newly acquired philosophical self, climbed into Godzilla's mouth and Godzilla gobbled him up. He belched and said, My goodness, he's tastier than his goats.'

'Not very funny. You should stick to filmy story and funny walks,' said White Alam.

Now they had finished the kebabs and the bottle of whisky and were falling asleep, but Bulbul said they couldn't finish the night without hearing Kabil's story.

'What can I say? Kabil is a dim fellow but a vigorous type, and now that his younger brother was dead, he had his pretty sister all to himself, fornicating more assiduously than his brother's billy goat. He should have been a happy bunny, but his head was going funny, and he imagined himself as a giant insect, buzzing about behind the closed door of his stinking room. His dear father – you know who he was, yes, Him, the big One – couldn't help being rather inconvenienced and cross, so he began pelting his insect of a son with ripe mangoes. When things calmed down, everyone agreed that the boy needed treatment; it wouldn't do to have a dirty insect living among a respectable family with mummy-daddy-sister and all. So, they sent him to Godzilla, the esteemed head-doctor. Mind you, this time Godzilla-san wasn't very pleased to see the presents they had brought him: gourds, beans and pumpkins. Damn peasants, Godzilla roared, what do they think I am – a damn vegetarian? But his loyalty to his vocation and kind heart compelled him to take on Kabil's case.

'You've been a naughty boy, said Godzilla-san, fornicating with your little sister, but it's no good being an insect, no good at all. A little birdy might eat you up. But don't worry, I'll correct your head in no time. Anyway, shall I call you Mr G? No doctor, I'm K for Kabil. Yes, yes, of course, you are, said Godzilla-san, how could I not know Habil's brother? Something, though, is somewhat puzzling, continued Godzilla. I don't see any family resemblance. Perhaps your dear mummy was a bit naughty with a lecherous jinn. Never mind, said Godzilla. No time to waste. Let's get down to correcting your head. It wasn't an easy case, but Godzilla convinced Kabil that he wasn't an insect but the son of his father, a proper man and as good as any human that ever lived. All seemed well, and in the tranquil moment that followed, they had a long philosophical talk about his misguided brother who'd lived too long in a cave. Before discharging him, Godzilla asked: Who are you? I'm a human, Kabil said, the craftiest animal there is, and I know the time of what has been and will be, and I'm so glad to be a human, the master of all living things. Happy that his methods had worked, Godzilla said goodbye to Kabil at the door and went inside to sit on his giant tail.

'But not even a minute had passed when Kabil ran back, his body trembling. What's the matter with you? asked Godzilla. A little birdy is out there. He's skulking among the branches, said Kabil. So what, you're a human, not an insect, so you've nothing to fear, said Godzilla. Of course, I'm a human. You know it, I know it, but does the little birdy know it? Godzilla shook his head and asked: Who am I then? Why, you are my head-doctor, said Kabil. No, I'm Godzilla, and he gobbled up Kabil as he had gobbled up his brother, saying: My goodness, he's tastier than his brother.

All three of them screamed Godzilla and rolled on the floor.

After the official registration of Noor Azad and Dipa Kaiser's wedding, the reception was held at Sweet Canteen. Since love-marriage was still taboo, the event seemed illicit, and only a select few people were there. Apart from Dipa Kaiser's father, Ratan Kaiser, Bulbul and the Sweet Canteen's staff, the other guests were Noor Azad's few outcast poet friends and a similar number of Dipa Kaiser's foreign-educated, bob-cut friends who harboured new views about themselves and the world. Dipa Kaiser, as a concession, wore a red silk sari and kohl on her eyes, and henna on her hands, but refused lipstick and rouge. Her friends were in casual salwar kameez.

The cook wanted to cook for the occasion, but Noor Azad wouldn't have it. He wanted the cook, Dula Raihan and the two serving boys to be guests, relieved of labour and properly looked after. He brought in the famous Haji biryani from old Dacca and meesty-sweet from Moran Chand and hired staff from a canteen down the road to serve.

Unknown to Noor Azad, two of his poet friends had arranged a troupe of musicians to come and play. They were a rock/folk group led by Great Khan, not a descendent of Genghis or Kublai but a long-haired, ganja-smoking rebel from new Dacca. While they were waiting to play, the group's members sat in a corner strumming and plucking their guitars and dotaras, softly beating their dhols and breathing into their flutes to Great Khan's humming. They were smoking chillums of ganja, its aroma drifting over the rest of the canteen. Not sure about his role as the main man, and feeling uncomfortable with Noor Azad's poet friends, Bulbul went to sit with the musicians. When they offered their chillum, he took it and after several rounds he was decidedly high. Later, much more at ease, he spotted the renowned sculptor, Ratan Kaiser, sitting alone. With his long white hair and beard, and his long white punjabi, you could mistake him for a sadhu.

'I'm a big admirer of your work, Sir,' said Bulbul.

'Thank you. Are you a friend of Noor Azad or Dipa?'

'Both, Sir. I've known Noor for over three years. I met Dipa only recently.'

'I've nothing against love-marriage, but I hope they are not too hasty,' said Ratan Kaiser.

'They might have known each other only briefly, but they look like a good match. A modernist poet and a progressive journalist. They share a passion for French things.'

'I worry about the influence of imperialist culture. Many young minds are derailed under its influence. They end up being apes rather than being original. Mind you I'm not advocating unthinking nativism, but a deep and critical engagement with it.'

'Dipa is politically too conscious to be a naïve victim of imperialist culture,' said Bulbul.

'Yes, of course. But how about Noor?'

'Noor is a good poet, Sir.'

'I see,' said Ratan Kaiser and began to play with his beard.

At the dinner, Bulbul sat beside Noor Azad, surrounded by his poet friends. Dipa Kaiser was at another table with her father and friends. The musicians sat with Dula Raihan, the cook and the rest.

'I see you've been talking to the old man. What did he say?' asked Noor Azad.

'Well, we talked about his artistic philosophy. He likes you,' said Bulbul.

'Good,' said Noor Azad.

Haji's biryani from old Dacca was delicious as ever, and in the interlude before the meesty-sweet, Dipa Kaiser stood up to speak.

'I know it's not customary for anyone to speak at our wedding events. Let alone a woman. But it's about time someone broke these traditions. You may ask, by marrying aren't we, Noor and I, submitting to tradition? Yes, we are. But can we see each other without marrying? You know the answer to that. But my main reason for standing before you is to remember my mother. Hers was a love marriage, too. Since I was eight, my father has been both my father and mother. Thank you, abba, for taking care of me. And loving me. I love you more than you can imagine.'

There were tears in Ratan Kaiser's eyes; he wanted to say something, but his voice choked. Noor Azad looked glum. Perhaps he expected Dipa Kaiser to say something about him or express her happiness in marrying him. He got up and asked Bulbul to say a few words. Bulbul had not prepared anything.

'Well, what can I say? Dipa is such an amazing woman. Noor is so lucky to have her in his life. To Dipa and Noor.'

Bulbul knew he should have said something about Noor Azad's genius as a poet, his amazing generosity, and their friendship, but he couldn't. Noor Azad looked even gloomier.

He looked happier when the musicians got going. Great Khan, his long hair swirling, was belting out traditional folk songs in rock mode. Though the guests did not stand up to dance, they twirled and bounced their feet.

'Thank you, Bulbul. What made you think I'm amazing? I wish we were having this party in Paris. I could've danced with you then,' said Dipa Kaiser.

'Because you are amazing.'

'A circular argument.'

'Everything about you is amazing.'

'Everything? Infinity is unfathomable and meaningless.'

'Well, how about the dimple on your left cheek?'

'What about it?' asked Dipa Kaiser.

'It speaks of a delicious *élan vital* that, well, seems to be in a critical dialogue with that powerful reasoning machine of yours.'

'Should I take that as a compliment? Or are you hiding something behind that gobbledygook? Anyway, it's nice that you think I'm amazing,' she said, her cheek dimpling with a smile.

Bulbul wandered around without wishing to talk to anyone, but spotting Ratan Kaiser alone, he went to sit with him.

'Don't get me wrong. I'm not against creative syncretisation. It has always existed between cultures, but this group lacks creativity. They are just mimicking Western rock form and forcing the folk content into it. Very sad,' said Ratan Kaiser.

'They are pioneers, Sir. You've got to admit that a group like this are bringing our folk songs to the youth. Hopefully, a new musical idiom will emerge.'

'Maybe. But we have to be wary of the imperialists. Once they have sneaked in their culture and colonised our desires, nothing will budge them.'

'But Sir, you managed to overcome them and produced work that's absolutely native. Our own. Yet, traces of other cultures and traditions can be found in it, too. Am I right, Sir?'

'I'm not saying you can't learn from others. Even from those from imperialist citadels. I've learnt a lot from Rodin and Henry Moore. Two working-class lads from the very bottom of their societies. Henry Moore, for instance, was inspired by Toltec-Mayan sculptures. He could either imitate them or, coming from an imperialist centre, more likely than not, appropriate them. He wouldn't have been worth bothering with if he'd done either. But he took them to the Yorkshire landscape of his childhood. That gave him flow and undulation, the distinctive marks of Moore. What can I say about Rodin? He was basically a mason – a craftsman of material things. He might have learnt a lot from classical sculptures, but his distinctiveness emerged when he put those forms through the materiality of things his hands worked on. His thinker is not a Cartesian figure engaged in mind-on-mind games. He thinks through the sheer materiality and density of his body – its mass, its tensions, and its folds of matter. I looked at Moore and Rodin among many others. I looked at the murti-making tradition of our craftsman. Then I sat down by the paddy fields for days, looking at people ploughing the land, sowing, harvesting, carrying loads of rice on their heads, and focusing on their muscles, veins, and torsion. If I've done any worthwhile work, it lies in there. Sorry, to be rambling on.'

'Not at all, Sir. Thank you. I've always been deeply affected by the muscularity of your sculptures. The people's labour and way of life speak through them. We're blessed to have you among us, Sir.'

The musicians had stopped playing, and some of the guests had already left.

'Very unusual wedding. Never seen anything like this. Very modern, isn't it?' said Dula Raihan.

'I suppose so. I hope you've enjoyed it,' said Bulbul.

'Very educational. Never been to a love marriage before. To a non-religious wedding, either. If I told my family about it, they wouldn't believe it. They might think I read it in a book – about how the heathens get wedded in Feringhee lands.'

'There's nothing wrong with it, is there?' said Bulbul.

'Noor Sir and journalist madam are very modern. A perfect match.'

'Yes, yes, too perfect,' said Bulbul. He was rushing to the door when Noor Azad caught him.

'Thank you, Bulbul. For being with me today. Another thing – I don't know how to put it.'

'Just say it. You don't have to measure your words with me.'

'You know the flat. It's a bit small. It would just about be enough for Dipa and I.'

'You want me to move out. No problem.'

'No rush. I will stay at Dipa's house for a few days. Thanks for being so understanding.'

That night, alone in the flat, his last night, because he would move out first thing in the morning, even if he had to stay in a hotel for a few days, he couldn't help thinking that perhaps his friendship with Noor Azad was over, but how could he forget Dipa Kaiser? He cursed himself for acting like a stupid moron, speaking like Professor Giyani, and hiding behind abstruse jargon. Yes, if he'd had the courage, he should have said: Dipa, your dimple drives me crazy; I want to squeeze you tight between my arms and join our lips. No, that would have opened a can of worms. Perhaps she, too, would have had to confront her feelings for him, which he was sure were there, veiled, unspoken, but there. It wouldn't have been right to complicate things now that she was married. She should have the chance to be happy with her choice, and he should move on. But that was easier said than done.

CHAPTER 20

He found lodging with a widow with a teenage son. She was Munir Mahmud's sister. She lived in a large house in the city centre and within walking distance of *The People's Voice* office. When he heard about his homelessness, the editor offered to help. 'Let me have a word with my sister. She has a lot of room to spare.' Within an hour, he called Bulbul to his office.

'It all settled. You can move in immediately if you want.'

'The rent. How much do I pay?'

'My sister's a rich woman. Apart from her share of the family inheritance, which was substantial, her husband left her enough to see her through life comfortably. She doesn't need rent. If you help my nephew with his schoolwork, she would appreciate that.'

'What do I do about food? Will I have access to a kitchen?'

'Don't worry about food. You'll eat with the family. She might ask you to help her out with some official business from time to time. She has a driver, Kala Mia, who runs errands for her, but sometimes she needs someone more capable and educated.'

'Editor, I work for you full-time, would I have time for all this?'

'I'll make sure you have time. Besides, it won't be much. Perhaps just seeing her lawyer a few times. She has a dispute about some of the properties her husband left her.'

Despite his misgivings, he took up the offer of the lodging. The widow sent her driver, Kala Mia, to help him with the move. It was a red-bricked, two-storey colonial house with a large garden. He was given a room downstairs, between the kitchen and the lounge. Tendrils of bougainvillea coiled around its windows in an explosion of purple and red. If he looked through the gaps in the bougainvillea, he could see the spreading canopy of a custard-apple tree.

Munir Mahmud's sister was in her late forties. She was tall, but unlike her brother, she was slim with a well-proportioned head, neck and face. She looked elegant and dignified, wearing thin-framed, round glasses. Zahanara Islam was known as Zahanara Madam and simply Madam to most of her inner circle and subordinates. Her son, Khoka, was thirteen; he was as bulky as his uncle and wore thick glasses. As well as the driver, the household had a cook, Kazli Booa – a woman of the same age as Zahanara Madam – and Zorina, a young woman of about fifteen or sixteen who did the cleaning and chores around the house. Both came from Munir Mahmud's ancestral village in the north.

It was a busy time for Bulbul. Apart from covering the upcoming election, he was trying to dig into Criminal's case. For two afternoons a week, he helped Khoka with his schoolwork. Though

232

he wasn't much help with maths and science subjects, his enthusiasm for Bangla, English and history rubbed off on the boy and he was doing well in those subjects. Sometimes, in between his sallies across the city on his reporting and investigating missions, he visited the lawyer to inquire about the latest on Zahanara Madam's cases, and occasionally to the electricity office about a long-standing dispute. At least three evenings a week, he went out to the Press Club, but he avoided Sweet Canteen.

This hectic schedule should have prevented him from dwelling on Dipa Kaiser, but when he woke up too early in the morning and couldn't fall back to sleep, he let himself imagine she had realised her mistake in eloping with Noor Azad and had walked out on him. Full of remorse, she would hide away and seasons would pass, but he would run to her if she ever called him. His voice would tremble as he told her how much he loved her. Sometimes, he got up to play a game in the dark. He would set a fixed point, say, the corner of the bed. This was the zone. He would set a number, say thirty. He would circle the bed, mumbling numbers, hoping to be perfectly aligned with the zone at the count of thirty. If that happened, his wishes would come true; he would have another chance with Dipa Kaiser. He knew it was a childish, stupid game – superstitious wish fulfilment. Besides, with a slight adjustment of the length of his steps and speed, he could have easily manoeuvred the desired outcome. Strangely, he never arrived in the zone at the exact number, always overshooting the mark or falling achingly short. Exhausted, it took him back to the sense of dread he'd experienced as a child gripped by fears of a nuclear holocaust.

In the world of the day, his election coverage was much appreciated by the readership of *The People's Voice*, but he wasn't making much headway in the labyrinth of Criminal's case. He bribed a prison guard to let him inside to talk to Criminal again. Criminal opened his eyes wide and smiled. 'Journalist, Sir. You're back. I've been keeping your bed clean. And don't worry, the mosquitoes will make friends with you this time. I was very cross with them for troubling you.'

'I'm not here to stay. I'm here to help you get you out.'

'Oh, you're not coming in then? I promise you I'll look after you better this time. Bring you nice fruits from the garden.'

'I want to get you out of this place. But you have to tell me your story.'

'Get out? This is my home. Criminal loves it here.'

'I know it's your home, but you were born in a village, weren't you? What was it called? Did you come from a large family? Brothers and sisters, very close, yes? And how about a wife and children? You miss them very much, yes?'

Criminal fixed Bulbul with his wide, open eyes. 'Father, mother? Criminal was born here. This is Criminal's home.'

Exasperated, Bulbul left. If Criminal couldn't help in his own case, he had to explore other avenues. He went around the prison asking if any of the old guards could tell him anything. They all told him that Criminal had always been there, that he had come long before their time, and there was no time when the criminal wasn't called Criminal.

'We all like Criminal. A proper gentleman. If you think he's mad, then you're not correct in your head. He's saner than the sanest and wisest of men,' said the guards.

'But why's he in jail then?'

'We can't tell you that because we don't know.'

'Surely there are records. Could you look in the prison files?'

The guards looked at one another with bewilderment. 'Files? We don't know anything about files. Ask the governor, he might be able to help you.'

It took Bulbul several days, using contacts through his editor, to set up a meeting with the governor. He was told it might not be enough, but a desirable gift would help. He bought a sizeable hilsa fish, fat glistening through its scales, and set off for the prison. Since he was a bit early, he dropped in at the lawyer's office to inquire about Madam's property case. This concerned a plot in the commercial district, by all accounts valuable, that her husband left her when he died about ten years ago. But its ownership was disputed by a prominent property developer with connections to the army, and the case had been rumbling on. Now that General Ayub Khan was gone, there was perhaps a chance of resolving the case. The lawyer, a round man with a thin moustache, was surprised to see him.

'Who are you? I'm very expensive, you know.'

'Zahanara Madam has sent me. From now on, I'm her liaison with you.'

The lawyer was ogling the hilsa fish. It took Bulbul several coughs to bring him around.

'Oh, yes. I've told the driver. What's his name? Oh, yes, Kala Mia. I must say a shallow type and exceedingly dim. I updated him on everything. If I've got to explain everything to you all over again, it'll cost your Madam extra. My time is not free, you know. But since have been very thoughtful – you know, bringing me a fine hilsa – I might let you have a bit of my time gratis, as the Feringhees say. You're not the new driver, are you?'

'I'm Bulbul. I'm the tutor to Madam's son.' He didn't know how to say the hilsa fish wasn't for him.

'Fine name. I bet you have a good ear for music. Very rare gift, I must say. It will be my pleasure to talk to a teacher. At last, I can speak in a manner befitting my profession.'

'Thank you, lawyer Sir. Now that General Ayub and his governor have gone, Madam thinks we can resolve the case quickly.'

'This is very wrong thinking if I may say so. Generals may come and go, but the court has its procedures. Very meticulous, you know. The British established them, and they knew a thing or two about law. You can't rush this sort of thing. What is the value of a length of time, even a very long one, compared to the correct conclusion of a case? We mustn't forget that truth is eternal, as is the law. Do I need to spell out the duration of eternity? Perhaps to an idiot like Kala Mia, but you seem an intelligent man, Mr Bulbul. You know the score. Your Madam's case is very tricky, but we have some good news. It has already gone through the lower court with only two higher courts to go.'

'What? In ten years, it has just passed through the lower court? I can't believe it. Madam will be dead before the case is resolved.'

'I'm disappointed, Mr Bulbul. It is not becoming of an educated man to show impatience. The uneducated class want hasty results – they know nothing of the virtue of restraint. That's why they languish at the bottom of the pile.'

'Well, I'll be seeing you from time to time about the case. Madam will appreciate it if you push it a bit.'

'I am pushing Madam's case. Very hard. Getting it through the lower court in ten years was hard. Since you've brought me a fine hilsa, I'll push it even harder. Normally, I'm a meat man. A bit partial to goat, but fried hilsa is hard to resist.'

Bulbul realised that he had to give the hilsa to the lawyer and rush to the market to get another one for the prison governor, and there wasn't much time before his appointment.

'I hope you enjoy the hilsa fish. It's from Padma.'

'Padma? Excellent. Let me fill you in on the background of the case. It constitutes a gripping narrative that lends itself, yes, yes, well to the art of a storyteller. I don't want to brag, Mr Bulbul, but I'm known – how can I put it? – as a virtuoso in the profession. Even judges are known to have cried or laughed like happy little boys by my way of telling stories.'

'I'm afraid I've an urgent appointment to attend and don't want to take up any more of your valuable time. Perhaps next time.'

'I don't understand your generation. Always rushing. No time for stories. I must say, I don't find that a very elevated philosophy.'

Outside the lawyer's office, Bulbul hailed a rickshaw and offered the puller double the standard charge to hurry up. The rickshaw-puller pealed his bells, stepped on the pedals, and zoomed his way through the crowded streets. By the time he got to the market all the hilsa fish were gone, so it had to be a rohu, so large he had to buy a jute sack to plunk the fish in and carry it on his back. He was ten minutes late for his appointment, but it was another hour before the governor showed up.

He sat in his chair, not looking at Bulbul. 'What's that fishy smell? I don't like unclean types in my office. I'm very particular about hygiene, you know.'

'It's a gift, Sir, for you.' Bulbul opened the jute sack to show the fish. Almost jumping up from his chair, the governor, a small man with an enormous belly, poked his finger into its gills.

'Oh, such a fine specimen. It smells delicious too. Nothing beats a fine rohu. Fried or curried. What did I do to deserve it?'

'My editor has been in touch with you. He regards you as a very honourable man. Solidly upright.'

'Ah, you're Mr Munir Mahmud's man. Your editor, he's from a fine family. Very respectable. But sometimes he neglects his duty and publishes all kinds of – how can I put it –

subversive stuff. It's not befitting a man of such standing to be a communist.'

'Mr Munir Mahmud, a communist? There are many who consider him a bourgeois liberal,' said Bulbul.

'Let us not go into jargoning tamasha. What can I do for you?'

Bulbul told him about his interest in the case of Criminal and asked if the governor could look into the files.

'Why do you want me to look into the files? It's not a done thing here. Not at all.'

'I understand, Governor, Sir. We just want to establish his identity. Who he is and why he's there.'

The governor sucked his teeth and became very thoughtful.

'Who are we? Why are we here? These are deep philosophical questions. Mr…'

'My name is Bulbul. I just want to know the real name of Criminal and the charges against him.'

'Ah, singing bird. Very nice name. Regarding the matter you've raised… You see, many people get confused by the circular nature of things. I don't blame them for it. It takes a lot of imagination to think in a… what's the big word? Yes, in a non-linear way. But I assure you, the criminal is called Criminal. And because he's a criminal, there must be some charge of a crime against him. Everything is tiptop, perfectly logical – yes?'

'Of course, but can you please look into the files? I just want to know the nature of his crimes.'

'Who doesn't, Mr Bulbul? We all want to know about the nature of crimes. Some say we're all born with criminal tendencies. Even divinely ordained. But I don't go that far as a man of law and reason.'

'Please, Governor, Sir. Any information on him would be helpful.' Bulbul took his fountain pen out of his pocket and pushed it towards the governor.

'A fine-looking pen. You're a thoughtful man, Mr Bulbul. A very perceptive gift. How did you know that I dabble in a bit of writing? With a pen like this one could compose an epic. Though I'm afraid my talents may not match Valmiki's.'

'Please, the files, Sir.'

'Yes, yes, files. For us, they are sacred documents. It's not right that they should be opened lightly. You must understand that, Mr Bulbul.'

Bulbul had had enough; he stood, picked up the rohu fish and was about to storm out.

'Mr Bulbul, don't be so hasty. Please sit down. To be frank with you, we've had some mishaps. The mismanagements of my predecessors. Incompetent governors with loose morals, too greedy for gifts. They didn't appreciate the sacred nature of files. Ah, the British, they taught us the value of files. Anyway, many of the files have gone missing. Very unfortunate. I tell you what, since you gifted me a fine rohu fish and a fine pen, I might be able to do something for you. There is an old inmate... His name is Batya Azam – Batya for his diminutive size, but a notorious bandit in his time. I believe he's from the same time as Criminal. Serving a life sentence. He might be able to shed some light on the matter.' The governor scribbled Bulbul a short note to show the guards.

'Just show the note, and they'll take you to Batya Azam. Perhaps, the next time, I can show you some of my compositions. I'm sure I'll be inspired after dining on this fine rohu fish and writing with this fine pen. Perfect literary combination.'

From the jail, Bulbul stopped by the electricity office. He had already been three times before. The first time, when he put the bill in front of the cashier, the man, without looking up, had launched into a tirade.

'Are you an idiot? How many times do I have to tell you that I don't want to see this damn bill again. Pay up, or we cut you off next week. We're not a charity, you know. What does she think she is, your Madam? She can't indulge in heavy consumption and not pay up. Bloody freeloaders!'

The second time, Bulbul had to cough for the cashier to look up.

'Who are you? What's your business with the bill?'

'I lodge in Zahana Madam's house. She sent me to inquire about it.'

'Nothing to inquire. Are you blind? Can't you see the amount? We've been very generous, you know. Normally, we would've cut off your Madam's supply months ago.'

'Thank you for your consideration, but you have to admit the bill is excessive. Common sense tells us that to run a bill like this you'd need to operate a factory. Any sensible person can see that the bill is excessive.'

'Your sensible person, your commonsense person – they are common because they don't get the point. I have no time for a sensible person. Stupid, average types. Of course, they can't see the legitimacy of the bill, otherwise, they wouldn't be sensible or commonsense types, would they?'

'I don't want to argue with you. Can you send someone around to check the meter? I'm sure the matter can be resolved.'

'What do you think we are? Do you think we've nothing better to do than check your meter? Tell your Madam to pay up, or we cut her off next week.'

On the third visit, Bulbul secured a meeting with the accountant in charge.

'Accountant Sir will see you. You don't know how lucky you are. A rare privilege. The Accountant, Sir, is a bit shy. He plays card games. When you go to see him, you have to play a card game with him,' said the cashier.

'What for? I don't like card games. It's strange that he should be playing card games during office hours.'

'What you like or don't like doesn't matter to me. If you don't play cards with Accountant Sir, the appointment is off.'

Crumpled up in his extra-large chair, the accountant did look shy, not daring to meet Bulbul's eyes when he entered the room. He was a small, thin man in an oversized black jacket.

'Are you here to play a card game with me?'

'Well, I'm here to discuss Madam's bill.'

'Yes. No hurry. Let's have a game first. It will relax our minds and we then can discuss the matter calmly and reasonably. Yes?'

Bulbul nodded and the accountant brought out a pack of cards. 'Do you know poker? Or any other card games?'

'No. I don't know any card games.'

'No problem. You are…?'

'I'm Bulbul.'

'Singing bird. Very clever. I see I'll have a hard fight on my hands.'

'So, what game are we playing?'

'Since you don't know any, let's settle for the one-card game.

Each of us will have one card. We'll ignore the difference between clubs, diamonds, hearts and spades for simplicity's sake. Only the values. Whose is the highest wins. You have the right to stay in the game or be out. Of course, you don't have to show your card if you're out. If you stay in the game, the stake doubles at each call. Shall we start with five rupees a round?'

Bulbul hadn't realised the game involved money and began to wonder what it was really about. Anyway, since the game seemed simple, and that he stood as much chance as the accountant to win, he decided to play. Each would take a card and look at its value, and then the accountant, who had the privilege of going first, would reveal his hand. All he had to do was to say he was in to continue playing. If he said he was out, the game would end, and he would lose the amount at stake. In the first round, the accountant had a queen and threw it on the table, face up, with glee. Since Bulbul only had an eight, he called out, and the accountant won the five rupees. In the next round, the accountant threw down a jack and Bulbul had a king. He stayed in the game and doubled the stake. With the stake now at twenty rupees, Bulbul called out, letting the accountant win.

'You're clever man, Mr Bulbul. I anticipate a very fruitful discussion of your Madam's bill.'

The accountant had a king in the following round, and he threw it down with a gesture of triumph. Despite only having a jack, Bulbul stayed in the game, only calling himself out after losing forty rupees.

'It's a pleasure to play with an intelligent man. It's the lower classes who don't know the rules. They always spoil the game.'

In the next round the accountant had a queen and Bulbul a king. This time, he stayed in. Now, the stake rose to two hundred and fifty rupees. The accountant looked very pleased, as though, if he weren't a shy man and given to restraint, he would have risen to his feet and danced with joy. Instead, he muttered, 'Mr Bulbul, you're a clever man. Very clever. Perfectly acquainted with the rules.'

But to the accountant's utter surprise, Bulbul threw down his winning king.

'Shall we discuss Madam's bill now? I'm already late for

another appointment. I promise I'll return soon, and give you a longer game.'

'Nothing to discuss. We'll cut your Madam off if she doesn't pay up soon. Good day, Mr Bulbul.'

'I thought we agreed to discuss the case if I played. I don't understand.'

'Yes, that's the problem. You understand nothing. Please don't waste my time. I'm a busy man.'

On the way out, Bulbul said to the cashier, 'I don't understand. I played a card game with your accountant. Yet, he refuses to discuss the bill with me.'

'Did you win or lose?'

'Win.'

'I see. Accountant Sir doesn't discuss bills with fools.'

Now, on his fourth visit, Bulbul came to pay it up. Even though the bill was totally unjust, Madam wanted to settle it to regain her peace of mind.

Seeing Bulbul at the counter, the cashier gave him a stern look.

'We're up to our necks with your Madam's bills. Total botheration. No more discussion. From today, it will accrue fines. Twenty rupees a day.'

'Don't worry. I came to settle the bill. Madam decided not to contest the bill anymore.'

The cashier squiggled a note on the paper in front of him, then sucked his teeth. 'Paying a bill is not an easy matter. Several papers need to be checked and corroborated. And it requires the signature of several officers. Takes time, takes time.'

'I don't get it. You've billed us. Despite it being excessive and unjust, we want to pay the full amount. I don't see the problem.'

'You don't see the problem and that's the problem. Do I have to remind you again that it is an official matter? We have our procedures, you know.'

'What do we do then?'

'Come back in two weeks. I'm sure it will be resolved by then.'

'How about the fines you mentioned?'

'Fine is fine. It goes up by twenty rupees a day. Nothing can be done about it. Rules are rules,' said the cashier and closed the window. When Bulbul kept banging on it, a security guard, a giant man with a handlebar moustache, came up, wielding his baton.

'If you don't vacate the premises immediately. I'll eject you by force. Do you want that?'

Bulbul always had his breakfast on his own, lunch at the canteen next to his office, and at night, Zorina left his supper on the table in his room, except for the two evenings he taught Khoka when he dined with him. He rarely saw Zahanara Madam except on Fridays when he had lunch with her and Khoka. She would inquire about Khoka's studies, the latest from the lawyer and the electricity bill. She wasn't surprised by the report on her property case; she sighed and said it was a curse that would run for generations. Over her electricity bill, she was angry.

'Allah, where have you brought us? We can't even pay our bills without paying bribes. It's hell. Not even a change of government will change this. It has entered our veins.' She instructed Bulbul to find a way of paying the bill – whatever it took.

Bulbul returned to the electricity office, but the cashier closed the window as soon as he saw him. He had to pay a bribe to the guard to have a word with the cashier, who in turn needed to be bribed to arrange a new audience with the accountant.

'It was hard to persuade Accountant Sir. He was most reluctant, you know. Anyway, he agreed to play a game of cards with you. This is your last chance. Don't forget the rules.'

Bulbul played the same card game as before but this time he lost a thousand rupees to the accountant.

'I see, you have learnt the rules. It's always nice to play games with reasonable people. Having considered all aspects of the bill and scrutinised it meticulously, as it rightly deserves, I concluded that there are no more issues. Excellent outcome, don't you think? Pay the bill on your way out, and the added fines.'

CHAPTER 21

Though six months had passed since he moved into Zahanara Madam's house, Bulbul felt he hardly knew her. Apart from

Friday lunches, their paths barely crossed. Usually, she stayed upstairs, and if she needed to go out, which she rarely did, Kala Mia would bring the car to the porch, and she would hasten into it without looking around. Recently, though, with the onset of summer, she'd started to spend her afternoons outside in the garden, under the large flame tree which, years ago, had been brought from Madagascar by the colonial officer who first lived in the house. He insisted on calling it flamboyant, but the locals loved it as krisnachura – after the dark-blue, flute-playing divine seducer. Madam called it 'old-man flame tree', sometimes just 'dear flame'. She would sit under its domed red canopy and read. If not reading, she would sit quietly, as if in deep meditation. Everyone in the house knew not to disturb her when she was with her dear flame.

She came from an old landowning family that had grown fat collaborating with the British Empire, then with the generals in Pakistan, who rewarded them with high positions in the civil service. She'd read the Koran as a child, but her education was primarily secular and Western. Although she wasn't sent to England like her brother, Munir Mahmud, she had a degree from Dacca University. Soon after graduation, she was married off to a civil servant from another landowning family, so she hadn't done much with her degree. Since her husband's death ten years ago, she'd lived a reclusive life; her outings were mainly to visit bookshops. At home, she didn't do any cooking or household chores and had little to do with her son, Khoka. He was looked after by Kazli Booa, the cook, and Kala Mia took him to school and back. Since Madam was a secular, educated woman she didn't spend time in prayer either.

'What does she do the whole day?' Bulbul asked the cook.

'She just reads books and writes. She paints. Sits down and meditates. Sometimes she sings,' said Kazli Booa.

'What kind of books does she read?'

'How should I know? I'm a no-reading woman. But I can tell she reads deep. When she's in a book, only Allah knows what happens. She goes funny. I could be in the room to ask if she wants moong or masoor dal cooked. She won't even notice I'm there. I think they're devil books. Taking her over.'

Although Bulbul's teaching made a difference to Khoka, they

hadn't become close, and spent hardly any time together outside the lesson periods. Apart from going out to school, Khoka rarely left his room. Even when his mother was under her dear flame tree, he didn't come out to be by her side. No friends ever came to visit him, nor did he play any games in the garden.

'That boy is funny. A mighty big eater, growing a baba Ganesh,' said Kazli Booa.

'Why do you think Madam and the boy are like this? What happened?'

'How do I know? I'm no mind reader, nor a gossiping woman. There are those – big, fat mouths – who say all sorts of things out of spite, but I'm not one of them.'

'Yes, I understand. But something must have happened to make them like they are.'

'Yes, even a fool can see that. Happening is always happening. Nothing happening doesn't make people – you know – go funny, but my mouth is sealed. Don't you go around poking your nose in it, acha?'

But Bulbul couldn't help being curious and sometimes Kazli Booa would let on a little more. Late at night, he would find her in the kitchen. Zorina and Khoka would already be asleep, and Kala Mia lived in a nearby shanty, outside the house. Although Madam's bedroom light would be on, she never came down to the kitchen at such a late hour. Hearing Bulbul's footsteps, Kazli Booa would hurry to retrieve her hidden stash of treats. 'That boy, Khoka, he's a greedy duck. I swear by Allah that he devours everything. If I don't hide them well, he sniffs them out.' She would offer Bulbul palm bread or rice pudding, make him a hot glass of Ovaltine, and talk until Bulbul would doze off.

Kazli Booa looked like an old woman despite being only in her forties. She'd come to Madam's parents' household when she was a child, and when Madam was married, she'd brought Kazli Booa with her. She had been Madam's playmate and close companion until the marriage. In the new household, she became the cook and the general carer. Sometimes Kazli Booa let slip comments about the marriage, such as: he was pure evil and may he fry in hell. If Bulbul asked in what way the husband was evil, she would stay silent, biting her lips. But he got the impression that soon after the wedding, things got worse by the day, and Zahanara Madam used all sorts of excuses to stay away from the house.

'What kind of excuses? Where did she go? Did he hurt her?' Bulbul would ask.

'I've said enough,' Kazli Booa would say, but then begin again, and Bulbul learnt that things had taken a terrible turn when Khoka was born. The poor boy had never really stood a chance. There were many things you could say about her, Kazli Booa admitted, but she wasn't a person to take pleasure in another's demise, but she felt it was Allah's blessing, a stroke of good fortune, that the evildoer of a husband was dead.

'How did he die?' Bulbul couldn't help asking.

She snapped, 'Why do you ask silly questions? How do I know? Am I a doctor or something?'

It was a hot, humid night. Though the mosquito net saved him from bites and muffled the buzzing, it made the night even more oppressive. Unable to sleep, he began to tell himself a story. He could have had anyone, but Zahanara insisted on being the heroine. What could a storyteller do but let his heroine have her way?

She was a bright young woman with much promise but married to a lousy son of a bitch. Everyone had thought he was a good catch: a charmer with dashing looks and a promising civil service career, but a slight scratching of the surface let loose a gambler, a drunkard and a womaniser who was prone to violence – in short, a beast. At first, Zahanara turned a blind eye to her husband's misdemeanours: his gambling and his drunken return to the house at late hours. The rumours of his womanising were harder to take. Perhaps this was how it was with men of his class, and thinking she could wean him off it with charm and intelligence, she played the supportive wife and waited. Instead, things got worse. If she dared to ask where he'd been when he came home drunk and smelling of other women, he would fly into a rage. Swearing obscenely, he would break glasses, smash windows, kick the dressing table, and then flop on the bed, snoring like a beast. In the morning, he would say, 'You're my precious flower. Where your petals fall, I kiss the ground. Just a few rounds at the table and a small glass with friends. Work is very stressful, you know. Can you find it in your heart to forgive me, my precious flower? Why would I look at another woman when I have your beauty and charm? Enough to make a man happy for a thousand years. God-damn-it woman, I love you.' Come the night, he would be at his games again: gambling, drinking and whoring.

Who knows what possessed her, but, one night, Zahanara, dressed in her husband's clothes, went out to follow him. Bulbul knew he shouldn't have done it – it's not right for the storyteller to follow his character on a private mission, but he couldn't resist it. Besides, something terrible might happen to her, and he wouldn't be able to forgive himself if she ended up dead in some alleyway.

On that night, the house was quiet. Zorina and Khoka were already in bed, and because Kazli Booa had caught a chill, she'd taken to her bed early. Seeing a figure tiptoeing towards the front gate, Bulbul knew it was Zahanara and followed her.

He hadn't gone far when the rain turned into a downpour. With the water level rising fast, the streets were empty and dark. He was sure Zahanara was on the trail of her husband, the beast, to catch him as he came out of the gambling club. From the way he'd kicked the door on his way out, it was fair to assume he had made heavy losses. Instead of confronting him, Zahanara followed him to the drinking den, staying only a few yards behind. Crouching under a raintree, she kept an eye on the door. He wasn't there for more than an hour but came out dead drunk. He staggered through the knee-deep water and, at one point, stumbled and fell face down. Seeing him drowning, Zahanara almost ran to his rescue, but he managed to get back to his feet, and headed for the whore house.

He came out of the whore house in high spirits, singing at the top of his voice. As soon as the beast turned the corner, Zahanara confronted him. It was terrible. The beast jumped on her, kicking and punching her, digging his nails into her face. Bulbul knew he should break cover and run to help her, but how could a story-teller do that? He was there to observe the scene, like a wildlife cameraman at a lion kill, letting nature take its course, but it wasn't nature. Bulbul told himself to hell with being the story-teller, and he was about to run to her rescue when the beast let her go and disappeared into the night. Still keeping his distance,

Bulbul waited to make sure that she was fine, and she was. She laboured her way home through the water. Who reached home first? Husband or wife? It was a stupid question, but Bulbul was sure the traces of that assault lingered on Zahanara's face. Faint scars, almost invisible, but they were there.

It reached the point when her husband didn't give a damn: he gambled more, drank more and stayed the nights at the whorehouses he frequented. Zahanara tried to ignore him when he was home, but he forced himself on her and beat her. Then she started to go out as if to a secret rendezvous. She would set off as soon as the beast was out of doors. Sensing a looming catastrophe, Kazli Booa must have been worried for her, but what could she do?

Where did she go? Perhaps Kazli Booa had good reason to keep her mouth shut. The scandal was the last thing a well-to-do family would have wanted – imagine the shame of it – but no one in their right mind could have blamed Zahanara if she was looking up an old flame from her university days. Was this why Madam called the flame tree in the garden dear flame? Perhaps, the tree spoke of a passion for her first love, before she had to play dutiful daughter and then abused wife? It was lucky that the old flame hadn't died of a broken heart – otherwise, where could she have found solace?

But was this storyline a bit too predictable, too soapy to be worthy of Madam's dignity? Had it shocked her old flame when she returned to him? Had he been dreaming of this day? She had no hesitation over leaving the beast and running away with the old flame; he was still madly in love with her and would do anything for them to be together. So, everything was arranged; they were to meet at a sampan with a blue sail. It would be waiting under the large flame tree that overhung the riverbank. She knew the tree very well; it was one of their favourite rendezvous when they were students. She'd always thought that if perfect love had a home to bloom, it would be there, among its red flowers, whose petals floated down the river to the sea.

Kazli Booa must have known what was happening. Bulbul was in no doubt that she tried to persuade Madam that this madness could lead only to catastrophe. Perhaps that's why she'd waited for Kazli Booa to have one of her chills and take to bed early?

Her flame had arranged a rickshaw to pick her up outside her front gate. It was a moonlit night. Since the beast rarely changed his routine, it was fair to assume he would have been on his way to the brothel. Feeling nauseous, her hands trembling, she got on the rickshaw. Without a word, the rickshaw puller stepped on the pedals, and they breezed through the streets and alleyways. Feeling the cold wind against her face and seeing the landscape in soft silhouettes in the moonlight, she relaxed. Together, they would sail away from this nightmare to a new life.

The rickshaw puller dropped her on the riverbank, some distance from the flame tree. Her first impulse was to run towards it, but she checked herself and settled on a steady but brisk pace. She heard birds squabbling in the canopy; dogs barked from the other bank. Her pulse racing, she hurried down the slope. A hurricane lamp hanging from the mast revealed a blue sail. She found him hunched when she entered the boat, facing away from her. She gently touched his shoulder. It was the beast.

Angry at his losses at the gambling tables, drunk and frustrated for missing his whore-house visit, the beast unleashed a savage fury on her. She took it in silence, frozen at the flame's betrayal. She could not bear to wonder how he could have done this to her.

When the child came, it only added to Zahanara's sorrows. The beast suspected that he might not be the real father and the fact that the boy looked nothing like him compounded his suspicions. Her only respite came during the hours when he was gambling, drinking and whoring; when Zahanara heard his car approaching the gate late at night, she would freeze like a prey animal under the paws of a carnivore. He would swear at her, drag her by the hair across the room, punch her and force himself on her. Outside their locked bedroom, Kazli Booa would sob.

At last, Bulbul felt he was falling asleep, and besides, he didn't want to go on with this terrible story, but how could he sleep without seeing it through to the end? Months continued of Zahanara's ordeal in hell, but one night, towards the late summer, the beast came home sober and in a jovial mood. He said he wanted to leave this dreadful episode of his mistreatment of her behind and begin all over again, but she knew that once a beast, always a beast. He'd made plans for them to visit his country home to mark his new resolve; she could not refuse him. The only thing she asked was that Kazli Booa came along with them.

He hired a large sampan and the days leading up to the trip were strangely calm, almost serene. He skipped the gambling and whoring and drank only a quarter of his usual amount and came home early. He would lie on the recliner and read the newspapers; she would be in bed with a book. He would kiss her forehead before they went to sleep.

When, after a week of downpours, the rain finally stopped and the sun came out, the beast thought it was an auspicious day for the trip. The sampan was divided into three sections. In the middle section, he and Zahanara would sleep with the baby's cot. The stern end was the kitchen where Kazli Booa would cook and sleep. The bow was for storage. There was a small boat hitched to the sampan where the two boatmen would sleep.

Getting to the country home would take two days, so they needed to stop somewhere for one night. The beast was jovial; he stood on the deck, climbed on the cabin's roof and sang at the top of his voice. He leaned over the hull to pick a lotus fruit and offered it to Zahanara. He had never looked at Khoka with any tenderness since he was born, but now he played with him, put on gooey baby talk, though the beast being the beast, this came out as harsh gurgling that made Khoka scream.

Despite the beautiful evening, Zahanara could see the beast's mood was darkening. He came into the cabin and slumped on a pillow. Kazli Booa prompted Zahanara to offer him a whisky. At first, he dismissed the idea. He had turned over a new leaf and brought no drink on the sampan. Zahanara, playing the loving wife who knew her husband's needs, brought out a large bottle of whisky from her suitcase and filled a glass. His hands trembling, he snatched the glass and downed it in one gulp. By the time Kazli Booa served the dinner, he had gone through the whole bottle and begun on another that Zahanara had tucked away in her suitcase. He burped and mumbled how beautiful and chaste Zahanara was and how much he loved her, but it was a pity she was a whore who needed to be taught a lesson. He tried to stand up to kick her, but gagged, threw up, fell sideways and began to snore.

After finishing their meal, the boatmen went to their boat for the night. Propping their faces in their hands, Zahana and Kazli Booa kept vigil over the beast. The night wore on; they looked at each other and nodded. The boatmen must have been asleep by now, tired after a long day's labour.

Kazli Booa went to the kitchen area and returned with a length of hemp rope. They stuffed his mouth with his handkerchief, tied his legs, then slid the hemp rope under his neck and looped it around. The beast was still snoring. Holding the rope on either side, Zahana and Kazli Booa looked into each other's eyes and pulled with all their strength. Apart from a slight thrashing, the beast didn't make much noise. Kazli Booa fetched the large sack they'd brought for the purpose, and they shoved the beast inside it, dragged it to the deck and pushed it overboard.

In the morning, following instructions not to wake up their passengers, the boatmen punted the boat away from the shore, then with a strong wind behind them, hoisted the sail.

When Bulbul finished telling himself the story, he was shaking so much that he stayed awake until dawn. When he finally fell asleep, he dreamt of his mother. Strangely, she had the same face as Madam.

He woke with a headache. After taking some pills, he went back to bed. Luckily it was Friday, and he didn't have to work. He remembered the story he'd told himself and felt dreadful. How could he tell such a horrible story about Zahanara Madam and Kazli Booa? What devil had possessed him, what sickness was eating away his insides?

At lunch he couldn't look at Madam. Keeping his head down, he nibbled at his food and got up from the table, saying he wasn't feeling well. Kazli Booa brought him fresh mango juice and wanted to massage his head, but he said no. He stayed in bed, trying to blank out the traces of the night, but the taste in his mouth was sour. In the afternoon, he got up and peeked through the curtains. Madam was sitting under her dear flame tree, reading a book. Why had he seen his mother in his dream last night? Why did she have Madam's face? If she'd lived, his mother would have been nearly the same age as Madam, but was that enough reason to take on her face? He was desperate to go out for a smoke but feared that Madam would see him. But then she seemed never to notice him, and if she did, pretended that she hadn't. There was no reason why it should be any different now, so head down, he went out of the front door and turned the corner to go to the back of the house, when he heard Madam calling his name. He froze and looked around to see her beckoning him. She gestured for him to sit on the rattan stool beside her recliner. She put her hand on his forehead and left it there for a few seconds.

'You don't have temperature now. Perhaps you have been working too hard.'

'Perhaps. Thank you, Madam.'

'Take some rest. I'll tell my brother to let you have a few days off.'

'I'm fine, Madam. With the election coming, it's a crucial time for a journalist.'

'I know. But they can manage a few days without you. Now go where you were going, but come back. I want to talk to you.'

He went to the back of the house and lit a cigarette. For a moment his heart raced, thinking that Madam had some inkling of the story he'd told himself last night. But that was absurd. How could she enter his head and read him like a book? He puffed on his cigarette so furiously it made him cough. What did she want? He had been living in her house for about six months and never before had she wanted to talk to him. She was taciturn at the best of times, even with Khoka and Kazli Booa. Had he done something wrong, but what? He returned and she gestured for him to sit by her.

'Sorry for not paying you much attention. I've this habit of drifting into another world.'

'You've been very kind, Madam. Forgive me if I've done anything wrong,' he stuttered.

'Wrong? You've done nothing wrong. You've done an excellent job with Khoka. He lives in his own world, too. Sometimes I can't reach him. But you've been wonderful with him. And the lawyer. He's such a lowlife idiot. He's showing some urgency because of your efforts.'

'Thank you, Madam. It's been a while since I've seen the lawyer. First thing tomorrow, I'll be on the case.'

'No. You rest for a while; that's more important. By the way, how are your parents?'

'My parents?' said Bulbul, as if this was the first time in his life anyone had asked him this question.

'Do they live in your home village?'

Bulbul went quiet, and his eyes travelled through the blankness of time and memory.

'My brother mentioned that you came from Mominabad. Perhaps they live there.'

'Dead. My parents are dead.'

'I'm sorry to hear that. If you don't mind me asking, when and how?' Madam removed her glasses and cleaned them with the edge of her sari.

'I don't know much. No one talked to me about them. It's all vague, but I understand that my mother died giving birth to me. My father – I think I was about one – I'm not sure about the circumstances of his death, but the riots of '46 had something to do with it.'

'You've been an orphan, my poor boy,' said Madam. She held his hand, and her eyes misted up with love.

CHAPTER 22

Despite the intense humidity, relieved only by sporadic downpours, Bulbul was having a calm and restful time. In the afternoons, if it wasn't raining, Madam would ask him to join her under the flame tree. She would offer him mangoes, lychees, jackfruit and sweet tea with thick milk.

'Munir and I also grew up without our mother. She died when Munir was only eight months old and I was two and a half. I remember feeling angry at everything and everyone. How do you feel about losing your mother?' Madam put her cup down.

Bulbul continued eating the mango, savouring its sweet, fragrant pulp, and then he scratched the side of his head. 'I don't know. I never knew her. She belongs to a time before me. The idea of her is abstract to me. I only know of other people's mothers, not mine.'

'Have you seen any photograph of her?'

'No,' said Bulbul.

'So, you don't have any idea what she looked like. Sorry to be nosey, but how old are you?'

'I'm twenty-three.'

'Your mother would have been proud of you. Twenty-three and already a staff journalist at a leading newspaper. I'm proud of you too.'

Bulbul didn't know how to respond. He kept staring beyond her at the custard apple tree. 'Thank you,' he said at last. A long silence followed as the wind picked up and scattered red petals from the tree on their heads, laps and hands.

'She would have loved you. We mothers, we can't help it.'

'Yes, I can see. Khoka, he's so lucky. To be blessed with so much mother love.'

She suddenly gripped the arms of her chair and twitched slightly, as if a toxic memory ran through her.

'Books. What kind of books do you read?' she said abruptly.

'Well, I am very eclectic. But right now, I've nothing to read.'

'You can look through my collection. Borrow whatever you want.' She got up and gestured for him to follow her. She led him upstairs, past Khoka's room and along a wide corridor lined with books, arriving at her private quarters. One of the two rooms, with a blue door, was her study, the other, with a green door, he wasn't sure. She led him into the study which, like the corridor, was stacked with books from floor to ceiling.

'So many books. One could easily get lost here,' said Bulbul, sliding his fingers over the spines of titles facing him in the high, red-brown shelves that framed the room.

'In a sense, yes. But I also find myself here.'

'How? You mean they show you the way? Once, someone gave me a book. In Mominabad, where I grew up. It changed my life.'

'These haven't changed my life, but they talk to me like friends. You see, I have no one else to talk to.'

Bulbul's eyes wandered across the vast collection of books, singular in the shapes and colours of their jackets, but in an assemblage that seemed to have settled into a strange, barely audible conversation.

'I like reading books. If you like, you can talk to me about them,' he said at last.

She didn't say anything, but a faint smile rose and disappeared down the corners of her mouth. Bulbul's attention drifted to the paintings on the wall, especially of a woman in three different canvasses. The woman looked identical except for the colours of the saris that draped her body: the two at the sides were blue and green, the one in the middle was red. It seemed a wind had caught the saris, twisting and turning them, making them collapse inward, then billow out, pleat after pleat to a vanishing point. Their movement and flow caught him. The woman had vermillion on her forehead, but she didn't look like a Bengali or Indian woman.

'Did you paint them yourself?'

'Yes. Do you like them?'

'Yes, amazing colours. The pleats stretch her out to infinity. If I hold my gaze more than a flicker, it has a dizzying effect. I didn't know you were a painter.'

'I dabble in it. That doesn't make me a painter.'

'Really, they are brilliant. Enigmatic. She seems to be contemplating something serious. Vanishing and yet coming back to herself. Who is she?'

'A self-portrait,' said Madam and laughed. 'No. Just joking. I can never get to her level, even in my dreams. Take a guess.'

'I don't know. From a distance she looks like a Bengali or Indian woman. Her exposed skin is pitch black. Close-up, I'm not so sure. The face is different.'

'You're very observant. Yes, she is Indian and foreign too.'

'I see. What were you thinking when you painted her?'

'Do you know Draupadi from the *Mahabharata*? The sari is hers, from the scene of her disrobing.'

'It rings a bell, but I don't know the *Mahabharata* well.'

'In the Dice Hall of Hastinapura, the Kaurava prince, Dussasana, the atrocious one, begins disrobing Draupadi. But the more he pulls, the more sari appears. On and on, until exhausted, he gives up. Her sari is endless, and her body is layered in infinite pleats.'

'Now I see. What does it all mean?'

'I can only give you my perspective. For me, it answers the question: what is the truth of a woman?'

'I've some idea from the painting, but I'd like to hear from you.'

'Unlike Phryne, a courtesan from ancient Greece who needed to be disrobed before the eyes of men to reveal her truth, Draupadi is folded in infinite pleats. She folds inwards and outwards at the same time. She reveals and conceals endlessly. In her infolding she pleats herself layer after layer into smaller and smaller monads. Windowless and infinite. In her unfolding, she billows out, orchestrating the entire universe. Between concealment and revelation, the woman's truth is an infinite journey. That's what Draupadi's disrobing says to me. Perhaps that's why the painting leaves you dizzied.'

'I can see what you are driving at. But I'll have to reflect on it to see what it all means. And what about the face?'

Madam looked into her painting as if lost in contemplation, then smiled like someone who'd found a lost friend.

'Despite the vermillion, the face is foreign. I imagined the face. I read her story in a magazine. *Reader's Digest*? I can't be sure. Anyway, the face represents Hypatia to me.'

'Who is she?'

'She was an Egyptian Greek. Like Cleopatra. She lived in Alexandria between the late fourth and early fifth century.'

'Has she anything to do with the library in Alexandria?'

'Yes and no. That library was already destroyed before her time. But she was a lover of wisdom and carried the idea of the library in her heart and never stopped rebuilding it.'

'She was a learned woman then, a scholar?'

'Yes. When religious fanaticism was on the rise, she stood for rational knowledge. Do you see the importance of the likes of her in the situation we are in?'

'Yes, I do. A book changed my life. It stopped me from accepting faith, to question everything with reason. Are you an atheist then?'

'I question things with reason but I'm not an atheist. Yes, Hypatia was a pagan and a lover of wisdom, but a Neoplatonist too. Our spirituality, our Sufism has its roots in Neoplatonist thinking. Philosophers like Ibn Sina and Al-Farabi, who were Neoplatonists, laid the path for our joyful relationship with the divine. I imagine Hypatia followed a path of love. Like our Lalon Shai, like our Bauls and fakirs. Like Hazrat Bibi Rabia Basri, from whom I learned the ways of love in my teens. She still summons me daily, and I sit at her feet as she showers me with divine light. Love of wisdom and the love for the One made Hypatia love everyone. You know, in Hypatia's times, Alexandria was riven by sectarian fighting between Pagans, Christians and Jews, but she tried to bind everyone in one love. It cost her life. Perhaps that's the wrong way of looking at it. Perhaps she gifted her life to posterity so that someone like me could find her after all those centuries. She was, above all, a teacher. Sometimes, in my vanity, I entertain the idea of being a teacher, but who would listen to this worthless widow?'

Was she asking him to be her student? Yes, he could learn many things from her, but the spiritual path wasn't for him. So, he decided not to respond. Instead, he said, 'An Indo-Greek-Egyptian then. Draupadi, the infinite, and Hypatia, the lover of wisdom and the One. Together they make many, but a single figure. I can't get my head around it.'

'Don't worry. Just look at the paintings. Draupadi and Hypatia are my stories. You're not bound by them. You must tell your own story. You don't even have to tell a story. Just look at the colours or the lines and let your body take you wherever it wants.'

Bulbul couldn't decide what to pick from the thousands of books on the shelves. Stopping abruptly, she took out a book and brought it close to her face, as if she wanted to smell it.

'The Birth of Tragedy'. You need a mother to give birth, don't you? I wonder who the mother is here?'

Taking the book, Bulbul stepped back and smelled it like Madam, as if in doing so he would find the answer.

'Obviously, the author, Friedrich Nietzsche. Or perhaps the tragedians like Aeschylus or Sophocles.'

Madam creased her brows, then cleaned her glasses with the edge of her sari. 'Has it occurred to you that these are men? How could they give birth? Or be the mother of books or tragedy?'

'I haven't thought that way before. I've taken it metaphorically.'

'Yes, metaphors like this vanish real women. Real mothers. Didn't your mother die giving birth to you? If this is a metaphor, it cuts in the flesh. Take the book. When you've finished, tell me what you think.'

★

The following day, he was feeling well and about to set off for work, when rain poured and a strong wind gusted. He waited for the rain and wind to subside and sat on the veranda looking at the fierce drops wreaking havoc on the flame tree, its flowers floating wildly in a fledgling pool. He didn't realise Madam was standing behind him. When he turned, he saw she was holding a letter. It was from the electricity board. She had another, even more unreasonable and excessive bill than the last one.

When the rain stopped, he phoned Munir Mahmud to say he would be late. Since he would be on errands in the city, the editor suggested he check out a curious case in the old town.

'The whole matter is laughable. Gossip and fabulation. It has been reported that a woman gave birth to a black snake.'

'What? Some superstitious nonsense. One hears this kind of story all the time. Should we waste our time chasing it?'

'I couldn't agree more. But the last few days have been rather quiet. Apart from the election, nothing much newsworthy is happening. Besides, this story sounds rather fishy. I suspect there is more to it than just gossip and superstition.'

'Fishy, you said? I'll check it out. What's the address?'

The place was very near Sweet Canteen, and his stomach turned over. He had avoided the area since Noor Azad and Dipa Kaiser's wedding. But his profession could not have no-go areas. On his way out, Kazli Booa came running with an umbrella Zahanara Madam sent because it might rain again later in the day. 'Madam is going funny. I never seen her fussing like this over anyone before,' she said.

Since the electricity office was the nearest port of call, he stopped there first. The cashier put his hands on his head and cried, 'No. Not you again. Your face still sneaks into my dreams. Gives me nightmares. What grief have you brought me this time?'

'It's you who are giving us nightmares. You're charging us at least three times our average consumption. This bill is even more excessive than the last.'

'Bill can never be excessive. It's always right. It's not our fault if you tripled your consumption. For all I know, your Madam might be drilling for oil in her backyard.'

'Look, I don't want to argue with you. Just send someone to read the meter. That will resolve the issue. Acha?'

'How do we know you're not tampering with the meter? We're not falling for that trick. Just pay up, and everyone will be happy.'

'Ok, you win. I want to pay up now. Madam doesn't care about money; she just wants her peace of mind. So, let's get on with it.'

The cashier looked puzzled, almost terrified; he scratched his head and stared at the bill for a long time.

'As you well know, everything has a protocol. You can't just walk over here and pay the bill. It's not a done thing.'

'I'm not contesting it. I just want to pay it. Acha?'

'I'm surprised that you haven't learnt anything. Even a latrine cleaner knows the rules. You have to play a card game with Accountant Sir. If you are so eager to pay, I can fix an express appointment for you. I know I'll get a scolding, but I'm here to help you in any way I can.'

'I've no wish to play games with the accountant. I just want to pay the bill and get the hell out of here.'

The cashier puckered his face and shook his head.

'What's the world coming to? No respect for the rules. If we don't play the game, there will be disorder and anarchy.'

'I've had enough of your nonsense. I will expose your little scam, your stupid game of bribery and corruption.'

'How do you plan to do this, if I may ask?'

'I'm a journalist. I can get it on the front page.'

'Journalist. I've a lot of respect for your noble profession. You might think me a mindless cashier, habituated to pettiness and given only to crunching numbers, an illiterate bumpkin and totally lacking moral sensibility, but it might surprise you to hear that I take delight in your exposure of social ills and often find myself in tune with your moral outrage. Very good. But let me tell you some home truths. Everyone plays card games with Account-ant Sir. Judges, lawyers, professors, holy men. And journalists and moral crusaders. Left, right and centre. They, of course, have their own games which everyone else has to play. There is nothing outside the game. If you're already in it, how can you undermine it? Do you have the moral authority?'

'You're twisting everything. It's obscene nihilist shit. I'm going to expose you, whatever it takes.'

'You do that, journalist sir. Good luck to you. I'll be the first to celebrate the ruin of our system of games. Three cheers for the end of games.'

Bulbul felt like pulling the cashier out through his hole, like a motherfucking rat. But he left. Outside it was drizzling. He didn't unfurl his umbrella. He needed to cool down a bit and the lawyer's office wasn't far. But by the time he arrived, he was wet; drops of rain trickled from his mop of black hair and his shirt was damp. When he saw Bulbul, the lawyer called the office boy to bring a towel and offered him the spare shirt he kept in the drawer. Bulbul was happy to use the towel but refused the shirt.

'Mr Bulbul, what can I say about your hilsa fish? It was simply superb. I can still smell it in my hand. Fragrance from heaven.'

'I'm glad you enjoyed the hilsa. Madam's case. How is it going?'

'Superb progress. Never been better. I've managed to move the files from the receptionist to the junior clerk's office. Allah willing, we can send it to the judge's secretary's office in few months' time. Super-fast trajectory, don't you think?'

'At this rate, it's going take another ten years at the middle court. Then, at the high court, Him only knows how long it will take there. Perhaps we will have Allah's final judgement before the resolution of this case. Just absurd.'

'Mr Bulbul, how many times do I have to tell you? With law you can't rush. One has to be extremely scrupulous with the procedure. Any faltering, the whole society will collapse.'

'Perhaps it should. The whole system is utterly corrupt.'

The lawyer opened his eyes wide. 'I can't believe it. An educated man like you saying these things. Should we welcome barbarism then?'

'Maybe we should. It can't be any worse than what we have now.'

'Mr Bulbul, I can see that you are upset. You are having a bad day. You must know that compared to other cases Madam's is moving very fast. Next stage could be even faster.'

'How?'

'I thought you might have brought me a new gift.'

'Gift? Madam has already paid you an enormous sum. Your

fees are increasing by the day. If this case is ever resolved and Madam gets her property, she'll have paid you more than its worth. You have no shame asking for gifts. This system can't collapse soon enough,' said Bulbul, storming out.

It was two in the afternoon, and he decided to have lunch before going to the prison. The restaurant was crammed with customers because of the rain. People were talking about the upcoming election and the birth of the snake child. From the table behind – what seemed like a gathering of friends – he heard a man saying that a giant king cobra had entered the house in the dead of night and copulated with the woman, who thought it was her husband. Someone else said yes, of course it was a giant king cobra, but it visited the woman in her dreams. A third man confided that the woman was young and unmarried, and that the thing indeed looked like a giant king cobra, but was the spirit of a lecherous landlord, long dead. No one doubted that the woman had given birth to a black snake baby.

'Perhaps we are heading for apocalyptic times,' said another.

After finishing his lunch, Bulbul ordered tea and approached the people behind him. Hearing that he was a journalist they were keen to have him at their table.

'You want to hear our story? Are we going to be in the paper? Oh, it's an auspicious day. We wouldn't have met you if it weren't for the rain,' said a man with a singsong voice.

'I'm here to find out about the snake baby. If it's true you will be in the paper.'

'Did you hear that? We'll be in the paper. Can't believe our luck,' said a man with a nasal voice; his tablemates nodded in unison. He stood up, stretched his arms to reveal his enormous frame and continued, 'I'm a stickler for truth. I'm known as a bulldozer when it comes to truth. I smash through rumours and fanciful tales, Mr Journalist Sir. This story about the snake baby – how can I put it? – absolutely watertight. Hundred and ten per cent.'

'I wonder where you get that extra ten per cent from. Never mind, I take it that you've seen the snake baby yourself. Can you describe it to me?'

'Journalist, Sir, what can I say? It's as good as seeing with my own eyes. In fact, more reliable. You see, sometimes I don't see so good. My wife's always pushing me to take a pair of glasses.'

'So, you haven't seen it with your own eyes?'

'His brother-in-law has seen it. A most upright man. No one makes a more truthful witness than he. The man's virtually a saint,' said another man.

'Have any of you seen it? I want an eyewitness.'

'What? My brother-in-law's not good enough for you. He's the most respectable man in the area. A hajji.'

'Where can I find your brother-in-law?'

'He's a hajji. Imagine the righteous character of the man. You can torture the man in Sodom, and you can't get any untruth out of him. He's away at Mecca.'

Men chorused that they had all heard it from the hajji.

'Yes, yes, of course, but I couldn't help overhearing you earlier. If you heard it from the same source, how come your versions differ?'

The men opened their eyes wide.

'Journalist Sir, we are getting confused. We don't understand your line of questioning. Just because we heard the truth from the same source doesn't mean we must tell it the same way. If we do, boringness will kill us all. We believe in literal truth. Our differences are simply matters of style. Our own signatures, if you like,' said the man with the singsong voice.

'Gentlemen, I'm afraid I can't put you in the paper.'

'Why not? You don't trust my brother-in-law? You don't trust us? Are you saying we are all liars?' He thrust his face so close that Bulbul felt saliva on his lips.

'I'm not saying any of this, gentlemen. We just can't print an extraordinary story like this without eyewitness testimony. Even that needs to be crosschecked. I'm sorry.'

'We know your newspaper. Always full of lies. Sometimes you print something that can't be true even in dreams. The other day, all the newspapers printed that a man went to the moon. We never heard anything so absurd. Where was your eyewitness reporter, your crosschecking, fact-checking tamasha then? Did your man on the moon meet the old lady? You know, the one with the spinning wheel? Did they have a nice cup of tea with her? Oh no, they can't find her. Very convenient. Utter lies,' said the man with the singsong voice.

'There are newsreels. Documentary evidence. Man has indeed been to the moon,' said Bulbul.

'All made up and lies. Are you an American spy or something? How much are they paying you?'

'Get the motherfucking spy, get the bastard, beat him to a pulp,' went the chorus. The nasal-voiced man growled like a dog and pushed Bulbul to the ground. His friends egged him on: 'Come on, Bulldozer, flatten him up, get the truth out of him.'

If it hadn't been for the restaurant owner, Bulbul would have received a serious beating. But he was told, 'You're a trouble-maker. I don't want to see you in my restaurant again. Now bugger off.' And he was manhandled out of the restaurant.

Late afternoon, he arrived at the prison gate and showed the guard the governor's note. He was taken to a small dark room and told to wait there. Another guard came and looked at the note and said, 'You want to see Batya Azam? Very dangerous inmate. No one is allowed to see him. I wonder how you got permission. Are you a relative of the governor? We don't like nepotism. This institution is at the heart of the rule of law.'

'I'm not a relative of the governor. It's in the public interest that I want to talk to him. I assure you it will further the cause of the rule of law. Please can you take me to him?'

'Well, it's not that easy. But since you want to strengthen the rule of law, I can be persuaded to help you.'

'What do you mean?'

'I don't have to spell it out, do I? You look like an intelligent man. Use your imagination.'

'If I'd known, I would have brought you a nice gift. I thought with the governor's note, there was no need for that.'

'You thought wrong. Like the governor, we also have the right to enjoy gifts. Anyway, I don't accept things or animals of any kind. We have to have standards – no? Only cash.'

Bulbul paid a bribe of one hundred rupees and the guard took him to another room, equally dark. He told Bulbul to wait there. Time was ticking by, and there was no sign of the guard. At last, another guard came in and Bulbul showed him the governor's note and told him about his dealings with the previous guard.

'I'm afraid you can't see Batya Azam.'

'Why not? I've authorisation from the governor himself.'

'If you want to talk to a dead man, you have to go to his grave. I think his body was taken to his ancestral village in the south.'

'Dead? When did he die?'

'Several months ago. After spending thirty years with us. We all wept when he died. He was small but a giant of a man. An original philosopher. We learnt so much from him.'

'But I saw the governor only last week.'

'Governor Sir is full of a sense of humour. He likes playing practical jokes on people. I must say he's excellent at it.'

Bulbul tried to phone the governor, but he was not available. He called Munir Mahmud, who also tried to get in touch, but to no avail. He knew from the guard that the governor was in the habit of walking to his house, just a few hundred yards from the prison. So, Bulbul waited by the main gate. After an hour or so the governor came out and Bulbul salaamed and introduced himself.

'Governor Sir, I came to see you last week. You permitted me to see Batya Azam regarding Criminal's case.'

'I don't remember you. And why would I permit you to see Batya Azam? The man died months ago.'

The governor lit a cigarette and strode away; Bulbul had to trot to keep pace with him.

'Munir Mahmud, my editor, arranged it with you, Sir.'

'What made you think I'm on talking terms with Munir Mahmud? He's a dangerous communist and subversive. He should be an inmate here.'

'Sir, I brought you a rohu fish for gift. Remember?'

'What? Were you trying to bribe me? That's a serious offence.'

'So, you remember me, Sir?'

'I didn't say that. I was talking about a hypothetical situation. Besides, I never forget a face. Yours is a face that doesn't ring a bell.'

The governor was almost in front of his house when Bulbul asked, 'Sir, how's your epic work coming along?'

'Very well, Mr Bulbul. The human condition seriously inspires me. Especially our tragic flaws.'

'So, you do remember me.' Bulbul handed over the note of permission to see Batya Azam.

'My God, I'm astonished by your audacity. This is evidence of serious wrongdoing. Forging a government document. You'll serve a long sentence for it. But you're lucky I'm in a good mood today. So, I'm willing to overlook it this time. Run along – before I change my mind.' And the governor went into his house.

Bulbul sat by the front door and began writing in his notebook. A burly man came out of the house with a large stick.

'Hey, don't loiter here. Bugger off!'

'I need to talk to the governor. It's urgent.'

'You motherfucker!' The burly man lifted his stick as if about to strike him. Bulbul scrambled to his feet and ran, and the burly man chased after him. Bulbul didn't slow down until he was on the other side of a market and when he paused to regain his breath, he realised he had dropped his notepad and the umbrella. He felt exhausted; his day had been getting worse by the hour. He thought of returning home but realised he hadn't yet checked on the snake baby story. He was sure that if he told Munir Mahmud about his day, he would be told to go home and rest, but how could he report his humiliation at the restaurant and at the hands of the burly man? It would only double it. So, he headed towards the house of the snake baby.

It was almost evening and still very humid. He would have to go past Sweet Canteen. The place was buzzing with customers – perhaps there was a talk tonight. Professor Giyani giving one of his abstruse lectures? Had Dula Raihan read enough books not to feel in a different orbit from the professor? He should have been in touch with him: how could he have been so callous as to sever all connections with Sweet Canteen and his friends? They must have wondered why he'd disappeared so suddenly without an explanation. How not to remember the wonderful times he'd had there with Noor Azad, drinking late into the night and planning to storm the city together with their words. Dipa Kaiser had come between them. Thinking this was no time for awkward meetings and explanations, he zoomed past, hoping no one had spotted him. He took the disused rail track and saw the market's sprawling outline in the twilight. Past the market, down the rail track, and veering right lay the shanty – his destination. Suddenly someone caught up with him from behind.

'Bulbul Bhai. I've been watching out for you. I thought you were coming to see us,' said Dula Raihan.

264

'I've some work here. At the shanty,' said Bulbul.

'Snake baby? I was sceptical. I know it goes against rational thought, but the more I hear, the more I find it difficult to dismiss.'

'I don't want to prejudge. I'm on my way to talk to the family.'

'But Bulbul Bhai, what's happened to you? No word. You just disappeared. Did we do anything to upset you?'

'No. You haven't done anything to upset me. Work is a bit hectic now. I wanted to stay near the office.'

'Noor Azad Sir is very worried about you. He wants me to look for you at the office. I'm planning to see you on Wednesday.'

'Don't tell Noor that you've seen me. Once things settle down a bit, I'll come and see you all.'

'What things?'

'Not now. Perhaps another time,' said Bulbul, heading towards the market.

After the market, he climbed down the rail tracks and came to the edge of the shanty. It was vast, with lines of rickety, makeshift shacks winding their way in all directions.

Suddenly, the sun went down and dogs barked in a menacing cacophony. From the shacks, lamps flickered like suffocating fireflies. The rumours of the place's savage and mindless violence had Bulbul's breath all jumbled up. Surely it was a bad idea to come here to offer himself as a sacrificial victim; perhaps he still had time to take flight from this hellhole. Shame on you, he told himself, for entertaining such thoughts, but how could he convince his heart to stop pounding? He bit hard on the skin at the back of his hand and quickened his pace, unsure what direction to take. Hearing voices from inside a shack, he tapped on it and the inhabitants went quiet, as if holding their breath for danger to pass.

'I don't mean any harm. I'm a journalist. I'm looking for the snake baby's house.' Bulbul waited for a minute, but hearing no response moved on. A boy came out from another shack with a bucket but hurried back inside when Bulbul called him. After several turnings, he saw an old man smoking a hookah outside his shack. He had a long white beard and looked like a kind soul.

'Uncle, I'm looking for the snake-baby's house. Can you show me the way?'

'You shouldn't be here. It's not safe. It could be anywhere and measuring you up with its tongue,' said the old man.

'What thing are you talking about?'

'It… you know. One mustn't speak its name. It slithers here as black as black can be. Oh Allah, the size of it. What can I say about its venom? It devours you whole.'

'So, the snake baby's still terrorising the neighbourhood? Can you point out the house where he was born?'

'Listen to me, young man. If you go anywhere near its house, it will ambush you. You'd better run. You might have a chance.'

'Have you seen the snake baby?'

'I don't have to see it. I know it's here. It's pure evil, the devil himself.'

'I believe you. Please, uncle, show me the house.'

'Remember, I warned you. But if you are so bent on killing yourself, what can I do? Go straight, then turn left, and left again, then right by the drain. You will see a goat tethered outside. The shack's wood panels are painted blue. Be careful, it will be following you. It's relentless and its appetite knows no bounds.'

Bulbul rehearsed the turnings the old man had told him, but was he getting the sequence right? With renewed resolve, he quickened his pace. He stopped and held his breath when he heard cracklings and rustlings coming from behind doors. People were securing their dwellings from the menace that roamed these paths. He lit a cigarette. Suddenly, the wind rustled the plastic sheets the shacks used as protection against rain. The smell of evil was everywhere.

He wished it wasn't true, but how could he deny his feelings? Yes, a giant thing was dragging itself along the ground, and the hiss was unmistakable, and it was coming his way. The thing stopped, then propelled itself faster. He could smell its noxious odour. How could such a bulky thing move so fast? It was gaining on him. He ran as fast as he could but realised he was running in a circle, always ending up at the same spot. Exhausted, and trying to jump across a drain, he fell face down. Lying there, facing the inevitable, he felt calm. The thing was almost on him, its cold tongue on his neck.

Bending down, the old man put his hand on his neck and said, 'I told you to be careful,' and gave him a tumbler of water. When Bulbul had recovered, the old man took him to the snake baby's shack. The father of the snake baby and his new bride were squatting on the floor, having their evening meal – by the smell of it, dry fish. Bulbul gagged a bit, and the old man touched his head. Such healing hands; he felt better immediately. The wife got up and brought two low stools. Bulbul sat on one, the old man on the other.

'This gentleman here is a big newspaperman. Tell him your story. He will pay well,' said the old man. Bulbul hadn't realised that he would have to pay for the story. The father, a skeletal man with dead eyes, squirmed and began to stutter.

'Don't worry. The gentleman is not going to harm you. All he wants is to hear your story for a fair price.'

Bulbul looked at the old man to inquire what was a fair price.

'Two hundred would do.'

'That's a lot. How about one-fifty?'

Caressing his long, white beard the old man laughed, then shook his head. 'You gentle folks. You've no shame. Have you any idea how much it'll cost this poor man? How much sadness and pain he'll suffer by reliving it? Allah have mercy on the poor man.'

Bulbul took two one-hundred-rupee notes and was about to give them to the father when the old man snatched them from his hand, kept one for himself, and gave the other to the father. When Bulbul looked at the old man, he saw his eyes were hard, as if he wouldn't hesitate to pounce on him with atrocious violence.

'Tell the gentleman what happened. Be absolutely honest. Be plain and simple. Truth doesn't need any props or fancying up. It shines on its own truthfulness. Acha?'

When Bulbul took out a cigarette, the father smiled solicitously and nodded to say that he wanted one and the old man too. The three of them lit up and the wife sat hunched with the sari over her head. In between taking puffs, the father told, matter-of-factly, what had happened. He was a simple man, a hardworking day-labourer. The blessing of his life was to be the birth of his baby, what he'd dreamt and prayed for, but there was something wrong with the mother. She was getting thinner by the day, like something was eating her up from the inside, so it was thought it would be good if the baby was born early. Mercifully, he came early, but as a black snake. Ya Allah, what was he to do? Still, he was willing

267

to hold him and call him his son, but he was the evil one, bit his own mother to death and slithered away and was still doing his nasty work.

The old man escorted Bulbul out of the hut and left him at the railway track. In the market he sensed someone was following him. His heart pounding, he thought of running but a woman's voice, fragile and gentle, stopped him. It was an old lady, leaning on a stick, shuffling towards him.

'Thank you, my son, for stopping for me. I saw you going into my son-in-law's shack with the old man. Both of them are evil. Murderers.'

'What? What do you mean?'

'Did they tell you about the snake baby? Of course, they did. It's all a scam. I wouldn't grudge them for making a few rupees. But it's meant to hide their evil deeds.'

'What are you talking about?'

'I'm a poor woman, but I had to promise him a bicycle. You know, for a dowry. From the day he took my daughter as his wife, he started to pester her for the bicycle. My daughter comes to me and cries, but what can I do? I'm a labouring woman. I break bricks for road builders. I work day and night. I still can't make enough to buy the bicycle for him. When my daughter was expecting the baby, I knew it would end up badly. My son-in-law is real evil.'

'If you had a hunch, why didn't you go to the police?'

'I tried, but they beat me with sticks. Called me a lying old hag.'

'That's typical of the police. Bloody fascists. Tell me the rest.'

'My daughter was seven months pregnant. It was then that he started to poison her. Very slowly. The old man helped him. When she was eight months, my poor daughter – may Allah take her to heaven – he beat her so badly that she lost her baby. My daughter was still hanging on to life. But the next day, he forced a big dose of poison into her and killed her. It was the old man, the real evil one. He advised my son-in-law to invent the story of the snake baby. How it had bitten its own mother to death and slithered away. They convinced everyone, but they couldn't close my mouth. They beat me up and told everyone that I was mad. Do I look mad to you? I'll keep on telling the truth even if it kills me. For my daughter. For my grandchild who couldn't even get born.'

Because Bulbul was thinking about the old lady, he didn't realise he was only a few steps from Sweet Canteen. Noor Azad was waiting for his return. Dula Raihan must have told him.

'Bulbul, my friend. Where have you been? I've been worried sick for you. Let us talk.' Noor Azad came close to embrace him, but Bulbul stepped sideways and just walked past without looking at him or saying a word.

That night he was so exhausted that he didn't bother to eat, didn't put on the mosquito net, and went to bed without changing his clothes. Despite the bites, buzzing and humidity, he fell asleep.

CHAPTER 23

The following morning, he slept past his usual waking time and woke up only when Kazli Booa knocked on the door.

'Madam is at the breakfast table. She wants you to join her.'

Bulbul wondered why, since she never came downstairs for breakfast. Feeling the itch on his skin, he realised the mosquitoes had feasted on him, leaving him with little bumps like chickenpox.

'What's happened to your face?' asked Madam.

'I didn't put on the mosquito net last night.'

'You didn't eat your dinner either. What's the matter?'

'I had a bad day. Things didn't go well at the electricity board or at the lawyer's. I've also been following two stories. They didn't go well, either.'

'I know. The lawyer phoned me soon after you left his office. Very agitated. Went into a long rant. The electricity board phoned as well. They were very rude and threatening.'

'I'm really sorry to let you down. I promise I'll behave better next time.'

'Don't be sorry. I'm sure they deserved whatever they got from you. It's I who should be sorry to put you through all this nasty business. From now on, Kala Mia will see to these things.'

'I don't mind doing them. I was a bit tired yesterday, that's all.'

'Truly, I mean it. By teaching Khoka, you're doing enough.'

'Let me do something else for you. I can do shopping or something.'

'Don't worry. Maybe, if you have time, we can discuss ideas. Sometimes talking to someone clarifies your thoughts. But if you're busy, don't worry.'

'I'd love to. But I'm not sure if I can be a worthy interlocutor.'

'Don't underestimate yourself, Bulbul.'

On the way to the office, he headed for the shanty. He knew Noor Azad wouldn't be at Sweet Canteen then, but he still took a rickshaw and put the hood down. The sky, laden with low clouds, was dark. Warm, humid wind clung to his skin. So many things had happened, and he had so much to think through, but Noor Azad kept coming back to him. How he'd behaved towards him was terrible. Perhaps he was a bit annoying at times, but Noor Azad was more than just a friend: he'd looked out for him throughout his university days, shared his flat with him, listened to his sadness and joy, trusted him with his intimate secrets, and made him feel that he would always be there for him, like a brother. How could he walk past him without a word?

It wasn't that Noor Azad had barged in and snatched Dipa Kaiser off him. He'd known her long before him and fallen for her, granted in his peculiar way, and she had reciprocated. That should have been the end of the matter. He hadn't even fancied Dipa Kaiser until Noor Azad declared his love for her. How could jealousy drive him? It wasn't worthy of him, of any human, or even a beast.

In the shanty, he knocked on many doors, and none of those who came out and talked to him would corroborate the old woman's story: that the husband had invented the snake baby to hide the murder of his wife. Instead, they repeated stories of their terrifying encounters with the snake baby, how it nearly sank its fangs in them, gobbled them up, and how no night had passed without its hiss giving them nightmares. At the mention of the old lady, they shook their heads and laughed. 'She is mad. No one understands the meaning of her words.'

It was midday, and the heat and the humidity had drained his energy. He was trudging his way between lines of shacks when

270

the old man, accompanied by two goons, jumped on him. One of the goons pulled a knife and they dragged him to a nearby shack.

'I helped you get your story last night. Saved you from the monster. And what do you do? Listen to some mad woman's foul mouth against me and the poor father. It's not right, is it?' said the old man.

'I'm a journalist. I have to listen to all sides of the story. Facts need crosschecking.'

'Yes, yes, of course. I hope you're satisfied now. Have any of the people you talked to not corroborated the father's account?'

'Yes, they did. But I feel the old lady is telling the truth and I intend to dig deep.'

'No, you will not,' said the old man, slapping Bulbul and spitting in his face. The goon with the knife brought the blade against his throat and asked, 'Shall I finish this motherfucker off?'

'No, but he needs to be taught a lesson.' The old man told the goons to urinate on him. While the goons soaked him with their hot, pungent piss, Bulbul thought he deserved this for being mean and nasty to Noor Azad.

'If we see you here again, I won't stop these fine young people. They are very upright, you know. They get very upset with people who peddle untruths. Now, get lost before I change my mind,' said the old man.

He ran through the streets. People, taking him to be a pant-pissing, smelly madman, stepped aside. Back at the house, his heart pumping in fear of meeting Madam, he was met by Kazli Booa. She said nothing but rushed to open the bathroom door and bring him a towel and a fresh set of clothes.

When he emerged from the bathroom, he wanted to set off for the office, but Kazli Booa stopped him. She brought him a cup of tea and biscuit and stood by him.

'Newspaper job is very nasty. It doesn't suit you. You're too soft and gentle,' she said, but didn't ask what had happened. Bulbul shrugged his shoulders and gave a strained smile.

'Why don't you come to see me anymore? I liked our talks,' she said.

'Sorry, Booa. I have been very busy.'

'But not too busy to spend time with Madam.'

271

'She's very lonely. She has been very generous to me. It's the least I can do for her.'

'Aren't I lonely too? I've no husband, no children, no relatives, no friends. I was brought to be with Madam when I was nine years old. That was forty years ago. I've been serving her ever since. She's mean and vindictive. I spend a little time with you in the kitchen, she can't stomach it. She had to take that away from me.'

'Sorry Booa. I'll find a way to see you. Promise.'

At the office, he went straight to Munir Mahmud and told him about his investigation of the snake-baby case.

'I agree that the old mother is telling the truth and that the story is a scam. But her allegations are very serious. She is accusing her son-in-law of murder. She's probably right, but I can't print this story without extensive crosschecking.'

'People in the shanty are either scared of telling the truth or taken in by superstition – which the goons exploit for all it's worth.'

'I understand. Since the mother has been branded a mad woman, she can't be a credible witness. If no further corroboration is possible, I'm afraid the story is dead.'

'So, we let injustice and crime go unopposed?'

'It shouldn't be. But the bottom line is that I can't print it.'

For the rest of the day, Bulbul followed various election-related stories and, in the evening, went to the Press Club to have a cup of tea in peace and write his column.

Seeing the one-eyed journalist, his heart sank. No one was sure that he was a real journalist or worked for any newspaper, but he would always be at the club, ready to pick fights with anyone. His last meeting with Bulbul had been horrible; he'd taken the patch off his bad eye and thrust his hollow socket into Bulbul's face, calling him all sorts of names. Bulbul hurried to reach a place as far away from him as possible, but he was spotted.

'Comrade. Come and join me. It's my treat,' said One-eyed.

'Comrade? Last time we talked, you said I was no comrade of yours.'

'That was last time. You're not still brooding over that, are you?' One-eyed called the serving boy to bring Bulbul some fish cutlets and a cup of tea.

'So, why do I deserve your fraternal greetings now?'

'Comrade, you are a sharp and intelligent journalist. I want to see you on the right side of history.'

'Which is the right side?'

'Why? Revolution, of course, Comrade.'

'I'm all for it, provided we can do it peacefully and with popular consent.'

'I see. You want to play Gandhi and spin your wheel. Do you expect the revolution to fall from the sky? Even for a romantic poet who's into – what do they call them? – oh yes, muses, it would be a fantasy too far.'

'Maybe. But blood only begets blood. I know democracy's imperfect, open to all kinds of manipulations and corruptions, but without democracy, you give free rein to psychopaths and megalomaniacs.'

'It's a pity you've fallen for sentimentalities and imperialist propaganda, Comrade. Reflect on these matters objectively and rationally. Correct path should be obvious.'

Bulbul was surprised by the relatively mild tone. 'Thank you, Comrade, for your kind advice. I hope my path never becomes too clear. Certainty can breed the devil in you.'

'You need devils to change things, Comrade.'

Taking leave of One-eyed, Bulbul found a quiet corner. He couldn't think what to write because both his stories had come to dead ends. How could he expose the snake baby story without at least another person confirming the mother's account? No one needed to remind him of his commitment to truth, but it would be foolhardy to risk another visit to the shanty. The old man and the goons would butcher him and feed his flesh to dogs.

He had no better hopes with Criminal's case. If he'd discovered who he was, he could have dug deep and established how and why he'd ended up in prison. It would have been the starting point of exposing the appalling state of the criminal justice system. But with Batya Azam's death and the governor turning against him, he could not make any inroads into the story.

He had been working on stories about the upcoming election and thought of doing a longer piece on it, but what could he write that hadn't been already covered in the daily news? He went home and found Kazli Booa in the kitchen. She was happy to see him, making him Ovaltine and cutting up a mango. He was telling her about his day but got up when he heard Madam's footsteps coming down the stairs. Usually, if she needed something she would ring a bell, and Zorina or Kazli Booa ran up to serve her.

With a concerned expression Madam asked if he was okay. He said he was.

'Take your Ovaltine. Let's go upstairs,' she said, picking up the plate with the sliced mango and heading towards the door. In his haste to follow her orders, Bulbul couldn't even exchange a glance with Kazli Booa to express his regret for leaving her. Madam led him through the blue door to her study.

Instead of chairs and a table, the study contained a low desk, like those used by ancient scribes, and cushions to sit on.

'Call it a mother's instinct, I'm worried about you, Bulbul.' Madam sat in a lotus posture, her hands on her lap.

'Work is a bit challenging. It's not easy being an investigative journalist. But I'm fine.'

'Perhaps you need something else in your life.'

'In what way?' Bulbul feared his eyes betrayed a hint of panic.

'Relax. It's all good. I'll come to that in a minute, but first tell me what you thought about the book.'

'Oh, yes, *The Birth of Tragedy*. A great goatee affair. How could you tell the difference between a great god and a great goat?' he said, laughing.

'I'm glad to see you laughing.'

'I'm sorry to be so flippant. I don't know what came over me. I'm sure the author – whom I imagine to be a very intense man – my god, the moustache on him! I've never seen anything like that. I suppose the only laughter he would approve of would be demonic. I don't have that kind of weightiness in me.'

'You don't know what you have inside you, acha?'

'It's a scary thought.'

'You're not alone in that. You see, life is a great commingling of pain and laughter. We ignore that paradox at our peril. Violence and peace. The sacred and the profane. Creation and destruction. Goodness and evil. Beauty and ugliness. Formlessness and form. You have to affirm all these things over and over. That's what the anklets of Shiva and the goaty songs of Dionysus tell us – their unspeakable truths. That's the power of the Chorus in Aeschylus and Sophocles that rends us in pieces and remakes us again. That's what Lalon Shai and the Bauls sing to us. That's what I heard in Hazrat Bibi Rabia Basri in my teens. Perhaps Santa Teresa of Avila heard her too. Otherwise, how could she have written those love songs to the divine and copulated with him?' Madam spoke as if in a trance.

Not daring to look up, Bulbul took sips of Ovaltine, and listened to the wind rattling something outside.

'I got carried away. Did I make any sense?' asked Madam.

'I get the gist of the book, but I couldn't follow what you were saying towards the end.'

'You must have seen it in our Jatra. In those moments of pathos. When we lose ourselves, tears flood us. In essence, it's the same experience of rapture and ecstasy that Hazrat Bibi Rabia Basri and Lalon Shai speak of. There are no other ways than to become one with Allah.'

'I'm not sure. I can see the role of rapture and ecstasy, but the concept of the One is a transcendent idea and I'm not comfortable with that. On the other hand, music and the pathos of tragedies take you deep inside your body. You don't go anywhere else but discover your own powers. Even the destructive ones. You harness those powers to become yourself.'

'I've no truck with such ideas. Totally egocentric. I shouldn't have asked you to read that damn book. Listen, I have been reading books all my life. The more you read, the more confused you become. Let's not read or talk of books anymore. Just think of the One as the beloved. Sit with him, walk with him, sleep with him, sing with him, dance with him. But above all, be silent with him. All you need is love.'

'What kind of love?'

'No amount of talking will take us to love. Let us sit in silence and keep the door open to Him, and love will come. Bulbul, that's what you need in life.'

Feeling awkward, Bulbul sat on a cushion and closed his eyes. He couldn't think of the One, let alone love Him, and his attempts at silence only produced noise and chatter in his mind.

Next morning, in the kitchen, he apologised to Kazli Booa for leaving her so abruptly.

'Madam. She's spiteful. Whenever I sit down to chat with you, she storms in and takes you away. I suppose you learned people have a lot to talk about. Heavy things. I'm just a servant and an illiterate donkey. Who would want to listen to me?'

'I want to listen to you.'

'Don't be foolish. I've been with Madam all my life. I've no stories of my own. I'm just a shadow under her body. Not worth bothering with.'

About a week later, he woke up one morning to the noise of a truck backing towards the porch. He went to the kitchen and Kazli Booa made him tea.

'What's the racket outside, Booa?'

'Madam is in one of her moods again. She's giving away all of her books.'

Bulbul hurried to the porch. Madam smiled at him.

'I should have given them away years ago. Books are useless. Knowledge doesn't lead you anywhere. It only breeds empty chatter and cynicism. You have to rely on your experience to be in love with the divine. Only there can you find peace.'

'You're getting rid of all your books?'

'I'm donating them to the university library. But not all of them. I am keeping Hazrat Bibi Rabia Basri and Santa Teresa of Avila. Also, the poems of Hafeez, Rumi, Attar, and Rabi Thakur. And the songs of Lalon Shai.'

'Can I have some of the books?'

'I don't think that would be a good idea. Come up to my study. We can sit down in silence. That's the only way.'

Back in the kitchen, Kazli Booa fried him an egg and some freshly made roti.

'So much money she spent buying those books. Now she gets rid of them. Just like that. That's rich, spoiled people for you.'

'She's on a spiritual path. She needs some peace in her life.'

'We cook and clean. Even look after her child. And she goes on a spiritual journey.'

'Your roti is very nice, Booa. Do you pray? Believe in god?'

'What kind of stupid question is that? Of course I believe in god.

Do I look like an idiot to you? But praying? Do I have any time for that? No. Serving and working are all I do. We poor people will end up in hell anyway. Everyone knows that rich people have already booked up all the places in heaven. Praying, building mosques, going to Mecca. Stacking up mountains of righteous credit. We have nothing to show. Not in this life or after.'

One evening, skipping his visit to the Press Club, he went upstairs. The corridor, emptied of books, looked naked, as if a layer of its skin had been ripped off. He knocked on the door to Madam's study. She opened the door without making any gesture of welcome and returned to her meditation mat. The bookshelves were almost empty, and the paintings were gone too.

'What's happened to the paintings?'

'I had to come clean to my conscience. They were indeed self-portraits. Works of vanity. They had to go.'

'It's a pity. I loved looking at them.'

'You should be looking inside. Love's journey begins there.'

'I'm not sure what exactly you mean by love.'

'I told you, didn't I? No amount of talking will show you the path of love. You have to listen to silence. As Mawlana Rumi said: the quieter we become, the more we can hear.'

'I understand, but I need something more tangible.'

'Well, this is the last time I'll speak on such subjects. I'm going on a forty-day-long silence retreat. Beginning this Friday. Will you join me?'

Bulbul didn't show it, but a spasm ran through his body. 'I'm sorry,' he said, 'apart from the job, I've many things to do. Besides, I'm not ready to embark on such a spiritual journey yet.'

'You will be ready soon. I can tell that your inside is well-disposed for such a journey. On the question of love, then. As I said, nothing meaningful can be said about it. If you don't want to listen to me, listen to Rabi Thakur: Love is an endless mystery because there is no reasonable cause that could explain it.'

'I get it, but please give me something. Some inkling of its nature,' said Bulbul.

'If you insist, but I can only give you bookish knowledge. In my vanity, I thought knowledge would give me truth. Then I came to realise that it was not so. So, I've decided to give myself completely to love. It's a very different love from the passion of the body that gripped Romeo and Juliet. That form of love is driven by lust and desire. Underneath it lies the instinct for reproduction. Lovers of this type tell each other fanciful stories of touching the depths of their being, merging into each other. All you have is a drama of the ego, possessiveness and jealousy that always ends in frustration and sickness. Nothing can improve on it, not even Vatsyayana's *Kama Sutra*. In fact, it makes it worse. That odious book is a fantasy of bodily pleasure and a code for dilettante living. Very calculating and sinister, like Machiavelli's *Prince* or Kautilya's *Arthashastra*.'

'But you need techniques and strategies, just as much in the art of life as in statecraft.'

'Yes, they are needed if you're into power-mongering for your ego. But the love of the Sufi way, Baul way, Vaishnava way is different. You seek the beloved and expect nothing back from Him. Absolutely nothing.'

'By Him you mean Allah?'

'Well. Allah is one of the names. Some call Him Baba, God, Yahweh, First Cause, Prime Mover or Nature, but the names always fall short. He's always beyond.'

'Isn't it impossible to grasp the beyond?'

'It's not a question of grasping and knowledge. The divine never shows His face. Like love, He can only be intimated in silence. In the depth of emptiness. Have you heard of Nagarjuna?'

'The Buddhism of the middle way? But I don't know much about it.'

'For Nagarjuna, things dwell in the eternal silence of the night. You might want to disclose, say, a red rose in the soft morning light and offer it to your lover as a token of your passion. Alas, the red rose is already dragged down by the neighbouring black rose, the tree that spreads it canopy over it, the meadow in which it blooms, and the whole universe of things which it is a part of. No matter how hard you try, no matter how beautifully you sing it, your red rose will always slide back into the silence of the night. Fariduddin Attar Nishapuri said the same thing when he spoke of the shoreless sea. Further beyond that sea lie love and divinity – the impossible that cannot even be imagined. Do you understand why they can't be spoken, but only be listened to in the depth of silence?'

'I still don't grasp how this love and the divine can't be spoken.'

'How often do I have to tell you it's not a question of grasping? That's why I didn't want to speak about it. You forced me to dish out the bookish language I've parroted for years. It's utterly meaningless. Hafiz says love is the funeral pyre, where the heart must lay its body. Until you disappear in the dense night of the beloved and swim in the boundless waters of fana, only then can you say with Mansur al-Hallaj, *Ana al-Haqq* – I am the truth. Kings, bureaucrats and fathers might torture you and burn you to ashes, but you will have already flown with the wind and found the eternal bliss of oneness.'

'This love of yours seems very frightening. I'm not sure if I'm up to it.'

'It's because we have no language to speak of it. Our language is very crude. It can only point analogically to something that lies beyond. Let us not speak of these things anymore. Let us sit down in silence and give ourselves to love. If it helps you find your way, follow your breath, intone *la ilaha ilallah.*'

He sat beside her on the cushion and closed his eyes. His mind began to wander – jumping images, snake baby and the old man chasing him to the end of time, Dipa Kaiser whispering in his ear, her breath touching his skin. Given that abyss between himself and the feeling of love, how could he intone *la ilaha ilallah*? How could he forget what he had learned from Mohan Ganguly and Scientist? Yet, as he could finally follow his breath and ride its waves, a calmness came over him. Then it broke him, drenched him in torrents of tears, with Madam holding him and telling him, 'Let it be, listen to how it tells a tale, how it sings of separation and then of union in love.'

That night he slept soundly and dreamt of his mother who again came to him with the face of Madam.

CHAPTER 24

Bulbul took the morning mail to Mominabad. Sanu would have met him at the station if it hadn't been for his wedding. This suited Bulbul fine because he wanted to walk through the place.

Just as he came out of the station, he was stopped by an old beggar whose hair and beard, both white, were matted in a dense bush. He smelt dankly of sewers. Bulbul stepped back, but the beggar edged forward and flung his arms in the air.

'I'm hungry. Give me money,' he said in a gruff voice.

Eager to escape, Bulbul searched his pockets, gathered his change and held it out to the beggar. Instead of taking the money, the beggar grasped Bulbul's hand and looked into his palm cupping the coins.

'Are you the one who came down from the train? Are you the one to announce that Him is dead?'

'Yes, I'm from the train but have no message. You have to look for a prophet. I'm not the one.'

'Very good. Only a bogus ape. Sicko-micko mental claims to know hisself. Very good. Eh, wait a minute. Do I know you?'

'No. I'm from Dacca.'

'Are you? A dandy man from the big city, eh? Damn liar. You are Fainting Shahib's grandson, aren't you?'

Bulbul realised the beggar was Keramot Ali, whose doomsday party he had attended with his grandfather. Tipping the money into his hand, Bulbul stepped sideways and sped past him.

'Run. Run like a skinny dog. You're turning nasty like your grandfather, that fundy-mundy Feringhee ass-licker. Oh, ho, he's frying in hell and loving it!'

In his haste, Bulbul could give only a cursory glance at the cinema billboard on which he had pasted the 'Scream' poster on the faces of the lovelorn matinee idols. It was now advertising some soap with the face of a model who looked more foreign than Bengali. On Ganginarpar Road, he settled into a leisurely pace. He passed a circular gathering and looked in; it was a teeth-man's show, not the old maestro, but a young man with a long bony face poking at a large pile of teeth. His language was matter-of-fact, his tone monotonous and the audience stood glum-faced. Further on, a man stood on a pile of bricks under the water tank addressing a small crowd. The speaker, belonging to the autonomist party, was urging the crowd to follow the Leader and vote to end the exploitation and the humiliation of East Pakistan. He was as dull as the young teeth-man. Bulbul looked up at the red water tower, gleaming in the late morning sun, remembering that night when he'd risked his life to put up that poster against military rule. Well, he hadn't really done it as a protest against the dictatorship, but for Scientist. How he wished Scientist was there to give him counsel. Was he a fool being drawn into the spiritual path by Madam? No, it felt right; he had to find a deeper meaning to life than aimless wandering. He should thank his lucky stars that he'd found Madam – a teacher of rare wisdom and compassion.

At the cinema hall he stopped before the billboard advertising the forthcoming morning show – *Planet of the Apes*. Sanu the Fat would have a field day playing those monkeys. He crossed the road and popped into the tea stall. Sanu wasn't in, but the serving boy took his bag and showed him to a table at the front.

'Fat Sir has instructed me to look after you, Sir,' he said.

'I suppose he's not coming to the stall today.'

'Fat Sir's wedding, Sir. I suppose you're here to eat the feast. Big arrangement, Sir. Many goats and chickens. The tent decorated with film posters. Very nice. No one likes films more than Fat Sir. You are to stay here, until Captain Sir comes for you. What can I get you, Sir?'

He brought Bulbul some dal puri and a large glass of tea.

'Do the Muslim League goons still come here?' asked Bulbul.

'Goon Sirs are keeping a low profile, Sir. If they come, they sit like scared cats, Sir. Very polite. If it weren't for Fat Sir, people would've given them a mass beating. We have all kinds of clients, Sir. But adda Sirs are the most regular. Every evening.'

Bulbul ate the dal puris, took sips of tea and looked out at the street: cows, goats and milling crowds among the rickshaws. Ah Mominabad and mufassil – he missed it so much. After an hour or so, White Alam came by in civilian clothes but in his military jeep. The serving boy came running and saluted him.

'A glass of tea and dal puri, Captain Sir?'

White Alam said no and took Bulbul to his jeep, and they drove away. He was to stay at White Alam's house. When his father, Stingy Traffic Policeman, died, his mother moved to their village home with his sister. So, the house was empty for most of the year except for the rare occasions White Alam visited. Leaving Bulbul to

281

freshen up, White Alam went out, returning by the time lunch arrived from Sanu's house. As they ate, White Alam told Bulbul about life in the military. He told him that the generals, despite allowing the election, would be reluctant to accept the results – especially if they went in favour of the autonomists.

'We might be heading for a Godzilla time. But let's not talk about such gloomy things. We're here to celebrate a happy event. Now tell me what's happening in your life,' said White Alam.

'Not a lot. Just doing my job. Covering the election.'

'Yes, of course. But I mean personally. Sanu the Fat is getting married. My mother is arranging one for me. Good family. Plenty of money and influence. I gave her the green signal. How about you?'

'I haven't found anyone yet.'

'You're not still hooked on love marriage, are you? I say, get married, secure the home front – and then play the field. There are plenty of willing women around.'

'I don't see things that way. Actually, that sounds terrible.'

'You're still the same old communist, eh? And a romantic? You live in cloud cuckoo land. Be real.'

'I am being real. What's wrong with looking for love?'

'I see, you're still hooked on that journalist woman. I wonder what you saw in her. Besides, she is a married woman now.'

'You'd never understand. She's very special. An incredible woman. But I'm not hooked on her. She doesn't mean anything to me now.'

'Are you sure? I hear you broke up with your poet friend over her. How can you put a woman ahead of your friend? Not proper. Not a Godzilla thing to do.'

They had a siesta after lunch, then went to Sanu the Fat's tea stall. White Alam wasn't keen to mingle with the crowds in the stall but he went in, on Bulbul's insistence, for a quick cup of tea. Sanu wasn't there but said he would sneak out sometime in the night to have a session with them at White Alam's house.

The tea stall was buzzing with customers and the adda men were there in force. Abid Ali, the journalist, stood up and extended his arms. 'Journalist, come and join us.' Beaming, Bulbul strode to join them, but White Alam felt nervous among the adda men with their erratic tongues and injudicious satire to which, as a military man, he was bound to fall victim. Samsuddin Gazi, the sawmill owner, called for two extra chairs and ordered glasses of tea and rasgollas and jalebis for them. Hakim Khan, the lawyer leaned forward to look at White Alam.

'You're Stingy Traffic Policeman's son, aren't you?'

'Yes, he was my father.'

'He was a legend. A man of old ways. His stinginess and his bribe-taking had something tragic about it. It was as if he was bound by some metaphysical compulsion to conduct himself that way. Otherwise, why couldn't he enjoy his immoral earnings?'

'I knew him a bit,' said Fazle Rabbi, the landlord. 'His devotion to extra earnings had something Herculean about it. He'd go out to work even on the foulest day. He never took a day off even when he was ill. I've never seen anything like that. Such singular devotion to bribe-taking. He was a hero on an epic scale, like Oedipus.'

'True, true,' said Hakim Khan. 'What marked the man was his lack of conspicuous consumption, the extravagant display of ill-gotten wealth that we find nowadays, especially among military men. They lack the tragic gravity of our Stingy Traffic Policeman. His corruption was a moral act. Not the nihilism and cynicism that we find today.'

Although White Alam was very thick-skinned and had never tried to lessen his father's bribing ways or hide his corrupt tendencies, he wasn't keen to offer himself as an object of amusement for long. He could take it personally, but it insulted his position as a military officer. He got up and said that he needed to be somewhere else urgently.

'Urgency is a life and death matter,' said Banu Gosh. 'Of course, one must attend to it. Time becomes fractured when facing such catastrophes. Obviously, it weighs on one. That's why I cultivate the art of fishing. Time dies when you sit with your rod by a pond.'

White Alam was already striding towards the exit. For a while there was silence, and then Abid Ali shuffled in his seat and cleared his throat. 'Doctor, to the world, you're a communist. You served time accused of being one. Such is the idiocy of the military with their islamo-mania and communalistic blindness. But we know you. We've nothing secret between us, have we?

You're steeped in capitalist ideology, a free marketeer par excellence. Time is money is the favourite tune of capitalists of all varieties. Am I not right? Now, how does that square with your fishing? The sport that hollows out the very passing of time.'

'Well, fishing hooks out the clock, its mindless tick tock, and releases us to the endless waves of duration,' said Banu Gosh.

'But doctor, you're not answering my question. All I wanted to know was how you square the productive drive of capitalism, its pursuit of labour time, with the waste of time, which, no matter how you put it, fishing is?' said Abid Ali.

'Journalist, you're trying to be too logical. It doesn't suit us adda men. Isn't fishing and adda very similar? We thrive on contradiction and paradox. Anyway, I'd rather hear from our young journalist friend from Dacca,' said Banu Gosh.

'Yes, yes, Mr Bulbul. We had such high hopes for you, our young friend, that you might join our adda group one day. But we don't grudge your choice. In fact, we're very proud of your success. Already a staff journalist at a national newspaper – and an English one. Very good,' said Samsuddin Gazi.

'My journalist friend here, Abid Ali, and you – our young friend, Bulbul – we've something in common,' said Banu Gosh. 'We all served jail time for political reasons. My political crime, as you all know, was not for being political but just for being a Hindu – which I don't practice. You might say I was jailed for what I ought to be but am not.'

'You were not even a shape without form, Doctor. You were a 'no man'. You didn't exist. So, they kept in jail 'nothing' instead of you. A super tamasha,' said Fazle Rabbi.

'Very apt point, landlord. As I was saying, Abid Ali, my journalist friend, unlike me you weren't arrested for being a communist, although you are one. You were arrested for naming the name: General Ayub Khan,' continued Banu Gosh.

'True, but I'm not really a communist,' said Abid Ali. 'Like most of us here, I have my share of bourgeois tendencies. We enjoy the finer things in life too much. Frankly, we adda men can't be communists. Aren't we the overseers of the republic and kallipolis? But it's true that I've got communist friends and share certain ideals with them. It's more as an aesthetically and ethically beautiful thing – not somewhere I want to live. As our doctor said, we're paradoxical men.'

'But we are not just bohemians and dilettantes,' said Banu Gosh. 'Haven't we suffered jail time? What was your crime, Mr Bulbul, our young journalist friend? What did you serve jail time for?'

'Well, it wasn't me that they arrested. At the demo, the police were capturing bodies. I happened to be one of the bodies. They didn't know who I was,' said Bulbul.

'I beg to differ, my young friend. They weren't arresting just any bodies, but bodies in a demo. You were a body in a demo. You placed your body there, didn't you? That makes you a demonstrator. Like I'm a lawyer when I put my body in the court,' said Hakim Khan.

'Your body in court is a handsome specimen, lawyer. Not to mention its power of eloquence. I wonder, though, how you continue to be a lawyer outside court. Never mind. Now, if I may turn to our young friend; Mr Bulbul, tell us the news from Dacca. Where is the country heading?' asked Fazle Rabbi.

'I've no more news than what you read in the papers. We report what we see and hear. We can't deal with the time to come.'

'Good journalistic answer. But where's your passion? Your fire to change the world? In a journalist's hand a pen could be an instrument of war,' said Abid Ali.

'I don't disagree. But first, I want to change myself.'

'Very good. But it's your involvement in changing things that changes you. You become a revolutionary by doing revolutionary activities. Just as you become a thief by thieving, not by thinking about it,' said Abid Ali.

'Let us hear our young friend. In what ways do you want to change yourself?' asked Samsuddin Gazi.

'I met a spiritual teacher. Someone like Hazrat Bibi Rabia Basri or Mawlana Rumi. Or like our Lalon Shai. A person of immense learning and wisdom and righteousness. The love of the divine radiates through her. I want to be on that path,' said Bulbul.

'Is the lady in question young and pretty? You seem to be in love with her,' said Fazle Rabbi.

'Not in the way you think. I love her as my teacher. My pir. My guru.'

'I also had a spiritual calling in my youth,' said Banu Gosh. 'Sometimes failure in love, I mean romantic love, pushes you in that direction. It's a kind of death wish. But medical science saved me, and if I need a temporary spiritual escape, I go fishing. A day by the pond amounts to weeks of meditation in a cave.'

'You have to die to come alive. Nothing matters other than the love of the One. You live the truth that way. Everything else is superficial and a mere passing of time. Illusory time,' said Bulbul.

'You disappoint me, Bulbul. I thought you were a person of reason and enlightenment, not the god business and religious fakery,' said Abid Ali.

'I'm not running to a mosque or a temple. It's personal. Something between me and the divine. My teacher acts as a guide.'

'The same old god business and supernatural nonsense. Of course, the beautiful poetry of Hafiz, Rumi, Attar, Khayyam, Gibran or Galib makes the whole thing seductive. And whose heart doesn't pine for transcendence listening to Lalon Shai's songs? But it's as misguided as any other religion. Only the love of reason makes you truly free. We are bound by matter and its infinite composition,' said Abid Ali.

'Maybe,' said Bulbul. 'I don't want to argue about it. It's not a question of knowledge and understanding. It's a feeling and one dwells in it in silence. Let's talk about something else.'

Abid Ali shook his head, and the rest kept silent until Hakim Khan spoke.

'Let me tell you about one of my clients. A woman in the body business. She was accused of severing the manhood of her boss man and shoving it down his throat. Secret nightmare of every man.'

'Was she supposed to have cut off the whole lot or just the long bit?' asked Fazle Rabbi.

'Yes, the whole lot. Pardon my language. Balls and all.'

'Good lord. The woman is a devil bitch. I hope she was hanged for it,' said Fazle Rabbi.

'Those were precisely the prejudices I was up against. Mind you, they were my own prejudices too. So, I had to overcome myself to defend her.'

'Why should we overcome ourselves to align with evil? It's

right that she should be hanged. Butchering your privates – my god, the horror of it,' said Samsuddin Gazi.

'A very universal view, I must say, among bodies with that dangly thing. As you know, my law practice is thoroughly ethical. I only take cases if I know the accused is innocent and haven't committed the crimes they were charged with. But what's the first thing the woman did? She confessed and showed no remorse. Not only was I reluctant to take her case on, I wanted to strangle her there and then.'

'The audacity of the bitch. Strangling her would have been too kind. I would have skinned her alive,' said Samsuddin Gazi.

'But breaking my long-held principle, I took her case. She did what she was accused of, yet I defended her.'

'We're all contradictory, as I've been saying, lawyer. Take me for example. My capitalist tendencies are no secret. Yes, I wholeheartedly subscribe to the idea of maximisation of profit. I run my surgery not as a charity but as a business. Yet, when I see a poor soul knock on my door, my philosophy disappears. I end up offering my services for free. Total contradiction. Total madness. Sorry to interrupt you, lawyer. Now tell us why you took her case.'

'I was about to throw her out. Then she said she would pay me for an hour of my time. Double the amount her clients pay her to use her body. Was I a whore to her? I felt outraged and pushed her out and locked the door. I thought she was gone when I didn't hear anything for a while. Then she knocked on my door one day and said: You misunderstand me, lawyer Sir, you don't have to take my case, but give me a chance to tell my story. I promise I won't bother you again. The rest is history, as they say.'

'Under capitalism, all workers sell their bodies. We're all whores, lawyer,' said Abid Ali.

'Journalist, you bring your communist philosophy into everything. Very unfortunate. Anyway, she told me her story. I took up her case, and she was acquitted.'

'What was her story then?' asked Fazle Rabbi.

'Well, she was a feisty woman, looked at me unblinkingly. I was unnerved by the power of her gaze. Yet, she was small and thin. I wanted to hear a tragic story, but she wouldn't give it to me. I wanted her to have destitute parents who were forced to sell her into the body business. I wanted her to have a sickly child so she was forced to sell herself to buy food and medical care for him. I wanted her to have a cruel pimp who locked her up in a cage, raped her, beat her. She looked at me with her fierce eyes and said: Lawyer Sir, these are your stories, not mine, and they have no bearing on the case. My past is mine alone.'

'A very intriguing female. Why did she kill her pimp then?' asked Banu Gosh.

'She was selling her body, but her boss, a local muscle man, a thoroughly bad type, was claiming half her earnings. At first, she needed him for protection and procuring clients. Gradually, she built up her business and acquired rich and loyal customers. She was more than capable of looking after herself. Yet, the boss hung onto her and claimed half the earnings. She tried to reason with him and was even prepared to pay him a lump sum to back off, but he wouldn't listen. He wanted to enjoy the fruits of her labour for eternity. So one day she decided to finish him off. She planned it all meticulously and executed it the way she wanted.'

'That's a premeditated murder. Surely a clear case for hanging. Lawyer, I wonder how you managed to get an acquittal for her. Besides, I still don't understand why you decided to defend her,' said Samsuddin Gazi.

'She's a worker. Why should a non-labouring top dog enjoy the fruits of her labour? Between these two classes, there has always been a war. I'm glad that you, my lawyer friend, decided to fight on the right side,' said Abid Ali.

'Journalist, unlike you I've never been into the rhetoric of class war. Aren't we petit-bourgeois adda men? We are given to aesthetic pleasure and amusement of all varieties. Some disparage us as superfluous men. I wouldn't be surprised if some liken us to that scrounger of a boss,' said Hakim Khan.

'So, it's guilt that drove you to defend her – a very corrosive sentiment,' said Banu Gosh.

'No, I can't explain it, doctor. She had such honesty and nobility that you felt she was extraordinary. Somehow, I was compelled to defend her.'

'She must be a witch and she hypnotised you. Otherwise, it doesn't make any sense,' said Fazle Rabbi.

'Perhaps she was a pure force, beyond good and evil. One trembles at such force but can't help being drawn to it. Perhaps it speaks to a secret desire to be like her,' Bulbul said.

'Young man, you're talking like Keramot Ali, the jute merchant. We know where he ended up. Anyway, lawyer, how did you convince the judge that she was innocent?' said Samsuddin Gazi.

'Well, I made her wear a burka. As I said, her face was fierce, her eyes unblinking and incapable of lying. Her face hidden behind the veil, she appeared fragile with her thin, small body. Then I told the story of her impoverished parents and how they were forced to sell her, and how the cruel boss imprisoned her in a dark dungeon, beat her with his belt, raped her whenever he wanted, sold her body to dozens of men a day, who were allowed to do the most abominable things to her. She was his beast but worse off than a domestic cow or dog. So I asked the judge: if a dog is treated like that and she snaps and bites the owner one day, would you blame the dog? I left it at that and wasn't expecting a positive verdict. When the judge acquitted her, it was a surprise.'

'She must have been very pleased,' said Fazle Rabbi.

'I don't know.'

'I suppose you haven't seen her since,' said Fazle Rabbi.

'Well, I remember her story because she came to see me a few days ago. Very well dressed, like a gentlewoman. Fine manners and a measured voice. She had some problems with one of her properties. She wanted to employ me. I told her that it wasn't my area as a criminal lawyer. Anyway, I asked her why she wanted to employ me. She told me that she needed a lawyer without any morals. One that was good at lying.'

'Such a bitch. She should have been hung,' said Samsuddin Gazi.

Instead of taking a rickshaw, Bulbul decided to talk to White Alam's house. He felt relieved to have got away from the adda men. It wasn't like the olden days when, during the cricket season, sitting behind them, he lapped up their every word and imagined how wonderful it would be to be a part of their group. Now, he felt irritated by their endless chatter. He cursed himself for telling them about his recent spiritual inclinations and Madam.

No doubt they would laugh at his expense and tell some ridiculous story about it. Like his grandfather, he would end up being a laughingstock in Mominabad.

As he neared Abid Ali's press building he heard an echoing voice from a loudspeaker. It was a public meeting in the compound of the American information centre, burnt down during the uprising against General Ayub Khan. The flags, banners and posters indicated that it was a gathering of the Communist Party. The speaker was a tall, handsome man in his sixties, with a deep but clear rhythmical voice. It was passionate yet logical and poetic. Though not a very large one, the audience seemed mesmerised by him. Bulbul didn't know who it was, but he was soon held by the speaker, his appeal to end the exploitation of man by man, his dream of a society where all men would be equal. Suddenly a section of the crowd broke out calling, 'Comrade Mohan Ganguly, red salam, red salam!'

Bulbul felt danger closing in on him and that he must run to save himself. For years, he'd tried to imagine the face of the man whose notebook had made such an impact on his life. Why should he experience terror instead of joy at seeing him? Was it because he had been betraying Mohan Ganguly's teachings? Imagine how disappointed he would be to hear of his recent spiritual leanings. *Comrade Bulbul, how could you be such a dope and fall for spiritual claptrap, that life-denying, miserable escapism*?

He felt he was suffocating and almost ran to cross the road and hurried on to White Alam's house. His friend was on the veranda.

'You look so scared. Did the adda men give you rough time? Such a good-for-nothing lazy lot. Gobbing all day and feeling superior to everyone. If their beloved communists come to power, they'd be the first to get shot.'

'A bit tired. I'm fine, really. Adda men communists? Only Abid Ali, the journalist, has left leanings. Even for him it's no more than an aesthetically pleasing thing, like an exquisite cover drive.'

'Bloody cricket. I never liked the game. Heaven-made for lazies and anti-production types. Anyway, Sanu the Fat will come with dinner soon. We're going to have a Godzilla time.'

Bulbul went to shower, then lay on the bed. On the ceiling was a gecko, immobile as ever, its eyes unblinking. Fixing his eyes on it, he tried to stop thinking about Mohan Ganguly and his own cowardly behaviour. He should have stayed, said hello to him, and come clean about his spiritual leanings. If Ganguly rebuked him, he should have taken it on the chin. Nothing should distract him from his spiritual path. He sat on the floor on a pillow in half-lotus and closed his eyes. He followed his breath, in and out. He felt calm but couldn't bring himself to call the name of Allah, let alone be wrapped in his love. Were Mohan Ganguly's teachings barring his path to the divine?

White Alam knocked on the door; Sanu the Fat had arrived with tiffin carriers. After dinner they sat in the drawing room and White Alam brought out a large bottle of whisky, served three glasses with ice, and raised a toast.

'To Sanu. We wish you a Godzilla wedding tomorrow.' He downed his glass and Sanu did the same but Bulbul lowered his glass without touching any of the whisky.

'What? You're not drinking?' asked White Alam.

'My stomach's feeling a bit funny. I'll give it a miss.'

'You will get better, I promise. Pure Scottish whisky. Cost me a fortune.'

'You two carry on. I'll wait a bit.'

After their second glass of whisky, White Alam asked Bulbul if he was ready for it, but Bulbul shook his head.

'What is this? We're supposed to have a Godzilla time. What's the matter with you two? Sanu, you're keeping your mouth shut, and Bulbul, you're not touching the drink. I don't get it.'

After his third glass, Sanu the Fat perked up and started talking.

'Too many things on my mind. Maybe my filmy days are numbered.'

'For god's sake, Sanu, you're marrying Mizan Ali's daughter. Nothing to pay anymore. All totally free. Morning show, matinee, late night show. Now you can go in with your wife. You will make a romantic duo, just like in the films,' said White Alam.

'Maybe. Godzilla,' said Sanu.

'Yes, Godzilla. Here we go,' said White Alam and began to laugh. Sanu joined him, but Bulbul was still looking serious.

'You're not still thinking of that journalist woman? I told you, didn't I, that you should have gored that damn poet to death. No good feeling miserable for yourself now. Let's have a Godzilla time one last time,' said Sanu the Fat, screaming like Godzilla.

'I'm not thinking of her. It's over,' said Bulbul.

'What then? What's making you so miserable?' asked Sanu.

'Sorry. I should've come clean with you two earlier. Actually, my stomach is fine. I got into something.'

'What? You're not thinking of becoming a saint again?' asked Sanu.

'No. That thing in Dambarpur – that was a fraud. Now I've met a real saint.'

'That saint thing in Dambarpur was a good earner. I would've kept it. Anyway, who's this saint of yours?' asked White Alam.

'Well, not quite a saint. Though she has all the qualities. She is more like a teacher,' said Bulbul.

'Singing bird, you are in love again, aren't you? And she told you not to drink and, like a good boy, you're obeying,' said Sanu.

'Not the way you think. She showed me the way to spiritual love. The love of the divine.'

'I thought you'd done with the god business. It would be funny to see you running to the mosque. Even Godzilla would have a bellyache laughing,' said Sanu.

'I'm not going to the mosque. I'm taking the Sufi way. The Baul way of Lalon Shai.'

'Whatever, you still have God, Allah, Brahma. I thought you got rid of that nonsense long ago,' said White Alam.

'Well, it's not the same kind of god. He doesn't belong to any religion. He's nothingness beyond, whose love created the world. And I want to join him in love.'

'Just fancy language. If you want to be religious, go ahead. Don't cloud it with mumbo jumbo,' said White Alam.

'Have one last drink with me. For Godzilla's sake,' said Sanu, and Bulbul took a swig of whisky.

'It's good. The best whisky I've tasted,' he said and continued drinking and was soon as drunk as his friends.

'Singing bird, it's no good loving a saint woman. No good will come of it. You will have only pain and no pleasure,' said Sanu.

'She will take him to heaven. There he will enjoy seventy-two houris. Singing bird, you greedy, lecherous son of a gun,' said White Alam.

'My Madam is my divine guide. She will take me to the truth.'

'Madam? Your saint woman is a madam? Singing bird, you naughty boy,' said Sanu.

The next day, at the wedding ceremony at the bride's house, surrounded by Bulbul and White Alam, and sitting on a raised platform, wearing his silk sherwani and pagri, Sanu the Fat looked sombre. He sat with downcast eyes, sweating in the humidity of the afternoon. Sanu, who was usually unashamed of his huge appetite, could not even bear to look at the whole roasted goat served before him.

'For Godzilla's sake, eat something. You'll need your strength for the honeymoon night,' said White Alam.

'The whole thing's too much for me. I feel like fainting.'

His discomfort was compounded by his bride's gaggle of cousins who'd come, as customary, to tease him.

'Brother-in-law, why are you so fat? Can you eat five pots of rice in one sitting? My god, with your huge belly you're sure to flatten our poor sister. She'll end up a paan leaf,' said a skinny little girl who pulled on Sanu's sherwani. He gave a weak, forced smile.

'Brother-in-law, is it true that you snore so big that crows fall dead? Oh, our poor sister. She'll be broken to pieces,' said a naughty-looking boy who knocked Sanu's pagri off his head. Sanu gave the same weak, laboured smile.

'Brother-in-law, they say you act funny, like a big lizard. Give us a show,' said another boy, much older than the rest. He put a grasshopper on Sanu's head and began to laugh.

'Yes, Godzilla!' Sanu popped his eyes and gave a fearsome, low Godzilla grunt. It was enough to scatter the teasing cousins. After that, he regained his appetite and began devouring the goat.

Seeing the adda men approaching, Bulbul moved away; he went to sit on the parapet by the raintree and lit a cigarette. It was there that White Alam found him.

'I was looking for you everywhere.'

'Why?'

'A messenger from Dacca. He came to my house looking for you. Not finding us there, he came here.'

'What message?'

'I don't know. It must be urgent. Come. I'll take you to the man,' said White Alam.

It was Kala Mia, the driver.

'What's so urgent?' asked Bulbul.

'Munir Mahmud sent me to bring you back to Dacca.'

'Why? I've got leave for another week. I'm going to Dambarpur tomorrow.'

'Our little Sir, Khoka, is no more,' said Kala Mia.

'What? What's happened to him?'

'He was found dead in the school pond. Madam is acting funny. So Munir Mahmud Sir sent me to fetch you.'

CHAPTER 25

He found Madam in her study, darkened save for a dying candle. Her back straight, knees folded, eyes closed, she swayed her head back and forth and rhythmically intoned *Allah hoo*. She didn't seem to have noticed Bulbul standing behind her. Only when he turned to leave did she beckon him to her side. He took his place on the rug and folded his knees as she did. At first, he felt awkward, his breath erratic, but as time passed he was drawn into her loops. He began to breathe to her rhythm and intoned *Allah hoo*. He felt a caressing wind on his face as if a flight of butterflies were fluttering their wings of love over him. *Allah hoo*.

Now the candle was dead and the room pitch-black. He began to sob, and Madam held him, then lowered his head on her lap, and breathed *Allah hoo* on his face. Such was the caress of divine breath and mother love, he couldn't stop sobbing.

'Were you remembering your mother? She is with Allah. Khoka too,' said Madam. He looked at her as if searching for something in her face, perhaps a faint, lost memory. She began to hum a Lalon Shai song: *I've never laid my eyes on him – Next to my house in the land of mirrors – There lives my neighbour – If only he were to touch me – All my pain will wash away – He and Lalon live in the same place and yet a chasm is between us.*

In the morning, he woke up in his bed. He had no idea how he got there. Kazli Booa brought him a cup of tea and told him that she and Madam had brought him down last night.

'Can I tell you something? Stay away from Madam.'

'Why? She has only been kind to me.'

'Nothing good will come of it. Especially for you. Let her mourn her own child.'

'Poor Khoka, he was such a sad boy.'

'Yes, yes, he was. Doomed from the beginning. Someone like him never stood a chance.'

'Why not?'

'What? What do you take me for – a gossiping woman?' Kazli Booa scurried off.

Still in bed, Bulbul thought that he should go out to look for a place to rent. Now that Khoka was dead, he had no reason to stay. He went up to Madam's room and found her praying. When she'd finished, she asked him what the matter was.

'Nothing, really. Sorry for being a nuisance last night.'

'Not at all. In fact, you helped me. I felt as if Khoka was with me. Together we are walking towards the divine light.'

'Khoka. I'm so sorry about him.'

Madam sighed and took to her beads, muttering *Allah hoo*. Head down, Bulbul stayed silent and bit his lips.

'I've been thinking,' he said.

'What?'

'Now that he's not here, you don't need a tutor anymore. I'll move out in the next few days.'

'You don't have to. We have a lot of rooms in this house. What am I to do with so many rooms?'

'Thank you, but it's for the best.'

'Well, do what's best for you. But can I ask you a favour?'

'Yes, of course.'

'I want to go north. It has been a yearning for some time. To be by the Mazar, to lay my eyes on Shai-ji's resting place I don't know who else to ask. Would you come with me?'

What else could Bulbul say except, 'Yes, of course'? He still had a week's leave left; it was the least he could do for her.

After breakfast, he headed for the Press Club, hoping to find a colleague who might give him a lead on a flat. As usual, One-eyed was there in a hard-to-avoid spot.

'Comrade, long time no seeing. Come, come, join me.'

'Thank you. What's made you so cheerful?' asked Bulbul.

'Oh, the news. The imperialists are reeling, Comrade. Little Vietcongs are smashing up the cowboys. And the Blacks – let us not forget the Blacks – I hear they are putting an end to the 'yes massa' tamasha. They're putting their stuff out there, limbo dancing, yes, right on Uncle Sam's imperious buttocks. Yes, the righteous train is just around the corner, Comrade.'

'Yes, that's all very well. But can we catch it? Without spiritual enlightenment?'

'There you go again. Talking the mantras of bourgeois escapism. It makes me sad. Are they massaging your brain with that shit? That editor of yours and his sister?'

'No one is brainwashing me. You'll always miss the train without divine love in your heart.'

'What? You've gone, totally gone. Kaput. It makes me sad, really sad. Only Mr Devil will have a blast. Yes, he will.'

'You and Mr Devil have a good day,' said Bulbul and moved away. He ordered tea and waited for a familiar face, but he wasn't expecting Dipa Kaiser. He would have escaped if she hadn't spotted him and dashed towards him.

'What's the matter? Why did you disappear? Noor has been so worried. Me too,' she said.

Lost for words, Bulbul rubbed the back of his neck, and looked blankly at her.

'Dipa,' he said at last.

'What do you think I am? A ghost? Not a word. You just vanished.'

'Sorry. I'm really sorry. But it was for the best. For all of us.'

'I don't understand. I feel sad that I lost you. Noor too. Did we do something wrong?'

'Forgive me for disappearing like that.'

'But why?'

'If you haven't worked it out already, well…'

'Oh,' said Dipa Kaiser, her head down, and she began playing with her orna.

'Anyway, let us put it behind us. Soon, I'll come and see you all.'

'Good to hear that. We've missed you so much.'

'Did you?' said Bulbul and then went silent, as if trying to pick up the thread of a long-lost story.

'What are you thinking?'

'Oh nothing. I've been rather preoccupied lately.'

'Yes, I heard about your landlady's son. Such a tragic story.'

'Yes, very sad. I was his tutor.'

'Are you staying on there?'

'No. I'm moving out.'

'Where will you go?'

'I don't know. I'll find somewhere.'

'My father's house is virtually empty. He likes you very much.'

'I don't think it would be a good idea.'

'Why not? He appreciates you. It will help him too. He misses company. Please consider it.'

'Ok. I'll think it over.'

'Good. Now tell me what you have been up to?'

'Apart from work, nothing much. Exploring spirituality, a bit.'

'Spirituality – that's interesting. I never thought of you as a spiritual type.'

'Well, I never thought of myself that way either. But there it is. And I'm serious about it. Anyway, what did you think I was?'

'For a start, a materialist. Of the dialectical kind.'

'Yes, I'm that too.'

'I don't understand. Dialectical materialism. How do you square that with spirituality?'

'I'm not in the squaring business anymore. All I can say is that Materialism without a soul is dead matter. Only rotten things will grow on it.'

'Yes, you've a point there. I've seen many comrades flaunting their materialism as a bloody – how can I put it? – truth machine. Becoming robotic themselves, without any feelings or care. I've wondered if we can build a just and equitable society with people like these. On the other hand, spirituality might push you to care just for your own soul. You can become very self-centred.'

'Yes, there is that danger. But if your heart is full of divine love, you'll want to share it with everyone else.'

'Love, yes. But I'm not sure about divine love. His love always seems to strangle us women. It has been a cursed love for us. Made us cower beneath His feet. Shall I tell my father you'll call on him?'

'Give me a few days to think. I'll call you.'

'Promise,' said Dipa Kaiser.

Bulbul thought Kala Mia would drive them to Lalon Shai's resting place, about two hundred miles north, but Madam decided on the train. She wore a simple white sari and wrapped her belongings in another white sari. She could have been mistaken for having humble origins if it weren't for her smooth hands and face. At the station, she asked Bulbul to buy third-class tickets. When he looked at her inquiringly, she said, 'We're on a pilgrimage. Shai-ji would disapprove of flaunting wealth. He hated all differences – between rich and poor, races, men and women, and religions. He sang of oneness and equality among all.'

'He sounds more like a communist than a mystic poet.'

'What's the difference? None, I say,' said Madam.

Bulbul took the male carriage next to Madam's female compartment. He sat by the window next to a young man whose mother was in the same carriage as Madam.

'Are you going to the north? All the way to Kustia?' asked the young man.

'Yes,' said Bulbul.

'We're from Kustia. My mother works as a domestic in Dacca. I am a baby-taxi driver. And you?'

'I'm a journalist. It will be my first time in Kustia.'

'Journalist? How come you're with us in a third-class compartment? I thought you high-up people only take first class.'

'We're visiting Shai-ji's resting place.'

'You're a Baul, then? Is your mother too?'

'Who?'

'The lady in the next compartment. I saw you helping her. Does she also take the Lalon path?'

'She's the real devotee. It's her trip, and I'm only escorting her.'

'If you don't mind me asking, what religion is Lalon?'

'Well, he has no religion. For him, all humans and animals and things, all of nature and everything is god,' said Bulbul.

'So, a stone or a plant is a god? A dirty little hog? And we humans too? Hasn't God made us? And Him beyond and above us?'

'Everything together is god. We are all part of Him, and He is part of us. That's the Lalon way.'

'I'm not a big book reader like you people. High thoughts are beyond me. But Lalon sounds like a godless, sinful type to me.'

'No one loves god more than Lalon. He can't stand being separated from Him.'

'You're confusing me. I can't get my head around it. My local mullah says Lalon and the Bauls are godless low types with very bad morals. No washing and smelling very bad and addicted to ganja.'

Bulbul looked out of the window. The morning mist had almost lifted, and villages, marooned among vast brown fields and watched over by lines of tall betel palms and clumps of bamboo, were coming into view. Children came running towards the tracks to wave at the passing train. Sensing that the baby taxi driver was still awaiting his response, Bulbul pretended to have dozed off, but his mind was racing. He felt so muddled. He was like a blind buffalo going over a cliff with this spiritual thing, but it would be cowardly to blame Madam for it, downright unfair, for she had treated him like her own son and only wanted what was best for him. And what of Dipa Kaiser? Now that he was on a spiritual path, it wasn't fair for her to barge into his life again. But how could he not think about her, the smell of her hair as she leaned across the table at the press club, and, as always, that dimple on her left cheek?

He opened his eyes when the train stopped at the next station. Along with new passengers came hawkers selling digestive concoctions, Bombay mix, large, round aubergines, boiled eggs, coconuts, newspapers, magazines, and much more. He bought a coconut and a packet of Bombay mix and took them to the women's compartment. Drawing the edge of her sari over her face, the woman next to Madam chewed on her paan and said, 'You've a good son. My son never brings me anything.' Madam took a sip of the coconut and said that Bulbul was a good boy.

'I bet he's a good earner too. He'll fetch you a handsome dowry.'

Back in his seat Bulbul bought two boiled eggs and offered one to the baby taxi driver, who thanked him and said, 'I like you Lalon and Baul people. You have simple hearts. God or no god, you're kind people.'

A newspaper and magazine seller came onboard and launched into a long, loud promotion of his wares: hot latest news, fresh and steaming, no exaggeration, no fabulation, no gossip-mongering, fakery and tall tales, just solid truth of exceeding accurateness, though truth, if truth be told, is stranger than any make-believe loud talk. Now, gentlemen, have you heard of that Amrikan hubshi fellow, Muhammed Ali is his name? Not only by name but by deed too, a Muslim of the highest order. Gentlemen, don't miss the special feature on him, which is only in today's edition. Yes, his mummy-daddy were slaves in iron collars, but Allah gave him the hands to wrestle with alligators and tussle with whales, and he did so to glorify Allah's name and to break the iron collars from his mummy-daddy's necks. He's a man, now you see him, now you don't, and what more can I say about him? Allah was just as bounteous with his tongue as He was with his hands, and no wonder he became a butterfly to float the skies and swoop down to sting the wicked like a bee, the slavers of his mummy-daddy, a miracle of a man you might say, but true, and the same can be said of our Leader, our imam, his finger pointing to the promised land, his tongue mowing down the wicked slavers who came from Punjab to rob us off our tongues. Gentlemen, read the reports from up and down the country, from Chittagong to Rangpur, people are already queuing up to vote for him. But righteous war will soon be upon us, the forces of devil slavers will descend on us like the army of Yajuj and Majuj, but the Leader, walking tall on stilts, his head touching the sky, yet his back scraping the ground, will face them like his brother Muhammed Ali. So, gentlemen, get your copy; it's a bargain, two mighty slayers of evil in one edition.

When the hawker had finished, the baby taxi driver pointed to Bulbul and said, 'Do you know who this gentleman is?'

'No,' said the hawker.

'He's a top newspaperman from Dacca.'

'How come he's travelling in third class?'

'To spot people like you. So you become a story in the newspapers.'

'I don't want to be a story. Sorry, Sir, sorry,' said the hawker, and hurried away.

In Kustia, they booked into a hotel and visited Shai-ji's resting place. It was late afternoon and the dust clouded much of the sun. They passed male fakirs with matted locks, draped in white lungies and alkhals, their female foils in white saris, strumming their ektaras, making melodies on dotaras, tapping dhols, and singing. Around the white-domed Mazar, they pushed through a milling crowd, pivoting around Lal Fakir, his long red locks whirling, his voice soaring to the sky.

A journalist from Dacca spotted Bulbul. 'Are you here to cover the mela?'

'No. It's a private visit.'

Bulbul turned to look at Madam, but she wasn't there; he lifted himself on his toes and stretched his neck to look over the crowd. She was nowhere to be seen.

'Shall I help you look for your mother?' asked the journalist.

Bulbul gave him a puzzled look but didn't say anything. He began searching for Madam, describing her and asking anyone who crossed his path whether they'd seen her. No one had. Late at night, he returned to the hotel and phoned Munir Mahmud.

'You're an investigative journalist, aren't you?' her brother said.

'It's a missing person's case. It's police work, Editor.'

'No excuses. Just find my sister. Take it as an assignment.'

Bulbul slept little that night and set off in search again in the early morning. By the afternoon he was exhausted. He sat under the banyan near Shai-Ji's Mazar and had almost dozed off when he spotted an old blind lady. He had seen her the day before among a group of female Bauls, beating cymbals and singing in her rasping voice *Which way to go, which way to turn, I don't know*. He went and sat by her, and she extended her arm and touched his head.

'What brings you to me?'

'I was with a lady, and I lost her. I'm looking for her.'

'We're all looking for the lost one. Don't look outside, look inside.'

'A well-born lady from the city. Smooth face and hands.'

'My eyes don't see, yet I see everything. She you seek has taken the path and is on the road.'

'Which way to go, how can I reach her?'

'Go inside and take your own route. That's the way. But for now, go behind the market, find the kapok tree, then south along the tobacco fields, two shrines away.'

He rented a bike, set off south on the mud path between tobacco fields and reached the first shrine. A group of male Bauls were in the courtyard strumming their ektaras and dotaras, tapping the dhol drums, clearing their throats for the musical journeys ahead. He asked them about Madam.

'The new mother. The one with smooth hands and face. She is with her sisters,' said one of the Bauls.

'Where can I find her?'

'They set off for the next Mazar early in the morning, where the bodies of the three mad ones are still shaking the ground.'

The Mazar of the three mad ones lay tangled in banyan roots, and behind it, under a krisnachura tree, he found the female Bauls at their ease. Squatting on the mud floor, Madam was engrossed in rubbing coconut oil into the long locks of a young female Baul.

Seeing Bulbul, she said, 'Singing Bird, what are you doing here?' Bulbul opened his mouth wide because Madam had never called him that before.

'Singing Bird,' said the young Baul with the long locks, 'are you the new brother? Have you come to be our bulbul? Breathing sweetness into Shai-ji's songs.'

'No. I can't sing. Sorry to disappoint you.'

'He's a newspaperman from the city. But his heart always trembles at Allah's name,' said Madam.

He walked with Madam to the pond where they sat on the ghat.

'Editor Sir, your brother is very worried about you. Me too.'

'Why worried? I am with my sisters. On Shai-ji's path.'

'Editor Sir wants you to return to Dacca with me.'

'I've found my home here. Along the path Shai-ji laid for us with his songs.'

'You're not used to this kind of life. So much hardship and danger.'

'I've changed. Hazrat Bibi Rabia Basri came to me. So did Draupadi the infinite. They all pointed to Shai-ji's path. Mawlana Rumi, Attar, Hafiz, Kabir. They all sing through him. So do Krisna and Saraswati.'

'I can't go back without you.'

'Yes, you can. I've found my way. Go and find yours, now.'

Munir Mahmud wasn't pleased. 'You come back to the office without my sister. You left her in the jungle among drug-addict scoundrels. Now, I have to go all the way to Kustia to fetch her.'

'Editor Sir, she has found her path. She's not coming back.'

'We'll see about that. Now, back to work. There's a big cyclone coming. Find out about it.' He narrowed his eyes at Bulbul.

Bulbul had heard about the cyclone raging on the southern coast. He phoned the radio station, fellow journalists, government officials, but they were still waiting for further information. Munir Mahmud wanted details of the wind velocity, the storm surge's height, government efforts at relocation, and possible casualties.

'Editor. The information is very sketchy. Just the report of a cyclone on the south coast.'

'I can't run a headline: Cyclone on the south coast. And have nothing to add to it. It's lazy journalism. Damn lazy.'

'I phoned around. No one knows much.'

'We're not no one. It's our business to know. Make the silence yield its secrets. I don't want to hear excuses.'

'Sorry, Editor.'

'Lazy journalism. Damn lazy. Now, take the first steamer to the south. Give me something to run a story. And don't come back empty-handed. Damn lazy journalism.'

The following day, a chilly November morning, Bulbul still felt Munir Mahmud's harsh tone churning acid in his stomach. Until then, he had always been considerate and sometimes affectionate towards him. Since he'd come back without Madam, Munir Mahmud seemed to blame him for his sister choosing the path of a wandering Baul.

Bulbul took a rickshaw to the old town, heading to Sadarghat.

As he passed Ratan Kaiser's house – its betel-nut trees still a long and floating paling in the mist – he wondered whether he should come and live there. He liked Ratan Kaiser, a secular man of enlightened ideals, and could learn so much from him. Besides, he would get to see more of Dipa Kaiser, who, despite his best efforts, still breached his barricades whenever he slackened his guard a bit – in moments of sleepiness, in dreams, and when the passion of his body trampled his mind. He should have fought for her, as Sanu the Fat had said. Sometimes he could be so passive, so in denial of his feelings. Perhaps it was time to own up to everything he felt and be his own person.

At the launch terminal at Sadarghat, he was about to buy a ticket for a cabin on the upper deck, but opted for the lower deck, thinking of his trip to Kustia with Madam, with Lalon Shai singing of oneness and equality between all. It was a rickety old paddle steamer. Down the stairs, in the vast open spaces of the lower deck, families were sprawled on the floor, hunched up with grim faces, some crying. He guessed they were going home to search for their relatives. He put his bags down next to a young man, Suraj Mia, a rickshaw puller in Dacca. He was travelling with his sister, Tula Banu, a domestic servant. They were heading for their ancestral home in Bhola. They feared for their family, more than fifty in number, all living in a village called Tazumuddin, near the mouth of the river Meghna. Between the sister's sobs, they prayed.

'I'm also going to Tazumuddin,' said Bulbul.

'Are you a government official, Sir?' asked Suraj Mia.

'No, I'm a newspaperman.'

'Do you think everyone is dead there?' asked Suraj Mia, and his sister broke into louder sobbing.

'I don't know. I'm going there to find out. I hope your family members are safe.'

When the sun broke through the mist, he went up to the upper deck and noticed a female figure holding onto the railings and looking out over the river. She wore a white cotton salwar, kameez, and a black orna flying over her shoulders. Feeling he shouldn't disturb her, he was about to head some distance away when she turned in profile. Dipa Kaiser. Was it a coincidence or a strange twist of destiny? Whichever, he wouldn't run away from her now.

'What are you doing here?' he asked.

'Probably the same as you. Chasing a story. I've a feeling that this cyclone is a big one. Yet, no one knows anything about it.'

'My editor insisted I check it out.'

'Good that he did. You know how things are. A woman journalist on her own, especially a local one…'

'I'm happy to escort you anytime, Dipa.'

She looked at him as if that were news to her, then quickly averted her gaze to the river, to the orange ripples from the east. Soon, the deck seemed full of people staring at them, perhaps thinking they were a couple in love on a secret rendezvous.

'Perhaps we shouldn't be seen together. You know how gossip starts,' said Dipa Kaiser.

'No one knows us here. We can put on our journalists' badges if you're still worried. Display our cameras. Be seen as a journalist team out to cover the cyclone.'

'That's all we are, aren't we?' said Dipa Kaiser.

'Are we?' said Bulbul.

It was early evening when they arrived at the Bhola terminal. It should have been thronged with relatives welcoming their loved ones from Dacca, but now only a few mangy dogs darted about, looking for scraps. Even the hawkers and beggars hadn't bothered to turn up. They saw broken shacks, roofs blown away and gaping holes in their sides. They sought out the official in charge, a portly man with thin, short legs, a cone of a tummy sticking out, and jowls hanging like a toddy-pot under his chin. He told them that the damage where they were was nothing compared to further south, along the banks of the Meghna.

'Real hell out there, especially towards the river's mouth. In villages like Tazumuddin, we think nothing survived – men or beasts. Water would have got them if they didn't perish in the 185km wind. Mountain high. Dragged them down into the sea.'

'Can we get there?' asked Bulbul.

'Nothing is running between here and Tazumuddin. Roads are impassable. Fallen trees, houses, and dead bodies blocking everything. The ferry boats and passenger sampans were either washed out to sea or dumped inland, miles from the shore.'

'I'm sure you'll agree that this news must reach the whole

country. The world must know about it. Otherwise, no help will come. Survivors will die of cholera or starvation.'

'I can see that, but what can I do?'

'I'm sure a man in your position has many resources. We'll mention you in the papers. Prominently. You'll be a national hero,' said Bulbul. Dipa Kaiser lifted her camera and began framing a shot, until the portly man stopped her.

'Let me put on a new shirt. Clean my face a bit. One can't be in a national newspaper looking like a pauper. A man must show his status in life.' He disappeared behind the door and returned wearing a white suit, red tie, and smearing talcum powder over his face.

Thinking that she was seeing a giant frog and unable to stop her giggles, Dipa Kaiser hid her face behind the edge of her orna.

'You look very handsome,' said Bulbul.

'I know. In my youth I had the ambition of going into films.'

'You could have become quite the hero,' said Bulbul.

'One mustn't blow one's trumpet, but I'm often complimented on my good looks.'

Keeping the shutter shut, Dipa Kaiser pretended to shoot him from various angles. The man pulled in his cheeks and pressed his chin against his neck, making his jowls even more prominent.

'Very handsome. I'm sure the nation will get a proper hero.'

'Yes, that's what we want, don't we? But isn't it a bit dark here?'

'Our cameras are the latest on the market. Work even in total darkness. Very modern,' said Dipa Kaiser.

'Very good. I'm a modern man. Very forward looking, you know.'

After he'd posed for his final shot, Bulbul asked about the speed boat.

'It's night now. I'll arrange a bunk bed in our office dormitories, Mr Bulbul. You can sleep there. First class facilities. For the lady, we have a spare room in the staff quarters. Very clean. Will you two dine with me tonight? Yes? Even in hell, Zulmat Ali gets the best fish. Please don't forget to spell my name correctly. I'll see what I can do about the boat in the morning.'

In the morning, Zulmat Ali announced that he was making the port's only working speed boat available to them.

'A man must do whatever he can in a national emergency. The

world must know of this disaster. But make sure that my name is spelt correctly. And put my picture in profile. They say I look my best that way.'

'Thank you, Mr Zulmat Ali. Profile it will be. The name and the face will live on forever in our national memory.'

Zulmat Ali had also arranged two tiffin carriers full of food for their lunch.

'Men must eat even in a hell hole. This is the curse and the pleasure of being an animal. Obviously, I prefer the latter. For your nourishment there are puris, aubergine bhai and bhuna chicken. Keep it well hidden from wretched hungry mouths.'

Outside, on the way to the ghat, Dipa shook her head and said, 'I feel sick for humouring him. I should've taken his pictures to show the world. The face of a wretched pig.'

'Yes, I agree. But at least he has given us the boat.'

Near the mooring for the speed boat, Bulbul spotted Suraj Mia and Tula Banu, squatting by the water's edge. Usually there were small boats to ferry passengers to Tazumuddin, but today there were none.

On Bulbul's insistence the speed boat driver allowed them to come on board. On both sides of the river it looked like a nuclear catastrophe, with houses mangled in heaps, boats perched in trees, and bloated bodies of humans and animals drifting down-stream. Bulbul had never thought he would stumble into a more disturbing vision than those he suffered in his nightmares when he was a boy, fearful of an impending nuclear holocaust. What he saw was much worse than his dreams ever delivered.

Near the mouth of the Meghna, Tula Banu screamed, and the speedboat stopped. All the familiar landmarks of their village were gone, except the mosque, its brick-built minaret, encrusted in mud, standing solitary under the sky. Without it, Tula Banu would not have recognised her village. While the driver steered, Bulbul and Dipa Kaiser used long poles to push aside bloated bodies to clear their passage to the mooring place. Hearing the speedboat's engine, a dozen people rushed towards them, the survivors of a village of about a thousand people. It was the first visit they'd had. Since the day the water came from the sea, riding on the wind, they'd had nothing to eat and were sick from drinking contaminated water.

Dipa Kaiser and Bulbul looked at each other and ran back to fetch the tiffin carriers. At first the people stood in dazed silence, then they fell upon the food all at once, the young men claiming the lion's share, women and children scrabbling for the leftovers scattered on the muddy ground.

'Where are the government officials? Where is the relief? People have been forgotten and left to die like beasts. Pakistan must pay for this,' said Dipa Kaiser.

Soon after dropping them, the speedboat driver left; he would return to pick them up in the late afternoon. Suraj Mia and Tula Banu headed up the riverbank. Bulbul and Dipa Kaiser followed them. Only the mud platforms remained in a large compound – the huts had flown god knows where. Screaming and calling the names of their loved ones, Suraj Mia and Tula Banu ran zigzag across the compound. No one answered their calls. They called for the stray dog that hung around the compound – Kutta, Kutta – but that too fell on deaf ears. They slumped to the ground, not crying anymore but staring at nothing with nothing in their eyes. Surely someone must have survived of their family of fifty? Bulbul and Dipa Kaiser looked around the compound but couldn't find anyone.

It was afternoon and the sky was blue and empty – not even a vulture circling it. At first, no-one noticed a man who came in silence and stood behind them.

'Suraj Bhai,' said the man. Suraj Mia and Tula Banu jumped to their feet, looking at him as if he couldn't be real, a ghost.

'Where have you been?' asked Suraj Mia.

'Looking for food. Nothing to eat here.' The man was their cousin, Fonu Mia.

The brother and the sister recited the names of their parents and other relatives, asking what had happened to them. Fonu Mia looked at the sea and pointed.

'Where are the bodies?' asked Bulbul.

'Only a few returned from the sea,' said Fonu Mia.

'What happened to them?'

'They are by the mangrove.'

There, they found the group of survivors, squatting, staring at the bloated corpses floating at the water's edge or trapped between the mangroves. One of the survivors stood up and asked if they had any more food. When Bulbul told them they had none, the group stood up and left. Fonu Mia was too hungry and exhausted to help; he sat with his hands cupping his face.

The floating bodies were beginning to smell. Suraj Mia, Tula Banu, Bulbul and Dipa Kaiser walked out into the water. Treading water up to their chins, the siblings turned each body face up. They screamed with recognition and dragged their loved ones to the shore. Bulbul and Dipa Kaiser pulled bodies ashore but felt helpless because there were so many of them and they had nothing to dig graves with.

Among the twenty bodies they brought ashore were Suraj Mia and Tula Banu's brothers and sisters, but their parents weren't among them. Fonu Mia still sat impassive, as if he was in the middle of a dream. Not once did he look at the bodies of his loved ones piling up around him. Suddenly he lifted his head and said he was hungry. Tula Banu had rice cereal and date palm sugar in the bundle she'd brought along for the journey. Hunched over the rice cereal like a lion guarding his kill, Fonu Mia set about eating with such passion and intensity that Bulbul and Dipa Kaiser turned their eyes away because it was obscene to watch.

It felt even more obscene to take photos, but they had to tell the world of this catastrophe and the callousness of the government that failed to inform the people properly or relocate them away from danger. No one had come to their aid, sent food and medicine, and buried the dead.

When they came back, they found Fonu Mia weeping over his wife's and his daughter's dead bodies. He told them that he survived by clinging to a tall palm tree. He didn't know where he had found the strength to cling on, but the storm surge was too strong for the others.

It was late afternoon when they heard the speed boat approaching. Suraj Mia and Tula Banu refused to leave their dead relatives, but Bulbul and Dipa Kaiser knew they had to inform the world of what had happened and bring help.

Back at Bhola, Zulmat Ali was waiting for them with rice bread, cream milk and meesty sweets, but despite not eating the whole day Bulbul and Dipa Kaiser had no appetite. They needed to call their newspapers in Dacca and send out the photos.

'It's important work, I admit. But one can't do good work on an empty stomach. I learnt that lesson from my grandfather. He served in the colonial police during British times. An upright man and a legendary eater.'

'We'll eat something once we finish the work,' said Bulbul. 'But you could do something for us. You will be a national hero. People will know of your good deeds.'

'Just name it. I'll do anything for you. I will have biryani cooked for your dinner. Perhaps fried hilsa fish. But don't forget to print my photo in profile and spell my name correctly. And my designation. You must get that right too. I'm the chief of this port. Yes, the very top man.'

'Of course. You're a very important man. We're honoured that you took us under your wing. Perhaps you can use your influence. I hear students are already going from home to home collecting food, medicine and clothes for the survivors. Go around the town and gather as much as you can. Apart from food, medicine and clothes, we need spades and earth-cutters. There are so many to bury. And volunteers to go to the disaster zone.'

'Students, they're only good for talk and mischief-making. Very troublesome, you know. But rest assured, I'll use my influence. At this dark hour, it's my duty. Oh, yes, don't forget the dinner. Eight o'clock sharp, and it will be a full menu.'

Zulmat Ali also made available the only working telephone, so Bulbul and Dipa Kaiser took turns telling their respective newspapers about the scale of the disaster and what they had seen. They also managed to send the film of the photos they had taken on the night steamer so it would reach Dacca the following day.

While Zulmat Ali went around to see the town's traders and businessmen, Bulbul and Dipa Kaiser met up with the student volunteers who had already collected a lot of food, clothes and blankets. On hearing about Tazumuddin the students wanted to set off immediately to take relief to the survivors and help bury the dead, but they didn't have the means to get there.

'Let us go and lay siege to Zulmat Ali's office. We mustn't budge until that motherfucking fat pig gives us a boat,' said one student with thick, black-framed glasses.

'Yes, let's hang that corrupt son-of-a-bitch upside down until he gives us a boat,' said a skinny student with a nervous tick.

'Yes, yes, let's do it now. Let's get that ass-licking bastard,' said a tiny student, who seemed to be too young to be rousing a mob.

Alarmed at the students' lynching mood, Bulbul told them that Zulmat Ali was helping with the relief effort. Right now, he was out canvassing donations from the town's well-to-do.

'I don't trust that fat bugger. He's bound to gobble up half of what he'll raise,' said the student with the black-framed glasses.

Bulbul persuaded the students not to do anything rash and wait until the morning.

'We'll get the boat. So, gather things at the port. Ask around for shovels, earth-cutters and any digging materials. There are a lot of graves to dig.'

At eight, they met Zulmat Ali on the veranda of his bungalow.

'Come come, I've been waiting for you. Even on a dark day, one mustn't be late for dinner. Hot hot from the cooker is the best.'

Dipa Kaiser asked if his wife would be joining them.

'Wife,' sighed Zulmat Ali, 'I've no luck, no luck at all. She died a year after we were married. She had a first-class mind and was a charmer. I might be partial, but people say she was a rare beauty. Allah showered His bounty on her but took her away from me. I don't complain – that's destiny for you.'

'I'm so sorry,' said Dipa Kaiser.

'My mother and sisters begged me to marry again, but I wouldn't hear of it. She was my ocean of love. I could swim several lifetimes and still not reach the end. Let me correct myself. It was wrong of me to say – incorrect to say – I've had no luck. I feel blessed to have had the company of such a wondrous person and known such love even for a brief period. Very lucky indeed.'

'I wish I could have met her. She sounds amazing,' said Dipa Kaiser.

'Yes, yes. Anyway, we're getting late for the dinner. Hot hot is the best,' said Zulmat Ali, who led them to the table. It was piled with biryani, bhuna beef, dal with fish head, fried hilsa fish, and aubergine bhaji as main dishes. Both Bulbul and Dipa Kaiser felt sick; they couldn't erase the images of the survivors falling on their tiffin carriers like beasts and Fonu Mia going god only knows where on crumbs of rice cereal among the rotting bodies of his family. Yet, at Zulmat Ali's prompting, they fell on their plates like those mouths on their tiffin carriers.

'Don't rush. There is plenty. People must show their status by the way they eat.'

'Sorry. Forgive our manners,' said Bulbul.

'Don't worry. Have your fill, then we'll talk,' said Zulmat Ali.

When meesty sweets came, Bulbul asked how his efforts had gone in the town.

'Mothers have given their saris, their sacks full of rice. Even goats and chickens. No one will go hungry or clothesless. Pharmacies have emptied their shelves. Even Doctor Ahad Khan, renowned as the meanest doctor on this side of the river, who would open a patient up and wouldn't sew him back until he got his fees, even he agreed to volunteer his time. You see I've influence in the town. And people do respect me.'

'Thank you. Now, how do we get things to the front line? The speed boat is too small,' said Bulbul.

'I know. I've already asked my technical team to work on the reserve steamer. One is in the dry dock. They'll work the whole night to get it ready by the morning. You see, I'm a man who anticipates problems and solves them while others haven't even seen the problem. I suppose that's why I am the chief. I don't like discussing practical matters over dinner, but on what page will you write about me? Show the photos of me?'

'The front page, of course,' said Bulbul.

'Yes, yes, the front page is good. Now, you two. Young lovers?' Zulmat Ali's mischievous smile made him look even more like a frog.

'We are just friends and colleagues,' said Bulbul, and Dipa Kaiser nodded.

'Yes, yes. You don't have to be bashful with me. I'm a modern man. Very forward-looking, you know. I know a pair of lovers when I see one.'

'Seriously, we're just colleagues. We came together to cover the story,' said Dipa Kaiser.

'Yes, yes. You need some privacy. I've seen to it. You'll have the VIP bungalow tonight. Just the two of you. My motto is: let love bloom like a thousand flowers.'

Bulbul looked at Zulmat Ali as if about to say something but didn't; Dipa Kaiser played with her orna.

'Have a very good night. In the morning, we began the relief effort. No one goes hungry when I'm in charge. And no one dies.'

On the way to the bungalow they didn't speak. Once inside, in the large sitting room with a ceiling fan whirring in empty space, Dipa Kaiser moved briskly ahead of Bulbul as if to escape from him, then stopped abruptly and turned around.

'What are you playing at?'

'What do you mean?'

'Why didn't you refuse the bungalow? Why weren't you more forceful? I mean, in denying it. You know, his stupid assumption.'

'Well, couldn't you have been more forceful too?'

'He was mainly talking to you. It's like a male thing going on between you two. So typical.'

'Anyway, what are you worried about? I'm not going to jump on you. I'll take the settee here. You can have the bedroom. If you want, you can lock it from inside.'

'Well, I might,' said Dipa Kaiser, quickly moving to the bedroom. Sulking, Bulbul reclined on the sofa and looked at a gecko glued to the wall. Its solitariness only heightened his. Suddenly, the gecko scuttled across the wall and launched its harpoon on something he couldn't see. Perhaps a fly or a mosquito. Bulbul sat up as if the deadly assassin had dragged him to another time and place. It altered his mood. He sat up and began drafting a piece on the cyclone, the devastation and the enormous casualties it had caused, but more than that, the callousness of the authorities. Perhaps it was the final straw that would break Pakistan.

After an hour or so, Dipa Kaiser came back. She'd had a shower and a change of clothes. She looked relaxed in her blue kameez and wrapped in a white shawl. She sat next to him and said, 'Sorry to be stroppy. It's been a tough day. Perhaps marriage does something to your head, but I trust you completely. You are a good friend. Besides, remember that I've been a student in Paris. So, I can handle these things. Sorry again.'

'Don't worry. Given how we men are, especially here, I don't blame you. Let's put it behind us. We still have a lot of work to do.'

'Yes. I've been thinking. You don't have to sleep on the sofa. In the bedroom there's a separate bed. You can take that. I don't mind at all,' said Dipa Kaiser.

'I'll be fine on the sofa,' said Bulbul.

'Not that silly chivalric thing. I insist that you take the bed. The matter is closed, yes?'

Next to the double bed where Dipa Kaiser lay, Bulbul took the single bed. No 'goodnights' said, they put the lights off. Nearly an hour passed and they were still awake. Bulbul was pretending he was asleep, not making any brisk movements. He tried to slow his breathing down to a ripple. Oh! if only he could become a gecko, no one would notice him. He could stay suspended in the wreckage of time and space. Dipa Kaiser, though, knew that he was very much awake and that his mind was speeding like hers.

'What are you thinking?' she asked.

'Strange. I have never slept in a room with a woman except my grandmother.'

'Seriously. So, you're? You know…?'

'You mean a virgin? Yes.'

Dipa Kaiser stayed silent for a while.

'We're supposed to be professionals. Stay calm, observe and report. I don't think I can do it anymore. I want to cry and scream. Throw petrol bombs. So much misery, so much injustice.'

'Don't worry. Our reports and our photos will be petrol bombs. The whole Bengali nation will be incensed. That will be the end of Pakistan.'

'I hope so. By the way, have you given the idea further thought? You know, coming to live with my father.'

'I don't know. You visit your father often, don't you? We'll bump into each other. I don't think it would do us any good.'

'Am I a monster? Do you want to avoid me at any cost? Is this why you ran away from us? Without even a word?'

'Yes,' said Bulbul.

Dipa Kaiser was silent again but breathing heavily. 'I didn't know you hated me so much.'

'Dipa. It's because I loved you so much.'

'Oh,' said Dipa and once more lapsed into silence. Both tried to stay as still as possible, but what were they to do with it now that it was out in the open?

'Sorry, Dipa. Sorry for everything.'

'You should have said something. I had feelings for you, too.'

'You must have known. I've no experience in this area, but people say somehow one feels these things.'

'I was confused. I thought you liked me. Then, when you didn't say anything, you didn't give me a sign, I thought you only liked me as a special friend. Or that you were jealous of Noor. So called mimic triangle.'

'I suppose, what you're saying... to an extent is true. But I couldn't quite confront that feeling that I loved you. So, I hid behind abstraction and jealousy. Pathetic, really.'

'I had a lot of feelings for you, but you played it so cool, I thought you couldn't care less. Well, if you'd been more forthcoming...'

'What would you have done? Whom would you have chosen? If I had expressed my love for you.'

'I don't know. I love Noor. We cultivated that love before you came onto the scene. He was so demonstrative. Still is. I thought we were made for each other and still do.'

'I know. And that's why I left.'

'Can't we just be grown up and be good friends? Noor misses you so much. He loved you more than a friend. Like a brother. He's sad losing you. Can't we have you back as a brother?'

'I don't know. I felt about you in a certain way. I don't know if I can change that.'

'You should meet someone. I've some nice friends. Perhaps I should introduce them to you. I don't want you to be alone.'

'Would it make you feel better?'

'Don't take it the wrong way. All I want is for you to be happy.'

'I'm happy, ok. Let's go to sleep.'

In the morning, they woke up tired and didn't ask each other how they had slept, let alone make eye contact. Silently, they went through their morning routines; they felt relieved when the call to the breakfast came.

'How are the young lovers?' asked Zulmat Ali.

'We're just colleagues. If you must know, I'm married. Very happily, too,' said Dipa Kaiser. Looking bewildered, Zulmat Ali swallowed up his eyes, puffed up his face and scratched his head. In an awkward silence, the three of them hurried through breakfast.

The boat was already loaded with food and other relief materials when they reached the terminal, and the student volunteers were on board. In Suraj Mia and Tula Banu's village, they buried the dead and fed the survivors, but they knew there were hundreds more villages with their dead and unburied, their diseased and starving survivors and no one to bring them succour.

That night, on the return steamer to Dacca, they kept their distance, but before arriving at Sadarghat, Dipa Kaiser came to look for him.

'Don't be like this. I still care for you. You mean a lot to me.'

'I am happy that you're happy.'

'You'll come to see us. Noor would be so thrilled.'

'So many things to do now. But I'll see.'

CHAPTER 26

Even before they arrived in Dacca, Bulbul and Dipa Kaiser's reports on the Bhola cyclone sent tremors across the land. Nationalist sentiments had already reached a fever pitch; their reports pushed them to a breaking point. It helped the autonomist party win a landslide at the general election.

Pleased with his work, Munir Mahmud promoted Bulbul to the role of the deputy chief investigating journalist. 'You've an eye for the story. Good work,' he said.

'Thank you, Editor.'

'I'm still not happy with you for losing my sister to the druggy scoundrels. But I'm a rational and a fair man.'

'Thank you, Editor. But Madam has chosen her path. None of us can do anything about it. I think she's in a happy place.'

'Happy place? Worse than a beggar's shed. Stinkier than an open sewer. Dog shit everywhere. Can't believe it. I go all the way to Kustia. Her only brother. She wouldn't even talk to me. Only smiled like an imbecile and gibbered. I couldn't make a head or tail of it. She's a well-educated, modern woman. Well-versed in philosophy, literature and the arts. She had a fine singing voice. Now she only sings that folksy gobbledygook, those damn Lalon Shai songs.'

'Sorry to differ, Editor. Lalon Shai is our greatest native philosopher. A humanist, a very radical one at that. If we are to build a secular, democratic society, bring harmony between all races, religions and classes of people, well, we can't do without him.'

'Enough of this nonsense. Go back to work.' He glared at Bulbul and returned to the piece that he was editing.

Bulbul moved to a small flat in the new part of the city. A woman came to clean the flat once a week, but he rarely saw her. Apart from a cup of tea and toast in the morning, he never cooked. He had lunch at the small café next to his office and occasionally at the press club. He always had dinner at The Grand Potbelly Eatery down his lane. He would get there, often very late, have his dinner and climb up to his flat, but sleep rarely came to him easily.

He was learning not to dwell on Dipa Kaiser. Sometimes their paths would cross at the press club. If he couldn't avoid her, he would give her a nervous smile and say how busy he had been, which was true because, after the election, the whole country was in the throes of a revolution. As an investigative journalist, he was trying to get to the stories behind the stories.

'See what the military is up to. I've a bad feeling about it,' said Munir Mahmud.

'You need the likes of the CIA or KGB for that, Editor,' said Bulbul.

'That's lazy talk for an investigating journalist. If you're not up to it, I'll find someone else.'

'Well, let me see what I can do. Give me a couple of days.'

'In a couple of days, we might all be dead.'

Bulbul thought that he should begin by visiting White Alam, now posted outside Dacca, about thirty miles away. But in non-cooperation lockdown Dacca there was no public transport. There were barricades throughout the city, and because of the threat of violence and danger, the baby taxis stopped working. A few rickshaws were still braving the streets, but White Alam's camp was beyond their range.

With this problem in mind, Bulbul entered The Grand Potbelly Eatery. It was almost empty except for Mr Potbelly himself and his three staff members sitting glum-faced at a dimly lit table. When he wasn't cooking, Mr Potbelly, the owner and chef, would often stand outside his restaurant. He thought his enormous potbelly – big enough for triplets – was the best advertisement for his establishment. His tactics worked most of the time. When Bulbul got to know him better, he asked him about it.

'Bulbul Bhai, it's simple really. They look at my belly, sometimes sneakily, especially those gentlemanly types. Ladies giggle behind their saris. Folks from the countryside want to poke at it. They all think surely good eating is to be had here. If the owner and the cook didn't find his own cooking so exceedingly delicious, how could he have grown such a potbelly? So, they walk in like zombies and, with Allah's blessing, none has been disappointed.'

Now, Mr Potbelly sighed, 'Bulbul Bhai, what nasty days. Hardly any customers. If it goes on like this my potbelly will turn flat. I'll be ruined.'

'Reducing your belly a bit wouldn't be a bad idea. You'd be in tiptop health.'

'Bulbul Bhai, you have some funny ideas. Have you been mixing with foreigners? People look at my belly and say: such exceedingly good health; may it continue with Allah's blessings. Now, what can I do for you? The usual?'

'No. I'll just have aubergine, potato bhaji and dal. I don't feel that hungry today.'

'What? No fish, no meat. Are you trying to ruin your health? I bet that's a no-good Feringhee thing. Oh Allah, they're everywhere. All right, all right, the customer gets what he wants. But Bulbul Bhai, you're not just a customer to me. I'm very fond of you. Never met someone with so much wiseness. Now tell me what's happening? Is General Yahiya Khan playing games with us?'

'I don't know. I feel that something fishy is going on.'

'If you newspapermen don't know, Allah help us.'

'I think the military is plotting something. But all very hush-hush. If I could get to my friend – he's in the army – about thirty miles away.'

'Take my bike. Go and see your friend. If the military moves against us and lays a finger on our Leader, this land will burn. Ha, it will.'

'Thank you. I could do it with the bike. Very kind of you.'

'It's not a matter of thanking. It's my duty. Go and find out what the military is up to. Very greedy lot they are. Once they put on khaki pants, their shit takes a wrong turning, ends up in their brains.'

It was a chilly morning; the mist hadn't lifted yet. Putting his shoulder bag on his back and securing it with a rope, Bulbul set off. Without motor traffic, the city should have been silent, but the workers and the students manning the barricades, even at these hours, were noisy. Their slogans told of their yearning for freedom and readiness to shed blood to achieve it.

By the time he'd crossed the city's outer neighbourhoods, the sun broke through the mist. He rode between lines of sugarcane, past endless mustard fields, whose yellow, vibrant in the sun, made him feel almost optimistic. He arrived at a bridge, but it was wrecked. Villagers, fearing army incursions, had dug trenches to the approach and set fire to the base. Made of wooden planks, the bridge was a charred wreck. He looked around but saw no one. He shouted. Receiving no response, he sat down, took some rice cereal from his shoulder bag and munched as he waited. Then a thin man with a goatee appeared on the other bank.

'Who are you? What do you want?'

'I'm a journalist. I'm on an important mission.'

'What's your mission? How do I know you're not a spy for the military?'

'I can't tell you about my mission. But you must know that it's very important. Anyway, do I look like a spy?'

'A spy doesn't look a spy. Any fool knows that. All he needs is a devious inside.'

'I assure you I don't have a devious inside. I need to find out what's happening and warn people.'

'We're expecting badness. We'll protect ourselves in any way we can,' said the man and disappeared. Time passed, then around midday, the man with the goatee reappeared on a small boat with four young men armed with spears and machetes. Jumping

319

ashore, they surrounded Bulbul and searched his shoulder bag. They were suspicious of his camera and note pads.

'What are these? For snooping around and evil doing?'

'I'm a journalist. These are my tools of trade.'

'You look too young to be a journalist? What newspaper do you work for?' asked the man with the goatee.

Bulbul told them he worked for *The People's Voice*, an English daily.

'Never heard of it. Anyway, we don't trust Feringhee papers. Full of foreign ways. They are always up to some badness.'

Luckily, he had a copy of the paper in his shoulder bag that featured his report on the cyclone; it had a lot of photos of the disaster and the victims. He showed them his journalist badge to prove he was the article's author.

'We don't know Feringhee's ways of writing,' said the man with the goatee and sent one of the young men to fetch the school-teacher. He, a timid man with a stutter, verified that Bulbul's name on the journalist's badge was that of the author of the article and said that the paper, despite being in English, was with the people.

'With even the people of foreign ways on our side, we will surely have victory. Allah willing,' said the man with the goatee.

They helped him across the river.

Cycling at top speed, Bulbul reached the camp at about two in the afternoon. It looked like an impenetrable fortress with a stern-looking military policeman guarding the main entrance. He sat under a tree some distance away hoping, rather absurdly, that White Alam would wander out. No one came in or out of the gate except speeding military jeeps. At last, gathering courage, he approached the entrance.

'What's your business here?' asked the tall, skinny military policeman in Urdu. He had a well-groomed handlebar moustache that spoke menace and violence.

'Captain Alam. A childhood friend. I came to see him,' said Bulbul in his broken Urdu.

'No visitors allowed now. Everything closed for a VIP visit.'

'It's urgent. His mother is very ill. In fact, dying.'

'We've mothers dying, too, in Punjab, in Sind and the frontier provinces. We can't see them because of you damn fish-eating

Bengalis. You're creating mischief. Now clear off.'

Bulbul had no option but to return to Dacca. Feeling disheartened because Munir Mahmud wouldn't be pleased, he felt like taking to his bed, perhaps picking up the novel he had given up reading, or listening to some music. It had been ages since he had done either of these things. Then he remembered the meeting at the campus.

He knew that both Noor Azad and Dipa Kaiser would be present. That didn't deter him. On the contrary, he felt compelled to attend because they would be there. Now that the signs of impending catastrophe were becoming all too real, it dawned on him that he might not get another chance to see them.

He still had Mr Potbelly's bike. He rode it through the mist-laden avenues, made darker because of the unlit streetlights, though torches danced like giant fireflies at the barricades. His journalist credentials allowed an easy passage. He could hear the slogans exploding into the night sky long before he reached the campus. Torches on long bamboo poles made the gathering a festive city of lights. There were thousands of people, mostly young, and their mood, despite the foreboding of tumultuous times, was festive too. It was as if they were there to celebrate their team winning the World Cup. Along the path leading to the stage, some youths, sporting wood or bamboo-made mock rifles, marched as if heading to the front line. Bulbul couldn't help being moved by these brave boys and girls. Would he have the same resolve to walk into the death zone? In front of the stage, groups of students leapt into the air; their slogans, merging into each other, became an enormous thunder of passion.

He knew that Noor Azad would be on stage at some point in the evening. He was billed as the leading poet on the programme, but Dipa Kaiser – what would she be doing? Would she be there to lend moral support to her husband? Or as a journalist covering the story? Or would she be like him, just an ordinary member of the public?

He made his way to the front and spotted Dipa on the stage. She wore a green salwar/kameez and a red orna wrapped like a scarf around her neck. Always the professional, she was taking many photographs. He waved, but she didn't spot him. Perhaps after the event he would seek them out. He was content to give himself to the poets and the musicians for now. After a couple of patriotic songs, which the crowds sang along to, the poets began to appear – mostly young and fiery and passionate.

Because Noor Azad was the best-known poet, he was to appear last. Thinking about what he knew of Noor Azad's writing, Bulbul felt uneasy. His friend might find himself out of sync with the crowd's mood. Recently, he had been writing abstruse, highbrow poetry about idiosyncratic, personal, inner experience. Following his French masters, he imagined the devastated land-scape of industrial capital and the coming of the machine age, where alienated flaneurs wandered in the ugly underbelly of emerging megacities, saying a lot in beautifully crafted, musical verses but not saying much.

Apart from the tiny bohemian arty lot from the posh neigh-bourhoods, this crowd, only recently emerged from the paddy fields, sought a collective, safe home. Bulbul feared that they, after their initial gesture of respectful silence, might lose their patience with Noor Azad and boo him off the stage.

It was unprecedented. The crowd, just as much as Bulbul, was stunned. Then they broke into euphoric dancing. Holding torches, their flames fluttering high in the wind, they whirled like der-vishes. Noor Azad appeared on the stage flying a flag: a dark green piece of cloth, its circular red middle had a cutout map of East Pakistan stitched on it. 'This is the flag of our Bangladesh,' he announced and ran across the stage, the flag flying like a sail across a tempestuous sea. Dipa Kaiser ran around him, taking camera shots from every angle.

Noor Azad then hoisted the flag on a pole set up for it at the front of the stage. He raised his hand to silence the crowd, which was now ready to lap up his every word. His poems were simple and direct: they spoke of people's hopes and aspirations, their determi-nation to live on their land on their own terms. In beautifully shaped images, they evoked the pastoral romanticism of green and riverine Bengal. He was now a people's poet, and the people took him to their hearts.

Afterwards, Bulbul went to look for Noor Azad and Dipa Kaiser and found them surrounded by a large group of admirers. Noor

Azad was soaking up the adulation of his fans and responding to their silly questions – which would have gotten on his nerves only a short while ago and unleashed his sharp, biting tongue on them. Now, he was patient with them. Standing next to him, Dipa Kaiser was at ease, no longer a journalist but a smiling, encouraging partner who was approving every word of her beloved comrade husband. Such a beautiful couple.

It was Dipa Kaiser who spotted him and called out his name. Noor Azad broke free of his fans and rushed towards him.

'Singing Bird, you came,' he said, hugging Bulbul. It was strange because he had never called him that before. They didn't have much time as he and Dipa Kaiser were due at a meeting.

'Things are coming to a head. We're not prepared, Bulbul. We're not prepared,' said Noor Azad.

'I have a bad feeling too. Who knows what will happen? I'm glad we met,' said Bulbul.

'Yes, yes. Don't you run out on me again. Acha? I missed you so much,' said Noor Azad.

'I'm sorry,' said Bulbul.

'Past is past. No explanation is needed. It will be like old times again. Only better,' said Noor Azad.

'I'm so glad that we found you again. Let's meet soon. Properly. The three of us,' said Dipa Kaiser.

Bulbul cycled back to The Grand Potbelly Eatery and again found Mr Potbelly and his staff seated at the same dimly lit table. The rest of the Eatery was empty, like a deserted station at the end of a godforsaken line.

'I knew you'd be coming. So we stayed open.' Mr Potbelly gestured him to join them at the table.

'Thank you,' said Bulbul.

'I don't like this thanking business. Very foreign custom. Anyway, today you're not a customer, but our guest. And none of that veggie-wuggie nonsense. Proper dining of Eatery style. All on us.'

'Why are you so kind to me?'

'There you go again. Perhaps I should call you my little brother, then you wouldn't bother with that botheration. Very tiresome.'

'You can call me little brother. I would like that.'

'Acha? Can't believe I have a high-class educated man like you as a little brother. You see, I don't know any reading-writing. When I was a little boy, a restaurant owner acquired me. It's a terrible history, but I don't want to go into it. Feeling bitter and sad are not my things. I began by doing the plates and pots. Then, as a serving boy. Finally, I learned my trade in the kitchen. Now, I own my restaurant. Very lucky. Anyway, enough of me. Little brother, how was your visit to the military.'

'Well, it didn't go very well. They wouldn't let me in. Saying VIP visits, high security. Things like that.'

'Very suspicious. Buggers are cooking up something. Your friend the captain. Any news of him?'

'No. They turned me away at the gate. Then I heard helicopters landing.'

'Very suspicious. Generals must be going around the camps. Giving instructions. Hush, hush like. I wouldn't be surprised if your friend was already disarmed and arrested. I hope they haven't killed him already.'

Dishes arrived at the table. A whole chicken roast, pilau rice, parathas, beef bhuna, goat curry, and large pieces of fried carp.

'So much. I suppose you people are starving.'

'We're not hungry. We've already dined. We'll watch you eat. That will be our pleasure, little brother.'

'I'm not very hungry. Anyway, I can't possibly eat all this.'

'I might be an uneducated cook, but I sense things. Bad times are coming, little brother. Eat your fill.'

With the eyes of Mr Potbelly and his staff on him, Bulbul felt uneasy; he nibbled at a piece of carp.

'Very tasty,' he said.

'Ha, but you're not eating much. Oh Allah, you're just skin and bones. To fight the military, you must be strong, little brother.'

'Can I keep the bike until tomorrow? I am thinking of trying the camp again.'

'Keep the bike as long as you want. Better, consider it yours. But I'm not sure about you going to the camp again. Dangerous. Buggers are planning something bad. Nasty lot.'

'Mostly rumours and hearsay. We've no reliable evidence yet. The Leader is still talking to General Yahiya Khan.'

'I don't like the look of him, that General. If you narrow your eyes, you see a devil's face. He's just buying time. Organising savagery on the sly. Ha, that's what he's doing.'

Despite being very tired, it took Bulbul ages to fall asleep. He thought of Noor Azad and Dipa Kaiser. If there was a perfect couple anywhere in the world, it was them; they were made for each other, but what a lousy friend he had been, walking out on them. Stupid, petty jealousy. He would make it up to them: perhaps invite them to The Grand Potbelly Eatery and introduce them to Mr Potbelly himself as his best friends. No doubt Dipa Kaiser would find him amusing and hide her giggles behind her orna, and Noor Azad would be keen to get along with him. He was sure that Mr Potbelly would make a fuss over them, saying your friends are my little brother and sister, too, ha they are. It's on me, dine until your belly aches, no veggie-wuggie nonsense, just solid Eatery dining. Ah, bright young people, our future, but things are not looking good. What will happen if the army unleashes its firepower on the people?

It didn't bear thinking. Bulbul felt as he did when he used to have nightmares and wake up screaming, and Dadu and Kona Boo came running to him. Dadu. It had been so long; he should have been to see her – what a useless grandson he had been, getting carried away with his work, stupid jealousy, and Madam and her spiritual fantasies. Sorry, Dadu, really sorry.

He woke up late, and the mist had already lifted. He rode out on the bike and arrived at the broken bridge by midday. He shouted for help, but no one came. He wondered what had happened to the goatee man, the teacher, and the others: why weren't they responding to his call? He waited an hour, then secured the bike against a dead tree, hid his bag under a rattan bush, and plunged into the river. Luckily, the current wasn't strong, and he crossed it easily. It was about ten miles until the next river, and he walked on and on. No one was around, only a few goats or cows doing what they do, paying him no attention as he passed. It was late afternoon and the sky turned bright red, then dark purple. A flock of herons flew over the bamboo groves nearby. Suddenly, it was dark. He had no torch but the road was straight. He walked until he saw the lights of the military camp.

The gate was shut. No military police were guarding it. Occasionally, the gate opened to let in or out a jeep or troop carrier. Everything told him he mustn't go anywhere near the gate. Something very dangerous was happening. It was already nine; too late to return to Dacca. Besides, now he had come this far, he couldn't go back without seeing White Alam. What had happened to him? Perhaps he'd been locked up or even killed, as Mr Potbelly seemed to think. But White Alam, well apprenticed at the home of Stingy Traffic Policeman, had always been devious and full of tricks. It would be him if anyone knew how to stay alive in such circumstances.

The night got darker. It was silent save for a few jackals howling some distance away. Suddenly, the camp became a giant orb of light, so bright he felt he was looking straight into the sun. Then the firing began. He crawled back several paces and stayed with his head ducked behind a mound. After half an hour or so, the firing stopped as suddenly as it had begun. The gate opened and the roar of engines shook the earth. Ten jeeps, at least fifty troop carriers, and many armoured vehicles sped out. They formed a long column through the night until the wind stopped carrying their sound. Now, even the jackals stopped howling. He lay there looking at the dark sky. Not even a star to offer him solace.

He waited for another twenty minutes, then crawled towards the gate, which was still open. He pricked up his ears but heard nothing from inside the camp. It seemed everyone had left with the convoy. The camp was still brightly lit, but no living soul seemed left there. What had happened to White Alam? Perhaps he'd gone with the convoy. But what was the firing for? In that half an hour, it seemed thousands of rounds had been shot. Who were they shooting at? He should have explored the rest of the camp, but his legs froze because it crossed his mind that something terrible had happened here. He didn't want to stumble on White Alam's body.

Jackals had started howling again. He thought he should find White Alam's body before they did. He moved through the camp – no one was there. Then he went around the back to a long barrack. It was dark there. He opened the door. His first impulse was to run away because the smell of blood was sickening. He doubled up, gagging. Several minutes passed; it was not the time to turn his back on his friend. It was not the moment to dwell on the past, but how not to remember Abid Ali, fire in his eyes, standing on a box before his burnt-out press and naming the name – General Ayub Khan – knowing that the military was coming for him? How about Dadu, crazy Dadu? Had she thought twice when she faced that mob frenzied for Kona Das's blood? No, she hadn't even batted an eyelid. And Dipa Kaiser. She was no less crazy than Dadu. God only knows where she got that strength to cling to the boy. Three burly policeman, all pumped up, and they still couldn't snatch the boy off her.

He fumbled for the switch. There were bodies in a flood of blood across the room. A big pile against the wall at the back. Perhaps several hundred. None of them had their uniforms on. All had their hands tied behind their backs. Now strangely calm, as if all emotions had drained out of him, he moved from body to body like a mechanical doll. All were Bengalis. It seemed that just before they left the camp, the Pakistani soldiers had executed the Bengali members of their units.

Now frantic, Bulbul went on turning the bodies but couldn't find White Alam among them. He started to scream: 'Alam, Captain Alam, it's your friend Bulbul, where are you?' He was about to give up when he saw a movement under a pile of bodies. Soaked in blood, White Alam appeared from underneath and said, 'Godzilla.'

CHAPTER 27

Before White Alam headed for the Indian border and Bulbul returned to his flat in Dacca, they lay under the night sky, watching fireflies dance in silence.

'You're thinking, aren't you? How did I manage it?' said White Alam.

'Yes, how did you do it?'

'Simple really. Just looked for the weakest link. Offered him a bribe. My watch, my radio, and the cash I had on me.'

'He could've just taken those things from you, then shot you.'

'Yes, he could have. But once I'd offered them to him as gifts, he was caught in the obligation trap. A vicious trap. As I said, he was the weakest link. You see, there is an art as much in giving as in taking bribes.'

'Well, I'm glad your apprenticeship with your father came in handy. I am so relieved. Happy to see you safe.'

'Anyway, how come you're here? I wasn't expecting a visitor in these terrible times.'

'We heard rumours that Pakistan was massing troops, preparing an all-out attack on us Bengalis. No one had any concrete information, so my editor insisted that I do a bit of legwork. Find out what's happening. I thought you might know something.'

'We knew alright. But you're too late. Far too late. The buggers have gone for a pre-emptive strike. Weeks ago they disarmed us, all the Bengalis in the regiment. Then they arrested us and kept us locked up in the barrack where you found me.'

'How did they manage to keep it a secret?'

'Well, they closed the camp. Completely sealed it off. Stopped using phones. Even wireless. Generals would come in on helicopters at night and instruct the local commanders. Yes, we had a pretty good idea of what was happening, but what could we have done? They kept us with our hands tied behind our backs. They had armed guards posted all around the barrack. If only one of us had managed to escape.'

'Sorry to be late. Now they must be out butchering people.'

'I also heard they plan to massacre our intellectuals, poets and artists. I know you're mixed up with that lot. Perhaps there's still time. You can warn them. And your newspaper. They hated all those liberal newspapers. Especially those sympathetic to nationalist causes, like yours. You need to warn the editor.'

He arrived back in Dacca about midday. The city was under curfew and the military patrols were the only traffic on the roads. Sporadic firing could be heard from various parts of the city. Bulbul used narrow alleyways, slithered along the ditches, crawled behind walls and parapets, and made wild runs where there was no other option. Hoped for the best. He was lucky.

Before going to his flat he knocked on the door of The Grand Potbelly Eatery. No answer. As he was about to leave, someone opened the door a tiny sliver. It was Mr Potbelly. He grabbed Bulbul and yanked him inside.

'What are you doing out there? They are killing everyone. What to do, my little brother?'

'I don't know. Maybe we should get out of the city.'

'There is a curfew. They are shooting anything that moves. It would be too foolish to go out. Let us wait a bit. Doing rushed things in an emergency is no good. You must be hungry. Let me give you something nice to eat. No more restaurant-wusturant hokum-tukum. Now you eat here like home. Ha, your own home.'

Bulbul had hardly eaten anything for the last two days. Yet, only now, at the mention of food, did he feel hungry. Mr Potbelly served him chicken curry, dal and a large plate of rice.

'Sorry. Not serving you many items and hardly any top-ranking items. The chicken. An old hen. She passed her laying days long ago and her meat's tough. Not good eating. She went about pecking and clucking the backyard like she owned the place. What to do? I had to slaughter her. No market to buy anything. No customers to feed. Bloody military.'

Bulbul nodded and tucked into the meal.

'Did you find your friend? The military man?'

Bulbul told him what had happened at the camp and how White Alam survived.

'Ha, that's the rule. In times like this, the good ones end up dead. Only the devious types survive. Anyway, I'm glad your friend made it. At least someone was there to tell the story.'

'He's heading towards India.'

'You should be doing the same. It's not safe here. Not at all.'

'First, I need to find out what's happened to my friends. Also, to my editor.'

'Don't do anything rash, little brother. Wait for the curfew to be lifted. I'll take you out. At least out of Dacca. No time to see friends. Acha?'

From all corners of the city came the sounds of gunshots, mechanical and insistent, some close up, then loud bangs of explosions, earth-shattering and terrifying, but Bulbul, so tired and emotionally numb, drifted into sleep. He dreamt of Dipa Kaiser appearing as a horse with wings. She put him on her back and flew across the sky. The following morning, he turned the radio on. The military broadcast announced that the curfew had been lifted until the afternoon.

He was making himself a cup of tea when he heard a knock on his door. He leapt up, thinking that it was the military coming for him. He thought of getting out of the bathroom window and then onto the roof. He could climb down using the pipe and run for it as they do in films. He went to the kitchen and carefully pinched the curtain enough to see who was at his door. It was Mr Potbelly who'd come with a tiffin carrier containing paratha, aubergine bhaji and the leftover chicken curry from last night. He also brought along a suitcase.

'Window has opened. Ha, it has. Let us take you out of Dacca. First, have breakfast. Nothing tiptop can be done on an empty stomach. My philosophy. On a well-filled tummy one can even conquer Everest. I bet Sherpa Tensing and Hillary had a full-up tummy before taking on that mighty mountain. Brought you some top-class breakfast. Now, little brother. Eat.'

Thousands of people on the road were using the pause in the curfew to leave the city. Like a typical husband, Mr Potbelly strode ahead with Bulbul a few paces behind. Bulbul was wearing a burka; he was playing Mr Potbelly's ailing wife. When Bulbul was reluctant, Mr Potbelly said, 'No time to be worried about gender-bender rubbish. You know your Bhola cyclone reports – first class they were. One of the regulars read them to me. I had tears in my eyes. You're a top-class journalist, little brother, but one of the reports had your photo on it. A good one. Rather handsome. When they see you, they might recognise you. It would be very dangerous.'

Panting slightly, with the laboured movements of an ailing wife, Bulbul followed. At the old railway line crossing the new and the old parts of the city, the guard at the checkpoint stopped them.

'Hey you, mother-fucking fatty, come here. Where are you going?'

'I'm taking my poor wife to her mother, Sir.'

'What's wrong with her? Why's she panting like a cow in labour? Have you been putting your whale of a weight on her? No wonder she's cracked.'

'She's very poorly, Sir. Spots all over her. I don't know if she will make it to her mother's. Ha, very doubtful, Sir.'

'How do I know you're not lying? I've had a dozen burka-wallis already. Telling the same goddamn story. All ailing and dying. I'll have to inspect your wife.'

'You'll be taking a big chance, Sir. Ha, you will. My wife's disease is very catchy. Very deadly too. Also, she's a rather religious type. Prays five times, reads the Koran all day and calls Allah's name. You wouldn't want to inspect such a woman. Allah's wrath. Allah wouldn't like you dishonouring a pious woman. I bet your wife is very pious, too. Pious women, they are Allah's gift to us. Acha, am I not saying the right thing, Sir?'

The guard was hesitating when his commanding officer came to see what was happening.

'What's the matter? Why are you taking so long? If his story doesn't add up, take him in. Otherwise, let him pass. So much traffic, we can't take the whole day on one damn case.' He summoned Mr Potbelly.

'Hey, you, what do you do?'

'I'm a cook, Sir. A good one, Sir.'

'I see. Do you make much money? Or do you gobble up everything you cook? You bloody rice-khur, fish-khur Bengalis. Lazy good-for-nothings.'

The officer poked Mr Potbelly with his baton.

'Sorry, Sir. Ha, Sir, I'm a bit partial to food. Allah has given me this gift of cooking. What can I do, Sir? One has to love one's own food. I bet your mother is an excellent cook, isn't she, Sir? A noble and pious lady.'

'This man is an idiot and a bloody glutton,' the officer told the guard. 'Let's not waste our time on him.'

Mr Potbelly wanted to take the shortest route out of Dacca, but Bulbul insisted they go by his friends' and the newspaper office. Reaching Noor Azad and Dipa Kaiser's flat, Bulbul ran up the stairs, Mr Potbelly trudging behind.

'Don't be so sprightly, little brother. You'll arouse suspicion.

331

Keep going with the ailing wife story. At all times.'

The front door was locked. Bulbul knocked, but there was no answer.

'They must be heading out of Dacca, like us.'

Bulbul wasn't reassured; he wanted to check on Sweet Canteen. Perhaps someone was there. No one was there, but the place looked ransacked. On the floor patches of thick blood were not yet dry. There were bullet marks on the wall.

'My friends. They must have killed my friends.' Bulbul slumped to the floor.

'You don't know that, little brother. They must all be on the road like us. Ha, they are.'

Bulbul touched the blood and said, 'What is this?'

Mr Potbelly almost dragged Bulbul out of Sweet Canteen.

'Let us not be foolish. Acha? The window is small. We need to make it out of Dacca by the afternoon.'

To get to his newspaper office, they had to take a detour of several roads and alleyways. Mr Potbelly wasn't happy and kept saying how foolish it was and how it would get both of them killed, but Bulbul wouldn't listen.

The doors to *The People's Voice*'s office were wide open. They went from room to room. Nothing untoward seemed to have happened: no blood, no bullet marks. Even the chairs and tables were in the same place. Munir Mahmud's green door was closed but not locked. Still in a zone of his own, Bulbul was about to rush in when Mr Potbelly stopped him.

'You stay here. Let me have a look first. Your editor is a clever man. Very educated. He must be already outside Dacca. Safe as a cuckoo in his nest, enjoying our country cooking.'

'Cuckoo building a nest?' said Bulbul, pushing past Mr Potbelly.

Munir Mahmud was still in his chair but slumped on his desk. His face was missing, blood everywhere. It seemed they'd shot him close up with a high-velocity gun.

'Little brother, let us go. There is nothing we can do here. Ha, nothing.' Mr Potbelly used his enormous bulk to drag Bulbul away from the room.

'We can't just leave him there. At least, we've got to bury him. He was my boss. My mentor.'

'Listen to me. We can't do anything for him now. He's just an empty body. Would he care if it's housed or not? I doubt it. Anyway, it's my duty to save you. Just obey your elder brother. Just for once. Acha? When I return to Dacca, I promise to care for his body. I'll do it for you.'

It was late afternoon when they reached outside Dacca. Bulbul took off the burka. When they made it to a small country market it was closed, and not a soul was around, except a few skinny dogs. Mr Potbelly knocked on several shops, but no one answered. Only the tea stall was open.

'Brother, a fine establishment you have here. War or no war business goes on. Ha, it does. Give us some tea. Thick milk and plenty of sugar. And some cookies.'

'No problem. We haven't seen you around before. Are you, by any chance, from Dacca? A lot of people have already passed through today. Too many sad stories,' said the stall owner.

'Ha, we are. Myself and my brother. Just wanted to get out of the city for a while. Until things settle down a bit. You and I, we're in the same business. War or no war, we cooks need to feed people. Acha, am I saying the right thing?' said Mr Potbelly.

'You've a tea stall in Dacca?' asked the owner.

'Sort of. I do some dishes on the side. Regulars wanted it. So, what can I do? Next time you're in Dacca, you come to my place. Acha? You enjoy my food for free. After all, we're brothers in the same trade. I have some rooms, too, if you want to spend the night. Enjoy a film in town. You stay at mine. Completely free. I insist.'

'Once things settle down a bit. I might take you up on your offer. Who wouldn't want to spend a night in Dacca? But not now. I hear Dacca is a killing field. Bodies. Thousands of bodies. Already rotting. They say even the crows have fled.'

'It won't last. In no time, all will be as usual. Ha, it will. I can already see you at my place. I'll do my top items for you. Do you want to do a few naughty things in Dacca? No problem. Life is for enjoying, that's my philosophy. Now, my little brother here needs a place to stay the night. You see, our village is too far. My brother will be gone early morning. He's no bother. Not at all. He's a very small eater. Hardly eats anything.'

The owner scratched his head but felt that he could not say no. He offered Bulbul the stall bench and said he would share with him what his wife had cooked.

'We can't do top items. We're just country folk. My home is just a room. Myself, my wife and two children. But the stall might not be big enough for you two.'

'Ha, you guessed right. I take up too much room. A cook can't help acquiring some bulk. It comes with the job. Would you eat at a skinny cook's place? I see you are acquiring a handsome paunch. Very good. In no time it will blossom. You deserve it, my brother. But didn't I tell you I'm not staying? My business needs me. Ha, it does.' Mr Potbelly took his leave, and Bulbul walked with him to the edge of the market.

'There will be curfew soon. You can't go back now. It's not safe,' said Bulbul.

'You know me. I always find a way. I'll be safe and sound. Snoring in my bed in no time. Strange beds don't suit me. Not at all. Promise me this – no risk taking – straight to your Dadu. Ha? Once things settle, I will come to see you. I bet your Dadu only makes top-class items. Little brother, I'm not a religious man, but I'm leaving you in Allah's hands. He will take care of you. Sure, he will.' Mr Potbelly disappeared into the night.

It took Bulbul two days to reach Dambarpur. It was Teeny Mullah who spotted him first. He was up in a palm tree cutting fronds to mend Dadu's hut's thatched roof. He saw Bulbul as he was coming down the slope from the bamboo grove. He slid down the palm tree and ran towards Bulbul, breathless. He looked even thinner and smaller than Bulbul remembered.

'Bulbul Bhai. Bibi has been worried sick for you. We are, too. We heard about the killings in Dacca. Thanks to Allah, you're safe.'

Teeny Mullah wanted to take Bulbul to the outer bungalow, but he insisted on going straight to the inner courtyard, to Dadu's hut.

'How have you all been? Kona Boo, fine?' asked Bulbul.

'We're all fine. But Bibi, we're worried for her,' said Teeny Mullah.

'What's wrong with Dadu?'

'Where do I start, Bulbul Bhai? Bibi is old. Diabetics, heart problems. The hips are gone. Glasses don't help her anymore.

Totally blind. She has been in bed for months. And worrying over you doesn't help.'

Bulbul sat on the edge of Dadu's bed and touched her feet.

'Who's that?'

'Dadu, it's Bulbul.'

'My little bird. Come closer.'

She tried to sit up against the pillow, but her body failed her. She extended her arms. When Bulbul came near, she put her arms around him and slid her palms over his face.

'You shaved the beard. Good. I never liked it. It made you look like a fakir.'

'How are you, Dadu? Sorry, I didn't come before.'

'My body doesn't listen to me anymore. It wants to go on its own way now. Acha, you remember the old barber? Horihor Napit. He used to do your hair when you were a little boy. He came around this morning to take his leave. He's going to India. It's not safe for Hindus anymore. Pak army is looking for them everywhere to kill them. If you kill all the barbers, who will cut your hair? The whole country will look like fakirs. Right tamasha that would be. Poor Horihor Napit. He's nearly as old as me. It's not the time to be driven from your home. He told me about the troubles in Dacca. Teeny and Kona. Such a bad lot. They tell me nothing.'

'Don't worry, Dadu. I'm here now. We'll get you on your feet in no time.'

'Little bird, you'll just fly away.'

'I'm not going anywhere, Dadu. You and me together. You have to tell me stories, though.'

'I've no stories left in me. You live in Dacca. Newspaper man. You've all the stories, now.' Dadu shouted for Kona Das. Hearing her, Teeny Mullah came running.

'Bibi, don't you remember? You sent Kona to the pond, to wash clothes.'

'Don't just stand around. Go and slaughter a chicken. My little bird is home. He can't eat dry fish and mooli. Hurry up.'

Lying on the recliner in the outer bungalow, Bulbul looked out of the window at the wind ricocheting off the pale green rice plants, field after field, which would be flooded in a few months. Kona Das came in with a cup of tea and palm bread.

'Bulbul Da, I was worried sick for you. I hear Pak soldiers are killing everyone. Especially looking for communists like you.'

'It has been terrible in Dacca, but I'm fine, Kona Boo. How are you?'

'I've been fine. Teeny built a hut just across the bush. Much nearer. I can't manage everything on my own and look after Bibi. You've seen the state she's in. Needs whole day care. I don't know what I could have done without Teeny. Besides, I don't remember you coming back. I feared Bibi might die without seeing you.'

'I know I've been an idiot. Workwise it was mad. The student movement. Cyclone. Election. But I am here now.'

'I bet you will be off soon. Many young men are going to India. They want to fight the Pak army. I also heard that the Pak army might come to villages like ours. It won't be safe for you. You're a communist, and you wrote bad things about the army in the paper. You would be on their list, on top, Bulbul Da.'

'It's you who should be going to India. Aren't you aware of what's happening?'

'I know I'm untouchable to most Hindus, and the Pak army and the mullahs see me as just a Hindu, but what to do, Bulbul Da?'

'They are killing, Kona Boo. Killing all Hindus. You must leave for India immediately. I'll find people to take you there.'

'I'm not leaving Bibi. If they want to kill me, let them kill me. I don't care.'

'You've always been a stubborn one. You've a knack for making things difficult for yourself.'

'What do you mean, Bulbul Da? Do you think I should have converted? Become Teeny's pious wife. Everything would have been alright then?'

'Yes.'

Kona Das looked at Bulbul's face as if she had only just noticed that he had shaved off his beard and cut his hair short.

'I wish you were still a fakir,' she said and left.

Facing massacres and arson laying waste to town after town, village after village, millions of refugees were escaping to India. The youth, driven by idealism and the fear of being slaughtered in their homes, listened in secret to independent Bangladesh's radio and were taking up arms. Everyone lived in fear that death would knock on their door at any minute. Bulbul, though, had become strangely detached. It was as if the war didn't exist or, if it did, was taking place far away. He didn't listen to any news and hardly ever talked to anyone apart from Dadu, Kona Das, Teeny Mullah and the imam. Even with them he avoided the subject of the war. Desperate to protect the village, the imam enlisted the help of Teeny Mullah, who again grew his beard and donned the skull cap and the long punjabi proper to a religious man. Together, they went to the nearby town to see the military authorities and the head of the Islamist-collaborationist forces – Mullah Omar Ali – whom Teeny Mullah knew as a fellow student from his madrasa days.

'You know Dambarpur is a place of pirs and saints. We freak out too much on spiritual matters to bother with freedom fighting and such nonsense. We're grateful to Pakistan for giving us the purity of Islam and letting us call Allah Allah the whole day. If any infidel comes to disturb us, they will be dealt with very harshly indeed,' said the imam.

'Yes, yes. That rings sweet to my ears. The more extreme the better,' said Mullah Omar Ali with divine menace. He turned to Teeny Mullah. 'My old friend, it's been ages. I remember you clearly from our madrasa days. You were a bit – how do I put it? – of a wishy-washy type. A bit too fond of material things. Islam was just a trade for you. Something to fatten your tummy. I'm glad that you've turned into a true believer. Don't forget that righteous violence is totally halal. Allah will be over the moon.'

Mullah Omar Ali took the imam and Teeny Mullah to see the military authorities to convince them there was nothing to worry about in Dambarpur.

'Sir, the village is our pukka bastion committed to extreme harshness towards the freedom-wallahs, the infidels and the Hindus. I assure you, they wouldn't bat an eyelid in committing harshness. They would take delight in cutting their throats. Excellent village, Sir. Pure symbol of our pure land.'

Almost every week, the imam visited Mullah Omar Ali and the military commander, always accompanied by Teeny Mullah, to report on Dambarpur's commitment to extreme harshness.

'So harsh that even our tongues tremble to name our deeds, Sir. Mr Hitler – some harsh fellow, wasn't he, Sir? – I bet even he would wet his pants to hear of our harshness,' the imam said.

Although many expected the worst, the imam's manoeuvres protected the village from military raids and allowed Bulbul to get on with his own extreme form of detachment. He wore a lungi, hung a gamcha-towel over his shoulder, and a broad-brimmed matla-hat on his head. Kona Das laughed at him. 'Bulbul Da, you look funny. Like you spent your whole life in the paddy fields.'

From her bed and using Teeny Mullah as her khansama and point man, Dadu still tried to control her estate. In average years, apart from the fishing lake, date palm sugar, the flock of geese and rice, she alternated between growing jute and mustard. These enterprises dwindled since the war drove away many of the farmhands, fishermen, date-palm cutters. There was no fishing and though blocks of date palm sugar were packed in baskets, they didn't reach the market. Kona Das looked after the geese as best she could and Teeny Mullah ran from field to field, making hardly a dent in their upkeep.

At the imam's azan in the morning, Bulbul would get up and head for the fields. He would squat, head bent and, moving like a duck, prune the mustard plants. The sun would rise and time would go by without him looking up, always bent, working the lines of mustard plants until Kona Das would bring lunch.

'Bulbul Da, you've soft hands. You're not used to this kind of work. You'll kill yourself.'

Bulbul would look at her with narrowed eyes, as if he were looking at the sun, and say, 'Kona Boo, don't worry. I'm fine.'

He preferred to sit alone under the star-apple tree, look at the rice plants dancing in the wind and eat his lunch – mostly salty-soaked rice with red hot, dry fish vorta. Sometimes, Teeny Mullah would join him. If he raised the subject of the war, Bulbul would stare at the rice plants as if he were deaf. Teeny Mullah would tug at his beard, mutter some Koranic verses, and change the subject.

'Bulbul Bhai, I hear you've become a Baul. A follower of Lalon Shai. Whatever way, I'm glad you found Allah.'

'Allah? Not my thing. I don't care much for singing and dancing to divine union. At one point, I was taken in by the idea of spiritual love. Now I realise it's a way of getting back to religion, I can't do that anymore.'

'Tawba, tawba. What are you saying, Bulbul Bhai? You're a godless, Allahless, nastic-ustic atheist. Are you not fearful for your soul? Of the eternal fires of hell?'

'No.'

'Don't you believe in anything, Bulbul Bhai?'

'Of course, I believe in a lot of things. I may not take the path of Allah and divine love as the Bauls and Lalon Shai would have us do, but I believe many of the things they are on about. I believe that the whole universe and everything is one. All things – us, the animals, the trees, the dust that gets into our eyes – are connected. There's no difference between them. All men, all races, all sexes and all things are equal.'

'You're still a communist then? A communist on the Baul path?'

'I don't care for labels, Mullah. Call me what you want. For now, all I want is to touch nature's bounty.'

'I can't believe it when I see you. Like you've always been a farmer. Maybe you're praying through the land. Mustard plant. Jute plant. Rice plant. Allah has mysterious ways.'

'Maybe. How about you? Do you still want to go to hell to be with Kona Das?'

'I don't know, Bulbul Bhai. I left it to Allah.'

When Teeny Mullah left him alone, Bulbul entered the jute fields to tend the young plants, pulling up weeds, and sometimes, without being aware of it, caressing a leaf as if he wanted to speak to it in the language of his skin. It had been a long day, but he wasn't done yet. In the late afternoon, with the sun almost touching the bamboo grove some distance away, he took to the rice fields. Usually, there would have been three or four men working the boat chutes round the clock, watering the parched, hungry fields, but now there was only him. He stepped on one of the boat chutes, pushing it down with his weight into the deep pool of water fed by the surrounding lakes and the rivers, and scooping up a brimful, he let it back up to slide the brown liquid into the fields.

At first, he felt the strain of his labour, his leg muscles screaming as if one more turn and they would burn to ashes, his heart thumping, and his lungs swimming in torrents and drowning. Then, as time passed, he felt nothing except a vague motion and the swish of the water rolling. Drenched in sweat, he went on and on, hardly noticing the orange afternoon giving way to the mauve of early evening, not even caring to look up to see the flocks of herons squawking and flying low above his head.

Kona Das stood watching him. Then she came to stand in front of him. 'Bulbul Da, what are you doing? Are you trying to kill yourself or something?'

He seemed to have woken from a trance.

'Kona Boo, it's you. What are you doing here?'

'What's got into you? You scare me, Bulbul Da.'

'Just doing my job.'

'Are you? Anyway, Bibi wants to see you.'

He went to the pond to bathe, and Kona Das followed him. While she stood on the ghat, he dipped under the water. When seconds passed by without him surfacing, she couldn't help remembering him drowning as a little boy. Then she had jumped in to pull him out. Would she have to do the same after all these years? She climbed down to the lowest step, her feet touching the water. She started to scream: 'Bulbul Da, Bulbul Da!'

It wasn't until she hitched her sari up and was about to jump in that he surfaced.

'Why are you scaring me? Has a wicked jinn possessed you?'

'Just enjoying the silence under the water.'

'What? Are you crazy?'

Dadu looked much better. Her hair had been oiled and her eyes had recovered some of their twinkle, even though she couldn't see a thing. She sat up, leaning on a round pillow. She called Bulbul to climb onto the bed and sit next to her.

'My little bird, what's happened to you?'

'Nothing. Just watering the rice fields.'

'It's not your job, little bird. Remember, you're a journalist.'

'You wanted me to be a farmer, to look after your land. Have you forgotten that?'

'That was when you weren't doing your schoolwork, didn't like reading books. Now you're a city gentleman. You took up writing as your trade. Farm work is not for you anymore.'

'Who's going to weed the mustard fields? Water the rice plants? If I don't look after your crops, they will be ruined for this year.'

'I know, but they are not your job. What can we do with the war? We have to let them go for this year.'

'I am not letting them go. As long as I am here.'

'Acha, what has happened to you? It's you who has been writing, telling us of the troubles of the war. Now that it's here, you pretend that it's not happening. I don't get it.'

'I don't want to talk about it. Tell me a story, Dadu.'

'I only know children's stories. You are not a child anymore. You were in Dacca, involved in so many things. Important things. It's you who should be telling me stories.'

'I don't want to talk about those things. If you don't want to tell me stories, that's fine. Shall I massage your feet?'

Kona Das brought in spicy puffed rice and Bulbul, taking Dadu's silence as yes, began to massage her feet.

CHAPTER 29

'I've been thinking. It's about time you got married,' said Dadu.

Bulbul didn't say anything. He shrugged his shoulders, which she took for consent.

'It must be all the work you're doing on the land. It's driving good sense into you. Maybe you were always meant to work on the land. I know your grandfather would have disapproved, but then he was an old fool.'

That night, Dadu had the old cockerel slaughtered to celebrate the news. She sent Teeny Mullah to invite the imam.

'Are you sure that Bibi has invited me to share the cockerel? I must say it's a fine-looking bird. No doubt full of flavour. But

Bibi has never invited me to the inner courtyard to share a meal before. What's going on?'

'Bibi is looking for a wife for Bulbul Bhai. I think she wants you to be the matchmaker.'

'Masallah, that is good news indeed. I'm always happy to serve the Syed family. After all, they're related to the Prophet and sainthood runs through their blood. After a suitable marriage, the young master might reconsider it.'

'Consider what?'

'Becoming a saint, of course. It'll bring prosperity to all of us.'

'Prosperity?'

'Yes, prosperity. What can be more halal than making some profit? Living it up a bit while doing Allah's work.'

The imam arrived with a pitcher of milk from his cow.

'I'm honoured to be invited to your inner sanctum to share salt with your esteemed company.' He stood grinning and rubbing his hands.

'Don't just stand there. I want to speak with you before my grandson comes in,' said Dadu.

'Your words are always significant, Bibi. Very weighty and full of meaning. My ears would indeed be blessed to lend themselves to their utterance.'

'No need for blathering nonsense. I'm looking for a bride for my grandson. Can I trust you with this assignment?'

'Inshallah. I'll secure the best. The most beautiful, accomplished, and dutiful for our young master. Very shy and pious too. And most pure – that goes without saying. I'm glad that the young master has come to his senses. I'm sure it's the call of sainthood.'

'Leave that sainthood thing alone. I haven't forgotten your mischief with it the last time. I'll pay you handsomely. I'll give you two sackfuls of rice and mustard. A fish, too, from the haor.'

'Bibi, your generosity is truly unparalleled. But a kid goat. One hasn't tasted a kid for a long time. Yours look so delicious. Fat oozing out of them.'

'Imam, is this your version of spiritual matter? Never mind. You can only have one of my kid goats after you fix my grandson with a nice girl. I don't want any burka-wallis. Don't forget that my grandson is city-educated. Very modern like his grandfather.'

'If I may say so, the burka is nothing, Bibi. It's just an outer garment. To show that one is keeping up with modesty. To ward off lecherous eyes. You can't trust our menfolk, Bibi. Full of dirty thoughts, even when planting rice or praying in my mosque. Imagine the dirtiness they bring to the house of Allah. Anyway, the real good in a girl lies within.'

'I hope you're an exception to those lecherous fellows. Do you have someone in mind?'

'Yes, yes. A wonderful girl. Her beauty is matched only by her virtue.'

'Come on, man, don't try to be a storyteller with me and keep me in suspense. Who is she?'

'You know Haji Azar, the imam from the next village. As it happens, his daughter is that rare thing: beauty matched by virtue.'

'Isn't he an Al-Badr? Collaborating with the Pakistani army?'

'It's a hard time, Bibi. We all have to play the game a bit. From the outside, some people will see us as collaborators, bloodthirsty Pak-lovers. Haji Azar has taken blessings from the house of Allah in Mecca and touched the grave of our prophet in Medina. There is no blemish on his character.'

'I hear he has always been a Jammat-e-Islami man. Didn't he also grab some Hindu property?'

'We mustn't pay heed to gossip, Bibi. Some are envious of his good fortune. The man has more land than anyone else in our swampland and a fine, two-storey house to dignify his station in life. I assure you, Bibi, he's an upright man.'

'The daughter, does she have an education? And her accomplishments, what are they?'

'I am sure, Bibi, you'll agree that attending school doesn't necessarily make one educated. You, Bibi, if I may say, are the wisest person I've ever met. Have you been to school? Her accomplishments? She prays five times daily and has learned a large part of the Koran by heart. An excellent cook. Once I had the fortune to taste her catfish boona with fenugreek and mustard. I still can't help licking my fingers. She's also very good at embroidery. If you see her Mecca in gold thread, your eyes will shed a tear of righteousness.'

'I understand. The girl's illiterate. But in times like this, one can't be choosy. Would Haji Azar be agreeable to our proposal?'

'He'll jump at making a relationship with the Syed family, with the blood of saints. He'll be freaking out with joy. He might have a few rupees, but in terms of bloodline, family prestige… Well, he'll pay any price to have some of it. Yes, if I may say so, a perfect situation for driving a hard bargain.'

'We're not in the market to sell ourselves but to get a decent bride.'

'I assure you, Bibi. You'll get precisely that. She's his only daughter. I know your Syed family is esteemed throughout the land and given to higher callings. Full of dignity and upright morals, as it should be. But he'll pay a dowry. Your grandson needn't work anymore in his life. I hear he only makes a few rupees scribbling for newspapers.'

'You ignorant fool. My grandson is a journalist. A staff journalist on an English paper.'

'Forgive my insolence, Bibi. But how many people read English newspapers in our country? Only a few, I hear. Limited to our deshi shahib types. People in the market call them monkeys.'

Dadu was about to say something but stopped when she saw Bulbul coming in. He was surprised to see the imam.

'What's brought you here?' he asked.

'You tell your grandmother nothing about this war. She's starved of information, so I'm called to bring news.'

'Cut the nonsense. I've asked the imam to share the cockerel with you. He'll be your matchmaker,' said Dadu.

Bulbul tightened his face and sat cross-legged on the rattan-mat on the floor without looking at Dadu or the imam. Looking somewhat sheepish and tugging at his beard, the imam joined him. Kona Das brought in the dishes and Teeny Mullah served.

'I hear our freedom fighters are doing well. Beating the hell out of the Pak soldiers. Our heroes were raised on rice and fish. Isn't it just amazing? Victory will be ours very soon, Allah willing.'

Bulbul ignored him and got on with his meal.

'I understand. You don't want to talk about the war. All right, how are the rice fields coming along?'

'Fine. We will have a good crop, but I'm not keen on this

hybrid variety. Next season, I'll grow only the native varieties.'

'I admit the native varieties are good to eat. Such excellent flavours and textures, but the yield is very meagre. They wouldn't bring in much income.'

'I don't care much about income.'

'Yes, yes, I understand your higher calling. But once you're a married man, you will have to care about income. Who's going to feed your wife?'

Bulbul did not reply, so the imam praised the cockerel curry.

'He was a naughty bird. I don't think he liked men of religion. He used to chase me as if I were his number one enemy.'

'He never chased me. He was fond of me,' said Teeny Mullah.

'Teeny – you a religious man? I say you're a daily sinning man. A boatful of them each day. Already, you are halfway to hell.'

'Enough of this silly talk. I'm getting a headache,' said Dadu.

'Sorry, Bibi. Thank you for sharing this excellent cockerel with me. I put it up there among the best,' said the imam.

'Never mind. My little bird, are you hearing me?'

'Yes, Dadu.'

'The imam thinks Haji Azar's daughter would be a good match for you. Go and see her.'

Bulbul didn't say anything; he just shrugged his shoulders.

Kona Das brought Bulbul's lunch to the jute fields the following day. They sat under the kapok tree, its enormous humps of roots protecting them from the dusty winds.

'So, you're going for a burka-walli. Daughter of a collaborator. It's funny, I thought you were a communist.'

'Dadu wants me to get married. I don't want to disappoint her.'

'That's a flimsy excuse. I thought you were an educated man. What did you learn from all the books you read?'

'I don't know what I learnt. But now I'm learning new ways of living and thinking by working in the fields. If my only guardian, Dadu, wishes me to be married, I won't quarrel with her. Isn't that the way among country people.'

'Not my way. Anyway, when will you see Sultana?'

'I see. She's called Sultana. I'll go when the imam has arranged it. Have you seen her? What does she look like?'

'I thought you didn't care what she looked like. Acha, how

would I know? She never lifts her burka. I only remember her as a child. She was quiet and unsmiling but had dark, enormous eyes – a bit scary.'

'I see. Should I not go and meet Sultana then?'

'She's a grown woman now. She might have changed. If you don't meet her, you will never find out.'

Bulbul leaned against the kapok roots and sucked a lump of hard palm sugar. Kona Das sat next to him.

'In Dacca, you must've met some modern girls. Bob-cuts, communists. I bet they smoke cigarettes, too. Couldn't you get one of them? You know, love marriage. It would suit you better.'

'Well, there was a girl I loved, but she married someone else.'

'I see. Now it makes sense. You're jilted in love. So, you've gone all sour inside. Going for a burka-walli, I tell you, it will turn out badly. A poisonous thing.'

'I don't care anymore, Kona Boo.'

'That's what I'm trying to say. If Bibi had suggested a devil of a hag, you would've gone for her, too. It's all very sad. I feel like crying for you. But that city girl. Did you tell her you loved her?'

'It's complicated.'

'You're an idiot, Bulbul Da. Even Teeny has more courage than you. He gave up everything for me.'

On Friday afternoon, the following week, Bulbul went to see Sultana. Accompanied by Teeny Mullah, the imam came to fetch him from the outer bungalow. Seeing Bulbul in his crumpled half-shirt and cotton pants, the imam shook his head in disbelief.

'You can't go and see your bride like that. At least put on a punjabi,' and he sent Teeny Mullah to fetch one of his. Walking along the ridges between the paddy fields, the imam leading the way, they arrived at Haji Azar's homestead. Orchards and gardens surrounding the two-story tin house spoke of the family's affluence.

Haji Azar greeted them at the outer fence and ushered them to the bungalow. Once they were seated on cushions on a carpeted floor, Haji's brother, looking exactly like him, joined them.

'I'm honoured to have a member of the Syed family in my house,' said Haji.

'You're a man of Allah. He blessed you with his bounty. We're honoured to be at your home. I can see a bridge of righteousness and prosperity between the two households,' said the imam.

'Indeed. Bulbul, my son, I bet you get up with Koranic verses on your lips, pray five times a day, and observe fasting during Ramadan. As a man of the Syed family, not to say the bloodline of the saints, I'm sure you have the utmost contempt for the so-called freedom fighters. Damn atheists, communists and Hindus. They deserve utmost harshness,' said Haji.

'Of course, utmost harshness. We practice it most rigorously in our village. But our Bulbul here is a very peace-loving type. No politics,' said the imam.

'I understand. Saints have higher callings. Now, shall I call my daughter?'

Sultana, wearing a black burka, came with a plate of sweets.

'My daughter is very pious and accomplished. Please ask her questions,' said Haji.

Bulbul tightened his face and looked down.

'Have you memorised the whole Koran or only half?' asked the imam.

Sultana kept her head down and her face hidden behind the burka; she showed no sign of opening her mouth either.

'More than fifty percent, I would say. It's not becoming of women to do one hundred percent. Would you like to see her embroidery?'

Teeny Mullah tugged on Bulbul's punjabi.

'No,' said Bulbul, so quietly no one heard him.

'There will be plenty of time for that. I see a very long marriage. A happy one too. It's all very wonderful and most blessed. A pious woman adding righteousness and prosperity to the Syed household. Who knows, she might even reignite the light of sainthood in our young master,' said the imam.

'You always speak my heart's desire, imam. Now, Bulbul Baba, I understand you write for a newspaper. In the Feringhee tongue. I hear that it's very easy to speak evil in that tongue,' said Haji.

'You must know that many Muslims now call Allah in that tongue. Even our holy Koran is translated into English. It's virtually now a blessed language of Islam,' said the imam.

'Allah's mysterious craft. He could turn a cutthroat into a saint. Perhaps, Bulbul Baba, you would like to see the face of our Sultana.

Normally, she would die rather than show her face to a man, but since you're going to be her husband, it's allowed. One hundred percent.'

On Teeny Mullah's prompting, Bulbul looked up, then the Haji lifted the veil off Sultana's face. For a brief moment their eyes met.

'Allah willing, everything looks auspicious. They will make such a blessed couple,' said the imam.

When Bulbul and Teeny Mullah returned to their village, the imam stayed to discuss the finer points and practical arrangements. Just after the sunset prayer, he came to report to Dadu.

'Bibi, Haji is overjoyed at the prospect of having a relationship with the Syed family. It will elevate his humble stock. He accepted all our demands. Two acres of land and a herd of buffalos. Fine specimens and givers of thick, rich milk. Best for our deshi cheese. He'll also throw in a foreign-made bike. Not a bad dowry in war times.'

'Have you talked about the date?' asked Dadu.

'We thought it would be better to wait. You know, for the war to end. You can't have a proper party now. This wedding deserves a celebration, something people will talk about for generations. Yes, Haji will spare no expense to arrange that. Anyway, the way things are going, this war will end soon.'

'The sooner the better. I'll also throw a big party for my grandson, but after the war. Imam, you've done a good job.'

'I'm always here to serve the Syed family. Bibi, if you don't mind, you know times are hard, can I have some of my payment now? A few sacks of rice and some mustard. The goat and the fish can wait until after the marriage ceremony.'

'Acha, you can have those. If this arrangement falters, you give them back. Do you understand?'

'Jee Bibi, jee. No chance of it faltering, I assure you. Haji wouldn't let a Syed slip through his fingers. It will boost his family's prestige by a thousand-fold. Our young master – I know he's very quiet, but I'm sure, deep down, he's very happy. Sultana, what can I say? Not only by name, but also by her beauty and accomplishments. Yes, yes, a queen. Besides, he'll have a handsome dowry.'

From sunrise to sunset, Bulbul worked tirelessly in the rice and jute fields. He pruned, watered, watched plants grow and waited for the rain to come. When it came, wearing a straw matla-hat, he stayed in the fields the whole day, even though he had nothing particular to do. He squatted on the narrow high ridge bordering the fields and trained his eyes on the arching stalks, their clusters of green grains, dangling above the rising water. It was as if he were watching over his babies.

He got a cold and that forced him to bed.

'Bulbul Da, what got into you? You know rice and jute can look after themselves in the rain,' said Kona Das, bringing him a glass of hot milk.

'I had to be there, Kona Boo. In case the stalks couldn't keep up with the rising water.'

'What would you do? Drink up the flood water? Your head is not right, Bulbul Da. Now, you're making your body ill.'

'I'm fine. It's just worry about the little plants. If it weren't me, who would look after them?'

'Enough of this crazy talk. How about Sultana? Your bride. Have you thought about her?'

'What? Nothing to think about her.'

'You're marrying her, aren't you?'

'Yes, of course. At the end of the war.'

'That could be soon enough. I hear the Pak army is on the run.'

'How is Dadu?'

'Bibi is not well, Bulbul Da. She has been making funny noises. She's been asking for you.'

'I must go to the inner hut and see her.'

'You can't go with your fever and all.'

Bedridden with high fever, Bulbul stayed in the outer bungalow and the rain continued to pour and flood the land. From time to time Kona Das brought home remedies, soft rice with yoghurt, and put wet cloths on his forehead. Teeny Mullah came to sit by him and recited Koranic verses which, mingled with the sound of the rain, made Bulbul think of weeping women in houses of the dead. Seeing Bulbul's pained face, Teeny Mullah said, 'Is Shaitan chasing you? Call Allah. He'll save your soul.'

Delirious with fever, Bulbul imagined devils dancing on the

roof, all poised to feast on his soul, but Sultana came to his rescue and drove them away. Shamelessly then, lifting her veil, she stayed on, next to his skin. What was he to do but let his body have its way, get drunk on her smell, take off her blouse, the folds of her sari, her pristine undergarments and dig his teeth into her skin? Strangely, she seemed only too happy to do likewise, and bit him even harder, drawing blood. He remembered nothing of those rainy nights when he emerged from his delirium.

At the onset of the winter, the war was almost over. On the dry fields, Bulbul planted mustard, stretching as far as the bamboo grove and the rail line. Almost in a dream, he walked through them, brushing against the petals, and then he stood on the mound of the rail line to have a better view of the yellow. His heart was as happy as his eyes. At first, he didn't notice that Kona Das was running towards him, but her cry alerted him to her presence. 'Bibi is doing funny things. I'm scared, Bulbul Da. Come quickly.'

He held Dadu's hand, and she looked at him as if looking beyond him, and died. He screamed and then went to the outer bungalow and closed the door behind him.

Within days of Dadu's death, the war was over. Fearing the wrath of the freedom fighters, Haji Azam fled the village with Sultana and the rest of his family.

'Are you going to look for your bride, Bulbul Da?' asked Kona Das.

'She's not my bride. I don't know her. She means nothing to me. I only did it for Dadu and she's not here.'

'But you promised to marry her. You can't break such a promise. It will bring bad luck. A poisonous curse will hang over you.'

'A curse,' said Bulbul, smiling nervously. He went for a walk through the mustard fields.

When he returned, he called Kona Das and Teeny Mullah to the outer bungalow.

'I'm going back to Dacca,' he said.

'Why? What's going to happen to the land and the haor? And the homestead?' asked Kona Das.

'I want you two to take charge of them. Manage them in whatever ways you see fit. I don't want any profit from them.

Consider them to be yours from now on. I want you two to move into Dadu's hut.'

'Bulbul Da, you know we can't move into Bibi's hut together. Remember, we are not married. I'm still an untouchable and he is still a... you know. They will burn the hut down, drive us out. Bibi is not here. You'll be away. Who's going to protect us?'

'Well, you decide. Whatever arrangement suits you best. But I'm leaving everything to you two.'

'You're not coming back to Dambarpur again, then?'

'I don't know, Kona Boo. I don't know.'

He arrived in Dacca in the late afternoon. He went to the building where he had his flat. With the front gate locked, broken windows, and dust and dirt smearing the facade, it looked like a ghostly place. He waited a while, hoping that some other tenants, like him, might be returning too, but no one did. Instead, he went to The Grand Potbelly Eatery. It looked much the same as before the war. He paused before the door, his hands shaking. He knocked, and getting no response, he pushed the door. The room was empty, but the tables were set with water jugs and glasses, green chillies, pieces of lemons, and salt. He walked to the cash counter and looked at the festoons of flags. Circular red with a squiggle of a map on a sea of green. A voice from the kitchen drifted in. 'Lucky you. You are my first customer in independent Bangladesh. You get the full menu free. Ha, you do.'

Bulbul ran to the kitchen and found Mr Potbelly cutting up a large rohu fish.

'My little brother, it's you,' said Mr Potbelly, 'When did you get back? You look totally tip-top. Like the war did you a lot of good. Special treatment tonight. You'll have the rohu head. Ha, you will.'

CHAPTER 30

Mr Potbelly gave him a room at the back of his restaurant.

'You do nothing, little brother. You just sit at the till. Scribble your stories, if you like. Everything's free. Lodging and food. You eat whatever you fancy. Fish head every day, if you like. And why not, why not? Acha, everything tiptop? Good times are coming, little brother, good times.'

No idea what he was to do, Bulbul sat at the till, head down, reading his books and receiving the takings. He hardly ever looked up at the customers, let alone engaged them in conversation.

'Your cashier is a sour one. Bitter as a green tamarind. What's wrong with him?' one of the customers asked Mr Potbelly.

'What kind of stupid question is that? We're just coming out of the war. Millions dead. My little brother had it bad. Badder than diabolical bad. Do you expect him to play a Joker? Like them films? Ha, a real silly-billy question.'

Along with Munir Mahmud, many of the staff at *The People's Voice* were dead. Only the shell survived of the office, clinging to its steel rods like a giant scarecrow. What hit him hard was the news that Noor Azad was dead, too. His closest friend, and he had walked out of his life over a stupid jealousy. Now he was gone, he'd lost his chance to own up to it and make amends. Dipa Kaiser was still alive, but it didn't bear thinking about the enormity of her sadness, her loneliness. She had lost both her husband and her father. He thought of going to look for her but felt dead inside. Once his cashier's duty was done, he stayed in his room, sometimes wide awake in the dark, muttering to himself. Mr Potbelly was worried.

'Go for a walk, little brother. How about a film? I hear Gulistan Hall has opened its doors again. You and I can go for a late show. Perhaps a comedy. Or you fancy them fleshy actresses? Some sexy dancing behind the trees? Whatever, it would be fun. Ha, it would.'

Bulbul always responded by saying tomorrow, but with each day's passing, tomorrow was becoming never, making Mr Potbelly ever more worried. On Monday, when the restaurant had its weekly closing day, Mr Potbelly, pretending to be on a visit to see his cousin, went to *The People's Voice*'s office. It was a busy building site with a forest of scaffolding everywhere, workers milling around, repairing, plastering, painting, and replacing shattered doors and windows. One of the rooms on the ground floor had been turned into a makeshift office. From there, the newspaper was bringing out slim editions. He asked about the boss and was told she wasn't arriving until the afternoon. He bought a large packet of peanuts and waited, munching. How could he not remember that he had seen Munir Mahmud dead, his temple blown up, and pieces of brain and blood all over the room? He could still feel bile in his throat. He wondered who the woman who took charge was. Since Bulbul told him nothing, he presumed the new boss must be the previous editor's wife.

When he saw a tall, elegant lady in a white sari getting out of the car, he thought she was the new boss. He was right. Seeing the ragged and portly figure thumping towards his employer, Kala Mia jumped out of the car and stood between them.

'What do you want?' he asked.

'It's private between me and the boss. Ha, it is.'

'Get lost. Madam has no time. She has a newspaper to run.'

Stepping past them, Madam rushed towards the stairs but stopped and looked back when he heard the name Bulbul.

'How do you know Bulbul?' she asked.

'He's a little brother to me. Ha, he is.'

'Where is he? How is he?'

'He's staying with me now, where he can stay as long as he wants. I look after my little brother, but he's in a bad way.'

'He's not injured? Or tortured during the war?'

'Na. It's a mind botheration. I think he needs to work. Ha, he does.'

'Yes, of course,' said Madam, asking for the address.

It was late evening and winter chill was in the air. Customers wrapped in chadors buzzed around The Grand Potbelly Eatery. Bulbul was at the cashier's stool, and Mr Potbelly was in the kitchen. When Madam walked in, a hush descended on the restaurant. It wasn't the kind of place where women went.

She looked around and headed straight for the till.

'Gather your things. We're going home,' said Madam.

Bulbul was too stunned to respond; he looked at Madam wide-eyed, as if she were a vision.

At last, he found his voice and said, 'Tea. I'll get you some tea,' and ran to the kitchen.

Soon, Mr Potbelly came back with him and greeted Madam.

'I love my little brother here. But the restaurant is no good for him. He needs a proper home. Ha, he does.'

'I'm glad that you've seen sense in it. I'll look after Bulbul.'

Standing between the two, Bulbul seemed nonplussed, but Mr Potbelly patted his back.

'I'm always here for you, little brother. You come in whenever you want to eat a top item, especially fish head. Now go with the kind lady. Acha? You need a bit of homely treatment. Ha, you do.'

He was given his old room on the ground floor. He didn't bother to unpack his things and lay on the bed and looked at the gecko. Immobile as ever, it seemed frozen in time. Surely, he thought, it couldn't be the same old gecko. Kazli Booa came in with a cup of tea; she looked frail and much older.

'Madam got you again. I thought you had escaped. This is a cursed house.'

'Just for a few days, then I'll be gone.'

'Well, that's what they all say. Anyway, what did you do during the war?'

'I stayed with my grandmother in the village. Planted rice and grew mustard. That's all.'

'Good that you've survived. Our Zorina wasn't so lucky. Do you remember Zorina? The girl who used to do chores around the house?'

'Of course, I remember her. What's happened to her?'

'As you know, she and I are from the same village. I cared for the house when Madam went to the north to be a Baul. Zorina was back in the village. When the war started, I locked up the house and went there too. It was meant to be safer. One day, the army came. They took Zorina away. Dishonoured her. We found her body floating in the river. Poor Zorina. She was such a good girl.'

He felt unnerved by the story; he said he was having a headache and wanted to rest a bit. He went under the quilt and dozed off.

Kazli Booa came to wake him up.

'Madam's waiting for you at the table. Don't fall for her motherly tricks. She's very crafty.'

Bulbul didn't want to get up, and he wasn't hungry, but felt he couldn't refuse Madam's summons.

Madam got up from her chair and served him a plate.

'Is it the war? Something bad happened?'

'No. Nothing bad happened in the war. I was fine.'

'What did you do?'

'You mean in the war? Nothing special. I just grew rice and mustard. Things like that.'

'I see,' said Madam. An awkward silence followed and Bulbul, head down, shuffled rice grains with his fingers.

'It was a dice game with the devil,' she said.

'I wonder why the devil has spared us?'

'I don't know, but how I wish Munir were here. I could've continued with my spiritual journey, but *The People's Voice*, as you know, was founded by my father. I can't let it go under.'

'I'm glad that you're taking charge.'

'What are your plans?'

'I don't know. Perhaps I can come back to the office. If you'll have me.'

'Of course, I'll have you. I need good journalists like you to make the paper work. But there is no hurry. You take your time.'

Bulbul slept for days, but one evening, hearing Madam singing a Lalon Shai song, he went up to see her. He found her in the study which, without the paintings of Draupadi the infinite and Hypatia the lover of wisdom, and without the books, looked bare and soulless.

Putting the ektara away Madam gestured for him to sit by her on the rug.

'What's happening, Bulbul? Are you well?'

'I'm fine. But I want to go back to work.'

'Are you sure you don't want to rest a bit more? The job is yours. Always.'

'It would be best for me to work. I can't escape from life forever.'

'We went through a hell, Bulbul. We had to do what we had to do to survive. Now we have to build up this country. It's a bigger war.'

'We're just journalists. What contribution can we make?'

'You know very well we have a vital role to play. Without building a democratic culture, we will return to the same old days. Military strong man and all that nonsense. Can one build a democratic society without an independent, free, critical press?'

'When can I get back to work, then?'

'As soon as you want. I need you to take this paper forward.'

'I'll go out to look for a place tomorrow. As soon as I find one, I'll start. You can't live with your boss, can you?'

'It's not just the work thing. I care for you, Bulbul. You are like my…' She looked around, abstracted, scanning the empty wall. Bulbul thought that if only a gecko were there, he could have given himself to its timeless immobility.

'It's funny really. You wanted to be a Baul, and I wanted to be a peasant. Now that's behind us.'

'It's not behind me. I carry Lalon Shai's teaching inside me. Who could be a better guide if we want to build a humane society?'

'Maybe. But it comes with hefty baggage – this love of god thing. I don't feel easy with it.'

'Perhaps you misunderstand. His god is all of nature. Everything. Like Einstein's god, Spinoza's god. Anyway, let's not argue, Bulbul. I'm sure the Baul ways will guide you too – and the soul of a rice grower.'

He got lucky and found lodgings near the newspaper office. As an investigating journalist he got busy in no time: so many problems to report in this new country, many stories to cover, and so many truths to unearth. Madam maintained a strictly professional relationship with him at work, and he was happy with that, but she continued to invite him to have Friday lunch with her. Despite repeatedly refusing with various excuses, he eventually felt compelled to accept her offer.

He took the bus to Madam's house. Since it was Friday afternoon, it wasn't as densely packed as the rest of the week. The war's scars were still visible in the wrecked buildings, roads and bridges, and the tears of the loved ones of three million had barely dried, yet it felt to him as if it had happened a long time ago, during another lifetime. With the death of Dadu, his link with Dambarpur was gone. Now, he was alone, a true orphan at last. His time in the village during the war, his labour in the fields, his pulling of the canoe-chute to water thirsty rice plants, his tending of the mustard fields wearing a matla-hat, all seemed as if they were the stories of someone else.

He went to the kitchen and found Kazli Booa draining the rice.

'I told you, didn't I, to stay away from Madam? She'll devour you the way she did her son.'

'She's my boss. But I can come to see you, can't I?'

'I may not be a book-reader like you, but I'm no fool. When did someone like you visit the likes of me? Madam is in the garden.'

She was on the recliner under the flame tree, but it wasn't the season of flowers. She was browsing a newspaper, a strand of her loose hair fluttering in the wind.

'I'm making you our senior investigating reporter. You choose your own story and a better salary and conditions,' she said, without taking her eyes off the newspaper.

'Thank you. I hope I can repay your trust.'

'I think it's time for you to think of a family. A person can't always live alone. Do you want me to look out for someone suitable? Or perhaps you've already someone in mind.' She set aside the newspaper and peered at him over her glasses.

'Thanks for the offer. But I've been thinking of someone. Perhaps it's not the right time. She's a war widow. Her father was also killed in the war. So the wounds must be very raw.'

'I see. If you want to win her over, get in now. Offer your support and help. Eventually, though, you will need a guardian to take your proposal. I'll always be there to do that for you.'

'Thanks. But she might not want anything to do with me.'

'Did you behave badly around her? Don't be proud. Ask her forgiveness. Do whatever it takes to convince her that you care for her. Be sincere.'

'I will do. Thanks again.'

'Can I know who she is?'

'All I can say at this stage is that she's a friend's wife. He was martyred in the war.'

CHAPTER 31

He knew she had been living in her father's house. Yet, his nerves failed him every time, even within sight of the tall betel-nut trees. It was the whim of destiny that opened the doors to her. After work, he went to the press club for tea and samosa in a quiet corner and perhaps, if he bumped into a familiar face, a round of adda. He wasn't expecting Dipa Kaiser, but there she was, a queen bee among buzzing young men. His first impulse was to slink away unnoticed, but instead, he put his hands in his pockets, then took them out, looking at his fingers. How strange they looked, like two tarantulas ready to go out on a hunt. He sensed Mr Potbelly whispering in his ear: little brother, you do surprise me, ha you do, raising those wicked monsters right inside you, but it's time, little brother, you let them loose. Damn that timid little bird.

He walked over to the group, all young male journalists on Dipa Kaiser's daily. They knew Bulbul as a respected figure in the profession. They stood up and offered him a chair.

'Carry on. I just wanted to say hello,' said Bulbul.

Dipa Kaiser looked lost for words and smiled nervously at him. Oh, how not to notice the dimple, the crescent moon that shone briefly before dimming into the smooth brown of her cheek. Suddenly, feeling self-conscious, he hurried to the back of the room. He ordered a tea and samosa and sat alone, reading a broadsheet newspaper. It swelled like a sail, shielding him from prying eyes. He scrolled the front page, his heart pounding. Even before his eyes reached the end of a column the headline's meaning had melted in the air. He took a sip of the tea, biting the edges of the cup with force, almost cracking the enamel surface. Again, Mr Potbelly whispered in his ear: little brother, it's no good being a scaredy cat, follow those monsters of yours. He sprang to his feet and headed again for Dipa Kaiser's table. As before, the young journalists fell silent and stood up.

'Sorry to disturb you again. Dipa, if I may have a word with you.'

Without waiting for her response, he headed back to his table. Within minutes, she came and said, 'I knew you'd survived the war. So glad to see you.'

'Noor and your father. I'm so sorry, Dipa.'

Her eyes welled up and her lips trembled. She bent her head and looked at the edges of her sari, its geometric patterns in black and white, shaped like open petals in motion, marching back to back in strict lines. He wanted to extend his hand to touch hers.

Instead, he bent his head and slipped into her silence.

'It seems an eternity. How have you been?'

'I'm fine, but I didn't get to say sorry to Noor.'

'What for?' asked Dipa, as if she hadn't a clue what he was alluding to.

'You know, being such an idiot. Walking out on you two.'

'Our last meeting – before the war at the poetry reading. Do you remember that?'

'Yes, very well. I felt then that the door had opened between Noor and I again. I could ask his forgiveness.'

'Don't feel that way. Noor was very happy. He felt that you and he could go back to old times. Bosom friends again.'

'If he knew why I acted so stupid…'

'Don't torture yourself over it. Let's move on.'

'Move where? You know, my feelings for you haven't gone away. They are stronger than ever.'

'Let's not dwell on this anymore. Please. Let's be friends. I care for you. As a friend.'

What else could he have done? Absolutely nothing. From now on Dipa would be a friend and his life would run its course without being anchored down by her. During busy work hours things were fine. His only concerns were the stories he was covering. He was content to be weighed by unearthing their depths and secrets and how they should be told. Yet, there were the after-work hours, alone at home, on a bus ride, among jostling crowds, when he would be gripped, without the slightest provocation, by a terrible ache for Dipa. Sometimes, in bed, he would tell himself stories in which she could no longer deny her feelings for him and, risking everything and the shame that would be hers, she would tiptoe into his room and set his skin on fire. If only he could hold her tight and smell her hair, everything would be perfect, but she would be as elusive as ever, leaving him like the stray dog down his lane, whining and howling, and then just an inert lump of dead meat. It was getting too much. He couldn't bear it anymore, so he took a break. He went to Mominabad to see Sanu the Fat.

After lying low at the beginning of the war and spending a few months in a refugee camp in India, where he lost his wife to cholera, Sanu the Fat came back with his baby son.

'What can I say, Singing Bird? The boy is a real character. He was sickly but clung to life like a leech. His grandmother is taking care of him now. His aunt is even now giving him her milk. He loves it, the little rascal. A real Godzilla type. He doesn't need me, but I love him.'

Freed from the day-to-day care of his baby and single again, Sanu devoted himself to his café. He'd also rediscovered his love of films and their retelling.

'Let's go and see a film. A morning show like old times. It would be a real Godzilla time. No?' So they went to the old Aloka cinema hall and saw *The Planet of the Apes*. Afterwards, at the restaurant, Bulbul was expecting Sanu to begin his retelling with a funny monkey walk. Instead, he walked deliberately, as if in sombre meditation. He kept his lips tight. From time to time he shook his head, and the punters, expecting, like Bulbul, some comic gesture, looked at each other, baffled. As time passed, the silence, bolstered by Sanu's heavy, dull steps on the floor, was unnerving. Punters, fearing the worst, began to shrink in their seats.

'It's not funny. Monkeys are not funny. No way, my friends,' he said at last.

'What do you mean? Flaunting their red bottoms up in the air. Right in your eyeballs. Cavorting little rascals. Even fornicating flasher-masher billy-goat style. They aren't funny?' said a punter.

Sanu shook his head and smiled. 'Yes, yes. Monkeys playing randy goats. Fornicating. Animal by animal. What's that bloody bombastic word?'

'You mean metaphor?' said Bulbul.

'Whatever. But the thing is this. If you take a proper look, really, it's not funny.'

'Why?' asked a punter.

'If a monkey had more brain than you, wanted to ride you as his ass to the bazaar and wanted to cut off your balls, would you find it funny?'

'What? Monkeys can't do such things. Hasn't Allah made us the only master types? Top of the food chain. Top of the brain chain,' said a punter.

'So you think of yourself as the master, acha? That's really funny,' said Sanu. He put a serving bowl on his head, wrapped a tablecloth around him and took up a crab-like posture and a little boy's voice. 'Look at me. Here comes the master. Me a jolly good human. Master-blaster of the universe.' He scuttled around the room, stopped to pick his nose and licked his snot. He fell face down on the floor. Everyone burst out laughing.

'Funny. Humans are funny – well, what can you say – like humans.' He pulled himself back to his feet, puckered his lips, rolled his eyes, and gave a little jump, which swung his belly like a ball filled with water.

'Are you doing a monkey or a human?' asked a punter, giggling.

Instead of replying, Sanu went romping around the restaurant, swinging his giant belly: 'Me a jolly good human. Top of the food chain. Mega-mega-brain-wallah. Master-blaster of the universe.'

That night Sanu cooked beef bhuna and khichuri and sourced a bottle of local brew.

'My wife! My house is empty, Singing Bird. I don't feel like laughing anymore.' He poured the local brew into two glasses.

Bulbul touched his shoulder but couldn't find anything to say that would make sense.

'We shouldn't be gloomy, Singing Bird. Not tonight. Life goes on.'

'Are you thinking of marrying again?'

'What? Not now. Not thinking about such things. Who knows about the future? How about you?'

'I don't have a girl, do I?'

'If you want, I'll arrange you one. What kind of girl do you like?'

'Do you remember Dipa Kaiser? The journalist?'

'Don't tell me you're still hooked on her. It's no good, Singing Bird. The woman is married. Let her go.'

'Not anymore. Her husband was killed in the war.'

'Is that so? That's sad. Widowed at such a young age. Very sad, but you have to look on the bright side. It opens doors for you. This time, don't play the shy type. Timid little singing bird. Go in there like a bull. Big, nasty, raging bull. Gore down anything, anyone that stands in the way. Claim her. That's the Godzilla way.'

Back in Dacca, Bulbul was called into Madam's office.

'I want you on a special assignment,' she said.

'Of course. It's my job. What is it?'

'I don't know what it is. That's why I'm asking you to do a little digging.'

'Digging into what?'

'Well, I have a hunch. Not entirely speculative. I hear certain things and they're getting louder.'

'So, what have you been hearing?'

'Perhaps it's general knowledge, that there is a faction in the military. An Islamist wing.'

'Yes, I know. What about them?'

'You don't have to be an Einstein to realise they don't like our secular path. I feel they are up to something.'

'A handful of soldiers? We shouldn't worry about them.'

'They may be just a handful, but they have powerful backers.'

'Acha, who for instance?'

'I don't have to remind you of the Wahabi ideologues. They have money. Tons of money. Now the number one superpower is in league with them.'

'Isn't it weird that the arch-materialist, capitalist, number one superpower can be in league with Islamic fundamentalists?'

'I know it sounds crazy, but it's happening. The number one superpower thinks they can use Islamist ideology against pro-gressive nationalisms like ours. Against socialism. So, they are backing the Wahabis.'

'Do you think the number one superpower is behind the famine?'

'Of course there are local factors, like crop failure, but the number one superpower is blocking grain supplies to create the conditions for mischief.'

'So, what do you want me to do?'

'I hear you have contacts in the military. Find out what's going on. You can have the front page.'

He would contact White Alam, now a war hero and a colonel in the elite presidential guard, stationed in the Dacca cantonment. He phoned him from the press club.

'Who's that?' asked White Alam.

'Don't you remember your old friend?'

'Singing Bird! God-damnit, I'd no doubt you would live through the war. Anyway, good to hear from you.'

'What made you so sure about that?'

'Because we Godzillas don't die that easily. Remember, we're born in the nuclear dump. Totally toxic and virtually non-disposable.'

They agreed to meet the next evening at the Cantonment Club.

'They have a good stock of Scottish whisky. It will be my treat. I could do with a bit of nostalgia,' said White Alam.

Putting the phone down, Bulbul ordered a tea, then felt like a cigarette. Although he started smoking in his teens, he had never fully succumbed to it, and went through long periods without a puff, without ever thinking he had quit altogether. He scanned the room for a familiar face with a cigarette. He spotted the Reuters man who had relayed his and Dipa Kaiser's report on the Bhola cyclone to the international news media. He was a big whisky man and yet preached Islamist ideas. His name was Zubed Ali.

Zubed Ali invited him to sit at his table. 'How are you doing my lefty friend? Are your patrons from Moscow – or is it Peking now? – keeping you happy?'

'I've no patrons. I'm a democrat and a socialist. And, of course, a secularist.'

'Secularist,' laughed Zubed Ali. 'Damn Feringhee idea. I tell you, my friend, your time is up. Islam is taking over.'

'With the help of your friend, the number one superpower?'

'Why not? The number one superpower has always been a good friend of Islam. They love fundamentals. Look how they never cross the Saudis.'

'You've overlooked something, my friend,' said Bulbul, lighting the cigarette.

'What is that?'

'If you bring in the Islamists, your whisky-drinking days will be over.' Bulbul felt slightly dizzy after such a long break from smoking but kept on puffing. Outside the press club, he bought a packet of cigarettes and a matchbox. Lighting another, he started the walk to his flat. He stopped by the charred skeleton of Sweet Canteen and wondered what had happened to Dula Raihan and the cook. Had they survived the war?

He came to Dipa Kaiser's house and knocked on the door. The housekeeper, a plump young woman with twinkly eyes, opened up and said that her mistress was having a shower. He said he had time and sat in the drawing room. Her father's sculptures dominated it – half-naked peasants with bulging muscles squatting on the ground. Their faces were blank, but their bodies spoke of such power that Bulbul felt squashed in their presence.

Dipa Kaiser walked in, her hair lank and wet. She looked thinner and darker. Her face, despite the brightness of her eyes, looked immensely sad. Although he expected it, he was undone when a faint smile bloomed that dimple on her cheek. He stood up, his lips trembling.

'Have dinner with me. I'll be back in a minute,' said Dipa and disappeared. The housekeeper brought him a cup of tea.

'Are you a cousin of Dipa Bibi?' she asked.

'No. What made you think that?'

'You two seem… very close, like you've known each other for a long time. Are you the brother of Azad Sir?'

'In a way I am, but not a blood relation.'

After sipping the tea, Bulbul went out on the veranda to smoke. He listened to the betel-nut fronds whistling in the breeze.

'I never knew you were a smoker,' said Dipa Kaiser.

'I had a long gap. But started again this evening.'

'Why?'

'I don't know. Just felt like it.'

'Maybe you'll give up at the end of this evening.'

'If you want me to, I'll give up.'

Dipa Kaiser glanced at his mouth, dimly illuminated by the cigarette's ember, but stayed silent.

'You are staying for dinner, aren't you?'

'If you want.'

'I'm going in to lay the table. See you in a minute.'

At the dining table, two plates were laid at opposite sides. Apart from rice, there was dal, fried eggs and aloo vorta. Dipa told the housekeeper that she could leave now. They sat facing each other.

'So, what brought you here?' she asked.

'I just came to see you. Can't I do that?'

'Of course, you can. But I hope there won't be any misunderstanding.'

'What kind of misunderstanding?'

'You know. Feelings and stuff. I'm not ready for that.'

'I can wait.'

'I don't know if I will ever be ready. Let's just stay friends. Why make our lives complicated? Besides, I fear that I might lose you as a friend if we try to do something different.'

'You'll never lose me. I'll always be there for you, Dipa.'

'You walked out on us, didn't you? It really hurt Noor. He was racking his brain, wondering what he had done to offend you.'

'I'm so sorry. I was an idiot. Will you forgive me?'

'Let's not dwell on it anymore. We stay just friends. Yes?'

'All right. On Friday night some Bauls will be singing Lalon songs. Would you like to come with me?'

'I don't know. Spirituality is not my thing. Besides, I'm not ready to go out yet.'

'Please, Dipa.'

'Ok, let me think about it.'

The next day he was so preoccupied with Dipa Kaiser that he almost forgot his appointment with White Alam. Mid-morning he phoned her house and the young woman answered. She said that Dipa Kaiser was at a meeting with her editorial staff.

'Please tell her that I phoned. If possible, ask if she could ring me back.' He told the receptionist at work to let him know as soon as there was a call for him. He was trying to edit a piece he had drafted on democracy and socialism but was finding it hard to concentrate. He was looking at his watch and turning his ears to the corridor to pick up the receptionist's footfalls. By midday there was no call, so he questioned her.

'If there were any I would have called you, Sir,' she said.

He went back to his desk. Perhaps Dipa Kaiser was trying to avoid him – he couldn't blame her, he had been a coward and such a terrible friend. Perhaps she didn't find him sufficiently attractive to risk an emotional entanglement. At last, a call came for him. He almost ran to the telephone. It was White Alam phoning to tell him of a change of venue for their meeting that night.

'At the Sheraton, we will have more privacy.'

Bulbul stood by the reception desk, rubbing his face and then asked the receptionist if he could make a call. He dialled Dipa Kaiser's number, but there was no answer. He went to the balcony and lit a cigarette, thinking that perhaps Dipa Kaiser had instructed the housekeeper not to receive any calls.

Unable to concentrate, Bulbul left early. His appointment with White Alam was still several hours away. He could reach the Sheraton on foot in fifteen minutes. Not having a clear direction in mind, he set off wandering. He was sweating in the afternoon's heat and humidity. Wet patches sprouted on his shirt and clung to his skin. He scarcely noticed the crowds on the pavement who, as if in a rush to escape a catastrophe, almost trampled him. Finding a gap behind a lamppost, he lit a cigarette and set off again. No matter where he headed, which turns and twists of the road he took, it was always towards Dipa Kaiser's house.

He knocked on her door and the housekeeper opened it.

'Dipa Bibi is very tired. She is resting now.'

'Can I wait then?' he asked. Not sure what to say, the house-keeper stood looking at her bare feet.

'Can I wait?' he repeated. The housekeeper looked up, panic in her eyes, and rushed inside. He paced around and lit a cigarette. The housekeeper came back and showed him to the sitting room. A minute or so later, Dipa walked in, annoyance on her face.

'Do you want a cup of tea?'

'No, thanks. I won't take much of your time. Just wanted to ask you something.'

'What's so urgent?'

'You said you'd let me know,' said Bulbul.

'About what?'

'The Baul concert on Friday.'

Dipa Kaiser made a face as if she couldn't believe what she was hearing. 'I told you I'd think about it.'

'It's the day after tomorrow. Tickets are selling out.'

She played with her nails. 'I am very busy now. A lot to do. I'm not sure if I can spare the time.'

'Just an evening. It'll help you take your mind off things – for a while.'

'I don't know if I want to take my mind off things.'

'When would you let me know then?'

'In the morning I'll look in my diary. Call you then. Ok?'

White Alam had already ordered two glasses of whisky with ice at the Sheraton, .

'What's the matter? Why are you looking so gloomy?'

'Nothing, really. Just been a bit tired.'

'Is that so? Drink up. It will put you in a Godzilla mood. Cheers,' said White Alam.

Over glasses of whisky White Alam told him of his war exploits, fame as a war hero, and authority as a high-ranking officer.

'We're all very proud of you.'

'And you, what did you do in the war?'

'Nothing much. Just grew rice. Mustard. Things like that.'

'I see. Anyway, what did you want to talk to me about?'

'My editor thinks that something big is about to happen. Have you heard of any rumours or gossip?'

'I thought you journalists were into the truth business. Deal with facts. Why so interested in gossip?'

'At this stage we have nothing much to go on. Sometimes you have to start at the bottom of the ladder – with rumours that may lead you to facts. It's a matter of knowing how to go down, then up.'

'So, your editor thinks something's going on in the army. We have some young officers. A bit disgruntled. Their numbers are very few. Besides, they are just talkers.'

'Are they Islamists? Friends of the sheikhs with petrodollars and the number one superpower?'

'Money and power. Who wouldn't want to be friends with them? But I tell you, no one is planning a coup here. Your editor is a paranoid type. Now let's talk about something else.'

After several glasses of whisky, both were a bit drunk.

'How is your wife? I hear you have a daughter?' Bulbul said.

'Yes, four years old now. A chatterbox but lovely. My wife… What can I say? She's enjoying life being a colonel's wife. And getting fat.'

'Don't you love your wife?'

'What? What's love got to do with it? Wife is wife. Her father has good connections. Promised a handsome dowry. She's dark, a bit on the ugly side. But a man needs a family to prosper. Now, how about you? Thinking of tying the knot?'

'I'm an orphan, remember. Who's going to arrange a marriage for me?'

'I thought you were a romantic type. You don't need daddy-mummy to fix you.'

'Maybe. Once you've given your heart to someone. It's given.'

'You're worse than I thought. You're still hung up on that journalist woman, aren't you? For Godzilla's sake, the woman is married.'

'Well, she's a widow now.'

'My advice is stay away. She's not wife material. Bob-cut and women libber. She might make you do crazy things, like washing the dirty dishes. If the whim takes her, she might even go on strike. I mean sex strike. It doesn't bear thinking about.'

'You don't know her. She's the most amazing woman. I love her.'

'Singing Bird, you're totally messed up. Kaput. May Godzilla help you,' said White Alam.

He phoned the office in the morning to say that he would be late. He made himself a cup of tea and sat by the phone. He lit one cigarette, then another. It was nearly midday and still no call from Dipa Kaiser. He couldn't take it anymore; he called her. It took her a while to get to the receiver.

'I'm sorry. It's been hectic this morning. OK, we'll do the concert. But I can't stay long. So much to do.'

At the concert, they sat near the front; he'd bought the most expensive tickets available. She was tense and fidgeting. He became tense, too. The Baul, a young woman all in white and carrying an ektara, came onto the stage. She was accompanied by a group of male musicians playing a bamboo flute, a two-string dotara, and a drum-dhol. Without an introduction, the flautist played a soft, sad tune that floated over the buzz of the crowd, as if from another world. The crowd fell silent. Then the two-string dotara plucked the notes and strumming the ektara, the singer sang a slow, high, elongated phrase. Matching the beating of the drum-dhol, the singer, in synchrony with the other instruments, went into a fast rhythmic phase of the song. The audience began to sway their heads. Halfway into the first song, the music began to touch Dipa Kaiser and she eased into her seat. The following number caught her attention. It began with a question: *Lalon, what's your religion?* To which Lalon answered: *How does religion look? I've never laid my eyes on it.*

'What is he saying? I thought he was just a mystical poet?' she whispered.

'Lalon is many things, like the divine he sings to.'

Now the singer held her ektara high above her head, and dancing in little steps around the stage, she sang:

> *What is this talk about losing religion/caste?*
> *When you came to this world*
> *What caste/religion were you?*
> *When you leave this world*
> *What caste/religion will you be?*

Dipa Kaiser began to tap her feet and sway her head to the music. For the next number the singer stood still before the microphone, lifted her eyes, and sang:

> *Circumcision marks a Muslim man*
> *What marks a Muslim woman?*
> *A Brahmin is recognised by a holy thread*
> *How to recognise a Brahmin woman?*

Then the singer whirled away from the microphone and began spinning like a top, and the musicians drove themselves into a furious rhythm. Like Dipa Kaiser, Bulbul allowed his body to follow the tempo of the music.

When the musicians took a bow at the concert's end, Dipa Kaiser stood up, thumped her feet and clapped loudly. The rest of the audience followed her.

They got on a rickshaw together without knowing what they planned to do. When it arrived at her door, she invited him for tea, and he was happy to accept.

'Have you eaten anything this evening?'

'I'm not hungry.'

'I'm starving. I've some leftovers from lunch. Let's share it.'

His look accepted her proposal, and Dipa served him a plate and said, 'Thank you for taking me to the concert. I needed it.'

They ate in silence. Afterwards, Dipa made tea and they sat on the sofa.

'Noor,' said Dipa Kaiser and she broke into a sob. At first, Bulbul didn't know what to do, but he hugged her, and she sobbed on his shoulder.

At the door she said, 'I don't know if I can reciprocate your feelings. I'm not ready for a relationship. I doubt if I will ever be. But I like to have you in my life. You're very important to me.'

Since he'd learnt nothing significant from White Alam, Bulbul dropped his investigation into the military and focused on the corruption among the emerging elite. Madam went along with this, saying, 'If there is a conspiracy in the military, it's bound to involve the corrupt elite. So, your digging into the affairs of the corrupt might lead you to the military.'

From time to time Bulbul visited Dipa Kaiser, who always offered him some impromptu snack or dinner. One evening she said she wanted to go out of Dacca on a trip. He, of course, was happy to accompany her.

Taking a video camera and sound recording equipment, they took a bus to the forest outside Dacca. They would investigate illegal logging and the destruction of the forest. They got off at the midpoint of the forest and walked through dense lines of shal trees. As they went further inside, they saw more and more clearings – the sure sign of illegal logging. But that day, they wanted to leave their jobs aside and enjoy being in the forest.

At first, they were alarmed when a troop of monkeys surrounded them, but they proved friendly. Knowing that this might happen, they had brought bananas with them. They watched the monkeys squabbling among themselves for the pickings – the big alpha males chasing away the females and the young ones, and grabbing most of the bananas. They made sure that the lesser members of the troop didn't go without. They took turns to take each other's photos with the monkeys.

Further on, they came to the forest ranger's bungalow. The ranger wasn't in, but the guard and the cook, thinking they were journalists on an assignment, opened the doors for them. They also assumed they were a couple. They offered them snacks and tea and said they could stay in the guest room.

'The ranger, Sir, will be cross if we don't treat you right,' said the guard.

Bulbul said they couldn't stay, but Dipa Kaiser wanted to experience the forest at night.

'I know it's naughty, but I want to see the fireflies in the forest.'

'Do you think it's right for us to spend the night together?'

'Why not? We stayed together in Bhola. Have you forgotten? You are my dear friend. I trust you completely.'

When it was dark, they borrowed the hurricane lamp and walked along a narrow path between shal trees, which was muddy and clogged with branches and leaves.

'The forest is full of snakes. I hear the jackals here are vicious, too. Known to have attacked humans,' Bulbul said.

'Are you trying to scare me or something?' She laughed.

They didn't have to go far to find the fireflies. They were gathered in large numbers around a waterhole.

'Let's turn off the lamp,' said Dipa Kaiser.

They stood watching the fireflies looping their bright lights like shooting stars.

'Aren't they beautiful?' she said.

'Yes,' he said, wishing he could hold her hand.

Then jackals started howling, as if they didn't like intruders in their territory. 'We should go back,' said Bulbul, but Dipa Kaiser remained fixed to the spot. Now the howling was getting louder and closer. They couldn't light the lamp because they hadn't brought any matches.

Bulbul grabbed Dipa Kaiser's hand and began to run. Only a few meters on, he hit a tree, knocked himself out and fell to the ground. When he woke up, he found himself in the bungalow. Dipa was hunched over him, holding his hand.

'Don't get up.'

'What happened?'

'You wanted to run in the dark. The trees didn't like it.'

She helped him to some soft rice with milk and banana. After that, he fell asleep. Early next morning, he woke up beside Dipa Kaiser, who was still deep in sleep.

He felt fine but she insisted that they see a doctor.

Nothing to be worried about, the doctor assured them.

'Thank you for taking care of me,' said Bulbul.

'That's what friends are for,' she said.

Back in Dacca, the following Friday evening, Dipa Kaiser invited him to dinner. She also asked a friend of hers and her husband. The woman, Munira, was the same age as Dipa; her husband, Amu, was slightly older. They were both university lecturers: she in history and he in Bengali literature.

'Dipa tells me that you were a close friend of Noor. We miss him so much,' said Munira.

'I miss him too,' said Bulbul.

'Yours and Dipa's reports on the cyclone in Bhola were so crucial,' said Amu.

'That was another time. Before Bangladesh was born,' said Bulbul.

They had a traditional Bengali meal of rice, dal, dry curry of small river fish, and spicy chicken with small potatoes. They talked about the famine, the food blockade by the world's number one superpower and the Islamist conspiracies to undo Bangladesh's independence.

'I can see Bangladesh going the same way as Chile,' said Amu.

'We mustn't let it happen,' said Dipa Kaiser. Each silently contemplated the consequences of such an event. Munira broke the silence and turned the conversation to personal matters.

'Amu is such a romantic. He doesn't want any children. He thinks he will lose me.'

'I'm too jealous to share you. What's wrong with that? Besides, this country is already teeming with people. Hardly any room left to breathe.'

'Everything,' said Dipa Kaiser. 'You men still want to possess us.'

'I understand where you are coming from, Dipa. But it's not like that between us,' said Munira.

'If you say so.'

'Bulbul, what do you think? Do you believe in love?' asked Amu.

'I like to believe in it, but it seems it doesn't believe in me.'

'Don't be defeatist, my friend. It's work like everything else. Keep at it, and it will come.'

Munira sensed the conversation was making Dipa Kaiser uncomfortable. She tried introducing other subjects, but they seemed somewhat forced, and no one was willing to run with them.

Once the friends left, they remained awkwardly silent. After serving them tea, the housekeeper retired for the night.

'You mustn't give up on love,' said Dipa Kaiser.

'I can't do loving on my own, can I?'

'If you want, I can introduce you to some of my friends. Do you remember Jamila? I think you'd get on with her.'

'I don't know. My feelings for you aren't done yet. When I think of love, I can only think of you.'

'Can I have one of your cigarettes?'

'I didn't know you smoked.'

'You don't know much about me,' said Dipa Kaiser, meeting his eyes.

Outside, on the veranda, they smoked sitting side by side on recliners, staring at the dark sky and listening to the betel-nut fronds swaying in the wind.

'I loved you, you know. Still do.'

'I know, you said that before. Was it really love? Or were you just jealous of Noor?'

'What do you mean?'

'You wanted me because Noor loved me.'

'Maybe. But the feeling was very real.'

'I was intrigued by you. But I was swept along by Noor's passion. You did nothing.'

'Yes, I was a coward and stupid. But if you give me a chance, I could show you how much I care for you.'

'I've many friends who care for me. I know you care for me, too.'

'But I love you. I can't stop thinking about you. Like my mind, my body goes all funny.'

'I don't feel about you that way. You are a good friend, and I do care about you.'

Time went by as they smoked and thought their own thoughts.

'Sorry to be a nuisance. I won't bother you again.' Bulbul stood up to leave.

'Where are you going? Sit down,' said Dipa Kaiser, and Bulbul obeyed. Leaving him on the veranda she went inside and came back with two cups of tea.

'Give me another cigarette, and don't be so quiet and gloomy. We have to take life in our stride,' she said, humming a Tagore song: *Like a torn flower petal blown in the breeze. It fell upon my heart like a sigh of her body and whisper of her heart.*

Unnerved by her sudden changes of mood, Bulbul took rapid drags on his cigarette.

'Have you been with a girl?' Dipa Kaiser asked, with a hint of mischief in her tone.

'What do you mean?'

'Have you been intimate with a girl?'

'I had only feelings for you.'

'So, you're still a virgin then?'

'I told you that in Bhola. Don't you remember?'

'Yes, I do, but that was quite a few years ago. Before independence. I thought things might have changed for you.'

'Nothing has changed. I loved you then, I love you now.'

Bulbul lit another cigarette and rubbed the back of his head.

'If you want, you can be intimate with me.'

'You mean you can love me? We can be together?'

'Don't confuse love with it. Right now, I've no room in me for that kind of thing.'

'What then?'

'I don't understand how a grown man like you can be so stupid. I said you could do it with me.'

Bulbul stayed quiet, then got up and left.

CHAPTER 32

Madam suggested that Bulbul should join the RBC.

'Join the RBC? You must be a high-ranking official or mega rich to be allowed in.'

'Don't worry. Munir had a membership. You can have it.'

'But they have a strict vetting policy. Apart from money, you need to be big in something to be accepted. I'm neither.'

'No problem. My grandfather was a member. So was my father. The club secretary is an old family friend. I'll fix it for you.'

'It's a den of intrigue and corruption. I don't want to be part of it.'

'You said you wanted to investigate corruption in the elite. Where better than in the RBC? If a conspiracy is brewing, you will surely get a whiff of it there. So, please take it as part of your job. Undercover operation, if you like.'

One early evening, casually dressed, Bulbul walked through the well-lit approach road to the RBC, fringed with stunted coconut trees with their bases whitewashed, and reached the columned porch of an old colonial building. The door was open and there was no one in sight. As he stepped in, two men descended on him. He showed them Munir Mahmud's membership card.

'Munir Sir is dead,' said one of the guards, dressed like an old colonial peon.

'I have his card now. Do you have any problem with that?'

'Highly irregular, if I may say so. No one has briefed us about your inheritance. Are you Munir Sir's brother?'

'Do I need to respond to the question? Just let me in.'

'We can't do that without proper verification. This is a top VIP zone. The whole city wants to come through our doors. We are here to make sure that doesn't happen. Besides, you're not properly dressed.'

Bulbul then mentioned Pota Sarwar, the club secretary, whom Madam had already briefed. One guard stayed with Bulbul, the other one went to fetch Pota Sarwar.

'Everything will be fine if Pota Sir gives the nod. But even he can't break the dress code,' said the guard.

'You don't like the way I'm dressed?'

'It's not a question of liking, but a matter of tradition. You have to dress like a sahib. Do you think it's called the Royal Bengal Club for nothing? It sets its members apart from the rest of society.'

It took several minutes for Pota Sarwar to arrive. He was

almost bald but with curly fringes around his head; he had the air of a busy man much in demand.

'I was expecting you, but you should have phoned, and I'm afraid your dress won't do.' He sent one of the guards to bring in what he called the 'emergency supply'.

'Have you worn a tie before?' Pota Sarwar asked.

'No,' said Bulbul.

'I'll help you. Practise at home before the next time you come. I know it looks funny, but it's what makes us, us.'

When the guard arrived with the 'emergency supply', Bulbul was sent to the bathroom to change.

The coat, a black jacket of the type that lawyers wear, was too big for him. So were the white shirt and the beige trousers. The shoes, on the other hand, were too small. Facing the mirror, Bulbul took off his pyjamas, punjabi, and sandals and put on the 'emergency supplies'. The trousers were for a portly man with an enormous rice belly, and Bulbul had to tie the string of his pyjamas around his waist. After squeezing into the toe-crushing shoes and hanging the coat over the sail of a shirt, Bulbul called Pota Sarwar.

'A bit helter-skelter, but a code is a code. And this will do,' said Pota Sarwar, knotting the red tie around a shirt collar that would have easily taken in a neck double the size.

'I look like a clown.'

'Here, everyone respects the dress code. No one will laugh.'

Holding onto the trousers, slipping down even with the string tied tight, Bulbul followed Pota Sarwar into the club.

'Call me Pota Bhai. Everyone here does. Let me know if you need anything fixing, but don't expect me to divulge any secrets. Hush, hush is the code of conduct here. Let me get you a whisky to welcome you,' said Pota Sarwar.

It took them a while to get to the bar. On the way, Pota Sarwar chitchatted to everyone, introducing Bulbul. 'He's taking the place of our beloved martyr, Munir Mahmud Sir,' he said.

'Oh, our martyr. His blood made us free,' people said.

Only when they were in the bar did anyone ask Bulbul's name.

'What do they call you, young man? You're not by any chance the long-lost nephew of our beloved martyr?' asked Mia Zahan, an old bureaucrat, sporting a white linen suit and long white beard and a pair of round Gandhi glasses.

'No blood relation. I'm Bulbul.'

'Ah, singing bird. What do you sing?'

'I'm afraid I've no musical talent.'

'I mean, what do you do, young man?'

'I'm a journalist.'

'I see. Should I be worried? We come here to let our guard down.'

'Mr Bulbul is super discreet. He's one of us,' said Pota Sarwar.

'Good to hear. Welcome, Mr Bulbul. You can be what you want here. It's our zone of freedom. Speaking abol-tabol nonsense and doing the disallowed is allowed here,' said Mia Zahan.

At the bar, they sat on the tall stools facing the counter, and Pota Sarwar ordered whisky.

'If I were you, I'd buy Mia Zahan a drink. To survive here you need some allies. Will your missus be coming sometimes?'

'I'm not married.'

'Never mind, the ladies will love you.'

'I don't see any ladies here.'

'They're usually in their own room, next to the big hall. Gossiping, playing cards. Some of them even ask for drinks to be brought over. Have you seen a woman who's had a bit too much? Not a pretty sight, but they will love you. Never thought we'd see a bachelor here.'

Suddenly there was a buzz in the bar, and the drinkers hustled to stream out. Pota Sarwar was also on his feet, saying he had to go.

'What's happening?'

'Talukdar Sir is here. I mean Charity Magnet.' And Pota Sarwar ran out.

The bar was now empty except for Bulbul and Mia Zahan. Bulbul approached him.

'Can I buy you a drink, Sir?'

'I hope you don't want anything in return.'

'Actually, I do want something in return. I'll be happy if you bless me, Sir.'

Mia Zahan looked through his Gandhi glasses, his eyes narrowed, and he nodded to Bulbul to sit down.

'I'm a Vat 69 man. Make it a double peg.'

On the way to the bar, Bulbul smiled, remembering that only villains in Bengali films drank Vat 69; it sealed their badness and made them capable of rape and pillage. He sat facing Mia Zaman.

'Have you met our Charity Magnet? Our saint.'

'No Sir. I've heard of him. But what's he doing in a place like this?'

'What do you mean? Do you think this place is dirty, only for baddies? Anyone important is welcome here. No one is bigger than Charity Magnet. The man is a genius and a saint.'

Bulbul fetched another double peg of Vat 69 and asked Mia Zaman if he could introduce him to Charity Magnet.

'Why? Do you want to dig into him for dirt? Debunk him as a sham?'

'What made you think that?'

'That's what you journalists do. Can't stomach a good man, especially if he's saintly. You fellows work on the perverse notion that all men have flaws. Perverse thinking.'

'I admire Charity Magnet. He's a big asset for our country. I want to be touched by a saint and feel blessed.'

Now tottering, Mia Zahan led Bulbul through a large hall where a classical singer was performing a raga accompanied by a sarod and a tabla. They seemed accomplished but the audience wasn't paying much attention, laughing and chatting.

'The real action is in the cabins. Top VIPs frequent them and play high-stake games,' said Mia Zaman as they passed along a corridor leading to series of rooms with closed doors.

'What kind of games?'

'Don't be nosy. Here's not the place to bring your nose.'

As they were passing the women's room, Mrs Sarkar, a successful entrepreneur in the fashion industry and a divorcee, was coming out. She was in her fifties and looked fit and glamorous.

'Zahan Bhai, long time no seeing. These days you never leave the bar.'

'You should come there, and I'll buy you a peg or two.'

'You know how it is for us women. We need to hide in our room to have a drink. Who's this young man?'

'He's Mr Bulbul, a bachelor.'

'A bachelor? Welcome, Mr Bulbul. Fancy having a singing bird among us.'

'Thank you, Mrs Sarkar.'

'If you need anything, just ask me.'

When she'd gone, Mia Zahan told Bulbul to stay away from her. 'Very dynamic lady. She has an eye for young men.'

Across the corridor, past a large door, was the most exclusive section of the club. A peon was standing guard. Mia Zahan told him that he wanted to see Charity Magnet. The peon went inside.

'Why can't we just go in and say hello?'

'You can't see Charity Magnet just like that. He's a top VIP. Discussing sensitive issues with other top VIPs and making deals.'

'What kind of deals?'

'I told you, didn't I? Leave your nose behind. You won't get far in this place with nosiness. No seeing, no hearing is the motto here. And no smelling either.'

The peon returned and said that Charity Magnet was in a meeting and that they should come back in fifteen minutes. Mia Zahan then took him around the building, showing him the gym, the sports hall and the swimming pool. He showed him a door and said, 'There are three rooms inside there. You can book them for private meetings. Funny things go on there.'

'What kind of funny things?' asked Bulbul.

'No nose. No nose,' said Mia Zahan.

At last, they were back at Charity Magnet's door and the peon escorted them inside. What struck Bulbul was his saintly aura; he seemed like the embodiment of pure goodness. He stood up and greeted Mia Zahan with a smile that spoke of innocence, sincerity and kindness. He greeted Bulbul with the same generosity of spirit and humility.

Charity Magnet was wearing a rough cotton punjabi, pyjamas, and flip-flops. When Bulbul looked the second time at his clothes, Charity Magnet smiled faintly and said, 'You must be wondering how I evaded the dress code. I didn't. I wore a suit to get in. But it doesn't suit me. My insides become sick with it. So, as soon as I get into this room, I change into my normal clothes.'

Mia Zahan introduced Bulbul as a brilliant journalist.

'The country needs brave journalists to speak the truth.'

'Thank you, Sir. I'll do my best. Can I interview you at some time?'

'I'm not newsworthy, Mr Bulbul. I serve the poor. It's their story that you should be highlighting.'

'But the poor find their voices through you, Sir. I just want to know about your work among them.'

'No need to speak of these things. My work is out there. Go to the villages and shanty towns. They will speak more eloquently of what we are trying to do.'

Back in the bar, after more double pegs of Vat 69, Mia Zahan slumped on the table, snoring. Pota Sarwar, as if he had been keeping track of Mia Zahan all along, rushed in with one of the peons, and they took him away. Now on his own, Bulbul went wandering about the club. He felt like a cigarette and fresh air and went to the back garden to sit on a bench. Just as he was lighting up, Mrs Sarkar came up behind him.

'I saw you. I felt desperate for a puff. Would you?' she said.

'Of course,' said Bulbul and offered her a cigarette.

'It feels naughty to light up. Like an illicit affair.'

'I haven't seen a woman smoking in this country. Except two. You're the second.'

'Who was the first?'

'That's a long story.'

'I see. I hope she didn't kill herself. I don't want to end up that way.'

'What made you think of such a thing?'

'Sharing a cigarette with a girl always involves complicated feelings. Dangerous desires.'

'Are we in danger then?'

'You're completely safe with me. How long is it since you had a home-cooked meal?'

'It's been a while.'

'Come to my place. I'm a good cook, you know.'

'I'm sure you're a fantastic cook, but I'm not sure. Would it be a good idea?

'I'm not going to eat you up, ok?'

CHAPTER 33

He decided against taking the bus to Mrs Sarkar's apartment. He would walk the mile there. The evening was hot and humid, and the smog was made more ominous by swirling dust and fumes. He veered off the main road and took the zigzag alleyways. It would take longer, but he didn't have to arrive at a precise time. It was a dinner invitation and people ate late in the city.

Only when he was passing a meesty-sweet shop did it occur to him that he shouldn't arrive empty handed. He bought a box of chamcham and a pot of sweet, creamy yoghurt. Swinging the bags gently, he ambled along almost dark alleyways. He felt like a cigarette but didn't have a hand free to light up, so he popped into a makeshift tea stall, ordered a liquor tea, and lit a cigarette. A bold, clean-shaven man, the roundness of whose head matched the shape of his face, served him with a broad smile.

'I haven't seen you here before. Where are you heading?'

'I'm going to Gulshan.'

'It's a long way from here. You'd better go back to the main street and take the bus.'

'I'd rather walk. I've time.'

'Yes, good to have time. In our village we had time. Here in the city, I don't know. Everything's crazy. I get breathless just looking at people. Like they are running from a tiger.'

'So you came recently to Dacca?'

'We didn't have much to eat in the village. What's the use of time if you go hungry?'

Bulbul took a sip of the tea. With just a few brewed tea leaves, the cup felt refreshing, as if nature had made its home within.

'Thank you for making a delicious cup.'

'I'm happy that you like it. It's on the house,' said the tea maker, smiling like a crescent moon.

'So, you own the shop?'

'What gave you that idea? Owning doesn't come to people like me. I work here from morning to night. Then I sleep here to light the fire again in the morning.'

'I see. The tea is not yours then, I mean, to give away for free.'

'You are right, but who will know? It's a secret between us. You see, I haven't had a customer the whole day. I've been waiting, waiting. Then you came along. So I'm lucky.'

'Thank you for the gift. What can I do for you?'

'If you give me something, it wouldn't be a gift, would it? But we can talk. That would be gift enough for me.'

'Sorry, I can't stay long. I have an invitation and I'm already late.'

'You must have been living a long time in the city. Getting late is the thing to say here. I don't mind that. It's fine by me. But who invited you, if you don't mind me asking.'

'A friend. She said she's a good cook.' Bulbul puffed his cigarette, thinking he shouldn't have given himself away so quickly.

'A she? I see. Good cook is good. Nothing is as bad as bad cooking on invitation. I bet she is very beautiful, too.'

'Looks don't come into it. To be honest with you, I haven't looked at her properly. Just a friend invited me for dinner.'

'Is she married?'

'Of course she's married. Happily, and all,' said Bulbul, rubbing his eyes as if smoke had gone into them. The tea maker was not easily fooled.

'I hope the loving husband is away on business. You don't want him jabbering away and spoiling it. Let's hope he's a pukka city-man, a not-having-time type. It's better he's occupied elsewhere.'

Bulbul didn't say anything. Sweat crawled down his head.

'Come nearer,' said the tea-maker, and he brought out a small palm-leaf fan and began to wave it over Bulbul's head.

'Take a rickshaw. You don't want to arrive at the lady's house all wet. It wouldn't be proper.'

'Thanks for the advice. I must be off.'

'Yes, yes. You can't keep a lady waiting. She must have an electric fan in her house. I bet she will have talcum powder all over her. Perhaps some attar. If you don't mind me asking, what smell do you like in attar?'

'I don't like attar.'

'I understand completely. The smell of skin or her hair is attar enough. But what do I know about such things? I've never been with a woman. I bet a city gentleman like yourself has been with many beautiful women.'

'Yes,' said Bulbul, and began to walk away.

'Good luck. I hope the cooking is as delicious as you expect.'

For a moment he thought of taking a rickshaw and going back to the main road for the bus. But instead, he began to walk briskly. It was about nine when he arrived at Mrs Sarkar's apartment.

'Oh, you came. I was giving up on you,' she said.

'Sorry. Got a bit lost.'

Mrs Sarkar gave him a towel and showed him to the bathroom.

'You can't stay in wet clothes. Take them off,' she said when he came out of the bathroom.

Seeing panic in his eyes, she said, 'I'm not asking you to take your pants off. Just the shirt. Anyway, what's to see in a man's upper body? If you feel uncomfortable you can wrap this around yourself.' She offered him a long gamcha-towel.

He sat at the table with a red gamcha-towel wrapped around his shoulders. Mrs Sarkar took his shirt and undershirt, soaked them in a bucket, frothy with washing powder, and came back with two plates. Sensing Bulbul's surprise that there was no home help, she said, 'I have a maidservant and a cook. They only come when I am out during the day. I can't have anyone staying in my home. It compromises my freedom.'

Bulbul offered to help bring in the dishes.

'Thank you for the meesty-sweet. You're very thoughtful. A gentleman.'

She served him a large piece of hilsa fish, cooked in mustard paste, which she said she'd cooked herself. He looked at her and smiled nervously. All the dishes were delicious, and she fussed over him, filling his plate with more than he could eat. After dinner, they sat in the drawing room, decorated with modernist paintings. Mrs Sarkar brought out a bottle of whisky.

'I bet you haven't met many whisky-drinking women in the city.'

Despite being educated in Paris, Dipa Kaiser didn't drink whisky, and no one else came to mind.

'You're the only one,' he said.

383

'I know I'm bad. But I like it. If the mullahs find out they will stone me to death.'

They lit cigarettes, sipped on whisky and Mrs Sarkar told him how she had been married to a wealthy industrialist, who seemed to be pious but was a brute and into whoring in a big way. 'I had to end it, but he was vindictive. Now that I've built my business, he doesn't dare anymore. He still whispers that I'm a whore.'

'Do you have any children?' Bulbul asked, and Mrs Sarkar became quiet and tearful. 'I wish I had. But in life you can't have everything. I'm lucky. I've built up my business. Number one fashion brand in the country with healthy exports. But it hasn't been easy as a woman here. Now, they accept me even at RBC. Spineless men gossip about me, but not in front of me. Madam, you're a pioneer, they say, not daring to look me in the eyes.'

'You're a formidable person, if I may say. Who would dare?'

'Am I so scary to you men? Honestly, tell me the truth.'

'You've been very kind to me. But what made you invite me?'

'I don't think. I just do. I liked you and thought you needed a bit of home care. But at RBC, they would gossip. You know, how I took advantage of you, corrupted you.'

They had several rounds of whisky with mellow Tagore songs playing in the background. As the night wore on, Bulbul laughed out loud and said: 'Ah Godzilla.'

'What? I didn't expect you to be into silly monster films.'

'It's a long story,' he said.

The following day he woke to Mrs Sarkar humming a Tagore song. She had just come out of the shower, her hair wet and long. She looked more like a girl than a middle-aged businesswoman. Finding himself sprawled in the bed, naked, he pulled the bedsheet to cover himself. Mrs Sarkar smiled and said, 'You should have told me before. That you were a virgin.'

Bulbul smiled nervously.

'Now that you are not, you can get on with life.'

At the door, Mrs Sarkar touched the tip of his nose with her finger, then leaned back, pulling her wet hair, her eyes misting up. She said, 'Thank you', and when he gave her an inquiring look, she almost sobbed. 'I felt you there. You were there with me fully.

Like a songbird come to sing to me. Only me. No one has done that to me before. Thank you.'

On the way back, he took the same alleyways on foot, and as he passed the tea stall, the man called him. He wasn't in the mood for a chitchat but felt it would be rude. Smiling and rubbing his bald head, the tea-maker greeted him.

'Thank you, Sir. It will be my lucky day. Customers will queue to be served. Was the dinner nice?'

'Yes, very nice.'

'And the husband, was he nice too?'

'Yes, he was very nice. It was getting late, so he insisted I stay in their spare room.'

'He seems like a nice man. But it would have been nicer, you know, if he were away on business.'

Turning serious, the tea maker accepted the money and said he was a paying customer now, but yesterday he was just a stranger. Bulbul couldn't quite fathom his logic, but as he stood up, the tea maker said, 'Next time you come, you'll be a friend. You pay only half the price. Friend's discount, you know.'

It was late morning, and the sun was already fierce. His shirt and undershirt, dried overnight at Mrs Sarkar's, were getting wet again. But still, instead of taking a bus or rickshaw, he continued to walk. Strange that something so meaningful had come to pass last night and that it had happened so simply, as if he were taking his first step proper to his kind as an upright animal. Or when he first opened his mouth to speak and Dadu cried out: "My little bird is talking!" Somehow, and all by itself, his body had found a new means of expression at the touch of another. If only he hadn't been so drunk, he'd have taken more in and savoured the moment, like his first tamarind with salt on a rainy day. Yet, he was happy that his body had experienced something that it was made to do. It mattered little that it happened without any ritual of courtship, love or desire to make babies. Nor was it important that she was perhaps the same age as his mother, if she had been alive.

He was glad it was Friday, and he didn't have to go to work the next day. He put the fan on and went to bed in the shaded room. It didn't make much difference to the heat and humidity, but the whirring of the fan was soothing. He lit a cigarette and thought he should tell himself a story about last night. That way, he would perhaps create a lasting memory of a significant moment in his life. Damn it, why should Dipa's face come to him now? Did he have sex with Mrs Sarkar, thinking that it was Dipa? No, it had nothing to do with Dipa. Absolutely nothing.

It was definitely Mrs Sarkar. Didn't she say that he was with her completely, fully present? He wished it hadn't been dark, but Mrs Sarkar insisted on switching off all the lights, even the dim bedside ones. How could he then tell himself the story of what had happened? As always, there was touch, smell and taste. Bodies have their own ways of doing things and making memories. His skin and hers sliding over each other and the scent of her hair unleashing his beast, a bull elephant mad in musth, rumbling to shatter the sky. What could he say of the tangy taste that showered his tongue in wet flesh? All he could think of was a stray dog lapping on a piece of meat that set its taste buds alight. He laughed, imagining Sanu the Fat telling him, 'Singing Bird, it's no good. No good becoming a dog. If you want to become an animal, go for a giraffe or something.' Above all, it was the movements, his body going on its own to hers, like a wasp lured into an orchid.

He stubbed out the cigarette and opened his eyes wide, but it was too dark to see, and his ears could only pick up the fan's whirring. He knew the gecko was there. Silent and immobile as ever. He should fall asleep because trying to tell a story about what had happened last night was futile. It was the body's business. He could describe its movements as if it were a machine – parts in a giant iron factory assembled to make merchandise for markets across the seas. Not the cleverest of metaphors, but perhaps by taking another path he could spin something more elaborate, as if an excess of language could somehow take him to an elusive truth. Perhaps he should just tell a titillating story about an affair between an older woman and a young man who lost his virginity to her. Still, what could he do with the body's business? Nothing. Let it sing its own hymns. It mattered little if it sang of Mrs Sarkar or Dipa Kaiser.

The following day, he woke up in a cheerful mood. At the office, Madam called him in to ask him to look into illegal logging in the Sundarbans.

'Do you want me to go there?'

'Not at this stage. I hear big business is involved. Maybe also the military. See what you can find out.'

'My contact in the military wasn't much help.'

'Don't stop going to the RBC. You can log in your time there as work. Sooner or later, someone will spill something. Then it's just a matter of lapping it up.'

'It's full of nutcases. Total crazies. But if you want, I'm happy to spend time there.'

'I still have a gut feeling something is brewing. Some big conspiracy to reverse the course of our independence. Anyway, are you free on Friday?'

'What's happening on Friday?'

'It's Khoka's birthday. I thought of doing something.'

Wearing a blue suit and a red tie, Bulbul walked through RBC's main gate. The peons saluted him. Pota Sarwar, breaking off an animated conversation with other members, came running to greet him. 'You look like a pukka member now,' he said.

Bulbul offered him a whisky, and they walked into the bar. He spotted Mia Zahan at his usual table and waved at him.

'How did you get on with Mia Zahan?'

'Good. He was very kind to introduce me to Charity Magnet.'

'You're lucky. Not many people get to meet him. Did you feel his goodness? Every time I meet him I tremble with humbleness. We're blessed to have him in our country. No one loves the poor more than him.'

'Yes, I felt his goodness. I hear that foreigners are also much taken by it.'

'The Americans, the British, the French. You name any white foreigner, they're really into him. They love our poor. They channel that love through our Charity Magnet Sir.'

'I hear foreigners are pouring millions into his fund.'

'That's why Talukdar Sir is called Charity Magnet. His organi- sation is the richest in the country. But let's not talk about money. It demeans Charity Magnet Sir. He loves the poor like a mother loves… you know.'

They drank their whisky in silence until Bulbul asked him about illegal logging in the Sundarbans.

'We don't talk about such things here. If I were you, I'd keep quiet. Our members won't like it. They are very sensitive, you know. Another thing. Nothing goes unspotted in the club.'

'What do you mean?'

'You were spotted with Mrs Sarkar in the garden. A fine and upright lady. Worth millions. We don't want her name dirtied.'

Busy as ever, Pota Sarkar couldn't stay long. Bulbul went to Mia Zahan with the offering of a double peg of Vat 69.

'I like you, young man. You know how to treat a senior.'

'Thank you, Sir. It's a privilege to sit at your table. Who wouldn't walk miles to be touched by your wisdom and knowledge?'

'Enough of the flattery. What's on your mind?'

'Logging. I hear a lot of logging's going on in the Sundarbans.'

'Where there are trees, there will be logging. And the Sundarbans have a lot of trees. So, what's your point?'

'Illegal logging, Sir. I hear some big businesses are involved. Maybe the military.'

'Illegal logging, eh?' Mia Zahan took a large gulp of Vat 69 and went quiet, as if he were about to doze off. Bulbul brought him another double peg of Vat 69, and the old man perked up.

'Illegal logging, eh? I'm glad you didn't bring up our bureaucracy. We have honour, you know.' Gesturing Bulbul to come closer, he leaned forward and whispered something. Then he got up, saying he ought to be going because his wife was unwell. Bulbul sat and mulled over what Mia Zahan had told him. He should see Mrs Sarkar, and besides, he could do with some fresh air.

He sat on the same bench in the garden as before and lit a cigarette, hoping Mrs Sarkar would spot him and come over. Even after his second cigarette, there was no sign. He called an old peon hurrying through the garden with a bottle of whisky.

'What's your name?'

'I'm Shahabuddin, Sir.'

'What's your job here?'

'I'm a peon, Sir. Twenty years' service here, Sir. On special duty to Madams' rooms.'

'Where are you taking this bottle of whisky?'

'I'm not at liberty to say, Sir.'

'Well, I get it. Do you know where Mrs Sarkar is?'

'I'm not at liberty to say, Sir.'

Bulbul pulled out a hundred taka note. Shahabuddin stood rigid as a hanged man. When he offered him a five hundred taka note, Shahabuddin, his hand shaking, took the money.

'If anyone finds out, I'll lose my job, Sir.'

'No one will know. I give you my word.'

'Sarkar Madam. She has gone on a business trip. Some foreign place. Please, Sir, if anyone knows…'

Bulbul wondered why Mrs Sarkar would go on a foreign trip without mentioning it. But then why should she? He hardly knew her; she owed him nothing. That was for the best – no ties, no complications, just a casual affair. Yet, he kept wondering how it could be possible that the body he'd touched intimately, had lost his virginity to, didn't mean something. Bloody humans, what the fuck are we?

Shahabuddin came back and gave him a note.

'What's this?'

'I don't know, Sir. Mrs Imam Madam sent it.'

'Who's Mrs Imam?'

'Imam real estate, Sir.'

Of course, Bulbul knew who Mrs Imam was, though he'd never met her. She was a well-known socialite, the wife of Hiron Imam, a property mogul who owned half of Dacca and who'd died in mysterious circumstances about a year ago. There were innuendos and gossip but there was no evidence against Mrs Imam. Still, rumours persisted that Mrs Imam had used her vast wealth to buy off witnesses, the police and the judiciary. Not a week passed without her appearing in the newspapers, often beside Charity Magnet at events. She seemed overwhelmed with care while distributing food packages and clothes to the poor and was often quoted in the newspapers: 'Thanks to Charity Magnet Sir I have found myself. I found myself through my love for the poor. Where would we be without the poor?'

When Bulbul came out of the club, he looked at the note. No name, no address, just a telephone number. He took a rickshaw, and instead of going to his flat, he told the puller to take him to The Grand Potbelly Eatery. Most of the city was closed and the streets were almost empty. He leaned back in the seat with a gentle breeze cooling his face. He wanted a cigarette but couldn't find his matchbox. He must have dropped it in the club's garden. He asked the rickshaw puller if he had a match and he had.

'How long have you been in Dacca and pulling rickshaw?'

'About six months, Sir. In the village, there's nothing to eat. Here in the city, I work the whole day. Still not enough to buy food.'

Bulbul looked at the rickshaw puller and saw he was only bones. He would die on his paddle before they reached The Grand Potbelly Eatery. He asked the man to drop him where they'd reached and offered him the full fare.

'What's wrong, Sir? Do you want me to go faster, Sir?'

'Nothing's wrong. I just wanted to stretch my legs a bit.'

'Shall I follow you, Sir? You might get tired after a while.'

Despite his protestations, the rickshaw puller paddled gently behind him.

'Where do you live?' Bulbul asked.

'In the shanty, Sir. North of the city.'

'Are the people there going hungry, too?'

'Yes, Sir. Old people are saying it's like before the partition. Many of us will die of hunger.'

The customers had already left when he arrived at The Grand Potbelly Eatery. Mr Potbelly was in the kitchen, checking the stocks for the next day's breakfast.

'Little brother, I didn't know you were coming. I would've cooked fish head for you. Ha, I would.' Bulbul said he wasn't hungry, but Mr Potbelly insisted on serving him a plate of rice with leftover cauliflower, aubergine bhaji, and dal.

'Little brother, how come I don't see you much? It's too bad.'

'Busy with work, you know. My editor thinks something big is about to happen, but I'm not getting many leads.'

'Little brother, I'm not a thinking man like you. Ha, I'm not. But when I cook, some things bother me: why is the number one superpower stopping food from coming in? Why are they in love with the fundi-mundi forces? Are they desperate to go to Mecca for Hajj? It makes you think, ha, it does.'

'I know. Have you heard of illegal logging in the Sundarbans?'

'Little brother, what do you think? Everyone knows about it. Politicians, government officials, the military. They are all in it.

Ha, they are. You should print it in your newspaper.'

'I'd like to, but I have no concrete evidence, so I have been going to RBC to listen to gossip.'

'Na, not that place, little brother. It'll eat your soul up.'

'In my line of work, sometimes you need to do these things. Anyway, it's not all bad. I actually met Charity Magnet there.'

'Did you? Our saint. Our champion lover of the poor. I wonder what he's doing in a place like that. It makes you think, ha, it does.'

'Don't be so cynical. There are some good people in the world, you know.'

'There are. But some are too good to be true, especially if they love the poor so much – like they are your diamond mines.'

'So, you don't think much of Charity Magnet?'

'I'm not saying that. The man is a superstar. One of our richest men. Everyone loves him, even the Americans. Anyway, little brother, let us talk about you. What's been happening?'

'Work. Just work. So many stories to chase but not many leads.'

'Don't let work eat you up. It ate me up, ha, it did. What do I have to show for it? Nothing. Listen to me. Get a wife.'

'Wife thing is not for me. Anyway, who would love me?'

'What? What's love got to do with getting married? Little brother, have you been jilted? Some woman let you down? Tell me the truth?'

'Well, I had someone in mind, but she didn't want me.'

'Why didn't you tell me, little brother? I could've fixed it for you.'

'It's a matter of hearts. She just couldn't see me, you know, as someone she could love.'

'Little brother, you know nothing. Ha, nothing. I have tricks.'

'What tricks? You cook her a fish head and she falls for me. Is that it?'

'Don't underestimate cooking, little brother. I have other tricks too.'

'Anyway, it's done now. I've moved on.'

'Have you? Let me find you a wife. It will help you move on for real.'

It was past midnight when he reached his flat. He looked at the note and thought, you don't call people at this time of night unless it's a real emergency, and this wasn't. He went to bed but couldn't sleep. He tossed and turned, then got up. He meant to go to the kitchen for a glass of water but instead picked up the phone.

'I knew you would call,' said a woman's voice.

'Who are you?

'They call me Mrs Imam, but you can call me Bokul.'

'What do you want of me?'

'Nothing. I just wanted to invite you. I am a good cook, you know.'

'Thanks for the invite. I can do my own cooking.'

'Of course, you can. I thought you might be missing home cooking.'

'I'm not a sociable person. I don't take up invitations.'

'A little bird told me otherwise. I don't want to brag, but my dishes, you know, have more class than Mrs. Sarkar's. I am sure you'd agree if you tasted mine.'

The next evening, he went to the RBC and looked for Mia Zahan but he wasn't there. He sat in the bar and ordered a whisky, and soon Pota Sarwar joined him. Bulbul asked him about Mia Zahan and learned that he was by his seriously ill wife's bedside.

'I don't know how Mia Zahan Sir will cope without his Vat 69. Perhaps he'll bite the dust with his wife,' said Pota Sarwar. Bulbul felt deflated, fearing he wouldn't have the chance to ask Mia Zahan to shed further light on the cryptic remark he'd whispered in his ear.

'We can't have him dying,' said Bulbul.

'Why not? Why do you need him?'

'Why would I be needing him?'

'I don't know. You journalist lot are always after something. Maybe some gossip to bring someone down. Maybe some clues to a grand conspiracy. You know, the sort you lot always cook up.'

'I don't see him as an informant. Just an old man I like to talk to.'

'Don't forget what I said before. Be discreet. If you want to meet women members, just don't share cigarettes in the garden. We have eyes, you know.'

Concluding that it wouldn't be a productive evening at the RBC, Bulbul walked out. But before he reached halfway to the exit road, Shahabuddin came running after him to give him a note. It had an address and a date: Friday evening. There was no name, but he knew Mrs. Imam was inviting him. Her house was not far from Mrs. Sarkar's.

He still had two days to decide. On the way to work, sitting at his desk or at home, he wondered whether to take up Mrs Imam's invitation or ignore it. He couldn't say that it didn't tickle his desire, that an adventure might await him. He would be foolish to turn her down. After all, she was close to Charity Magnet, and he felt in his guts that whatever was happening somehow involved the saint.

CHAPTER 34

At work, Madam called him to her office.

'Charity Magnet's son has disappeared. I got it from a reliable source.'

'Are we releasing it in the paper?'

'No, not yet. I want you to find out more. The RBC could be a good place to start.'

It was late Friday afternoon. The heat and the humidity were as fierce as ever. Bulbul took a shower, put talcum powder on his neck and under his arms, shaved, and gargled with cloves-soaked water. He thought of attar, but that would be going too far. He looked at himself in the mirror in his red punjabi and decided against it. He settled on a green polo neck and a pair of jeans. At twenty-eight, he still looked boyish.

He headed for Gulshan on foot. He was thinking of so many things that he forgot about the tea maker – otherwise, he would have taken a detour to avoid him. He wasn't in the mood for his intrusive questions and the lies he'd be forced to tell. Too late, he had already been spotted.

'You're a friend now. So, a fifty percent discount, and I'll throw in a few cookie biscuits for free.'

Bulbul thanked him for offering cookies, but he only wanted tea.

'Are you heading to the same she for dinner?'

'Yes.'

'She must be very fond of you. Inviting you again.'

'Yes.'

'This time, I hope the husband is away on business. You don't want him spoiling things for you.'

'I told you, didn't I? I like the husband. We are old friends.'

'Good to hear. But times are not good. In the market, I hear the military are not happy. Do you know anything about it?'

'Not really. Tell me what you've heard.'

'Just market gossip. The military – anti-liberation ones – are trying to take over with the help of some politicians, government officials and big business. That's why they're creating the food shortage. They're very crafty, you know.'

'It seems you're more informed in the market than I am.'

'If you don't mind me asking, what do you do?'

'I'm a schoolteacher.'

'I knew it. You look like a proper book-reading gentleman. I'm so honoured that you want to be, you know, a friend of a humble man like me.'

'The honour is all mine.'

'I wonder what the lady will be cooking today. Perhaps fish head. You like fish head?'

Bulbul said yes and got up, pausing to light a cigarette.

'I wish ladies came to my stall. I'd serve them tea for free. Oh, what pleasure that would be, them drinking tea so close to me and laughing. I've never seen a woman's teeth close up except my mother's. Hers were dirty from so much paan chewing. I bet your lady never puts paan in her mouth. Only white teeth.'

Feeling anxious as he passed by Mrs Sarkar's flat, Bulbul hurried on and arrived at Mrs Imam's house within minutes. On a lane packed with high-rise buildings stood a solitary detached house, enclosed in high walls. It spoke of old money, its value quadrupled by the real-estate boom after independence.

When he rang the bell, a guard in uniform opened the gate and saluted him. The garden around the house had mature trees and well-tended flower beds, which a gardener was busy weeding. By the porch, he noticed a bokul tree with creamy, pinkish flowers covering the ground beneath it. The gardener said, 'I take special care of that tree. Our Madam is called after it.'

By the porch, a man was polishing an old Mercedes Benz. Two boys greeted him at the door and took him upstairs to the drawing room. It was decorated with paintings by well-known Bengali artists and a sculpture by Dipa Kaiser's father. A young girl brought him a glass of cool water with lime juice. The air-conditioning hummed in the cool room. Mrs Imam walked in wearing a simple cotton sari, looking sad. Bulbul wondered if the disappearance of Charity Magnet's son was weighing on her.

'Thanks for coming. I knew you would.'

'Sorry about the news.'

'I hope your newspaper people will show some restraint and not release the news yet. Charity Magnet Sir is devastated.'

'My editor won't release it.'

'Yes, I know. She's old family, isn't she?'

The serving boy brought two bottles of wine, one white, one red, and two glasses on a tray.

'Let's not talk about gloomy things tonight. It's been tough these last few days. I want to relax a bit. Are you a white man or a red man, Mr Bulbul? I hope you don't mind me calling you Bulbul.'

'Not at all, Mrs Imam.'

'Stop that Mrs stuff. It makes me feel old. Call me Bokul. Here we are: a singing bird and a night flower. What are you having? Red or white?'

Bulbul had never drunk wine in his life; his experience of alcohol was limited to whisky and the local brew.

'I don't know, what do you recommend?'

'It's hot. So, let us go for a chilled white. A fine vintage. I got it through a foreign embassy connection.'

Mrs Imam poured them both a glass and said, 'To us. I can see the beginning of a good friendship.' She pulled out a packet of expensive foreign cigarettes and offered him one. He offered her a light before she had time to look for matches.

'Thank you, you're a gentleman.'

As they drank their second glass of chilled white, the cook asked if Mrs Imam wanted to give the dishes a finishing touch. She left him, saying that he should carry on drinking. He slowly sipped his wine thinking that this variety of alcohol was to his liking. He scanned the room, pausing on Dipa Kaiser's father's sculpture: a peasant with bulging muscles carrying a huge pile of sugar cane on his head. When Mrs Imam came back, she found him examining the sculpture close up.

'Do you like it? Ratan Kaiser. He's an old family friend. Very talented, wasn't he?'

'So you know Dipa Kaiser?'

'Yes, I've known her since she was a baby. I was her favourite aunty until she returned from Paris, you know, with radical ideas. I became one of the haute bourgeoisie to be despised. Still, I feel sad for her. A widow at such a young age. And she lost her father too. I wanted to reach out to her, but she's stubborn. How do you know her?'

'Her husband Noor was my best friend.'

'So sad. We lost so many good ones in the war. Have you seen Dipa lately?'

'Not much. She seems very busy running her own paper. Besides, she's got her own circle of friends.'

'I know. She only mixes with feminists and ultra-leftists. Do you know anything about her going back to Paris?'

'As I said, I haven't seen her much and I'm not in her circle.'

When a girl he hadn't seen before brought in a bottle of cold water, Bulbul asked, 'How many people work for you?'

'Well, I have nine staff at home, including my personal secretary. They are very discreet and loyal. What happens in this house stays in this house. I've never had a breach. Unlike some other people, I don't hide from my staff.'

They were called to dinner when they'd finished the bottle of wine.

'Would you have a glass of red with dinner?' asked Mrs Imam.

'Yes, if you think it will go with the meal.'

The flavours of lobster, duck, dal, okra, and carp head with fenugreek and green chillies delighted Bulbul. Seeing the pleasure on his face as he ate a second serving of carp head and kept licking his fingers, Mrs Imam said, 'I told you, didn't I? I am a good cook. You need subtlety and imagination. Otherwise, it would be like, you know, cooked by some people I could name – just a fish head.'

After dinner, Mrs Imam asked her staff to clean up and serve whisky in her wing. This was a large bedroom with an attached bathroom, a sitting room with a TV and music centre, a dressing room, and a balcony with an overhanging mango tree. One of the boys brought a large bottle of whisky and soda water and left.

Mrs Imam closed the door behind them. They sat on wicker chairs on the veranda and watched fireflies dancing among the mango trees. Seeing the bottle of Vat 69, Bulbul laughed.

'I know it's a cliché. I know I am better than that. But when I drink whisky, I want to be all the clichés and be bad. Really bad.' She laughed, 'Don't look at me that way. I'm just joking. Actually, it's a good whisky.'

She served two glasses, and they toasted.

'You're the second woman in this city I know, I mean, I had whisky with,' said Bulbul, taking a sip.

'You don't have to be an Einstein to guess who the first one was. She's so stupid and indiscreet. What did she think she was doing when she went to share a cigarette with you in the garden? The RBC has eyes everywhere. I blame new money. No culture, no sophistication.'

'Let's forget about her. We are here. That's all that matters.'

'A singing bird and a night flower. It sounds so romantic. I don't mind what you do with her, as long as you're fully with me when you visit me. By the way, I wonder how many women there are with whom you've shared cigarettes?'

'Only three, including you.'

'I see. Obviously, I know one of them. But who is the third?'

'It's a long story. I'd rather not talk about it.'

'Yes, let's not complicate things. And don't ask me to divulge any secrets either. Right?'

'Right.'

When they ended up in bed, Bulbul wanted to turn the lights off, but Mrs Imam wouldn't have it.

'I want you to see me. A grown woman of fifty-eight years. I take care of myself. I've had a few cosmetics, but you will find a few places which show what time has done to me, perhaps in my neck, my hands, and the fold of my stomach. I want you to see them and be with me. I don't want you to be thinking of a young girl when you are with me. And don't you go chasing that third cigarette-whali in your mind. Acha?'

In the morning Mrs Imam brought tea to the bed.

'Thank you. You looked at me, and you were there with me. One hundred percent. This has never happened in my life.'

After a shower and a quick breakfast, Mrs Imam said she had to go out. 'I need to be with Charity Magnet Sir. If you want, I can drop you near your office .'

'Don't worry. I can make my own way.'

'Don't be silly. I'm going that way.'

When they turned onto the main road, the Mercedes Benz got caught up in a traffic jam . She asked the driver to turn up the air cooler and put on the radio, which was so loud that the car shook as if bombs were exploding in it.

'I wonder where they're keeping the boy.'

'Come closer. I can't hear you.'

'I was saying, I wonder where they're keeping the boy.'

'Can I trust you? Not a word to anyone. And definitely not in the newspaper. At least, not yet.'

'We have been intimate together. Will there be any bigger secret between us?'

'Acha, I get it. The boy disappeared in the Sundarbans. That's all I know.'

'How old is the boy?'

'A spoiled brat. He's ten.'

'I was about ten when my grandfather took me to the Sundarbans.'

'What for?'

'He wanted to hunt a tiger. He took me along.'

'Did he kill a tiger?'

'Well, it's a long story.'

'You seem to be full of long stories.'

The traffic eased, and the car moved on.

'Illegal logging… a lot of interests, I understand, from various quarters…' said Bulbul.

'I'm not surprised. It's easy money. And a lot of it.'

'Do you think the boy's disappearance has anything to do with it?'

'Are you insinuating something? Charity Magnet Sir is above these things. Money means nothing to him. The man is a saint.'

'You're getting me wrong. I'm not saying that Charity Magnet is involved in illegal logging, but miscreants might use it to implicate him.'

'I don't know. I'd rather not talk about it now.'

At *The People's Voice*, Madam called him in to her office and asked what he had discovered.

'Nothing concrete. Only hunches. I feel that Charity Magnet is somehow involved. The disappearance of his son might be related.'

'Related to what? You mean illegal logging in the Sundarbans?'

'Maybe. Maybe more. By the way, do you know where the boy is being kept?'

'Well, I heard that the boy disappeared in the Sundarbans. I presume he's still there.'

'Where did you get this information?'

'I've other sources too, you know. Anyway, I might have to send you to the Sundarbans. Not immediately. First, I want you to go back to your military friend. See if there are any developments.'

'I'll do that.'

'Don't forget Khoka's party on Friday.'

It was late afternoon and he found Madam under the flame tree. In front of her was a round table with two glasses of coconut water on it. She looked distracted, miles away. She nodded for him to sit down without looking at him.

'Am I early?'

'No, you are not.'

'Where are the guests?'

'I didn't want to share Khoka's memory with anyone else. Just you.'

'Thank you for inviting me. How are you?'

'You see me every day at work. That's all I do. I have no time for anything else.'

'Do you still think of Lalon Shai?'

'I don't think about him, but I know he's in me. Maybe one day you can run the paper, and I can disappear. Follow the Shai-ji's way.'

'It's a family newspaper. I'm not family.'

'Do you think only blood makes family? Not in my book.'

Kazli Booa, with the help of a young girl, served samosas and meesty-sweet on the table.

'How are you, Booa?' asked Bulbul.

'Why? Same, always the same,' she said, as if she couldn't be bothered to talk to him.

As soon as he could, Bulbul went to the kitchen.

'Do you need something?' asked Kazli Booa.

'No. I just came to see you.'

'Me? You gentlefolks came to see me? An old servant woman like me?'

'Booa, don't be cross. I've been very busy at work. Your body keeping well?'

'My body has not much left in it. It wants to leave me now, which would be a good thing.'

'Booa, what are you saying? Your body, ya Allah, is full of good meat and fat. Enough to drive a young man totally pagal.'

'Are you flirting with me?' Kazli Booa eased into a giggle.

'It's good to see you, Booa.'

'You've changed, haven't you? Only Allah knows how serious you were. Like our Madam. Dead serious. Good to see that you're becoming a bit naughty. Do you have a fancy woman somewhere?'

'What woman is going to have me? I'll die a virgin.'

'That's not funny. Look at me.' Kazli Booa turned serious and got busy with her chores.

Madam took him upstairs to her library after samosas and meesty-sweet under the flame tree. Bulbul was surprised to see that her bookshelves were filling up again, and the paintings of Draupadi the Infinite and Hypatia the lover of wisdom were back on the wall.

'There they are. I don't deny anything anymore. They are part of my life. Just as much Hazrat Bibi Rabia Basri and Lalon Shai. And how are you?'

'I'm happy now. Taking life as it comes. Good or bad.'

'It's good to embrace everything that happens to you, but in the process you mustn't betray what you are. Your core values.'

'Sometimes it's not easy. We humans are so complicated.'

'In what ways?'

'Left to its own devices, the body wants to run with its needs, its cravings. It's hardwired like a female mosquito. Can a female mosquito help herself not to suck our blood, infect us with malaria? No it can't. Good or bad doesn't come into it. It just does what it does. Our lives would have been easier if we were mosquitoes. Or geckos. Sometimes, I feel it would have been wonderful to be born a gecko and wait on the wall in silence. Time would pass without passing. But we're burdened with consciousness. It really messes you up.'

'Don't overthink.'

'It's hard not to, but I'm trying.'

'Good. But be careful you don't do something you regret.'

They sat on pillows on a rug. The room was filled with the scent of sandalwood as an incense stick burned. They faced a framed photograph of Khoka wearing his school uniform.

'I don't know why. I never wanted to have him photographed. This was on his first day at primary school. Munir took it. Now both of them are gone.'

'I know your brother was a keen photographer, but I haven't seen his portraits before.'

'On family occasions, we used to ask him to take our pictures. He rarely did. I don't know why he took this picture of Khoka.'

For a moment, Bulbul pictured Munir Mahmud, with his large body, small face and head, no discernible neck and his eyes squinting as he spoke. But maggots and bacteria had already done what they were born to do, leaving just his bones to endure.

'Bulbul, are you ok?'

'Yes, I'm fine.'

'I thought we'd just sit here in silence. I couldn't think of anything else for Khoka's birthday.'

For a moment Bulbul looked at Khoka's photo, then closed his eyes. At first, Madam was silent, then she broke into sobs, but that didn't distract Bulbul. On the contrary, it only helped him to be with Khoka, the poor boy who never had a chance. His body shook and tears rolled down his cheeks. Yes, he was with Khoka the way he had been with Mrs Sarkar or Mrs Imam. One hundred percent.

CHAPTER 35

While he was passing through RBC's grand hall, Pota Sarwar hailed him and suggested they go to the garden for a smoke.

'It's a delicate topic, you know. Our members are highly respected. Pillars of our society. We've got to be very careful.'

'What are you talking about?'

'Well, you sharing a cigarette with Mrs Sarkar. People are beginning to read something more into it. The last thing we want now is a scandal.'

'What's the big deal about it? I had a cigarette with a grown woman. Is someone complaining about it?'

'Yes. I had a female member. Very concerned.'

'Who's complaining? Who is she?'

'Not a very clever question. You know I'm not at liberty to name names. The RBC wouldn't last a day without confidentiality. I hope you understand that.'

'Ok, I'll never have another cigarette here with a female member. Happy?'

'Don't take it the wrong way. I like you. My job is to raise member's concerns. Keep everyone happy. You must also understand it's a very sensitive time for us.'

'In what ways is it sensitive?'

'I'm not at liberty to say. All I can say is it's serious. Very serious.'

'Is it something to do with Charity Magnet? What's happened to his son?'

'What's happened to his son?'

'Don't play dumb with me. Everyone knows. Poor boy.'

'Make sure that the news doesn't spread further – until we've a handle on it.'

'We're keeping it out of the newspaper. But you must understand that we can't help the boy until we know more. Know why he was taken and who took him.'

'I don't think these are the right questions. All they will do is throw dirt on Charity Magnet Sir's good name. Why do people find it so difficult to believe that there are good people in the world and that there are saints.'

At the bar, spotting Mia Zahan, Bulbul approached him with double pegs of Vat 69. 'I hope your wife is better now.'

'The damn woman's indestructible. Made to last till doomsday. Never mind, I hear you're quite a lady's man.'

'Lady's man, me? Where did you get that idea?'

'People in the club are talking, you know. You have been spotted.'

'It's absurd. All I did was share a cigarette in the garden with a lady member.'

'Yes, a puff of smoke. It coils up even if you can't see it in the dark. If you're sharp enough, you can read many stories in it. Our members are very perceptive, you know.'

'So, members are spreading gossip about me. That's nasty.'

'I'm afraid the affairs of the body are always a nasty business. Nothing good comes of illicit fornication.'

They drank in silence until Bulbul said, 'Charity Magnet's son. That's very sad.'

'Yes, very sad. Many people want to trap him. Bring him down.'

'So, you think the boy might have been kidnapped? Some people holding him for ransom or something?'

'I don't know. We mustn't speculate. It's a nasty business.'

From the club lobby, Bulbul phoned White Alam's house and was told he was at the Hotel Intercontinental. Since it was only a few minutes on foot from the RBC, he decided to walk there. He found White Alam at the bar with a group of men, all quite drunk.

'Singing Bird, so good of you to join us,' said White Alam and introduced his companions, all businessmen. Taking his leave of them, White Alam took Bulbul to another bar room and ordered whisky.

'The damn businessmen you just met are all forest monsters.'

'What do you mean?'

'I mean, they are the princes of illegal logging, and big in contraband trade. Don't get me wrong. I don't disapprove of them. These guys have the balls and the know-how to get what they want.'

'So you're becoming pals with them?'

'Just to let you know, I've been given a new command. The Sundarbans will be in my area. Those guys will come in handy to me then. As a serving officer, I can't get directly involved.'

'So you'll be using their mouths to devour the forest?'

'Don't be so dramatic, Singing Bird. If you want to stay poor and humble, that's your choice. Don't try to impose it on others. It's not the Godzilla way.'

'I don't know what the damn Godzilla way is.' Bulbul was about to say more, but he caught himself; he hadn't come to argue with White Alam but to gather information.

'Have you heard about Charity Magnet's son?'

'Of course. It's open knowledge. I wish he had disappeared somewhere else than in the Sundarbans. Now that I'm going there, I'll have to deal with the mess. It would be better if a tiger ate the brat. End of story.'

'I might be sent to the Sundarbans to investigate the case.'

'Stay away. Big games are being played there. You'll get burned.'

'What games?'

'All I'm saying is stay away from the Sundarbans. Big players are involved, and they are dangerous.'

'Is Charity Magnet involved?'

'You make your own guess. But I'll tell you, Charity Magnet is a genius. He's really cracked the art of parallel growth. Increasing wealth and saintliness simultaneously. Real masterstroke.'

When he reached his flat it was midnight. Within minutes, the telephone rang. It was Mrs Imam. She was sending a car for him to be picked up. Bulbul wanted to talk about Charity Magnet and his son, but Mrs Imam said, 'It's been a tough day. Let's go to bed.'

In the morning, she gave him a lift to work. As before, the air cooler and the radio were cranked up.

'Charity Magnet's son. Any news?' he asked.

'I don't know. But I fear it's bad news. Too many people are gunning for Charity Magnet Sir.'

'Do you think Charity Magnet is involved in something? The Sundarbans is ripe with illegal logging and contraband trade.'

'You don't let it go, do you? But for argument's sake, let's say

404

that Charity Magnet Sir is involved in all these. So what? He will only be making money to serve the poor. He will be a Robin Hood, as well as being a saint.'

As Bulbul was dropped off, Mrs Imam smiled sweetly, looking almost girlish and thanked him for being 100%.

'If I didn't know any better, I'd have thought you'd fallen for me. Madly in love. It wouldn't be a bad thing either – between a singing bird and a night flower.'

The next day, about noon, he was called to the phone. It was Mrs Sarkar.

'So sorry I had to go off without telling you. It was urgent. But I couldn't stop thinking about you. I felt like a stupid schoolgirl.'

She would cook him a meal that night, and he was happy to accept the invitation. For several weeks he alternated between Mrs Imam's and Mrs Sarkar's houses. Mrs Imam knew he was seeing Mrs Sarkar, but the latter had no idea about the former. In any case, they were as happy with him as he was with them.

Finally, the news of the disappearance of Charity Magnet's son hit the headlines. No one knew what had happened to the boy.

It was time, Madam decided, for Bulbul to go to the Sundarbans.

CHAPTER 36

Everyone said a tiger had taken the boy. Nothing unusual in it – humans becoming food for tigers, especially in the Sundarbans. It was easy meat for them, much easier than catching an agile chital deer or a wary macaque. Bulbul shivered, imagining the torn, tender flesh between the tiger's teeth. Not a nice way to end your short stay on earth.

Once the newspapers broke the story, it gave rise to feverish speculation. It was said that Charity Magnet was involved in many political and financial intrigues and that he had powerful international backers and enemies.

When Bulbul got to the Sundarbans, talk of a man-eater, more bold and ferocious than any before, had reached fever pitch. Fear crawled the mudland like the crabs that swarmed red at low tide. On the morning he arrived, the half-eaten body of a fisherman was discovered, taken from a flat-bottomed boat the previous night. Demon that he was and master of stealth, the tiger had taken the fisherman without so much as ruffling his companion's dreams, asleep beside him. He'd taken the man by the throat, swum the dark waters of the channel, and brought his human feast into the forest. That month alone, the tiger devoured ten people – fishermen, woodcutters and honey-collectors – all within a mile or so of the watering station where forest workers came for fresh water from the government supply ship, which Bulbul had arrived on.

'Mr Bulbul, it's an inauspicious time,' said the captain. 'Evil is lapping the mangroves.' He tried to dissuade Bulbul from setting foot in the mud.

'Someone has to do the job and get to the truth,' said Bulbul.

'Truth,' laughed the captain, 'it has more twists and turns than these labyrinthine waterways.'

Bulbul was to carry out his investigation from the forest ranger's bungalow. The boy had been taken from there. Most of the old Sundarbans hands – foresters and hunters – agreed that it was the work of a single tiger. They called him Wrath of God. Bulbul hardly slept that night, terrified of Wrath of God's silent prowl. Perhaps he was just behind the bungalow, waiting to pounce on the next human, as it had pounced on the boy. Occasionally, he heard screeching and the shrill barking of macaques, the sign of the tiger's passing. Then, a growl made him hold his breath and curl up under the quilt. It wouldn't take much for Wrath of God to jump the perimeter fence and break through the wooden planks into the bungalow.

He remembered when he came with his grandfather on the tiger hunt all those years ago. He hadn't intended it, but the fact remained it was he who spilt the beans on what had happened, and that had led to his death. How could he forget his grandfather lying dead, his eyes closed, his body stiff, his mouth twisted and open to show the pink of his toothless gums, and especially the moment when he touched his cold hand, which felt as if it was trying to grab him and drag him down to hell? He needed to escape from these terrible memories of guilt and horror. His body, almost as a tic, dragged him back to those moments with Mrs Sarkar and Mrs Imam, to the touch of skin, the bittersweet taste on his tongue and the aroma that drove him wild. Ah, these memories of sensation saved him, but why wasn't he tempted to summon Dipa Kaiser, over whom he'd obsessed for so long? It was as if she'd died for him when she offered her body without the promise of love. She couldn't have been unaware that the gesture would shatter him. She knew he was in love with her. Was it her way of punishing him for walking out on her and Noor Azad, or for continuing to pursue her even when her reluctance was apparent? Had he spoilt it with his sudden manic drive to win her over? He was hurt, angry, and guilty, so he pretended that she had never existed in his life. Yes, Dipa, you can go to hell for all I care, but let me alone.

He woke up in the morning to a great commotion. One of the armed guards on sentry duty was missing; telltale pugmarks were everywhere. A search party of several armed guards and a tracker were sent out to investigate. Only a few hundred metres away, by a mangrove along a dark, narrow channel, they found the half-eaten body of the sentry. It took only a brief look for the tracker to confirm that it was indeed the work of Wrath of God. 'He's a beast from hell. No one is safe here,' he said.

Bulbul made a sketch of the pugmarks; they were huge. When the half-eaten body was taken away for burial, Bulbul returned inside the perimeter fence of the bungalow and made a thorough search of the grounds. There were no pugmarks inside. What was the sentry doing outside the fence? Seeing the tracker sitting on the verandah and smoking a cigarette, Bulbul approached him.

'I don't see any pugmarks inside the fence. So, the sentry was taken from the outside. Am I right?'

'You don't know Wrath of God. He knows the way if he doesn't wish to leave any pugmarks.'

'And the boy. Wasn't he sleeping inside the bungalow, next to his uncle? Do you think Wrath of God took him?'

'Of course. That he was inside the bungalow and beside his uncle doesn't change a thing. If Wrath of God wanted to take the boy, he would have his way.'

It was useless talking to the tracker; he wouldn't get anything out of him. All the dimwit was interested in was this stupid mumbo-jumbo; perhaps he was being paid to peddle this super beast nonsense. Bulbul left him, went outside the perimeter fence, and looked at Wrath of God's pugmarks. It seemed that the tiger had circled the fence several times, but there was no sign that he was ever inside it. From whatever angle he looked, Bulbul was sure the sentry was taken from outside. But why was the tracker lying? He traced the pugmarks all the way to the mangrove on the edge of the dark channel, to the kill site. All life seemed to have fled – the macaques, the chital deer, even the birds; only the flies hummed on the traces of blood. Nothing moved or broke the silence, but he sensed that Wrath of God was watching him. How could he ignore its demonic power? Yes, Wrath of God could take the boy from wherever and whenever he wanted; right now, it could take him in one giant leap. He turned and ran. Mercifully Wrath of God didn't follow him – it had just gorged on a new kill.

Ziauddin, whose father had overseen his grandfather's failed tiger hunt, came to see him at the bungalow in the afternoon. Ziauddin, apart from hunting rogue man-eaters, had never practised his family profession. Instead, he had become an important member of the Save the Tiger Project, using his accumulated knowledge of tigers to find ways of protecting them.

'I thought you would look different,' said Ziauddin.

'In what ways?'

'My father described a skinny little boy. Scared and desperate to hide.'

'I'm still scared.'

'Maybe, but it doesn't show.'

Ziauddin set about examining the fenced compound and tracing the pugmarks all the way to the kill site.

'What do you think?' Bulbul asked.

'It was Wrath of God. No doubt about it, but the sentry was taken from outside the compound.'

'The tracker insists that he was taken from inside.'

'I'm not surprised. Some dodgy business is going on here. A whole lot is involved.'

'What do you mean?'

'Why would you go outside if a vicious man-eater was on the prowl? It serves someone's interest to peddle the story of a supernatural beast.'

'But surely you don't doubt that the boy was taken from inside the bungalow?'

'Sure, the boy was taken from inside the room. But I can tell you it wasn't the work of Wrath of God. In fact, on that night, there was no sign of tiger activity in the area. You are a clever journalist. You work out the rest.'

'Did you talk to the uncle? I heard the boy was sleeping beside him.'

'No. They bundled him out before I arrived. No one has heard of him since. God knows what's happened to that poor fellow.'

Ziauddin insisted that the bungalow wasn't safe and that Bulbul should move into his house on the forest's edge.

'If Wrath of God can't come inside the compound, then what's the danger?'

'Wrath of God is the least of your problems. Danger comes from elsewhere, my friend.'

Bulbul moved into Ziauddin's house and from there widened the scope of his investigation. He contacted two of the shadowy groups that operated in the Sundarbans, the smugglers and the bandits. From the smugglers, he learnt that many security guards and forest officials were on their payroll, helping to move contraband goods, like whisky and wine. The sentry, taken by Wrath of God, was one of them. He was supposed to be at a rendezvous outside the compound for his payoff, but Wrath of God had other ideas. His smuggler contact warned him to go back to Dacca because things were getting very messy and dangerous; they wouldn't be able to protect him for long. 'We trust you,' his contact said. 'But there are forces here who wouldn't think twice about cutting your throat. Some individuals, even among us, feel that all journalists are double-crossers, and want to get rid of you.'

He was assured that the smugglers had nothing to do with the boy's disappearance. 'We have no control over Wrath of God. He has taken many of us. I'm surprised that he went for the boy. He would have been a mere morsel.'

Bulbul wanted to ask if it was true, as he heard from other

sources, that the boy had been taken across the border and that the smugglers had a hand in it. He didn't ask this because he thought he might lose his relationship with them.

From the nearby town, Bulbul phoned Madam to report what he had found so far.

'I don't like it. It's not safe. Come back to Dacca,' she said.

'I'm perfectly safe. Don't worry about me. I think I am getting closer. Only a few more days and I'll be back.'

'Promise me if you feel any danger, you'll leave immediately. Promise?'

He asked Madam if she could send someone to talk to Charity Magnet's family to find out what had happened to the uncle and whether there had been a ransom demand.

He phoned again several days later.

Madam told him, 'Charity Magnet has gone underground. No one has seen him for days. We couldn't get anything out of the family.'

'How about a ransom demand?'

'Nothing. The police know nothing. I think Charity Magnet is up to something big.'

'I know. Do we have any contacts with the bandits?'

'Munir worked with Shiraj Dacoit. He was useful, but be careful. He's unpredictable. Ridiculously pompous and prone to casual brutality.'

After days of trying, Bulbul finally made contact with the bandits and was taken to their base.

Shiraj Dacoit appeared in combat fatigues, his hair gelled back, sporting a pair of dark glasses with the air of a Bollywood superstar.

'Thank you, Sir. Thank you for seeing me,' said Bulbul.

'Your editor, Munir Mahmud, was a fine fellow. He did an article on me. Called me the Emperor of the Jungle. I liked that. So, I'm seeing you only for his sake. Now don't ask any intrusive questions. I wouldn't like that.'

'It's an honour, Sir to see you. You're a legend, Sir.'

'I like you. You have manners. Just stay that way.'

Bulbul moved with the bandits for two days, during which time they attacked several boats, looted their contents, killed everyone, and had themselves photographed with their victims. Shiraj Dacoit had his photograph taken – gelled hair, dark glasses, and Bollywood swagger – while holding two butchered heads aloft in his hands.

'Munir Mahmud was a good man, but his photographs were bad. Out of focus. I looked like a cheap hoodlum.'

Bulbul had to promise good photographs of Shiraj Dacoit on the front page as a part of the deal.

'You stay with us. Enjoy our hospitality. After we see the photos in the paper, we'll decide. In the meantime, you are completely safe. No one will cut your throat. Yes?'

Bulbul wasn't an expert photographer, but his shots showed Shiraj Dacoit in a glamorous light. They were printed on the front page of the *Peoples Voice*, headlined as *In the Domain of the Emperor*.

'Not bad. A bit more in the profile would've been better. But I'm not complaining. Anyway, the boys said I look handsome. Acha, Mr Bulbul, what do you want to know?'

But just then Shiraj Dacoit halted the questioning because it was lunchtime. There were piles of roasted deer meat.

'You don't see any rice here. Why is that Mr Journalist?'

'Perhaps you can't get rice here in the jungle?'

'You don't know us. If we want, we can have mountains of rice. No problem. But we don't go for rice. Do you know why?'

'I don't know. Rice is our staple. We Bengalis can't do without it.'

'I tell you that rice is our ruination. Big belly. Weak constitution. You have to admit it makes a guy look ugly, spineless, like a skinny, domestic dog. Whining and yapping. So, I banned rice in my camp. Only meat. How do you like the dishes?'

'Very delicious. Finest meat I've tasted.'

'Good to see you're enjoying it. The more illegal, the sweeter to the taste, eh journalist? Deep down, I bet you've always fancied being bad. Now what can I do for you?' Shiraj Dacoit laughed uproariously, almost making his dark glasses fall off.

At last Bulbul could ask him about Charity Magnet's son.

'Yes, the boy. Nothing is beyond Wrath of God. He took some of my men, too. We sprayed him with our brand-new automatics. He just leapt and vanished. He's a demon, all right. But the boy was too skinny. Wrath of God is very particular about his choice. He only took my fattiest ones. You get my meaning, journalist? Sure, we'd have liked to take the boy. I hear Charity Magnet has made plenty of money. If we do a little robbing here and there to feed our poor sisters, we are painted as evil. But that charity bugger gets mega-rich selling poverty. And he's worshipped as a saint. No justice in the world, journalist. I tell you he's crafty, but we didn't take his boy.'

'But if not you, who?'

'You're boring me, journalist. I'm a man of super patience, but there's a limit to how much a man can take silly questions. Don't poke your nose into hot things, otherwise, you'll go home without your head. Your wife might not like it. No lips to kiss. Let's enjoy the illegal deer and make merry.'

Then Shiraj Dacoit laughed, took off his dark glasses, looked benevolently at Bulbul and suggested that he meet the Year Zeroists. 'Them guys are totally crazy. But they might give you what you're looking for. Make sure you don't mention you've seen us. They wouldn't be very pleased.'

The Year Zeroists were one of the best armed and disciplined forces in the Sundarbans. Their dislike of Charity Magnet was well known: the bugger wanted to eliminate poverty and how could they have a revolution without poverty? Comrades, he's class enemy number one. The Year Zeroists also hated the likes of Bulbul as degenerate hedonists and soft lefties: double-crossing snakes and spreaders of confusion – eliminate them. Despite sending messages promising to write a favourable feature about their heroic struggle to take independent Bangladesh to its pure, year zero, and his declared admiration for Comrade Pol Pot, Bulbul hadn't made any inroads with them. Once, he had received a message that they would meet him, but halfway to the rendez-vous, he'd turned back because he was tipped off that the whole thing was a trap. The Year Zeroists wanted to take him hostage, or hang him as a revisionist pig. His investigation seemed to have reached a dead end.

Ziauddin continued to follow Wrath of God's kill sites, always alone with his gun at the ready and half-naked, his fleshy body on display as the choice meat that the tiger surely couldn't resist. After several days of not encountering anything, he sensed a presence as he entered the mangroves from his dinghy one morning. He was sure that it was Wrath of God. He followed his hunch about the tiger's path. Before him lay the mangroves, their upturned roots, the channels lapping against them, the mud and the thick canopy that devoured almost all the sunlight. He was sure Wrath of God was prowling somewhere near, stalking a fisherman who had foolishly ventured into the forest or a poor honey collector. Ziauddin met only with silence, except for the gentle lapping of the water. All life, macaques, deer, lizards, and snakes seemed to have fled from this part of the jungle. Even the mudskippers and crabs were not coming to the surface. Ziauddin sensed that he was gaining on the tiger; perhaps he would come upon him unawares, take him by surprise and shoot him dead before he could leap.

But there were no signs or pugmarks, and Ziauddin was beginning to think he had been imagining things, then he heard a sound behind him, turned and noticed pugmarks following his footprints. His heart nearly stopped. Wrath of God had been following him. He ran and climbed up a large tree, but Wrath of God didn't appear or growl to betray his presence. Ziauddin stayed in the tree until dusk when villagers, carrying drums and torches, came to rescue him. They only realised that one the rescuers was missing when they returned to the village. No one noticed he'd been taken.

Ziauddin took to bed, shivering, with a high temperature. When Bulbul came to sit by his bedside, he was frail and barely able to talk. But he told Bulbul it wasn't safe to stay there any longer. Wrath of God was indeed a monster, and he should go back to Dacca, otherwise something terrible would befall him.

'He'll play with you. Then devour you.'

Bulbul, though, stayed on, trying to use some local villagers, whom the Year Zeroists trusted as supporters, to find out if they were holding the boy. Nothing came off it. Ziauddin worsened and had to be taken to a hospital in the nearby town. He told Bulbul he could stay in his house, though he feared for his safety.

'You've noticed the empty patches in the jungle? It took

hundreds of years for those trees to grow. Now they are butchered and shifted down the river like dead carcasses.'

'You'd have to be blind not to notice what's going on.'

'Influential people are involved, especially the military.'

'Do you think the reason for the boy's disappearance could be found there?'

'My gut feeling says yes. But a lot of things are tangled up in it. You'll have to do a lot of leg work. It will be very dangerous.'

Bulbul stayed in Ziauddin's house, wondering what Charity Magnet had to do with the illegal logging. He'd raised a lot of foreign money for environmental protection but was this just a cover? Bulbul wandered through the clearing in the forest, following the trails of trees being dragged to the riverbank. From there, they were taken on rafts and transported downriver to the coast and beyond. But no one would speak to him, and armed guards warned him to stay away. Letters were slipped under the door when he slept, telling him to bugger off or he would be hung from the trees he loved. Bulbul discovered that there were at least two powerful consortia of businessmen and political and army factions involved in illegal logging. But he still couldn't figure out how Charity Magnet fitted in with any of these groups. Did one of them take the boy?

By now, White Alam had taken up his command post. His brigade was now the most powerful armed group in the Sundarbans. One evening, he sent a speed boat to pick Bulbul up. Some officers were having a party and Colonel Alam wanted him to attend.

'What a Godzilla surprise. Fancy meeting you in the jungle.'

White Alam introduced Bulbul to his fellow officers as his best friend. One officer, Major Khondokar, took a particular interest in Bulbul, never straying far from him, serving him whisky and snacks. Major Khondokar wasn't good at holding his liquor. Even after his first glass of whisky, he looked unsteady on his feet, his voice slurring.

'It must be a tough posting here. Far from modern amenities, among mosquitoes, snakes and tigers,' said Bulbul.

'Not at all. You might not believe it, but there's huge competition for it. The posting here is very lucrative.'

'I don't understand.'

'Fabulous riches. If you know how to extract them.'

Bulbul walked to the verandah, and the major followed him. They sat on recliners, the mangroves now an immense blob of darkness.

'Are you here on Charity Magnet's case?' the major asked.

'Yes, I am. Do you know anything about him?'

'Who doesn't? He's very clever. He's the main man of the number one superpower. Very good position, you know. Handsome rewards. Many would sell their souls to be in his position. But no one comes close to Charity Magnet in the soul-selling business. The number one superpower was looking for someone to soften the cutthroat image of capitalism. So they championed Charity Magnet as the capitalist of the poor. You know, as a counterweight to all those do-gooders, priests, poets and what have you who are partial to the likes of Christ and Marx and are out to spoil the show.'

'Interesting. Actually, I'm looking into the disappearance of his boy.'

'I know nothing about the boy. I hear he was a spoiled brat. If the tiger ate him, I hope it didn't give him indigestion.'

Sensing that the Major's tongue was loosened, Bulbul pressed further.

'I wonder how you see things in the military. What's going on?'

'Lots of bloody stuff going on. It'll mess things up for all of us. Islamists, damn collaborators. There's a tiny but committed group. They're very fond of Jihad and cutting things off – heads, balls, everything. Then you have a Year Zeroist faction, too. Also tiny but very motivated. They want to stage a putsch to go back to year zero. Perhaps they want to bring back dinosaurs. Imagine poor Wrath of God facing a T-Rex. Ho, ho, that'd be some show. I tell you something: the godless Year Zeroists are getting into bed with the Islamists. Very bizarre.'

'Do the military high-ups know about this?'

'Sure, they know. But they're too busy lining their pockets and too fat to move their arses. They're playing a waiting game. If the move fails, they'll come down hard on the conspirators and win brownie points from the government. More pocket lining and fat assing will follow. If the conspirators win, they will want a large cut. Either way, it's a win for them. Crafty buggers.'

'How does Charity Magnet come into all this?'

'I told you, didn't I? Charity Magnet is pulling all the strings. Poverty and wealth are not enough for him. The saint wants to be the kingmaker now.'

'What does the boy's disappearance have to do with all this?'

'I know nothing about the boy's disappearance. I know the Islamists and the Year Zeroists will want a big share of power after the government is toppled. The boy goes to the Sundarbans… You work out the rest, my friend.'

'You mean the Islamists and the Year Zeroists have kidnapped the boy as a bargaining chip with Charity Magnet?'

'I'm saying nothing, my friend. Your speculation is as plausible or absurd as any other. Who knows?' The major tried to get to his feet but fell face down and started throwing up. Two young officers came to pick him up and take him inside. Bulbul stayed on the verandah and White Alam joined him.

'Poor Major Khondokar. Tomorrow, he'll swear on his mother's honour he'll never touch alcohol again. He speaks so much rubbish when he's drunk. I hope he hasn't spoilt your evening with his nonsense.'

'We just had a friendly chat. It actually made a lot of sense.'

'Listen, Singing Bird. I'm serious. This place is not safe for you. Go back to Dacca.'

'You're the commanding officer here. I have nothing to fear, have I?'

'You know I'd do anything for you. We're Godzilla brothers, aren't we? But the game played here is beyond my pay scale. If you got into the wrong hands, I don't know if I could save you.'

The sky finally broke. The last blade of grass disappeared under murky water. Snakes took shelter high up in the trees. Gale-force winds lashed the forest and the waves in the channels rose high.

One afternoon there was a report of a kill. A fisherman had been taken from a boat, but a young boy with him left unharmed. Thinking it could be Charity Magnet's son, Bulbul hired a sampan and two foolhardy boatmen to get around the jungle.

'It's not the weather to go out,' they warned, but Bulbul wouldn't be dissuaded. In high winds and choppy waters, the boatmen had trouble steadying the boat; it rose and fell in jerky movements, and all three were soaked within minutes. Although all the water courses had merged, the boatmen knew the shallow ones by the look of the lines of mangroves. When they turned the first bend, they heard macaques screaming and jumping from tree to tree across the canopy. A sure sign of Wrath of God swimming past. Then they heard a roar. Bulbul began to shiver, his teeth chattering.

Out of nowhere, two boats came upon them at lightning speed. On board were men with automatic guns and cane-cutters. As if they had practised the move to perfection, two men jumped onto Bulbul's sampan and ran the blades through the boatmen's throats. They thrashed about the sampan like fishes out of water, spurting blood, soaking Bulbul red.

They tossed the bodies into the water for the crocodiles, sharks, or perhaps hungry tigers – though they were not a worthy feast for Wrath of God. They blindfolded Bulbul and bundled him into one of their boats, then surged through the wind and waves.

CHAPTER 37

When they removed his blindfold, Bulbul found himself among a large cluster of boats in a narrow channel surrounded by dense, impenetrable green. He had no idea who had captured him and why. They left him bound to the boat's mast. In the afternoon, he had a visitor who seemed to be in command. He looked like a mild, thoughtful man with a kind face. He wore a lungi and a Punjabi shirt. He carried neither a gun nor a knife. He gave Bulbul a friendly, gentle smile; he reminded him of one of his favourite high school teachers, Mr Bose, who taught Bangla. He shook his head and instructed that Bulbul be untied.

'Sorry for the inconvenience, Mr Bulbul,' said the commander. 'You are our guest. We'll make your stay with us as comfortable as possible. Please don't hesitate to ask for anything.'

'Let me go, commander. I've a job to do.'

'You don't want to go out there alone, do you? Didn't you know? Wrath of God is creating havoc out there. It seems he can't get enough human flesh. Besides, I can't throw you to the bandits and the cutthroats.'

'Who are you?'

'We want to take the country to a new dawn. Our independence was a sham. We want a new beginning.'

'So, you're the Year Zeroists?'

'Yes. We'll speak more later.'

Bulbul woke up to a calm morning. The gale-force wind had subsided and waves had settled into ripples. It was overcast and the rain still pattered. The flotilla moved on. Bulbul was surrounded by armed guards, one on either side of the boat and two on the cabin roof. He wondered what they meant to do with him.

The flotilla was a moving encampment of thirty small boats with straw and bamboo cabins, each accommodating about five people. A large cargo boat carried provisions and provided cooking facilities. The commander lived on a small boat which stayed close to Bulbul's. He heard crackles of wireless communication and voices from the commander's boat but had no idea what was being said. The fifth man on his boat was one of the ambushers who'd cut the boatmen's throats. He sported a long, black, bushy beard, wore a skullcap and a long white Punjabi. He rarely spoke; if not praying, he counted beads and hummed Allah's name. He looked so peaceful, serene, gentle and polite that Bulbul couldn't comprehend how he could be such a vicious cutthroat. In the afternoon, after his prayers, when he was counting beads and looking out of the window at the lapping water, Bulbul edged towards him.

'Venerable Mullah, what are you looking at?'

The man didn't seem to hear him. He continued counting beads, his gaze fixed on the lapping water and the mangrove. He spoke when Bulbul was about to give up and return to his place.

'I'm looking at Allah's creation. It's so beautiful, I feel like weeping.'

'Yes, Venerable Mullah, it's so beautiful. We are so fortunate to lay our eyes on such a miracle of creation.'

'Allah's creation. He has given us so much bounty. Yet, we sin against him. Deny his existence. I hear you communists say: Allah is dead. We soldiers of Allah are here to close up those impious mouths for good. So, no more filthy sounds, only the praise of Allah's name and his prophet. Peace be upon him.'

'Sorry, I don't quite understand. How come you're here with the Year Zeroists? I'd say they are more Allah deniers than I've ever been.'

'Allah works mysteriously. Sometimes you must ride with the devil to do your work.'

'Can you ride a devil without taking on some of its ways?'

'What are you saying? I've become a devil?'

'Not at all, Venerable Mullah. Just making conversation. It's the vice of a journalist.'

'I see what you're getting at, journalist. Bad company rubs off badness on you. Very true. That's why you have to be very vigilant. Make double the effort to stay on the right path.'

'I suppose that's why you pray so much, never stop counting beads and calling Allah's name.'

'There's not enough time to call his name. I wish I didn't have to sleep or eat. Waste of time when I should be praying and calling his name.'

Bulbul found out that the man with the long, black bushy beard was the son of humble peasants, had gone to a religious school where the ideals of Jihad had inspired him to become a Mujahideen, a holy warrior who'd give his life one day for the cause of Islamic ummah. He had joined the collaborationist forces and fought against the liberation of Bangladesh. He had killed many Hindus, killed the nationalists, and taken part in the slaughter of writers, poets, painters and professors. Spreaders of confusion, he called them. It occurred to Bulbul that Noor Azad might have been one of his victims. He imagined hitting the mullah with one of the oars, shaving his black, bushy beard and hanging him from the mast.

In the evening, the rain and the clouds cleared, and the last rays of the sun trailed their way into the boat. The man with the long, black beard brought Bulbul a cup of tea and a lump of palm sugar. They resumed their conversation, and an ease flowed between them.

When the sun had almost disappeared, Bulbul asked, 'Venerable Mullah, what about women?'

'What about them?'

'You know, in war.'

'Heaven lies beneath the feet of mothers, but in war, on the other side, they are just enemy property.'

'Enemy property?'

'Yes,' he said, and went back to his bead-counting.

Bulbul couldn't help remembering what Kazli Booa had said about Zorina: how she'd been dishonoured before being killed, her body floating in the river. Perhaps, the man with the long, black beard, or someone like him, had claimed Zorina as his share of enemy property. He looked at the orange trail along the river, his body shaking. He imagined castrating the man and feeding his privates to the crocodiles that swam the Sundarbans' waters.

On the fifth day of his capture, the storms returned. It was fiercer than when he was first captured. The commander emerged from his boat, climbed on the cargo boat and addressed the flotilla. He told the men to move the boats into a cove surrounded by large sundari trees and tie them together. Even so, the wind that galloped in with surging water tossed the boats and ripped many masts off. Bulbul's boat escaped severe damage, but the rain poured in through large holes made by the wind. When the storm abated, the commander climbed again on the cargo boat and orchestrated repairs to damaged boats. Bulbul watched as men stripped to their lungies to do this. Two boats were too damaged and discarded; the rest were repaired. With no sign of the rain abating, the commander decided the flotilla should stay in the sheltered bay. The armed guards, who'd come into the cabin at the beginning of the storm, stayed on. Unlike the commander and the man with the long, bushy beard, they didn't seem to have any political or religious convictions. They moved to the far end of the boat, hung bed sheets and lungies as a screen and sat behind it, drinking alcohol. The man with the long, black, bushy beard looked tense and counted his beads even faster.

Bulbul became feverish, with a high temperature. The man with the long, black beard nursed him day and night as if he were his mother. Putting Bulbul's head on his lap, he fed him soup, massaged him, and wiped his face with his gamcha-towel. He took him into the mangroves for his bodily functions. Reciting Koranic verses, he blew their blessings on Bulbul's face. 'Allah, heal my little brother. If he has sinned punish me. But don't harm him. Please, Allah.' He fasted for Bulbul's recovery. One morning, after washing Bulbul's body with soapy water and a gamcha-towel and massaging his feet, the man said, 'When the commander gives the order, I've got to do it.'

Bulbul struggled to open his eyes; his lips moved as if to ask the meaning of his words.

'I've got to kill you. You know our method. It's honest and goes back to the purity of the old ways.'

The wind and the rain stopped. Wrapped in a quilt, Bulbul sat up, leaning against the cabin frame, his head still light and spinning. He looked out of the small rectangular window. The rain-washed mangroves looked greener in the sun, but the river was cluttered with flotsam from the storm, drifting in a tangled mess. He lowered himself and, propping his head on a pillow, slanted his eyes over the mangrove to the sky. It was blue and empty except for the sluggish drift of small islands of clouds. He looked hard at them as if he could nudge them into gathering speed to propel him into another time and place where the mullah wouldn't be waiting to end his journey on earth. But they were in no mood to oblige and seemed to have come to a standstill. Perhaps they knew his fate had been sealed. How would Dipa Kaiser respond to his passing? Maybe she would feel relieved that an annoyance in her life was gone. If he had accepted her wishes and not persisted in his need to be loved by her, so desperate and clumsy, they could have remained friends, but he wasn't worthy of her friendship. Friends don't behave the way he did. She had just lost the two men dearest to her, but instead of being there for her, unconditionally, as friends should, he had got carried away with his pathetic need for love. He wished he could believe in an afterlife like Teeny Mullah, even if he burnt in hellfire, to get a chance to meet up with her to say sorry, but this was the only world there was, and he'd messed it up. Sorry, Dipa, sorry for everything.

The flotilla was on the move again. Bulbul recovered, and the man with the long, black beard kept his distance. If he happened to be in the cabin, he never looked up, just counted his beads and prayed. He mostly sat on the cabin roof and looked out to the forest as if to spot a tiger. One day, he moved to another boat. Now Bulbul was only with the armed guards.

Early one morning, one of the guards woke him and said he was to go to the commander's boat for breakfast. He was sitting on a rug on the deck with two earthen bowls, two paper containers with rice cereals and date palm sugar before him.

'I'd appreciate it if you'd have breakfast with me. Sorry, we can't get milk here. I must say rice cereal goes quite well with just water and palm sugar.'

'Thank you for inviting me. Very kind of you.'

'I command brutes and religious maniacs here. It's a historic necessity, Comrade. I miss civilised conversation. I should be thanking you for your company.'

They had just begun breakfast when a small dingy moored alongside the commander's boat. A thin young man with huge eyes and a long face climbed on board, handed the commander a note, and left. The commander glanced over the note and put it in his Punjabi pocket.

'Don't mind this intrusion. It's a daily ritual at breakfast time. Our leadership sends me the instructions for the day.'

From now on, besides breakfast, he had lunch and dinner with the commander. In his subsequent conversations, the commander told him frankly that he was already sentenced to death by the high command. He knew too much. The order for his execution would come one breakfast with the thin young man.

'It's nothing personal, Comrade. Just historical necessity.'

'I don't understand your historical necessity.'

'I suppose you don't. Otherwise, you wouldn't have been a revisionist type.'

'So, Comrade Pol Pot is the true liberator of the oppressed?'

'I see you still have the bourgeois habits of parody and irony. No action, only fancy posturing.'

Since he had already been sentenced to death, Bulbul felt had nothing to lose by being reckless and challenging the commander. Yet, he also retained an irrational glimmer of hope that he might be spared if he stayed on amicable terms with him, so he continued with the casual, friendly conversation.

Over dinner, Bulbul learnt that the commander was a bachelor and a virgin too.

'My love is for the revolution. I look at women comrades as soldiers in arms. Not as objects of lust.'

'How about love? Love for a woman?'

'It's just a fancy word. A stratagem if you like. A way of fooling women to give away their bodies so you can satisfy your lust.'

'How about women's lust? And how about your love of revolution? What are you lusting after?'

'There you go again, Comrade, with your bourgeois trickery.'

It was hot and humid. Under a fluttering lamp, with swarms of insects buzzing, he and the commander, their sweat dripping on their plates, mixed rice with dry fish and, between mouthfuls, continued their conversation. He learnt that the commander had come from a poor sharecropper family from the north of the country, that he'd been taught to read and write by the landlord's son, and that led him to think for himself and made him feel strongly about the injustices of the world. He became a revolutionary at eighteen; that was twenty years ago, in 1955. Since then he had worked underground for years, organised peasants and workers, and led armed struggles against landlords, the bourgeoisie, and rival parties.

'What is historical necessity now, Commander? You have Islamic fundamentalists, criminals, and pro-number one superpower, pro-Pakistani rightists among your group here. I don't understand.'

'Yes, I admit, comrade. They are a bunch of medieval reactionaries, imperialist lackeys and vicious class enemies. But they are just the stepping stones to where we want to go. I don't like it, but that's what historical necessity dictates.'

'Where do you want to go, Commander?'

'Ultimately to begin again. But for now, to get closer, one more stage.'

'What is the nature of this stage, Commander?'

The Commander hesitated, his face red in the fluttering light from the lamps dangling from the cabin's roof. He said, 'You'll see it soon, Comrade. Let's eat now. It's getting cold.'

The Commander served Bulbul more rice and dry fish.

'I like you, Comrade. I'm an avid follower of your columns. No one exposes the crimes of the ruling classes like you.'

'Then why am I your captive, Commander?'

'It's a historical necessity, Comrade.'

'Would you enlighten me about the nature of this particular historical necessity?'

The Commander stayed silent for a while, then said, 'You should have stayed away from this case. Your digging into the disappearance of Charity Magnet's son. Very unfortunate. It could sabotage our mission.'

'I came to dig for the truth, Commander. It's my job. But I don't understand how it sabotages your mission. Anyway, isn't Charity Magnet the main man of the number one superpower? Is this also another case of historical necessity?'

'Exactly. We know who he is. For now, we… well, let us not talk anymore.'

'I'm your captive, Commander. A dead man soon. On your command. So, whatever you tell me will go to the grave with me. That's if you want to dispose of my remains that way. I don't care.'

'This conversation has ended, Comrade.'

The flotilla stayed where it was, lapped by the waves. The man with the long, black bushy beard returned to Bulbul's boat but he avoided eye contact with him and remained silent. When the guards left the cabin, Bulbul approached him.

'What is happening, Mullah?'

'You don't want to know.'

'I'd rather know, though the knowledge will be of no use to me.'

'Well, if you insist. Has the Commander said anything to you?'

'He said many things. I am not sure what you're referring to, Mullah.'

'Has he told you about it?'

'About what? Whatever it is, you can tell me.'

'He's a coward, like all you communists. But I like to give a man time to prepare. If you want to ask for repentance and come into Allah's fold, I'm here to help you.'

'What are you talking about, Mullah?'

'We are very near to our objective. Perhaps only a few more days. I have to kill you. So, you've only a few days to be a believer again. You can still go through the gates of heaven.'

'No. Thanks for the offer, Mullah. I've been looking forward all my life to dwelling in your hell. You don't expect me to give up on my ambition now, do you?'

'You're a strange one. Arrogant to the last. Prepare for hell then.'

As darkness descended on the forest, Bulbul was having dinner with the commander again.

'Is this my last supper, then, Commander?'

The Commander examined his nails and scratched his stubble.

'Not yet. I don't want to lie to you. It could be soon. Very soon. Sorry.'

'Nothing to be sorry about, Commander. Let's not be gloomy for our remaining days.'

'Yes, I agree. We will have the finest fish and meat the Sundarbans can offer. I've also procured some local brew. I hear you're fond of the stuff.'

'Thank you, Commander. It's really a grand way to go. Illegal meat and illicit liquor. I'm so lucky.'

It was a large bottle of local brew. Deadly stuff. The Commander served Bulbul a large glass; he didn't have any.

'Are you a good Muslim or Year Zeroist, Commander?'

'What do you mean?'

'You don't partake – I mean of alcohol for religious reasons. I see you're still a good Muslim at heart, Commander.'

'Don't be ridiculous. I'm known to have a few glasses here and there, but command is an onerous responsibility. I need to be vigilant at all times.'

'Have one with me, Commander. A last wish, if you like.'

Once the commander started on the drink, he matched Bulbul for the speed at which he was going through each glass. Soon, he was tipsy.

'What do you think about Wrath of God, Commander?'

'The Sundarbans always harbour one or two man-eaters. Nothing unusual about that. The rest is superstition. Mumbo-jumbo, if you like. I must say the myth of Wrath of God greatly helped our cause. It diverted attention from our activities. If we wanted to get rid of the man-eater, we could've done it months ago. Contrary to popular delusions, he is neither a beast of monstrous proportions, nor very clever. Just an old, hungry tiger. You don't believe in all that nonsense about him, do you, Mr Bulbul?'

'I only see and listen, Commander, then report. The fear in people's eyes is real. So are the half-eaten bodies.'

Already, they had gone through more than half the bottle; the Commander was slurring his words.

'Of course, it's real. A man-eater doing his thing. What do you expect? If you're looking for a monster, you'd better look inside at your own fear, Mr Bulbul. Your own fantasies.'

'Wrath of God is peripheral to my story, Commander. I was actually looking for the boy.'

'I know, that's why you are in this mess. That's why we can't let you live and tell your story.'

'Well, whatever happens will happen. I'd like to know, though, what has happened to the boy.'

That day, the supper was illegally hunted deer-meat curry and crayfish from the river. The Commander swayed slightly as he sat down to eat. He served Bulbul and himself large plates.

'You want to fatten me up before you kill me?'

'Since the Mullah will have your head soon, I suppose there's no harm in telling you. But honestly, I don't know where the boy is now.'

'But he was here, and he disappeared. Am I right to assume as much, Commander?

'Of course, he was here. He was even in my flotilla for a few days.'

'So, it's you who had him kidnapped, Commander.'

'No, I just had him for safekeeping. It was the military and the logging interests. They wanted to make sure that Charity Magnet and his international backers didn't get too greedy. We all had a meeting and came to an understanding. It's not ideal, but the revolutionary road is never straight. You must know that, Comrade.'

'So, you've got soft communists, socialists, nationalists and democrats as your enemy. And you make pacts with the devil to get rid of them. I tell you, Commander, it'll backfire on you. The military, the illegal loggers and the Islamists will have a field day. Anyway, what's happened to the boy?'

'As I said, he was with me for a few days. I don't know what happened to him after he left. Perhaps the father sent him to the land of his international backers. Who knows?'

Bulbul carried on having breakfast with the commander. Each time, he felt it was the end when he saw the dinghy, carrying the thin young man with big eyes and long face, emerging from the morning mist. From that moment, everything would be set on an inevitable course. First, the young man would moor his dinghy with smooth deceleration and tie it to the commander's sampan, then, as if taking care not to disturb the commander and Bulbul in their tranquil moment together, he would come on board, cross the deck with languid steps and, with head bowed, hand over the note to the commander. Pausing his breakfast, the commander would take the note, glance over it, then put it in the pocket of his Punjabi shirt without betraying any emotion. Everything would begin to spin, and he would feel the boat, the river, the mangrove, and the sky becoming just a tiny speck of light and entering Wrath of God's mouth.

'You can relax. Nothing will happen today,' the commander would say with a faint, gentle smile. 'Are you scared of death, Mr Bulbul?'

'Yes, commander. I'm not very brave.'

'You are a materialist, aren't you? Fear comes only if you believe in religious nonsense. So, you have nothing to fear.'

'Yes, Commander. I'm a materialist. I'm still scared. Have you seen a goat or cow being slaughtered?'

'Yes, of course.'

'Haven't you sensed their fear? I don't know what they believe in. I bet they are absolutely materialists. Born as materialists and die as materialists. Yes, Commander. I'm terrified.'

'You are confusing the issues with your bourgeois obscurantism, Comrade.'

That morning, it was beautiful on deck. The sun rose but it wasn't hot because a cool breeze drifted in from the sea. There were flocks of birds in the clear blue sky, perhaps migratory cranes from distant Siberia. Minutes passed, and the commander stayed silent,

427

as if in deep contemplation, then he looked up, rubbed his chin, and asked Bulbul, 'What did you do during the war?'

'I ploughed the land. Grew mainly rice and mustard.'

The commander didn't say anything; he just looked at Bulbul with contempt. From then on, he didn't see the commander.

One evening, the man with long, black bushy beard brought him jamberries.

'The order came this morning. The commander just told me. I'll do you tomorrow morning. If you like, we can pray together the whole night.'

'Thank you, Mullah, for your kind offer. I'd rather not.'

'Why not?'

'I lost my faith in my teens. Although I've tried many different things since then, I've never regained it. Now at this last moment I'm not going to give in to panic. I want to stay who I have been.'

'You're not scared?'

'Of course, I'm scared. But do you think it's right to disown how you've lived?'

'Just foolishness. Do whatever you want; I'll pray for you.'

Bulbul sat by the window, looking beyond the river to the mangrove, darkening with the setting sun. The man with the long, black, bushy beard performed his evening prayer, then sat on his mat, counting his beads and calling Allah. From time to time, he would weep and mutter something.

Now that it was finally to happen, Bulbul felt strangely calm. He fell asleep and began dreaming of being in a house in a forest of tall trees, guarded by his good friend, Wrath of God, who, being ever so thoughtful, wouldn't bar his way to Mrs Sarkar, then Mrs Imam. If only he could have seen their eyes, everything would have been perfect, but they came faceless. Still, they came with their skin on, their smell, their bittersweet taste, and time just rolled on, stretching his body along the trees, their flowers burying him. Then he heard a loud, mechanical noise that woke him up. A flood of light engulfed the flotilla. It came from a military formation, composed of a gunboat and several landing craft packed with troops. There was uproar and loud cheering: the plot had succeeded – a section of the military and its assorted allies had taken over the capital city. After an hour, a military escort arrived at Bulbul's boat and took him to the gunboat to meet the officer in charge, who was discussing urgent matters with the commander.

'Who's this man, Commander?' asked the colonel, without betraying any surprise.

'He's Mr Bulbul. You must know him, Sir. A well-known journalist. He's been meddling in our affairs.'

'The name rings a bell. What do you plan to do with him?'

'I've orders to execute him, Sir. As soon as morning breaks.'

'If you don't mind, Commander, I'd like to take over his case. A dead journalist is no good to us. We might get some valuable information from him.'

'I've strict orders from Dacca, Sir.'

'Do you understand what's happened? We've taken over, Commander. We're in charge now. The entire Sundarbans is under my command. I'm having him, Commander. That's the end of the story.'

With Bulbul on the gunboat, the colonel ordered his formation to move on. Then he asked one of the guards to escort Bulbul to his private quarters. The colonel arrived after ten minutes and closed the door behind him.

'Fancy seeing you here, Singing Bird. You don't know how lucky you are,' said White Alam.

'Yes, that's me, Alam. I never thought you'd be my saviour.'

'You're my Godzilla brother, aren't you? I can't let you die like that.'

'They won't like it. You could face a court martial.'

'So what,' said White Alam.

CHAPTER 38

Because bandits were operating along these border parts, they had to take a detour. Now the water courses weren't familiar to the honey-collecting brothers. They punted and used their oars, but they were getting deeper and deeper into unfamiliar parts of the Sundarbans. They weren't even sure whether they were still in

Bangladesh or had crossed the border into India. Sometimes, they would travel the whole day only to arrive back at the same place they had started.

'I told you, didn't I? The Sundarbans is a maze. Even we get lost here. But the tigers, they never get lost,' said the younger one.

'Do you think Wrath of God is still here? Following us?' asked Bulbul.

'I don't know. He's so silent. He could be only a few yards from you, but you would never know. Only the macaques can tell you of his coming. Unfortunately, there aren't any macaques in this part of the jungle. Sometimes, though, he roars,' said the younger one.

For two weeks, Bulbul had been travelling with the honey-collecting brothers. He would have perished on his own by now. If crocodiles and snakes spared him, tigers would have eaten him up. Besides, he didn't have the know-how, he couldn't have gathered food to survive. The honey-collecting brothers knew how to source the nectar of the forest. They knew how to draw rainwater from the hollows of which trees and how to catch crabs at low tide. They kept Bulbul alive.

Finally, they reached a familiar spot.

'We know this place. The border is only a few hours from here. Allah willing, we will cross with you tomorrow morning,' said the elder.

They moored the boat in the middle of a large channel and secured it by digging in their long punts. On both sides of the channel lay the green fringe of nipa palms, their fronds touching the water. Beyond were the dense ridges of sundari trees, their white, pinkish flowers in full bloom. While the elder brother cooked crabs, the younger one and Bulbul sat on the cabin roof and looked at the evening sky changing colour in the water. Playing with the transistor radio, the younger put on the news, crackling but audible.

Between the news of the newly installed, military-backed government, the newscaster told of the execution of the renegade Colonel Alam. The Colonel, announced the newscaster, was not only corrupt but of the most despicable character. He had broken discipline and undermined the military, for which he was subjected to a summary court martial and executed, not by firing squad, as would be customary for high-ranking officers, but by hanging. It was further reported that the Colonel was such a lowlife that even his family didn't come to claim his body, but only a fat man from his hometown.

Bulbul kept staring at the sky's changing colour in the mirror of the water and imagining Sanu the Fat carrying White Alam's body back to Mominabad for burial. Noticing his trembling lips, the younger man asked what was the matter.

'Nothing really. I just remembered some friends. Once I went to see a film with them.'

'What kind of film?' asked the younger brother.

'Just a silly monster film.'

'Bora Bhai and I go to town sometimes to see films. We like love films. You know, hero and heroine falling in love. Bora Bhai cries, don't you, Bora Bhai?' said the younger brother.

During the night Bulbul hardly slept; he tossed and turned thinking of White Alam. He could have been alive and thriving had he not saved him, especially now that the military was in control. Why did he do it, why had he been so stupid? He couldn't stop thinking about Sanu the Fat taking the body to Mominabad. Perhaps he called a rickshaw to take them to the railway station from the cantonment in Dacca. He was clutching onto the body, and people were staring at him, a fat man with a corpse, perhaps asking him questions. How did it happen, who is he? How would Sanu the Fat respond? Would he tell a story of the Godzilla times, doing his funny walk, thumping the floor and roaring?

Towards morning, Bulbul fell asleep, only to be woken by the roar of a tiger. The honey-collecting brothers were up already.

'It's Wrath of God. It looks like he's just made a kill,' said the younger brother.

'What?' said Bulbul, struggling to open his eyes.

'Wrath of God. He made a kill, but it's good news for us. He won't come after us today,' said the younger brother.

In the morning mist, nothing was visible, but the honey-collecting brothers didn't need to see this part of the jungle to navigate their course.

At the border, Bulbul said, 'I don't even know your names and where you live.'

'We are just honey collectors. All that matters is that you're safe,' said the elder brother.

'Thank you for bringing me here,' said Bulbul.

'No need for that. We have seen your face. We had to bring you to safety. That's all,' said the elder brother.

Syed Manzurul (Manzu) Islam was born in 1953 in a small northeastern town in East Pakistan (later Bangladesh). He has a doctorate and was Reader in English at the University of Gloucestershire, specialising in postcolonial literature and creative writing.

His writing grows out of his memories of Bangladesh and the experience of working as a racial harassment officer in East London at the height of the National Front provoked epidemic of 'Paki-bashing' which terrorised the lives of many Bangladeshis and other Asians in the area. Experiences from these years fed into the stories in *The Mapmakers of Spitalfields*, which reflect both the trauma of racism, but also the creativity and achievement of Bangladeshis remaking their lives in Britain. Equally, the stories that reflect on memories of Bangladesh focus both on the bloody atrocities of the civil war which brought Bangladesh independence from Pakistan and of a rich culture which sustains the exiled imagination in the deepest ways. He is the author of the novels *Burrow* (2004) and *Song of Our Swampland* (2010).

He is also the author of *The Ethics of Travel: from Marco Polo to Kafka* (Manchester University Press, 1996) which explores the question: how is it possible for us to encounter those who are different from us – racially, culturally and geographically – and what are the consequences of such encounters?

The Mapmakers of Spitalfields
ISBN: 9781900715089; pp. 144; pub. 1998

'There are many who date the day he took to walking as the beginning of his madness. But others mark it as the beginning of that other walk when, patiently, and bit by bit, he began tracing the secret blueprint of a new city...'

He is Brothero-Man, one of the pioneer jumping-ship men, who landed in the East End and lived by bending the English language to the umpteenth degree. He, 'the invisible surveyor of the city' must complete his walk before the mancatchers in white coats intercept him and take him away.

These stories, set in London's Banglatown and Bangladesh, bring fresh insights to the experiences of exile and settlement. Written between realism and fantasy, acerbic humour and delicate grace, they explore the lives of exiles and settlers, traders and holy men, transvestite hemp-smoking actors and the leather-jacketed, pool-playing youths who defended Brick Lane from skinhead incursion. In the title story, Islam makes dazzling use of the metaphor of map-making as Brothero-Man, 'galloping the veins of your city' becomes the collective consciousness of all the settlers inscribing their realities on the parts of Britain they are claiming as their own.

Chris Searle writes: 'a luminous collection, a work of rare empathy and moving insight into the minds and hopes of new Londoners.'

Burrow
ISBN: 9781900715904; pp. 320; pub. 2004

Tapan Ali falls in love with England and a student life of pot-smoking and philosophy. When the money to keep him runs out there seems no option but to return to Bangladesh until Adela, a fellow student, offers to marry him. But this marriage of convenience collapses and Tapan finds himself thrust into another England, the East London of Bangladeshi settlement and National Front violence. Now an 'illegal', Tapan becomes a deshi bhai, supported by a network of friends like Sundar

Mia, who becomes his guide, anti-Nazi warrior Masuk Ali, wise Brother Josef K, and, sharing the centre of the novel, his lover, Nilufar Mia, a community activist who has broken with her family to live out her alternative destiny.

Tapan has to become a mole, able to smell danger and feel his way through the dark passageways and safe houses where the Bangladeshi community has mapped its own secret city. He must evade the informers like Poltu Khan, the 'rat' who sells illegals to the Immigration. But being a mole has its costs, and Tapan cannot burrow forever – at some moment he must emerge into the light. But how can a mole fly?

Manzu Islam has important things to say about immigration and race, but his instincts are always those of a storyteller. Using edgy realism, fantasy and humour to compulsively readable effect, he tells a warm and enduring tale of journeys and secrets, of love, family, memory, fear and betrayal.

Song of Our Swampland
ISBN: 9781845231705; pp. 336; pub 2010

When the killing starts in Dhaka, the villagers know the army from West Pakistan will soon be in their area, but unlike the other young men, and his beloved stepsister, Moni Banu, Kamal cannot join the resistance. Born with a hole for a mouth, most people, except Abbas Miah, the teacher who adopts him, his friends and Moni Banu, regard him as the village idiot. With Abbas Miah, Kamal embarks on a Noah's ark journey, with the motley survivors of the massacre that inevitably comes, to find refuge in the distant floodplains until the war is over. Along with a bombastic old actor, the village mullah, the village cutthroat, two Hindu boatmen, a foul-mouthed old woman, and a pious Islamist, who might just be a collaborator, Kamal discovers that there can be no escape from the war and the issues it raises.

As our guide to the painful emergence of the new nation of Bangladesh, Kamal is forced both to observe the face of evil, the complexity of betrayal, and look within to discover whether he has the capacity for true community, whether he can follow the injunction: "If someone knocks on your door, you don't ask who it is. You don't even look at their face. You just do everything you can for them."

Peepal Tree Press has been decolonising bookshelves since 1985 with our focus on Caribbean and Black British writing. We are a wholly independent publisher and part of the Arts Council of England's national portfolio since 2015. In 2024, we established a partnership with HopeRoad Publishing.

Peepal Tree's list features fiction, poetry and non-fiction, including academic texts and creative memoirs. By the end of 2024, we will have published 490 books by 320 different authors, including those published in our anthologies. Most of our titles remain in print. Our books have won the Costa Prize, T.S. Eliot, Forward, OCM Bocas, Guyana and Casa de las Americas prizes.

From the beginning, women and LGBTI authors have been fully represented in our lists. We have focused on the new by publishing many first-time authors and have restored to print important Caribbean books in all genres in our Caribbean Classics Series. We have also published overlooked material from the past as a way of challenging received ideas about the Caribbean canon.

We see decolonisation as about overthrowing and repairing oppressive, economically exploitative and racist power relationships. Many of our books explore the halting, difficult process of overcoming four hundred years of colonialism in the Caribbean in the post-independence period. But we also see decolonisation as needing to happen in Britain. We are committed to ending British amnesia over the destructiveness of empire and colonialism, including our role in the irreparable damage of nearly three centuries of slavery , and promoting an understanding of how Britain's long relationship with the Caribbean has contributed to the making of British society in ways that persist into the present. As a publisher, we have taken a stand on supporting Palestinian rights for freedom from a colonial occupation and denial of statehood.

We hope that you enjoyed reading this book as much as we did publishing it. Your purchase supports writers to flourish. Keep in touch with our newsletter at https://www.peepaltreepress.com/subscribe, and discover all our books at www.peepaltreepress.com, and join us on social media @peepaltreepress